A RELUCTANT MOTHER

A RELUCTANT MOTHER

a novel

DEIRDRE SIMON DORE

RONSDALE PRESS

RONSDALE PRESS
125A — 1030 Denman Street, Vancouver, B.C. Canada V6G 2M6
www.ronsdalepress.com

Book Design: Julie Cochrane
Cover Design: Dorian Danielsen
Editor: Robyn So

Ronsdale Press wishes to thank the following for their support of its publishing program: the Canada Council for the Arts, the Government of Canada, the British Columbia Arts Council, and the Province of British Columbia through the British Columbia Book Publishing Tax Credit program.

Canada Council for the Arts Conseil des arts du Canada

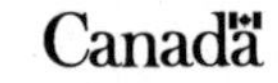

Library and Archives Canada Cataloguing in Publication

Title: A reluctant mother / Deirdre Simon Dore.
Names: Dore, Deirdre, author.
Identifiers: Canadiana (print) 20240289560 | Canadiana (ebook) 20240289579 | ISBN 9781553807100 (softcover) | ISBN 9781553807124 (PDF) | ISBN 9781553807117 (EPUB)
Subjects: LCGFT: Novels.
Classification: LCC PS8557.O7288 R45 2024 | DDC C813/.6—dc23

At Ronsdale Press we are committed to protecting the environment. To this end we are working with Canopy and printers to phase out our use of paper produced from ancient forests. This book is one step towards that goal.

Printed in Canada

For Vicki and John

PART 1

House of Crow

We sometimes encounter people,
even perfect strangers, who begin to interest
us at first sight, somehow suddenly, all at once,
before a word has been spoken.

FYODOR DOSTOEVSKY, *Crime and Punishment*

CHAPTER 1

It's never too late to have had a happy childhood. You rearrange your memories, you pick and choose, you lie to yourself, invent or exaggerate fond moments or steal them from books. You push dark nights aside to make room for sunny days, swap out heat for cold and vice versa until you realize the abundance of your luck and can look back happily at the sweetness of your infancy. It's doable. And I have done it. But can that same ability to rewrite your childhood be applied to the whole of a person's life? That's the question I ask myself now.

My psychiatrist is speaking in the hallway. I recognize her voice with its melodious Indian accent describing a pedicure she had done, with a tub of tiny fish nibbling away at her toes. Now they're banning the procedure. Difficulties with infections and also the poor *Garra rufa* are starved to the very point of eating callouses. She continues, I feel quite guilty that I had that done. But it worked, you know. No infection, none. And my feet were never so clean. But to do that to a sentient creature for the sake of beautiful feet? She chuckles. I brace myself for her visit and the earnest, sympathetic face she will quickly don in my presence, but she walks on and I am spared for the time being at least.

The bed is narrow; the room, but for electronic hums, is silent. It smells of Lysol and orange blossom, a scent I associate with my lawyer who is dutifully building a case for my release. My arms are connected by IV tubes to plastic bladders of golden liquids. Groggy with sleep or drugs, I leave my hallucinatory world behind in which I am young and horribly famous and wake to a pretty strong conviction that I will never be sufficiently punished for all the various crimes I have committed against anyone who has ever known me, appendicitis notwithstanding. I tell my lawyer, my appendix was a pocket full of feelings and past memories, everything that defined me. And now it is gone, and gone with it is my identity.

Nonsense, she says, it was full of bacteria. But what does she know.

Now my little lawyer has fallen asleep in her chair; the blogs and emails, journals and general ramblings I had delivered up as testimony in the trial have dropped to the floor. I call for the nurse, I call for morphine, I call for the bedpan and she wakes.

Read to me, I say. Tell me who I am again and where I stand.

She sighs. Why she has stuck by me remains a mystery, certainly not for the money, of which she has seen very little.

Your name is Frida Frank Brooke, she tells me. Named Frida either after the Mexican painter or a rich old aunt, not quite sure which. Your mother, Lulu Frank, is quite famous and you are both artists. Does any of that ring a bell?

Not what I am hoping for, but it's a start. And truth be known, the sound of her voice is more comforting than the words.

As it happened, my artist mother did name me after the painter Frida Kahlo, presuming I too would follow along that artistic path and wished to direct the muse. The old aunt, Frieda, left her fortune to a cat. But the similarities with the famous Frida are uncanny. Because, like her, not only am I an artist but I am also childless and, from an early age, familiar with hospitals. Do the similarities end there? Perhaps. Give or take this limp and a scar or two. I am now almost at the midpoint of my life expectancy, just a few years younger than Frida Kahlo was when she died.

Checking the time on her phone, my little lawyer asks, Can we continue? I nod.

She clears her throat and selecting a page from the top, reminds me of my first encounter with Tully.

Blake and I were hosting a party. I had just come home from a disappointment at a juried exhibition in Edmonton in which my submission received merely an honourable mention and not the prize I had hoped for. Blake brushed it off with a platitude, every closed door opens another, but I saw no open door beckoning. We were living at the time in a new-to-us old wood frame house outside the small town of Hope, British Columbia. After several years in Vancouver, Blake had decided that we needed a bigger place, not to mention that nature might be good for my mental health. I agreed when I saw a picture of the chicken coop and realized I could convert it into an art studio. So we bought the place sight unseen. Five acres of shrub and field and huge cedar trees all around. Plus three bedrooms, one for me, one for Blake, and one for my grandma, Roxanne.

The town itself is an old one, a fat bubble of civilization bulging into the Fraser River to the west with the towering Cascades to the east. A sportsman's paradise, I suppose, but I admired these natural wonders from a safe distance, not being the sporty type. I always knew Hope as a place you drove past while gaping at the Hope Slide. Major highways, important rivers, railroads, they surrounded and converged and crossed through while the township itself sat amicably apart, its own universe.

So much history here, Blake said. The Stó:lō for a millennia or more, the Fraser River gold rush, Fort Hope. And for a small town, it had every usual convenience really, even a quarry. But we lived about ten clicks south of the bubble, far enough away from the centre that I didn't have to deal with the towny-ness of it on a daily basis. A mountain view, the Fraser River a stone's throw away. And close to the airfield; he wasn't about to go hang-gliding, so I suspect Blake really settled on Hope because of the Rambo movie *First Blood*, which was filmed here. He had watched it with his dad a thousand times, and it was like a homecoming for him. So we dined out at Stallone's maybe once a month, took pictures of the mountains, watched the river flow and called it done. It certainly rained a lot.

It was our third Halloween there, and our tenth wedding anniversary, and Blake decided to celebrate. He said, This will cheer you up. You can finally make friends with the neighbours and dress up as Frida Kahlo again. I was forty-one years old and it had hit me hard to realize that aging doesn't stop at the dreaded forty. And he was right. I did take pleasure in pretending I was F.K. Not just for her beauty and talent, but I felt reassured by the tragedies she had suffered, how she had turned them into art and fame, albeit with an early demise. I held no illusions about making friends though; there had been an invitation once for coffee from a local truck driver, I forget her name. She sat me down at her kitchen table in front of pickles and cheese squares and homemade buns, sliced hot dogs pierced with frilly toothpicks. Two girlfriends already seated; they watched me eat. They looked strong, these women. They looked fearless and mentally stable. So stable. They said, We meet here every Tuesday. They added, For coffee and "poetry." They were kidding so I laughed. Really we just like to catch up on all the goings-on in town. They asked, Got any kids? I said no and the conversation died. When I left one of them handed me her business card, a local driving service, River Crossings.

But Blake had met a couple in town a few days earlier whose acquaintanceship he believed I should cultivate. They were setting up an art gallery, a summer "feeder" gallery here that would augment their main operation in Seattle.

Here? Why here? I asked.

I think the wife grew up in Hope, he said. Went to high school here. Has something to prove to the locals? Who knows? I wouldn't look a gift horse if I were you.

Blake would be Diego. I had a baggy brown shirt, soft and collarless for him, a long white cloth to knot around his neck and a paintbrush for the breast pocket. I dug my costume out of the closet. Elasticized and loose, it still fit. And so as not to seem utterly forlorn and friendless, I went through the local phone book to conjure up warm bodies. Seven thirty, come in costume.

All day I prepped for the party, vacuumed and dusted, while Blake left to confirm a contract for a computer upgrade at the pizza parlour in town. He was a systems analyst guy, an IT guy; opportunities in Hope for his line of expertise were few but he remained optimistic. Red hair tamed, Blundstones polished, he packed up a new motherboard and promised to be home in time to uglify himself as Diego.

I put a plastic pumpkin on the porch. I set out platters. All the food groups covered. Brie and prosciutto for the gallerists and hot dogs for the coffee klatchers. A temporary black rinse on my light brown hair which I adorned with a silk gardenia. I gathered my canvases and propped them up against the walls, very casual, and I had just finished thickening my eyebrows when I heard a knock. Six thirty, much too early for a guest, and I almost did not answer. Do I wish I had not? Then I realized that it might be a trick-or-treater. I picked up the bowl of jelly beans and answered.

When I opened the door expecting a six-year-old hooker or warty witch, I came face to face with a woman, about thirty-five or so, shoeless, on the frosty step, in opaque black tights torn at the knee and a very short black miniskirt with what looked like a broken zipper if the safety pin was any indication.

She looked me up and down and said, Do you have a gun?

I felt a chill of excitement or perhaps dread slip through me.

What?

She repeated her request. Then she added, I hit a deer, or more correctly it hit me. Ran straight at me, as if on a suicide mission. It needs to be put out of its misery.

She grabbed a handful of jelly beans and one by one popped them into her mouth.

She was instantly compelling in a rag doll sort of way, slouched and slender, her spiked, raven-black hair cut ragged, the ends dyed pink. A purplish cardigan, the cuffs worn, was draped around her shoulders over a dull green loose-necked sweater stained with something dark red on the sleeve. The sweater was tight enough to reveal the boyish quality of her chest. Her slanted eyes were large and dark as an animal's, that clear, that wary. Her dun complexion marred with gashes — a car accident? Cat fight? Tribal markings? Perhaps she was in costume. When she spoke, her voice was so carefully modulated that I wondered if English was her first language. No native speaker took such care with each consonant, every vowel. Yet no accent was definable.

She pushed a wayward strand of hair behind her ear, which was silvered with earrings, a dozen small silver hoops around the delicate lobe. The currency of beauty. My own ears, a tad on the big side, sported plastic skulls which dangled and clacked against my neck.

The woman helped herself to a few more jelly beans from the bowl I was still holding and said, Well? Hello? Earth to lady. A gun?

I came out of my reverie. Jesus, I said. Wait here.

I left her on the step and went for the rifle that we owned but had never used. It had been a housewarming gift from Blake's dad. Our new surrounds, he told us and the locals echoed, were alive with vicious cougars, starving coyotes, savage wolves, bloodthirsty raccoons and enraged mama bears. Every creature with only one desire, to rip the jugular right out of your throat. We accepted the rifle just to placate Blake's old man and had dutifully gone for our firearms safety courses. To date, I had seen quite a few blackbirds thonking in the trees, several dozen squirrels and mice unnumbered. I was still thoroughly ignorant in the ways of the blood and meaty guts of the real world. So this would be my first lesson.

The rifle was locked in a cabinet in the basement. An open-sighted 30–30 Winchester. I found the shells that belonged and carefully, as I had been taught, loaded one into the chamber with a click.

I called up to my aged grandmother, Roxanne, abed in her room on the upper floor: Roxanne, if you hear anything, just ignore it.

The Buffalo, her caregiver, stepped to the top of the stairs, looking down at me with suspicion.

You too, Buff, I said, with the rifle in my arms. Just carry on.

And the Buffalo lifted her heavy brows and backed away.

In my painted red boots, long swishing skirt and embroidered blouse, I stepped out into the drizzle of Halloween and followed the barefoot boheme up the road to where her car, an old VW van with a crumpled fender, was stopped, half in the ditch. The shivering body of a doe, prone on the road, struggled. The deer appeared to be in shock, her eyes glassed over, unblinking. I noticed her nipples, elongated and deeply pink. When I looked out to the trees I caught sight of the fawn. Staring, silent, unmoving. And beyond the fawn the flash of a magnificent buck, sprinting off, his antlers glistening in the rain. The doe shivered again in fear or pain and flung her legs uselessly in the air in an effort to stand and failed. Both hind legs bent at awkward angles. Her eyes were huge, the same shade of brown as the woman's. The deer snorted, her tongue lolled out of her mouth as she banged her head against the ground. Still, the fawn stood, immobile, watching.

I put the gun up against the doe's cheek and pulled the trigger and felt the concussion against my shoulder. The doe slammed its head against the pavement and convulsed in shock. I reloaded and shot again, just behind the velvety ears, and the animal let out a long gasping bleat, air whooshing from her ass and then finally, mercifully, lay still. Slow dark blood seeped into the ditch, staining the wet pavement blood red.

When I looked up to the trees for the fawn I saw only the flash of its tail as it flagged through the woods, then disappeared.

The woman stood silent. We stared down for a moment. She said, Well there we go. And then, I like your red boots, Frida.

She put her hand in the pocket of her ghastly sweater and pulled out a lipstick and smeared the waxy purple over her bottom lip, then top, then mashed her lips together and ran her finger over the lips to spread the colour.

How do you know my name? I said.

Frida Kahlo? Your costume?

Overhead a raven cawed, landed on a tree top and settled, its eye pinned to the carcass below. I shivered.

Your first kill, right? She gave me a sympathetic pout.

It was then I noticed that there was a child in the front passenger seat of the van, a girl of about eight or nine, and next to her was a small white dog with tawny eyes. The red-headed child and the white dog were staring at me with something akin to pity.

The girl rolled down her window. Mama.

The woman ignored her. Instead, she nudged the fallen deer with her toe. Are you sure it's dead?

I nudged it as well. Nothing. No response. My ears were still ringing from the shot. My shoulder bruised, the ropy scar that traversed it, pulsing.

Mama, the child called out again.

What?

I have to go. Again the child trained her narrowed eyes on me. As if I were the cause of this calamitous series of events. Glared at me as if I were also the cause of her urinary problems. It wasn't me who hit the deer, I wanted to remind her.

Number one or number two? the woman asked.

Number two! she shouted.

Can't you hold it?

No.

Oh my god, she said, such a pain. She turned to me. Do you have a bathroom?

I was that tempted to say no.

CHAPTER 2

I ushered the pair into my house and pointed to the guest bathroom, into which the child and her mother disappeared. I ran through a litany in my mind of what they would find in there. Lavender-scented soaps. Embroidered hand towels. A plastic spray can of Febreze. Where the hell was Blake?

On cue, he stepped through the door. About to apologize for being late, until he saw what I was holding and stopped.

What are you doing with that gun?

I had barely begun my explanation when, from the bathroom, a flushing sound.

Who's in there? Blake asked. Whose van is that? What's going on?

A lady and a kid, I said. I shrugged. She hit a deer.

Where? Here? What's going on? Is it dead?

It is now, I said. I think I told him to relax, that I had taken care of business, though I felt far from relaxed myself. In fact, in the aftermath of that killing, I felt fully alive. More alive than I had felt in years.

At that moment, the bathroom door opened and the woman, naked shoulders on display, poked her head out to ask, Do you have any bath towels?

Behind her, a sloshing.

Under the sink, I said.

Tampons?

No.

Shit.

I turned to Blake to roll my eyes. This is unbelievable, I whispered, pretending nonchalance I suppose, though a tingling had started under my skin as if my flesh was aware of something that my brain had yet to decipher.

The colour drained from his face and he nodded, then went upstairs to change into his costume, and before long our guests of honour arrived, the gallerist and his wife.

Joel was a tall round-shouldered man, good-looking enough in a middle-aged way, dressed smartly in a cashmere sweater and grey slacks. And his pretty wife, Marguerite, short, petite and several months pregnant. As I greeted them, the gallerist's eyes darted to the gun I was somehow still holding.

Is that loaded?

I nodded.

From the gun, his gaze travelled to my breasts.

For a moment I basked in his admiration until I looked down and saw the blood splatters on my white blouse.

Ummm, is the safety on?

Yes, I said. I put the safety on and set the gun down in the corner.

He turned to his wife. I told you this would be fun.

Want a drink? I blurted. Got any kids?

Yes to a drink, and yes to the kids, Joel said. Two, from my first wife.

And one on the way, said his second wife. She giggled.

He took his phone out to show me pictures, boys in hockey gear.

From the bathroom came the sound of water running in the bathtub.

The other guests began to arrive. The sheep farmer, the rancher, the coffee klatch women with their husbands.

The Buffalo appeared with a tray. She had somehow managed a costume though I'm sure I had not suggested it. A sexy French maid. The tiny white apron and ruffled black miniskirt exposing her ample, gleaming thighs. Joel took an egg roll; Marguerite, a carrot stick. The truck driver — forget her name — piled a wedge of brie on a cracker, and I grabbed a hot dog, found a glass of wine and drank.

Roxanne appeared, covered head to toe in one of my good white sheets with a hole cut out for her ancient face and slits in the sides from which protruded her skinny, mottled arms.

Is today the day you feed me? she asked.

A gasp from someone until I replied, No, you get fed on the first of the month, that's tomorrow and then nervous laughter from the party-goers. Roxanne smiled in approval but our brand of humour was obviously not to everyone's taste.

That Blake was making himself scarce certainly occurred to me.

Marguerite, the poor woman, big belly swollen with fetus on her tiny frame, had settled heavily into the former owner's red leather couch. The house had come fully furnished with the old man's things. Slick couches, dusty white lamps, a china cabinet, piano. A miss is as good as a mile, I told the agent at the time, and we settled in without further thought.

Marguerite was reminiscing: I remember this place and the old couple who lived here. They had chickens; my mum used to buy eggs from them. Is that chicken coop still standing?

It's my art studio now, actually.

Oh my god, what a cute idea. Me, I'd be freaked about chicken mites but you're apparently quite the brave soldier, aren't you? Almost like the real Frida.

I poured myself another glass of sparkling white (not quite champagne), drank it down and when I saw her watching, offered her a glass.

Oh no, she said, I'm pregnant. I can't. She grinned and patted the bump.

Of course you are, I said. I'm so sorry.

But, she added, maybe just one. She took the glass.

Hypocrite. And everyone too full of themselves to even put on a costume.

I proceeded to get drunk. Finally, Joel found the stack of paintings I had leaning up against a wall and began flipping through them. I watched him surreptitiously while he rambled on to no one in particular about the advent of Mexican Modernism as opposed to clichéd renditions of identity, beauty, sexuality. We're looking for an artist in residence for our gallery in Seattle, I heard Marguerite tell the chicken farmer. She glanced over at one of my abstracts and continued, To be spearheaded first by a solo exhibition. My heart skipped a little beat, but the way Joel shuffled through my canvases so quickly did not strike my heart as encouraging.

Until Roxanne, who was looking on as well, floated up to him, ghostlike. Boo, she said, and Joel started.

She laughed. Lulu B. Frank, she said. And after a pause. Ever heard of her?

Joel's eyebrows darted up into his forehead. Lulu Frank the artist? Of course. Hasn't everyone?

The coffee klatch poets all shrugged.

She lives in Paris, doesn't she? he asked.

Yes.

What about her?

Lulu is my daughter. Roxanne beamed.

Really? he said.

Really.

Nice one, Joel said.

Roxanne's wrinkled face poking out of the sheet was gleaming with pride.

Not to mention, I added for the record, technically that makes her my mother.

I was just about to say that, Roxanne said.

I saw Joel's eyes flip back to my work then with interest, or doubt, I'm not sure which. He said, Well, we all have mothers, technically.

Marguerite leaned forward and pointed at Roxanne. Actually, from the pictures I've seen on the internet, you look just like her.

Do I? Roxanne, glowing with pride.

Hardly, I muttered. And I began to tell them all about my mother's great talent and how as a toddler I had sat on the floor and watched her paint. I even told them that once she had dressed us in matching mother-daughter dresses. What was I trying to prove? Does talent rub off on offspring? Does maternal love demonstrate itself in matching dresses? While I talked Marguerite stumbled, laughed and Joel apologized for her.

My sainted pregnant wife is a little bit tipsy, said Joel. Just ignore her.

A pause and then, Congratulations Maggie! The truck driver raised her glass in toast.

She prefers Marguerite now, Joel advised.

I headed into the kitchen for a private snack and a private alcoholic refill. Blake was seated at the table, glassy-eyed, listening to the chicken farmer — I think his name was Tony, or maybe Tom — bemoan his egg-candling mishaps. Kids, these days, he said. They couldn't spot an embryo in a haystack.

Huh, said Blake.

Tony/Tom had brought a six-pack of beer. He handed one to Blake, who took it mutely. So where did you guys meet? he asked.

Who? Blake said. He looked a bit alarmed.

You and your wife.

Oh, Vancouver, Blake said. Frida was at Emily Carr and I was at UBC. We met at a frat party.

I looked at Blake blankly.

You don't remember the frat party? The purple dress?

I don't. And if I don't remember it didn't happen.

That's an interesting concept, Blake said. I'll have to remember that one.

Anyway, we didn't really connect until we met again in London, Blake said.

The chicken farmer nodded, I hate Ontario.

I explained that Blake meant London, England, at my mother's art exhibition at the Saatchi, in Chelsea. I still have the poster, the *Orange and Pink Show*, fractured, cubist. Her hair matched her canvases. Blake was star-struck, wanted to take her picture and get an autograph.

And I married the girl next door, Tony/Tom said. Ain't the world a funny place.

No, Blake said, it was Frida, the statuesque scowling presence behind Lulu that I was interested in. Been together ever since.

Our farmer mused on about his wife, how small she was, how amazing on a tractor, and I mused in turn about our first week together in London, the fish and chips, the fucking. Blake blushed.

I was raised on the prairies, Tony/Tom said. The Prairies, Canada.

My little lawyer is writing this all down and says, And what about this? Is this all true? She reads: In Toronto Frida had gotten a job as a taxi driver, volunteered at a children's burn clinic and shuffled her resumé around until landing a job at an ad agency.

Drawing logos for deodorant and cat food, I add.

My diligent lawyer nods, scribbles cat food. Carry on.

The faucet in the sink began to drip and Blake turned to watch it.

Tony was saying something about cornfields and running through them. Even Blake was annoyed, Well not everyone has the luxury of a cornfield at their disposal. Nor can they run.

Tony/Tom stared at him.

Don't forget to tell him about the scar, George.

It's just skin, Martha, he retorted.

Now I'm all confused, the farmer said.

Never mind, Blake said.

But Tony wants to know, now that you've piqued his interest.

No, no, said Tom.

I took a breath. I began to tell Tony an abbreviated account of my tragic childhood, a memory blunted by the years that had passed and yet potent again in the retelling. I set a little fire, I told him, when I was five, and unfortunately, depending on your perspective, I was the lucky little kid who survived, and my baby brother was not as lucky, but while I was escaping I broke my tibia but no one in the hospital noticed till it had healed badly. It shames me now to admit that I may have been using my tale as a way of bringing Blake closer to me, in sympathy I suppose, fearing rightly that he was drifting. But my ploy, no matter how unconscious and spontaneous, did not work and Blake stiffened in annoyance until I stopped speaking very nearly mid-sentence and Tony said, Okee dokee... doctors, and shook his head in sympathy.

Yeah. Doctors.

Tony: 'Cause me, when I have a medical problem, I call a vet.

We let that bit of wisdom gel. I thought to myself, Imagine, I could have married Tony, those golden fields of grain, coveralls drying on a laundry line, a cow mooing. For a moment I felt completely bereft.

The door to the guest bathroom remained closed, more closed than I had ever seen it. And then Tony asked if we had any kids and somebody said, Zippo.

The farmer picked up his beer, studied the label.

Susanna and I used to harrow the cornfields side by side, he said, until she gave in and let me have my way with her. Not as romantic as an English pub I suppose, but it did the trick. For a while. Till our sixth was born with red hair. Soybean farmer next section over.

In the silence, Blake said, We don't harrow. Never have.

Well, good luck to ya, anyways. He drained his beer, took it to the sink, rinsed it out and put it in his jacket pocket.

From the guest bathroom, another flush, splashing. Cabinet squeaked open. Water running.

By the way, the name is Ted.

Right. Ted.

Blake and I were suddenly alone in the kitchen.

Well, that was fun, I said. I returned to my guests.

Joel looked bored. Poor Marguerite kept swinging her huge belly around and downing another drink. She was on to cocktails now, entertaining her old chums with a story of what she and Joel had done on their anniversary a month before.

We went to a very expensive hot springs lodge. As in very. Bedroom fireplace. View of the lake. The bathroom, you should have been there. Heated floor, electric toilet. Couldn't figure out how to turn the bidet off. Sat there screaming, my butthole getting pummelled in streams of water. Until Joel told me, Just hit the red button.

The little crowd laughed. I mixed Joel a martini and saw his eyes light up.

Finally, I said, You know that's precious cargo in there and the Surgeon General has guidelines which do not include martinis.

Have a smoke, Mrs. Lead Coffee Klatch shouted.

Marguerite laughed. Joel winked. And I guess everyone had realized but me that she was in costume.

Just like the egg farmer who was dressed as a sheep farmer and the sheep farmer who was dressed as a cattle farmer and the coffee klatch women who were mostly dressed as whores, all of us dressed in our alter egos. The joke was on me.

That was when the woman of the dead deer stepped out of the bathroom with that glowering child in tow. The chatting, such as it was, stopped. The pair of them were so clean they squeaked.

Blake stood.

The child's expression had not softened. She reeked of the rose-scented hand cream that I had left on the top of the sink for the use of guests. Her mother meanwhile had found my emergency makeup kit under the sink and had availed herself of it and now glowed, gilded and rouged.

The entirety of the gathering instinctively created a circle around them as the pair advanced into the centre of the room.

I'm sorry, I don't actually know your names, I said.

Tully, she said, and smiled. Short for Anatole.

The silver hoops in her ears twinkled. The tops of her tiny breasts and the cleavage between them had been powdered, rosy and inviting, absolutely blemish-free.

And this is my daughter, Clarabelle.

Clare, the girl corrected. She wore baggy long johns under her grimy yellow dress.

My little crowd of merrymakers waited for an explanation.

I said, She hit a deer in the road and stopped here for a gun to put the deer out of its misery.

Which you shot, the child said, pointing at me.

I scratched at the stains on my embroidered Mexican peasant blouse. The deer's blood had dried. Unsalvageable.

You shot a deer? the sheep farmer asked, staring at me. He nudged Ted, and I rose a notch in their estimation.

Yes. It was suffering.

Aren't we all, chirped Roxanne.

I went to the door and opened it. I think your car is okay to drive?

The woman, Tully, was still barefoot, still threadbare, still as compelling as a plucked daisy, but somehow she was not moving towards the door that now stood ajar letting in all sorts of cold air. Fresh, cold air that I wanted to be out in.

I guess we should be going, she suggested, unconvincingly, to her daughter.

Oh, must you? From me, even more unconvincingly.

But I'm hungry, the child declared.

And Marguerite had the nerve to say, How could you be hungry with all this food?

Tully nudged her daughter. Go, eat.

And the child wandered into the living room and poked her fingers around the canapés until she found one to her liking and took a tentative bite. Yuck, she said, spit it out and tried another.

Everyone chuckled. Kids. Everyone that is, except me, and Blake.

Finally, the tattered creature almost made as if to leave.

But the child, who was hanging backwards upside down over the old man's loveseat, her spine curved in a perfect C, her red hair dusting the floor, said, But Mama, dessert!

I marched into the kitchen, picked up a profiterole, stuffed it into a plastic Tupperware. Said, Here, take it with you, no need to return it. A moment I cringe to look back on.

The child fell onto the floor with a thud and a cry of pain.

Marguerite rushed over to console, Roxanne hobbled over to console, and even the farmers clucked in sympathy. The child wiped her runny nose on the cashmere blanket draped over the couch, opened the Tupperware and stuffed half the sticky pastry into her mouth.

I'll keep the rest for Fancy, she said.

Tully poured herself a glass of red.

Had I ever seen Blake so feverish?

Are you coming down with something? I asked him.

He wiped the sweat off his brow. Hot in here.

I pulled my paintings up off the floor and set them out on display. The chicken farmer stood back and looked and then stepped up close to look again. All of them were abstracts, not entirely in the style of my mother. She didn't own polka dots after all.

The chicken farmer said, But what do they mean? Is that a dog? Is that a toe?

And Marguerite, God bless her little heart, said, They are abstracts and should be assessed in terms of colour and shape and line and texture and value and organization and how they occupy space and create emotion and make us look and look again.

The sheep farmer rolled his eyes at the chicken farmer and Marguerite shut up.

They ate the egg rolls, they ate the ribs, they pointed their greasy fingers at the murky green triangles and dotted circles of beige and black. No one bought or offered to buy. I stopped flirting with Joel, who had not settled on any of my pieces, was rambling on about painted skin, tapestry, Joan Semmel and Elizabeth Peyton until I finally snapped my canvases away from him. Art without money is like sex without orgasm, I thought. But my thoughts have a way of being vocalized.

Everyone stared at me.

That might be in the category of too much information, Blake said.

I was about to respond when the child charged at the piano. Lifted the lid and started banging on the keys. Marguerite joined her on the bench. She said, It's a piano, not a drum. Let's start with scales. But the girl would not stop thumping. I kept my cool until my cheek muscles ached. The child was quite a hit, the guests charmed by her antics, her loose high laugh, those oval auburn eyes, the chubbiness, the little gap between her teeth. I lowered the lid over the keys, letting them pull their fingers free. So noisy, I said. Right? I turned to the party-goers for their affirmations, which were quite lukewarm. I turned to Blake.

It's our tenth today, Blake. Do you want your gift?

Before he could answer I handed him the stainless-steel mugs I had ordered online, engraved *Happy Tin Anniversary, Frida & Blake October 31, 1997.*

Clapping.

Blake had a funny look on his face. He handed me a frying pan and I said, Oh thanks, aluminum.

It seemed hours upon hours until our little crowd of merry-makers finally departed, though it was barely nine.

We were left alone with Tully and the girl. No one concerned themselves with the dog in the van.

I had had more than enough of these two. No more beating around the bush. Blake had managed to get himself even drunker than me and the Buffalo had left with a large doggie bag of my food.

We're off to bed now, I said.

We've been so rude, Tully declared.

I kept my mouth shut.

Blake was on the couch with his head in his hands.

You see, the thing is, she said.

Oh god, there's a "thing."

CHAPTER 3

It's late, the hospital seems quiet, just the whir and breath of machines. I'm exhausted from the retelling but my little lawyer doesn't want to quit.

There's always a thing, she says. She has put the pages aside and waits for me to ramble on with bits of the story that I have almost forgotten.

I reach for the Jell-O cup on my bed tray. Could you crank me up?

You're already cranked. She waddles over to the window and opens it for fresh air though I find it chilly in the room and am shivering.

Are you gaining weight? I ask her.

So much. And another week to go.

Week to what?

The birth, silly. She is pregnant and I have not even realized, or remembered.

She waddles back to her chair. Tell me about the thing.

The thing is — Tully's visit was not accidental. She had deliberately come to our little outpost to find someone, to find Blake in fact. She had a vague address and had been driving up and down looking for his black Dodge pickup truck. Then the fog came in and then she hit that deer and knocked on my door and found him.

Like serendipity, Tully said at the time

You know the opposite of serendipity? my little lawyer asks.

I know nothing.

Zemblanity. And she looks at her phone. It's the faculty of making unhappy, unlucky but expected discoveries by design. In other words, the inevitable discovery of what we would rather not know.

And what I would rather not know was this: Tully wanted Clare to finally meet her dad.

Blake and I grew still when Tully made that announcement. Behind me, I heard a soft dripping. Roxanne, diaperless in her ghost sheet, was dribbling urine on my hardwood floor.

Ten minutes later, Tully was seated on the couch, not quite in tears, but pretending to be. Pouting. Whining. Bent towards Blake, her small youthful breasts enjoying the momentum of gravity, hanging loose, on show.

Clarabelle was on the floor leaning up against her mother's leg, studying a portrait of me that hung above the gas fireplace. It was a blown-up photograph Blake had taken about twelve years earlier when he was still in his photographer stage. My hair was long and thick and dirty blond, hanging down the side of my face in a tangle, uncombed. My strong nose lifted to the sky. I was wearing a flimsy thrift-shop peasant blouse, one shoulder nearly bare and was staring out of the photograph with a look of irritation. I remember that moment, how long it took him to focus, how he kept telling me to move into the light, then out of the light, smile, then not smile. The look of aggravation was not forced. I held a single flower in my hand, a weed actually; it drooped. I had wanted a rose or even a daisy, but Blake had balked. Too cliché. In effect, the weedy thistle, which he had positioned over my scar, very nearly stole the show.

The child asked, But who's that supposed to be?

My wife, of course, Blake said. That's Frida when she was young.

Tully, looking back and forth from me to the photo, lifted one eyebrow.

I had a rag and was mopping up Roxanne's mess. Roxanne had seated herself on the floor next to the child; she was trying to play pat-a-cake.

The fifteen pounds I had gained over the years felt like a hundred. I was a fat giant in a room full of Lilliputians. The child and Roxanne started rock-paper-scissors. I scowled at them.

Me: How old is she?

Tully: Eight. Her birthday is today.

Me: Our anniversary day.

Tully: Happy anniversary.

Clare: This is my birthday present. Meeting my dad.

The child smiled at Blake. She scooted away from Roxanne and settled back against her mother. She put her finger in the hole of her mother's tights, worrying it larger. Tully slapped her hand away, but the child paid no attention and started again.

Stop it, Tully hissed.

And then the child turned to me and said, What happened to your shoulder?

None of your business, I replied.

It had taken all of my adult life for me to realize this was the only answer I ever had to supply. Besides, there was nothing wrong with my shoulder. And if she could see my breast, there was nothing wrong with that either. The scar had faded and would continue to fade, give or take a thick layer of concealer and a turtleneck sweater. Most people were polite enough to ignore it. Not that there was anything to ignore. And anyway, I had pretty well stopped mixing with most people.

My little lawyer raises her head from the pages. The gall of some people's kids, she says.

Of course, she is testing me but I refuse to take the bait.

So you didn't tell her about the fire?

No. I had done enough talking about the fire.

I steered the conversation back to the issue at hand and waited for Blake to set the record straight. I went and stood in front of him, both of us facing Tully and the child. I hoped he would be kind to her. But not too. I wanted to feel his hands on my shoulders when he told her, firmly, that she had to leave, the child was not his, and her presence in our home, barging into our home like this, was completely unacceptable. I would shrug a little in apology. I conceded that there may have been an encounter, eight or so years ago, in Calgary. Blake at a week-long computer convention. He had come home to Vancouver with a big bouquet of flowers and a hangdog face, told me about some woman, confessed it all. Tears, shouting, broken plates and then pretty good sex. I had forgiven but not forgotten. Some leeway there for my own infidelity, should it ever come to that.

I was still holding the urine-soaked rag and Blake did not put his hands on my shoulders in solidarity. Rather, he stepped out from behind me and asked the most ridiculous question.

Tully, he said, how did you find me?

Just hearing him say her name made me a little crazy, and I'm ashamed to admit that I wrung the rag out on his foot. He didn't even notice.

I got it from your business card where you used to work. They had your forwarding address. She nudged the kid on the floor. This is Clarabelle. And I am off the deep end exhausted with being a single mother.

The child shrieked, Don't call me Clarabelle!

Tully: See what I mean?

What should we call you? Roxanne asked. Clare? She began to

sing in her squeaky old lady voice, "Au clair de la lune, mon ami Pierrot . . ."

And what I finally had to blurt, because nobody else was coming up with it, was that Blake was sterile. Blake had had a vasectomy ten years ago when we got married, and ergo the kid was not his.

A Michael Jackson song started playing in my head. I poured myself another drink. A strong one. Scotch. I hated Scotch. I drank it down. I glowered at the little girl. Particular eyes she had. I did note that. I threw the rag down and waited.

Tully chuckled. Tully pouted. Tully stared at the floor and moved her toe around in circles. Nothing more was said, no sound from anyone. Roxanne cleared her throat and I hissed her into silence. A small scratching sound as the child continued worrying the hole in her mother's tights.

I felt as if I was underwater, listening to fish, to the silence of piranhas. At the window, the resident raven had landed on the sill outside, peering at its own reflection. Furious at the sight of a rival it could not get at. Furious and confused.

I broke the silence. I'm sorry, I said, for the deer. I'm sorry for the damage to your car. I'm sorry for your daughter. Buy her a bicycle and go through your calendar again. Try to find another likely suspect. Because Blake is sterile.

Blake flinched. Tully sighed.

The girl looked up at her. Mama? Did you make a mistake?

It happens, I said to the child, and I flapped my hands up and down at her, come on, come on, come on, until the girl stood and the woman stood and I escorted them, decisively, to the door.

I watched them walk down the wet driveway to their car, the child leading the way. The white dog in the car barked. Back inside I went to the table and picked up a sausage roll. I ate it. I ate two. Did Blake see them to the door? I can't recall. I was too busy eating. I finished the platter.

I gave Blake a wide berth. He sat immobile at the table, waiting for me to say something, I suppose. I said nothing. I went to bed first. I took my Frida Kahlo costume off and stuffed it into a bag for the thrift shop.

I spent the night flat on my back, staring at the ceiling. Counting the number of times a fake knot in the fake wood was repeated in the pattern. And I presumed that he did too. I hoped so. Him in his bedroom, me in mine. Though when I passed his room, door partly ajar, I heard snoring. I farted loudly. He did not wake. So that's how it goes, I thought. I remembered when we hitchhiked to Mexico and he had stood in the street and juggled oranges for coins and I had painted little watercolours. The warmth of his skin, how I always welcomed his arms around me. His big, interesting eyes.

CHAPTER 4

When Blake and I decided to never have children and sealed that decision with sterilizations (our insides pasteurized, disinfected, decontaminated), we had made the hardest but best decisions of our lives. I remember the moment.

We had been stuck in a lineup in a supermarket behind an army of haggard mothers and their sniffling children. We were hungry, stoned, we were newlyweds. We just wanted to buy our cookies and chips and apple juice and get home. We hated waiting behind this horde of humanity and watched those women with a sort of horror. The toll on their bodies, the sagging flesh, the veins, the tiredness. The chit-chat at the till. Is Billy liking kindergarten? How is Susie's eczema? Sure, the parents thought their kids were little messiahs come to save the world, but any honest look at the snotty faces, filthy hands, whining and stubbornness, any clear eye could see the truth. Meanwhile, poor Mom, in her "Mom Hustle" baseball cap and sweats, had given up all hope of fashion or career or professional life. All hope of making a mark in the world.

We retreated to our lair that night and named off every great artist we knew who was childless: Frida Kahlo (yes, her), Georgia O'Keefe, Emily Carr, even Dolly Parton for fucks sake. Their art was their progeny. Consider my own mother, a famous artist herself who had shipped me off to Roxanne to raise. Didn't that prove the point? I admit that it might have been me who steered the conversation. The idea that some people did not deserve children, and maybe that I was one of those undeserving people, was an idea I was loathe to investigate. Like a mosquito buzzing about my brain, I swatted it away and convinced myself it was about creativity — and art. What I knew, and Blake did not, was that I had been two months pregnant at the time of this decision.

We could live in Paris ourselves, I told Blake. His eyes shone with the possibility and we let that hang in the room until it dropped of its own considerable weight, ate more cookies, made love. And then, like children joining a secret society, we pricked our fingers, smeared blood and decided.

In the morning after Tully and the girl's visit, I heard Blake leave the house early. His fledgling computer business necessitated a part-time job with the local plumber. It was still an hour before light and I was in no rush to greet the day. I fell back asleep and dreamed I was kneeling on the ground wrapping wild daisies in shredded paper. I had given that man an ear of corn for his birthday. Everyone was waiting with gifts. Hooded bowls of yellow pudding. The twists and turns of emotions the way dreams do and then leave you on an endless highway. There is never a giving up. Relentless obstacles to push against.

When I finally got up, he had left me coffee in a thermos. His note said, Gone to snake the lint out of some woman's washing machine hose. Be back at dinnertime.

Upstairs, Roxanne was banging on the floor. The Buffalo was not due for another hour. I gathered up some leftover party food, made a plate and took it up. I barely knew her anymore, could no longer see the glamorous grandmother she had been. She was wasted and small. Every day I was confronted with my future self.

Rain battered down on our tin roof. I came back downstairs and turned the TV on while I threw the rest of the party food into the garbage and later, hungry, wished I had not. I watched the clock until Blake came home. He smiled at me. He said, You look so sexy in that outfit. I had put on my painter's smock. Loose, long, buttoned to the neck. It had nothing to do with painting and everything to do with my current disguise.

He added, Because I know what's underneath. He wiggled his eyebrows at me.

I put a plate of boiled macaroni in front of him.

I said, You smell like a clogged washing machine.

And he washed again and sat at the table, wet hair slicked back, the bald spots at his temples on display. He put his fork into his plate and brought it to his mouth.

I said, That poor woman. That poor kid. Single mom, no father to fall back on.

He chewed and swallowed. Any coffee left?

You'll have to microwave it.

He poured himself a cup, put it in the microwave. Stood there while it heated.

But what a nerve, I continued, that she would come here and accuse you.

The microwave dinged.

Is that the woman you met at that computer convention?

A big glug of cream, sugar.

What computer convention?

The one you went to when I was stuck taking care of Roxanne.

A pack rat, I kept everything. While he had been at work I had dug out an old calendar from 1999. For March, a glossy picture of a black bear and her cub. Friday, March 5, Blake off to Calgary for a Y2K computer conference. I'm stuck with Roxanne. Wednesday, March 10, Blake home!!!

I showed it to him. Remember?

He had come home carting a big bouquet of flowers for me.

And I had given him my self-portrait. I remember it clearly because his eyes teared up when I gave it to him.

Same? Referring to the woman from the convention.

Maybe, he mumbled.

You don't know?

I haven't spent a lot of time thinking about it. I'm not good with faces.

Good with bodies?

He stirred his coffee loudly and dropped the milky spoon on the table.

I wiped the dribbles. Or maybe she's not the same woman, I said. Maybe she's just some crazy person. I narrowed my eyes at him.

He set his coffee down. A little nod. You're right. You're always right. She's just some crazy person.

I don't like the gun. I want you to get rid of the gun.

He agreed.

And I don't like this house. I don't like this wilderness that you have brought me to. I don't like the old man's furniture and I don't like this life.

He agreed.

And I don't like that woman.

He agreed to everything. I flung my plate of spaghetti into the sink. Our special French china bought in Paris so many years before. The plate broke cleanly in two.

It is quiet in my room: just the squeak of a nurse's shoes, a ringing phone, a distant cough and now the loud gurgling of a nearby baby.

My little lawyer has given birth. Some days, or maybe even weeks have passed, completely lost to me. I'm in a different room, with a different view of the parking lot. I don't feel any better. In fact, I feel worse. My little lawyer glances down at the sleeping bundle in the basket on the floor and frowns. Paris, she says. You are so lucky.

Am I?

Although my formative years were spent in Paris, I never really knew the Paris life except as a vague paradisiacal remembrance of things past. The hard edges smoothed over, the scene painted rosy in a child's memory. Baguettes and chocolate, Mom laughing. Smoke maybe? Maybe smoke. A man's hug, my father? Hairy arms. But vague because at the age of five, it all quite suddenly ended. An ambulance, a hospital. Doctors, bandages. Floral wallpaper. Watching my mother sleep. Then shipped off to live with my strange grandmother who was bedded down in Vancouver with an out-of-work film director. Why I was shipped off is still a mystery to me; there was a new baby brother and then there was not a new baby brother. Phone calls, tears; dolls and clothes jammed into a little Samsonite suitcase. Carsick in the cab to Orly, airsick on the flight to Toronto. Earaches on the plane to Vancouver. Not a popular passenger. And then, all around us, man, woman and child alike speaking English or Chinese and living in grey condos that stretched up into a grey sky. Why dwell? At the time of Tully's arrival, I had already pushed past forty with my own set of values and choices under my belt.

I look at my little lawyer. Her red hair is striped in purples and greens. She is coating her eyelashes in a third coat of mascara.

Going out tonight?

It's Friday, she scowls. As if that means anything at all to me.

And the baby?

She rolls her eyes.

For a month I locked him out of our house. He slept in the truck, in the driveway. I threw two old blankets into the gravel, a pillow, a tube of toothpaste, his asthma pills, his sleeping pills, his Viagra. A winter parka, gloves. It wasn't like I was killing him. The tools in the canopy could be pushed aside. There was room to almost stretch out. Music on the radio, news, he could still connect with Wi-Fi. Neighbours drove by, slowing down as they passed, gawking. Take a picture, it lasts longer, I shouted at them. He would sneak in for the toilet and the shower when I was at my easel. All my energy, my talent, drained away. I drank. I took pills. One day he found me on the floor, laughing, in tears, unable to stand. He helped me up. I hugged him around the knees. The rough cloth of his jeans against my face, my need for him overwhelmed me. I could not let go.

Please, he said, it's okay, you're okay.

Am I though? I tried to give him a blow job.

He did not protest. He moved back in and we resumed in a sort of truce.

My little lawyer frowns. Were you intimate again? She has been watching *Judge Judy* reruns.

No. Not intimate. Unless blow jobs count?

I'm not sure.

But he had his room and he kept to it.

Good.

My foolish pride.

In fact, we were like two passengers on a train, familiar faces to each other — shared a newspaper, passed the sugar — but barrelling down the track towards decrepitude. All we had to do was take note of Roxanne to know the destination. But not intimate. Intimacy is the experience of being truly listened to and responding in kind, repeated time and time again.

Listened to closely, I tell my little lawyer. I read that somewhere but it was put much more wisely.

After the party, I did not hear from Joel for quite a while, though Marguerite phoned from Seattle to thank us for the very entertaining evening. It annoyed me to remember how they all gathered around the child, patting her head, admiring her freckles, feeding her my expensive chocolates. Poor little fatherless child of a waif. I heard that word go round. All so proper. No one had the balls to say whore.

How does a person get what they want out of life? For that matter, how do they even know what they want? I had decided I wanted to be an artist. All the art books on my shelf, all the workshops say, Find the soul of the piece. Some say, Play. Others say, Persistence, just show up. No one ever talks about the talent-less. They are too busy selling their own brand of aid to the desperate. Am I one of those? Whatever happened to the five-year-old me so full of ideas, so lauded? Child prodigy. My ass. I still remember the last time my mother drenched me in that look of pure love.

Pre-fire of course.

After, those were difficult years. Roxanne had a lot to say about my weight, my grades, my friends. She bragged continually about her daughter, Lulu, and pushed me in that direction, to make something of myself. I wrote long letters to Mummy. I wanted to tell her everything, told her nothing. I never mailed them. I turned twenty. The men I chose to keep me company at night were older, artistic hacks, horny and rude. I got an STD. I got another. Roxanne had landed a tiny role in *Last Year at Marienbad*, a pretentious movie that I never did understand, after which she never missed a chance to tell me that I was the albatross for her own artistic endeavours. She stopped financing my lifestyle. I dropped out of Emily Carr. I moved to Toronto. And on a whim one day, I flew to London for my mother's show and ran into Blake again. He was there taking photos for an art magazine he worked at. Mummy loved it, catered to his camera, but to me? Gracious, polite, as if I were one of her many fans. Blake took his photos, then put his camera away and stuck by my side. That night he lost his virginity and sent a huge bouquet of flowers.

After the extraordinary effort Roxanne made at the party, she sank back into a typical slump. Sleeping till ten. Demanding eggs when she got oatmeal and French toast when she got eggs. Blake and the Buffalo humoured her. I did not. The tea too hot, the tea too cold. Not enough brandy in her milk. I avoided her as much as possible and let the Buffalo do what the Buffalo had been hired to do, keep my grandmother as comfortable as possible until her demise.

Roxanne called me into her room one afternoon and said, Are you ready?

For what? I put a blood pressure pill into her mouth.

For trouble.

You're the trouble, I said. Of course, I'm ready.

That black-haired woman with the child. That's the trouble. Mark my words.

I gave her another pill and left.

Blake wanted to forget Christmas that year. But I went to the Home Hardware and bought one of everything I could find. I went whole hog. And to give him credit, he manhandled the work. He set out my huge inflated snowmen in the yard, an inflated Santa, inflated reindeer, strung lights and baubles between the trees. The child-like childless couple. I wasn't going to hide out here on our little patch of paradise off the highway. Yes, it was too big, too cold, too wooden a house, with too many trees and mountains and way too many stars above, and not a neighbour in sight to admire our yard, but it was our duty to honour the charade.

At least Roxanne seemed to love it. She and the Buffalo sat by Rox's bedroom window looking out at the lights and sang "Away in a Manger" till I wanted to choke them.

Blake and I didn't sing, but we did drink as much of the Christmas booze as our little throats could swallow. Wine, whiskey, Baileys, champagne. I felt sorry for the bedraggled mother, I told Blake. But to be played the fool like that? We argued, I probed. What was she wearing? What did she do in bed? What did she say? Was she pretty, was she funny, was she skinny? Let it go, let it go, he said. I could not let it go. I wanted all the details of their years-old intimacy. When? Where? How many times? But every image I drew from him was like poison, a delicious poison. I knew she would one day return to haunt us.

Booze all gone, the inflated reindeer and inflated Santa deflated. Blake received a hand-drawn Christmas card in the mail from the child. A green tree with red presents underneath.

That smelled trouble and I knew it. With hardly a word from me, Blake decided he would go and read Tully the riot act. Be gentle, I told him. Don't have to be cruel. But she must be made to realize that the child is not his, ergo, we will not be accepting visits or any other nonsense. The woman lived outside Kamloops, apparently. It was a two-hour drive from us, in good conditions. The day he left was a foggy, softly snowing day in early January. I made turkey muffins while he was gone. Then I shovelled the path out to my coop studio where I lit a fire, put my smock on and tried to work. The coop took a long while to heat up and my hands were clumsy. Finally, I left my brushes dirty in the sink and texted Blake. Well? All good, he texted back. Home tonight.

He arrived home late, with flowers. A bouquet. A big tall smelly bouquet. For me. Another bouquet. Nothing but bouquets. It's a done deed, he said. I fell into bed with him, hungry.

The hard gristle of him, the warm peach of me. Like the old days with caveats. But as always my own satisfaction was elusive.

In the morning she sent him a text: I have your scarf. Did you want to come back and get it?

So much for closure, I said, loudly. So much for done deed.

Life does not come with guarantees, Blake said loudly back. The man rarely raised his voice. He'd had enough of me. I took note and quietly reminded him that there's always the guarantee that everything will go to shit.

I went up to my room and prepared for bed. He came in.

Look, if it makes you feel better, I'll go back and —

And what? Didn't you explain about your vasectomy? Didn't you take your medical records?

I should do that, he said.

Yes, you should. Not to mention, gestation is nine months, not eight. Not that it's relevant in your case.

I watched him count the months out on his fingers.

The next day, another four-hour round-trip drive, another tank of gas, Blake came home with his scarf: no flowers and no comment on how sexy I looked in my smock.

CHAPTER 5

Months passed, winter whooshed away without consequence or progress or calamity or joy. I buried the thought of Tully and her child under a thick layer of denial, robotically performing domestic and marital duties.

My budgeting skills were not top-notch. Nor were Blake's. But we had three credit cards and managed to juggle between them although winter was not being kind to us. Blake was busy enough with clogged pipes but that didn't pay much, and his computer business was still taking its time getting off the ground. He started going to the local poker games at the Legion. Claimed he was breaking even. The only part-time jobs I seemed to qualify for involved cleaning, babysitting, dogs and booze. Blake told me to stay home and paint. Isn't that your goal in life?

Occupational therapy? I asked. Truth being, the promise of Joel and his support felt like pie in the sky. But I kept a hawkish eye on his website and Facebook page and saw no indication of his having found another artist to champion. The progress on the opening for his Art in the Valley Gallery also looked to be in limbo, although Blake seemed to know that Joel was still interested.

But my art practice in fact merely involved a whole lotta shopping. Acrylics, pencil crayons, gessoed canvases. Sable brushes, Sennelier pastels, Golden Gels. Everything still tucked away in their boxes, sight unseen. Until one cold and wet afternoon, when the house was vacuumed and the dishes washed and the beds made and dinner prepped, I ran out of procrastinations and succumbed to the allure of fresh paints waiting for me in the coop.

First I arranged my brushes by size in a beautiful canvas roll-up bag with leather ties. I set up the mahogany easel. I created still lives of wine and oranges, knives and lace. I tacked up a postcard of Frida Kahlo, her self-portrait as a deer. The chicken coop lost its chickenness and cheered me on. Even the wildlife gathered, not merely to graze but to encourage. In the woods beyond, a coyote howled in appreciation, a raven cawed. Hours passed, I was in the zone, my brain flooded with dopamine.

When I could ignore my aching leg, my hungry belly no longer, I put my supplies away, admired my work and returned back to the house where smack dab up against my renewed and buoyant confidence was Roxanne, who was not doing well. She slept most of the day, threw up this morning. We were on baby applesauce now. The Buffalo informed me that getting her to brush her teeth or wash was almost impossible. Leave her be then, I told her. Who was going to get close enough to notice anyway? But the Buffalo had her standards and Roxanne was hauled under the shower every morning, howling in protest. I felt the end was near. The Buffalo confirmed this. I supposed there would be an inheritance and that was okay because we were having terrible money problems. But the old woman would be missed. Of course, she would.

Then Blake came home one day and told me he had just come from a conference with Joel and Marguerite about the computer networking system that they needed to connect with their gallery in Seattle. I tried to hide my hunger.

Blake was excited. It'll be a great job.

And the space?

It's a great space, Blake said. Lots of light, and high walls, clean, modern and rustic at the same time, crying out for art. They're still looking for an artist to represent.

My heart went crazy with a pit-a-pat thump thump, the kind of vibrational drumming that comes from inside and that you read about and think is just a cliché until it happens to you and you know you really are still alive.

He told you that?

Yup.

And what did you say?

I said, Hmm . . . keep my eye out.

The man had the sensibilities of a clam.

Well, next time he asks, I said. Hint, hint.

Next time what? He knows you're an artist, relax.

Be subtle, I said. Don't be too obvious. But don't be too subtle.

Blake packed up his little computer tool kit and left to work at the gallery.

But I could not relax. I bought a blond wig and a dress with pictures of Marilyn Monroe printed all over. I could not shake this feeling of impending triumph.

And though I had quite recently been enveloped in the sodden comfort of big bottles of reduced-price Chilean wine, stuffing myself with potato chips in front of the television, mesmerized by bad news, cooking shows, *schadenfreude*, I knew without a shadow of doubt what time it was and that change was on the horizon. Yes, there were volcanoes erupting, planes crashing, floods and forest fires, but in spite of all that I felt manic with impending success, absolutely Napoleonic.

One might wonder who would care for art in such tragic eventualities? I'll tell you who — the survivors, the wounded, the lost lives.

My little inquisitor shakes her head and bends wheedling over the jumbo baby.

In the mail the next day came a flyer from Buy-Low, a Publisher's Clearing House notification of sweepstakes winnings for

Roxanne, a telephone bill, a Visa bill and a card with childish handwriting on the envelope addressed to Blake.

I opened the square envelope. Inside was a drawing of a spaceship zooming through the sky with a deer standing on top of the ship. Or maybe it was a flying cucumber with a dog. Or maybe it was a fish with a leggy wart on its back.

I showed it to Blake. I said, Boy she doesn't give up, does she.

I dropped the card on the kitchen table where it sat radiating its innocent menace.

Well? I asked.

Blake said, Since when did you start opening my mail?

I said, Since when did you start getting any?

We both stared at it, as if it would levitate.

Near the house, a tire hung from a branch by an old, nearly rotten rope, an anachronism from another time. A walk up to the marshy swamp — is that an oxymoron or a redundancy? — it had those scouring rush things growing all around, pushing their way into the water, nature doing its nature thing; deer tracks, the cottonwood trees tipping over the trail, thinking bear and seeing none. The previous owners, the old people, had left a wooden boat at the edge there, tipped upside down, painted green, a planked rowboat of long ago. A talisman of sorts, of little use on the river that I could tell, but quaint and evocative on the shore. The name *The Green Horse* painted on the stern. And again a blackbird, scolding me.

And then an email from Joel.

My grandmother, the woman who raised me, might be shrinking away upstairs in that room awash in the turpentine smell of urine with half her faculties on hiatus and the other half lightly scrambled, but I went to her with a bag of marshmallows for advice. Or maybe just to gloat.

It's happening, Roxanne.

What? She looked startled. Am I dying? Is it now?

No, no. It's about me.

You're dying?

No. Stop it. I need a little advice.

She smacked her lips together. I handed her her teeth.

Joel, remember him, the gallerist? He's coming around to see what I've got.

Roxanne looked me up and down. Do you want to borrow one of my push-ups?

My art.

Oh, that.

Just wondering, what would you suggest? I mean, I can do anything, but I'm not really sure where I should focus, still lives, abstracts, landscapes . . .

Nudes, Roxanne said without a second's thought. Men like nudes.

I gave her a marshmallow and put out an ad in the local paper.

When Minnie showed up, a straight-backed, busty matron with curled and dyed brown hair and her purse held firmly in front of her, I gestured grandly for her to enter.

She looked around. Isn't this a chicken coop?

Not anymore, I said. It is my studio. Welcome to Studio Coop.

You're not planning anything funny, are you?

She had made herself up with twin slashes of blush on her cheeks and dark foundation that stopped at her chin.

I gave her the fifty dollars I had promised and offered a glass of white or red. She said, I brought my own and pulled out a can of diet cola. She popped the tab. I put my artist's smock on and suggested she take her purple down jacket off and lay it on the cot. She did. I pointed her to the slightly raised platform and the dressing screen to the side. I said, I hope it's warm enough in here.

Oh yes, she said. It's nice and toasty. And it was, it was terribly hot in fact.

I said, Are you more comfortable seated or standing?

Oh, I'm on my feet all day. I prefer a chair.

I gave her a chair. She sat, legs crossed, and smiled at the horizon.

Perfect, I said. Remember that pose. I gathered a palette. You can take your clothes off behind the screen.

Minnie's eyes narrowed. My sweater you mean?

Yes, your sweater and your clothes.

My boots?

Your clothes, all your clothes. Down to that little pink bottom I know you have hiding in there.

Minnie stood. She set her diet cola down on my art table with a bang. Walked up to me and slapped my face. She put her purple jacket back on, picked up her purse and left.

The next day a restraining order arrived, registered mail.

It took a few moments to get past my merriment over this turn of events before I realized the other option, the option most available, the option always staring me in the face.

I went out to the coop. I put a full-length mirror up against the wall, set out my palette and undressed.

I was in the kitchen boiling apples for Roxanne's bedtime snack, mentally composing the blistering retort that I should have given Minnie after she slapped me (and *I* got the restraining order?) when Blake got home from work and said, Now don't take this badly.

I knew immediately that I would take it very badly. I threw the wooden spoon into the sink, turned the stove off under the apples and said, What the fuck now?

He looked sheepish, explained, While I was at Joel's working on his computer system, I got another text from . . . you know who.

Good for you, I said. I turned the stove on again. At least Blake had the good sense not to say her name out loud.

Are you listening?

Not really. I thought nostalgically of the old days when bad news came slowly via Canada Post or an actual face-to-face. Now, in two seconds flat your whole world can fall apart.

She's not letting this go.

Too bad.

He put an apron on, one of mine, yellow with daisies. I gathered it was his turn to make dinner. I didn't keep such careful track of those things. He pulled an onion out of the pantry, peeled it and began to chop.

Speaking of Joel, he came by yesterday, I said.

His eyes began to water, possibly from the onions. I ripped off a paper towel and handed it to him.

I said, They're trying to have a baby. I asked Joel, Aren't there enough babies in the world? Besides, don't you already have two boys with your first wife?

Everybody's different, Blake said. Everybody's got the right to make their own choice.

As soon as he said that he realized the hole he was digging.

I'll let that go, I said magnanimously.

He tossed the onions in the pan.

He actually wanted to buy a painting.

Really? He peeled another onion. Like with real money?

I fanned out eight one-hundred-dollar bills.

His eyes widened. Which painting?

A new one. He's not fussy. Twenty-eight by thirty, earth tones, nature theme. He's letting me decide. Do you want to see what I've painted for him?

I returned with my self-portrait. In it I am sitting cross-legged on the ground, nude in the forest. I'm calling it *Nature Heals*. On my lap, I have painted a baby wolf, which is suckling at my breast. I watched Blake's eyes widen even further, glance my way, then back to the frying pan he was tending.

He put a spoonful of sugar on the onions. Stirred. I watched him scrape the burnt bits of onion off the sides of the frying pan. His mouth was set in a grim line, the furrow between his eyebrows deepening as he fussed at the pan.

Are you jealous? I asked him.

He stopped stirring without looking up, then resumed. No, of course I'm not jealous. Should I be?

Well, you sort of owe me one.

He threw the spatula down on the counter. Is that how it works? I owe you one?

Oh, relax. I'm only kidding. The point is — I scooped up the leftover pile of chopped onions and dropped them into his pan — I'm so glad we never had kids. Aren't you? Because here we are completely not tied down. I pointed to the portrait's belly. Not to mention, no stretch marks. If you ever cared to check that out.

Not tied down for what? We don't go anywhere anyway.

Well, we could. Especially if my career takes off.

I was reigniting a long-lost dream which now seemed attainable, within my grasp. Against my own better judgement and everything I had ever believed about the power of a jinx, I expanded on the dream and spoke it out loud, to the sizzling oil, to the wind against the window, to my husband, to the universe.

Anything. Everything. Artist in residence, Vancouver gallery, Seattle exhibition, Paris, New York, London. Remember our days in London? We could pack up, we could move. There's nothing holding us here. And people actually have computers in those cities. Real computers with real technology and real viruses that need fixing. Put this place on the market and we're free to follow our destiny. Sorry to sound so corny but . . . I miss the city, don't you? I took his face in my oniony hands and kissed him. I whispered, Joel's a pretty sexy guy but he can't hold a candle to you, Mr. Hard Drive.

Blake extricated his face from my grasp and opened a package of raw meat and dumped it into the frying pan.

I'm going to Buy-Low with this money, I said, and buying T-bone steaks. I can only imagine how tired you are of spaghetti.

Not at all.

I am. In Paris we'll eat duck, in Seattle we'll eat salmon.

I like spaghetti. It's good. It's cheap.

I turned and looked at him. You hate spaghetti. You're on low-carb.

Thing is —

NO. I don't want to hear "thing is." In the sudden silence that bloomed after my outburst, I grabbed a can of tomato paste, opened it and sliced my finger.

Oh god. Now you're bleeding, he said. As if I had done that on purpose.

It's only blood.

He went to the fridge for a beer.

I said, It's just that I can't concentrate anymore. When we're in bed I keep thinking —

Stop.

Never mind the sex, I can't even concentrate on my art. Can't even hardly pick up a paintbrush since that . . . person . . . came into our lives. And now you say she's emailed you again?

He said, She wants another face-to-face with me. She's adamant.

Bully for her.

I have to, Frida. But this time, I'll be plain, he said. Plainer.

Yup. Whatever you say, cabbage.

My little lawyer has fallen asleep. Through the window I watch the rain flatten the snow. Cars in and out of the parking lot. Wheelchairs. A big lady with a blue cast hobbling unaided into her van. What I wanted but could not articulate was a union of concern, a pulling together, a common goal, a fusion that would demonstrate and even reinforce the reality of his love for me. More than the way a man might fiercely love his country or a hockey team or a dog. I didn't want patriotism or loyalty. I wanted us to be a "we." Without it, I felt adrift.

Blake turned back to the meat sloshing about in its own blood and injected water, and while he fried, I envisioned the face-to-face he would have with Tully.

He would drive to Kamloops and on the way he would stop at Wendy's or an A&W and buy a Mama Burger and a Papa Burger and a Jr. Bacon Cheeseburger with a Frosty. After they had eaten, he would clear his throat. He would say, Tully, I hate to say this . . . I have something to say that you're not going to like. She would still be eating those fries, squeezing ketchup out of the little plastic packet, licking the red goo off her fingers. She has heard things she did not like hearing before. He would continue that, yes, he may have been the most likely suspect but was certainly not the father, could not be. Not only was he incapable but she had claimed to be on the pill, etc., etc., etc.

Of course, after those introductory remarks, he would remind her that she had promised to leave him alone. He would pick up the Coke then, slurp it down. And she would pout. I had seen that pout myself. It had no power over me, or over any self-respecting man, but Blake was susceptible. Always has been.

All the while the child would be twirling around in the stuffy little apartment they probably lived in, gathering all the bliss of the unbroken home into her heart, her tiny little guileless, uncomplicated child's heart. My imagination failed me then, or rather propelled me into that child's body where I was the guileless one dancing. I clamped down firmly on the imagery and plunged forward into the next scene that would undoubtedly play out: the two of them in a tangled bed together, everything smelling like beeswax, the grunts, and skin to skin, and sigh, scream, whimper of release and finally Blake leaving some money on the table. How much? He would tell me if I asked. He was honest in that way. And generous. Certainly more money for the child. And then he might request (demand?) her assurance that she was done harassing him. Harassment after all is an actionable offence. He would not use those words. He would be gentle, consoling. Empathetic. His mission? An utter failure.

From the corner of my eye, I saw out the kitchen window that the crow had appeared in the yard and was watching me, head tilted. Expectant.

Did you hear me, Frida? She's not gonna let this go.

I opened the window and tossed a bowl of kitchen scraps out into the snow. The bird swooped down and pecked at the tasty bits. The bruised tomatoes and rotten banana. Then cawed in complaint at the bay leaf and onion skins. I sucked my bloody finger.

I came up behind him and said, You need a hug.

I felt the tension in his body ease as I pressed my breasts against his back.

Thank you, he whispered. I knew you'd understand.

You're welcome. You're very welcome.

The meat sizzled and burned. The kitchen filled with the smells of scorched apples and burnt flesh.

The next day, I drove to Kamloops.

CHAPTER 6

With instructions I had read in Tully's email to Blake, I mapped my journey. Two hours winding along a slick freshly plowed road. Past lakes, gas stations, turning off one highway onto another, I saw the sign announcing Kamloops and I exited the highway. I turned left after the Esso. Past the Bottle Depot, onto Battle Street for three clicks, another left and then right at the sign that said "Mutton for Sale." I followed the rutted driveway past the big house till I got to the structure at the end. I stopped the car and studied the abode. Far from being an apartment, Tully's home looked like a barn. A decent enough place for old milk cows or mules, now unconvincingly converted into a domicile for human beings.

On the barn wall, someone had nailed the dead, fly-blown bodies of two ravens. Limp-necked, heads and beaks hanging groundward, eyes glassed over, the feathers still blue-black but with no lustre. Tully, who had been warned by Blake of my arrival, opened the door and saw what I was looking at.

Not me, she said. My landlord.

I felt queasy looking at these carcasses but pretended nonchalance. Some people hang wreaths or wind chimes. Whatever.

He raises sheep. Ravens are vicious on lambs. Does it bother you?

I pulled my gaze away from the bodies and looked at Tully. She was staring at me with the same penetrating gaze in her hooded eyes that I remembered from the night we stood in front of that stricken deer.

If you see a raven eating carrion, she said, it means a death is near. But if one comes into your dreams, some big change is coming.

And what is the significance of raven carcasses nailed to your door?

It's just a warning, she said.

A warning to who?

To the others.

Above us a lone raven circled. A rasping sound, a clacking.

Listen, she said. They fly around, they know; it's all very freakish and bizarre.

She turned to go in, expecting me to follow, and I did. Accustomed as I was to our log home with its low ceiling, I was affected right away by the great height of the roof overhead. Twenty feet or more, it felt cathedral. Old timbers criss-crossing the expanse, a sloped gambrel roof. A wooden ladder leaned against a platform suspended in the air with what looked like a mattress up there covered by a thick rumpled quilt, a lamp beside it. Electrical cords ran across the floor. The makeshift kitchen to the side and living area all open, all one big gnarly wide-open space. The place was cold. The heat was probably trapped up there in the ceiling. An old Fisher stove against the wall. Tully, this time in woolly-lined boots, wrapped her arms around herself and shook the cold off. Damn wood is wet, she said. She crossed to the stove, pulled a piece of firewood from the pile stacked against the wall and opened it. A puff of smoke came out. She stoked it, fiddled with the damper and corrected the draft. The barn was old, cobwebbed and drafty, unadorned, unembellished, inconvenient, impractical, hard to heat, harder to clean.

It's better than our last place, she said, a moldy basement suite in Nanaimo. But the landlord's a jerk.

On top of the wood stove, a cast-iron pot was bubbling. From the smell, I imagined some kind of stew. Garlic, meat, beans. But another smell, more pervasive than garlic and smoke, her woman smell.

At least he keeps us in meat.

No TV? No computer? No running water? I said.

She cocked her head. An outhouse. Do you need it?

The nurse comes into the room. My lawyer (little Sancho Panza) is away and I miss her. The nurse wants to look at my belly; blood has soaked through the bandages and there's a redness, a swelling; it feels infected. She is not gentle. A crust has formed. She scrapes it clean.

An intravenous of something, antibiotics perhaps. I long for a drink. I long to be home.

Where is my lawyer? I ask.

Your who?

My visitor!

She's tending her infant, the nurse replies. The baby has diarrhea.

And my husband?

I know nothing about your husband's bowel movements.

And now I am alone again.

I gather the pages I have written for my little lawyer from the bedside table. Pages, old journal entries, things written newly from memory. Words I have written in my defence. Or should I say offence? But in defence of what? To be honest, I don't know. But I suspect that if I don't play along, they might think me a real nutcase. So I play along.

I heard a rushing sound beyond the thin walls of the barn, the sound of melting March snow sliding off the roof. I had another two-hour drive ahead of me to get back home. I was there to stop the train wreck. I had a document prepared that she would sign. Would it hold up in court? Who knew. She might be naive enough to believe it would. I pulled it out. But before I could state my case, my rehearsed spiel, she began.

Listen.

She sat on the floor in front of the stove, the only warm place in the barn. I recall exactly what she was wearing: leggings, a man's cotton shirt in a faded checkered pattern, buttoned off-kilter. Blake had one just like it. Those worn-out woolly boots. A grey cat crawled up onto her lap. The white dog, the dog I would know later as Fancy, curled at her side. There was no place for me in that tableau. She pointed to a seat at the side of the stove. I sat on a thin cushion that had been placed on top of a stump of wood. I was carefully coiffed, faux elegant in a cream linen pantsuit, earringed and lipsticked, a beautiful mannequin, ridiculous. Overdone as a pot roast. I felt my skin breaking out. I felt the hairs on my face, those little menopausal hairs, beginning to sprout. I felt the sweat pooling under my breasts and in my armpits. Nervous sweat, that sour stench. I watched as Tully stroked the cat and the dog in turn. Her nails bitten down, dirty. The splash of freckles on her pale arms. Those will turn into age spots, I thought meanly, hope you're ready for that. Her face unmasked, an animal face, guileless. I could not have been more envious. I pulled my lips apart and tried to remember how to breathe.

I am not a prostitute, she began. Not now. I have a child after all. But money was not always the best with me. She held her hands out, palms up in a helpless gesture, coy. She smiled. She wrinkled her nose. You would not understand.

The stump I was sitting on was hard through the thin pillow. My back was aching with the strain of sitting without support. I slouched forward.

Tully looked in my direction, not at my face; her gaze travelled over my body, from my shiny black boots up my trousered legs to my breasts to my broad shoulders, down my arms and landed on the gold bracelet on my wrist. She sighed. There are always possibilities, she said. Adjacent to the ones we already exist in. Like a chess game. Where a piece can move sideways, or backwards, or leap over, instead of what the pawns do, only forward little bit by little bit. Your husband, I think, saw me as that sort of possibility. And in his precise, gentle way he shifted sideways.

My heart was pounding. To hear her talk of my husband in such an intimate way. Not intimate physically, but as if she had been privy to his thought processes. When was the last time I had considered him this deeply?

She continued. We met at a convention, in a hotel in Calgary. One of those cheap places full of lukewarm buffets and too much liquor. I was there with a friend, Yolanda. Another model. She told me that the men there lose themselves for a weekend, like schoolboys set free. I was broke. I hadn't been called in for a photo shoot in weeks.

She scowled. And tried to smile.

I stood to leave. Never mind, I said. I know what I need to know.

But she looked up at me and I was rooted to the spot. Closing my eyes in surrender, I sat down on the stump again and waited.

Ummm, you okay? she asked.

I nodded yes.

So when my friend finished with Blake in his hotel room, she found me in the lounge. She told me he couldn't get it up, but he paid her anyway. She flashed the hundred-dollar bill in her hand. She told me his room number. She said, He's clean. And sort of funny. After another beer, and then another, the bartender, who liked me, slipped a grasshopper my way, on the house. So sweet and green and delicious. Have you ever had?

Yes, when I was sixteen, I wanted to say. I pursed my lips in disapproval instead and nodded.

I went to his room, up the elevator, down the hallway, forget the room number.

Doesn't matter.

And knocked. No answer. I had to pee so I knocked again. He was watching TV. I forget what, some business show, something about stocks. He looked angry. At first, he didn't want to let me in, but I told him I just needed to use his bathroom. He had seen me at the bar with Yolanda so I wasn't a complete stranger.

I remembered her daughter had said she had to pee the first time I met them. Maybe that was their modus operandi.

When I came out of his bathroom, I told him, We don't have to do anything. I told him, I don't care if you're soft. I told him, I'm not a virgin, but this is my first time in a stranger's hotel room. I told him, I should probably just leave, that I understood, which was not truthful. I understood nothing, I was so hungry. Do you understand hunger, how powerful it is?

She was scoffing at me. At the flesh on my bones. I vowed to myself another diet, then realized that, yes, I did know the power of hunger. I pulled my shoulders back. Then what?

Then he said, Sit. There was a chair but it was taken up by a suitcase, so I sat on the bed. The room was so hot. We watched TV while he talked. He told me about you. He said you were beautiful. Too good for him but he had won the lottery. He said you were a chameleon, tall, blond, elegant one day, dark-haired and regal the next, always in disguise. And that made him lonely. But you were an artist, and he was proud of you and jealous. I hated you intensely. I had no power over anyone. Your husband saw that in me. That with me he would be in control. A possibility missing in his own life.

So, did he get it up this time?

I don't need to answer that. The proof is in the pudding.

The top buttons of her old plaid shirt were undone. She leaned forward to stoke the fire, her small breasts, braless, on display. I felt sickened, aroused. The smell of her in the room again. So my husband seduced her with stories of me. Slanted reality to suit his purposes.

She stirred the iron pot on the stove with a long wooden spoon. Are you hungry? she asked. Lamb and beans. My landlord raises sheep.

Yes, you've said. The ravens. The sign on the driveway, "Mutton for Sale." Not hungry.

But it smelled good, delicious. She licked the gravy from the spoon.

I opened my leather purse. I had come equipped with four one-hundred-dollar bills. I pulled out two. And the one-page document I had prepared. An affidavit of non-contact.

I want you to leave us alone. Just because you had a liaison that one night in —

One night? She snorted. It was a week-long convention.

I pulled out another bill.

She took the money. I'm sorry, she said.

For what? For fucking my husband? For this charade? Standing there in her presence I felt pathetic. More than that, I felt destructive but managed to keep myself from saying out loud what I was thinking. I wanted both more of her and less and tried to defend my conflicting emotions with a belittling tone that embarrassed me even as I spoke.

How do you even support yourself? I mean between "modelling jobs."

I clean. I'm a cleaner.

I looked around the barn. I may have snorted.

She laughed. For other people I am. This place is impossible.

The spiders and the mice. And in summer I mow lawns. Or I babysit. Walk dogs. Anything really. I'm not particularly trained. Very good at math though. Blake recommends me to people. I also work at a gas station on weekends.

Blake recommends you?

He did once. It didn't pan out. The problem is, I need a break. Rent is due. And I'm really sick of mutton. I'd like to go shopping. I wouldn't mind a nice pair of leather boots myself. A night on the town.

Her chest was freckled, pale. Her skin smooth as an egg. I imagined my hand on hers. Her small hand. I thought of that poem. The rain poem. I hid my own hand, large-boned, a simple gold band with a tiny diamond. I pulled the last one hundred from my wallet. A shiny green leather wallet. I placed the bill on the stump.

She stood, unbuttoned her shirt the rest of the way.

I owe you something, she said.

I looked at her. She leaned into me. For what? To kiss me? I could smell her breath. Meaty, and sweet.

I open my eyes to the sound of my hospital door opening. My little inquisitor is back. She holds her baby on her hip. The baby is huge, cannot yet hold its head up. Little wisps of pale rusty hair on its scalp. Some sort of dandruff showing through. It is blinking in astonishment at the blue lights of my monitors pulsing against the wall.

Interrupting? she asks.

How do you interrupt a probably dying person in the middle of a breakdown? Where have you been? My voice hoarse from neglect.

Don't be like that, she says. I've been boning up.

By boning up she probably means reruns of *Sex and the City*.

She pulls the earplugs out of her ears. I hear the strains of what sounds like Taylor Swift, or Justin Bieber. They all sound the same to me. She lays the jumbo baby at the foot of my bed where the infant presses against my ankle under the blanket. If I move my foot slightly I could kick the baby onto the floor. My little lawyer is ridiculous; a trusting, foolish mother.

So where was the daughter all this time? she asks. School?

No. The child was home-schooled. The day I showed up at Tully's she was out chopping kindling.

A girl that age with an axe?

Well, why not, I thought. We learn by doing; on that Tully and I seemed to agree.

Didn't you see her outside then?

Jesus, you sound like a prosecutor.

Friendly question.

The kindling was finished I suppose, and she was taking Fancy for a walk.

But you said Fancy was in the barn with the cat and Tully.

Did I say that?

What do I remember, really? I want to remember it true, but there are lapses and reversals that do not make sense to me. Tully was so relaxed, not a bit nervous, but somehow confrontational, as if I were the transgressor. She smoked a cigarette right down to the filter and stubbed it out savagely on the floor of the barn, I remember that. There was a hard edge to her, a desperation. She said she wanted the child gone. Did she? Did she say that? She scratched at herself. She said, Fleas. The dog was not there. Was the scratching from fleas? Or something else?

I squirm my foot under the jumbo baby. My leg aches. But I'm afraid to move. The baby squawks.

Hush, Tinker.

Or maybe she was taking Fancy for a walk. Vivid imagination. The fairy forest.

CHAPTER 7

When the child, Clare, came in, a small bird that was trapped in the rafters above flushed awake, flapping to the other side of the barn to re-roost. Had given up looking for escape. The girl was like a big breath of fresh air breezing through a fetid hollow.

I remember thinking that, then dampening the thought. The child was rude, clumsy. She tracked mud, kicked her boots off helter-skelter. She took up a lot of space. She began chattering to her mother, who listened listlessly.

Fancy found a dead frog in the fairy forest! Under some fairy leaf blankets. It was so dead, stiff and cold, but when I touched it, it opened its eyes and blinked. It came alive! We brought it back to life.

I doubt that, Tully said. You're making things up again.

It's true! It came back to life!

Whatever, Tully said. We have a guest, did you say hello?

Hello, I said.

She glowered at me.

Did you kiss it? I said. Is the frog your prince?

The child scowled. No. It was a dead frog and it came back to life as still a frog, obviously. Why would I kiss it?

Oh, excuse me. I thought you were demonstrating how a fairy-tale myth as expressed in the story of *The Frog Prince* might manifest itself in real life. That's all. My cheeks flamed as if slapped.

The girl marched over to the wood stove, opened it and looked inside. Did you let the fire go out, Mommy?

It's not out. There's still coals.

Barely.

The girl chose a piece of wood from the little stack against the wall and put it in the firebox. Again a plume of escaped smoke drifted through the room.

Damper, Tully admonished.

The girl yanked the damper out viciously, and without looking at me, demanded, What's she doing here?

You should ask her yourself.

Fancy suddenly leapt to her feet, barking at the window. Outside, a crazed raven swarmed by, thonking furiously at the carcasses nailed to the wall.

In the corner was a rifle. It looked exactly like the one I had used to shoot the wounded deer. I had told Blake to get rid of it.

Tully saw my glance. I should shoot that raven, put it out of its misery as well.

Why misery? I could barely breathe.

Oh, I think those dead ravens were her babies, her fledgies.

And then a knock on the door, and without waiting for a response, it opened. Standing there was a big man, muscled, unkempt, his ponytailed hair grey and tangled.

March third, he said. Rent. Did you forget?

Clare cringed.

The man glanced at the bills I had left on the stump and smiled. That's a start anyway. He looked at me and winked. But you'll need more than that I'm afraid.

Tully turned to her daughter. Clarabelle, go play outside.

No.

Go. Now, she shouted.

The child looked around the room, even at me as if for rescue, found none and with head high and surprising dignity, she stepped outside.

As she left I heard her whisper, I hate you, but to whom it was addressed I had not a clue.

Tully shrugged. Children. They see things with their own eyes, don't they?

My little lawyer picks her daughter up off my bed. The jumbo baby is sneezing, farting, drooling. My lawyer kisses the stubby, snotty nose and licks the mucus off her lips.

They live in a world without time, she says. Without even knowing where they end and the rest of the world begins. Everything is possible: the future, the past, the present, it's a giant swirl of life. Look at her. She beams. I'm going to keep her a baby forever.

The baby might have something to say about that, I offer.

You tell me, cabbage, you got the head. You got the head. She waggles at her child. You got the head, you got the head.

The baby thinks this is hilarious and my little lawyer babbles on. God help me. I have somehow put my fate in her tiny hands.

May I continue?

Please do. What happened next?

What happened next was that Tully leaned over and picked up the paper. She collected the money I had put out. She scrawled her signature on the affidavit and handed it to me. Here, she said. You got what you came for. Now go.

Of course, there are things my lawyer is not apprised of. Personal moments that would only confuse her. That confound even me. To this day.

Later at home, that night, I remade Blake's bed with fresh sheets. He was downstairs watching TV. We had not spoken yet. I suspect he was afraid to go there. Or maybe that was my fear I was projecting. From the look of the sparkling clean kitchen, he had made himself a solitary dinner and cleaned up. There was a plate of food under wrap on the counter for me. A chicken thigh, boiled potato, boiled carrots. I put it in the fridge. I was thinking of the power of hunger and my new diet. I opened the fridge again and in the fridge light, standing, I wolfed down three of Roxanne's pudding cups. I waited at the table, and in the darkened room lit only by the small lights above the stove, I drank a glass of wine. I drank another. I heard the TV go off. Blake slipped by the open doorway without coming into the kitchen. He called out, Good night, Frida. See you in the morning. In the hallway, I took off my yellow linen pantsuit. Dry clean only. I threw it into the washing machine. I undressed completely and threw it all into the washing machine. I could smell the smoke of the woman's wood stove on my clothes, even on my hair. What had I left her to? Her and the child. The landlord taking his pound of flesh while the girl waited in the snow.

I went up to Blake's room and climbed into his bed, the sheets heavenly with bleach and fabric softener and Blake's particular man smell. He rolled over and looked at me. Well? he asked.

I'm sorry I yelled at you.

Did you yell?

I'm sure I did.

I mounted him. I rode him until he climaxed. I told him after, It's taken care of. She's on her own, she won't bother us again. I stayed where I was, moving against him until he wilted and grunted under the weight of me, and I imagined her, a feather on his body. Weightless as a black raven feather floating above him. The noise she would have made, those female sounds. I faked it until Blake said, Don't.

Tully. I could have swept her up into my arms, I could have crushed her. But I ran. I just ran.

What was she wearing, again? my lawyer asks.

Clothes. What difference does it make?

Relax. I'm just wondering.

I am angry. I try to sit up in bed. A sharp pain stabs at me from my groin, my thighs, my abdomen. It's a pain I can't locate and cannot therefore tend to. The tubes in my arms pull my skin taut when I move. What's wrong with me? I whisper.

Just stuff, my little lawyer sighs. That's the thing with hospitals. They just keep looking until they find stuff. My advice to you is stay out of them as long as you can.

Sometimes she impresses me, my brilliant advisor, with the veracity of her world view.

Sometime later I went back. I turned in at the Mutton sign, one wretched sheep sleeping under it. Her old VW van was parked at the landlord's house. I beeped as I passed and waited at her barn for her to return. Twenty minutes ticked by. She looked ragged, exhausted.

He's such a slob, she said. The toilet was gross. And he's a brute.

The side of her face was red, as if she had been slapped.

She looked me over. So what is it now? Here again with guilt money? Another affidavit to sign?

Not a good time?

It's no matter, no difference to me.

We went inside. I had my satchel of paints and brushes, a sketch pad. A canvas. Charcoal pencils. One sitting, *alla prima*, I said. I won't come again.

I was dressed in a suit and tie from Blake's closet and his wool overcoat

Clare, you let the fire go out!

I'm sick.

No, you're not. You are a liar.

Clare coughed. Phlegmy and real. She was in the loft, in that bed. Did they share it?

Tully stuffed newspaper into the smouldering fire. She blew it into flames.

The light in the barn was good. It was coming in from windows high up on the wall. North windows. A good light to paint in. The room was still cold and I was not inclined to take Blake's overcoat off. Nor the scarf.

Then Tully, clearly exhausted, squinted up at me. Did you bring any food?

I ate on the way, a chicken club at the Red Beard.

Of course, she said. Stood. Nude, right? Dropped her clothes.

Skinny. Bones, ribs. Shivering. Skin glassy. The fire had not caught yet. The child up in the loft.

You artists, she said. Shall I sit? Stand? Lie down?

Anything.

It's your painting. She turned her face to me, the side of her slapped face, pulled her hair back behind her ear.

Put your clothes on. It's so cold in here.

She laughed. We like the cold, don't we, Clare?

Clare coughed again.

She knelt to the fire again, blew on the coals, picked up the hatchet, chopped more kindling. She did things. She moved. She complained up to her daughter about dirty socks dropped on the floor. She walked into the kitchen side of the room and picked up the same cast-iron pot. Lifted the lid and smelled it. Tossed her head around in a way that suggested it would do, put it on the stove.

I sat on my old stump, set my sketch pad on my lap and began gestural sketches of her actions.

An hour passed. The room grew warm. Warmer. The girl climbed down the ladder. The mother showed no embarrassment over her nudity

What exactly do you want? she said when the stew was bubbling. Your money back? I have left Blake alone, now you two leave me alone. Stay away. Unless you have come to take this kid, stay away from me.

I brought takeout, I told her.

My annoying lawyer interrupts: I thought you didn't bring food? You ate a chicken club at the Red Beard and didn't bring food.

But I did. I'm sure of it now. Sandwiches from — from where? Did I?

Tully whirled on me, furious, threw the sandwich in my face.

The woman was clearly unhinged.

Yes. No.

I put a hundred on the hardboard table.

Tully looked at it, tilted her head to the side. You know, when I had this baby, she was the light of my life. I would have killed for her. Then she grew. Not a bad child, not at all, but not the light I once basked in. Hormones, I guess. Pheromones. Something strong in me, something fierce just sort of drained away.

Clare coughed.

On a bureau in the corner of the room was a photograph I had not noticed before, a black and white of Tully standing naked in a long field, grey sky above her, and in her hand a flower.

I left. The hem of Blake's overcoat brushed through the muck in their pathway. I heard bleating in the field. A raven circled overhead. I heard a rifle shot but the raven flew free. I sat in my car until I saw the smoke coming from their chimney. I drove the highway home. Followed a snowplow going breakneck speed, bits of gravel and salt pelting my windshield. Another chip. On the radio a volley of voices dissecting Katrina, oil spills. Another missing woman on the Highway of Tears. It didn't touch me. Nothing touched me.

The next morning, after I had slept like the dead, I went to Blake and woke him. He sat up in bed. He was growing a beard and it was coming in thin and red. His lips were chapped in the gap. I imagined her kissing him.

No, he said.

But I had not asked a question.

No, he said again.

No, what?

She's not right in the head. She's a dangerous woman. You don't know what she's capable of.

What does that mean? I probed.

It means, leave it alone. Leave her alone.

Are you afraid of her?

He would not answer.

But the light her child had thrown, it was with me.

Did that meeting really happen? In my universe it did. It may have been another place, another year, another woman modelling for me. That frightened matron who fled from me in fear and loathing. As if I would have attacked her. Or seen her for who she truly was. All her flesh and folds hanging loose and free, not tucked away and disguised under layers of spandex and Lycra. But Tully was different. Her body was a gauntlet thrown down, daring you to look away.

But still, I cannot separate the fact of memory from the fantasy of dream. Was it a story told to me? Did she model not for me but for Blake?

Yes, I think it is Blake's memory I have commandeered. And he with a camera, and his bloody heart beating so loud in the room that there was no need for music or talk.

Though Blake always left his door open in invitation, I continued with our habit of separate bedrooms.

In the morning I limped outside down the snowy trail into my studio. Every paint and pencil lined up in rows, all the blank canvases. I chose a pot of rose madder, the cap stuck on with dried paint, and banged it against the work table until it cracked. I dipped my fingers in and smeared my smock with pink. I put it down. I picked up a charcoal pencil, snapped it in half, scribbled on a sketch pad, black eyes, a blackbird, then tore it up. I prepped a canvas with gesso, stood in front of it for an hour, for two. Outside a north wind was blowing. Another spring storm on the way. I mixed a puddle of a deep merlot-coloured red.

I waited a week, maybe two before I changed the sheets on his bed again. Sweated and stained. A hole torn in the bottom sheet, near the foot. I said to him, Can't you cut your toenails? You're ripping the sheet to shreds. But it pleased me to see evidence of his restlessness and I hoped his sleep was loaded to the gills with guilt. Did he know what he had done to me? To Hera?

My little scrutinizer stops reading, rubs her hands over her face, then drops them and studies me. After a moment she shifts her gaze to the window. It's raining outside; the jumbo baby is asleep.

She says, Last night I dreamed of a green horse. The wind in my face, ice slick and hard, street lamps coming on and I was lost, looking for landmarks. Then came a beautiful green horse. Its coat was as creamy as milked grass. A pale foal at her heels.

I look down at her sleeping baby. I offer a smile. A moment passes. Hera: the goddess of women, of family, of childbirth. Madly jealous over Zeus's lovers, his illegitimate children.

I know that, she says. I know.

When I close my eyes the green horse is there. With its wide-open wild eye pinned on me.

Spring thaw descended with buckets of rain and a gluey earth that I knew enough to steer clear of. When the ground finally dried out we tried again to plant a small garden in the old people's weedy plot. Threw some seeds around, dug some dirt. Who were we kidding? At least the deer and the moles and the slugs got fed. July's harvest brought four half-ripe tomatoes and a zucchini that we ate for a week till Blake made pickles and banished them into the pantry.

Finally, it was late August, a warm beautiful day with more than a hint of our summer ending. I stepped out to enjoy it and found waiting on the step a basket of wormy apples from a neighbour and three giant zucchinis on top. Next to it a box from Amazon with a new computer for Blake. Lucky you, I said to him. I bit into an apple.

Oh, it was time, he replied as he set it up. The old one was filling up with junk, slowing everything down. He was hunched over his desk transferring files, but when I stepped up behind him he shut the lid and said, Don't chew in my ear.

After he had left for his hang-gliding lesson, I opened his old computer and went into trash and found a score of emails, from me, from his sister, from Amazon, from Swagger. A bunch of junk. But there was a folder marked family/personal and in it a tax receipt for a donation to the Canadian Alzheimer's Society and an email from Tully dated 1999 with news of the birth. I closed his laptop, then opened it again. Clicking and reading. There were more. Several more, and recent ones too. We are not child people. We are too old now. We don't know how it works.

It's not rocket science, Tully had replied.

And Clare, would she be happy suddenly living without her mother? With strangers? Think it through. I have a job.

I have a job too, Tully wrote.

My wife has her art career. We are already taking care of one infirm oldster. You promised you would never contact me. My wife is not the most mentally healthy person in the world. She's angry. You have to understand that.

Clare raved about your house. All that food. How big.

Then: I can send you more money. But you've got to find other resources. There are resources out there for single moms. You've got to look into that. I cannot help you. I'm sorry.

Tully's latest arrived just one week ago. If your wife is so unstable, why don't you leave her?

I hit reply. I am warning you. Do not contact me again. It would not be in your best interest.

I hit send.

I heard the Buffalo thunking around upstairs in Roxanne's room. I heard a muffled shriek from my grandmother, then: You're hurting me, you're hurting me!

I stayed at his old computer and waited for her reply. None came. And when Blake got home, flushed with wind and adventure, he said, Wow, what a rush up there. It's like flying. It's like being a bird, so free and scary but so exhilarating. You should try it yourself, Frida, really you should.

I think not, I said. I get enough exhilaration just sitting at home. I watched as he tossed his old laptop into the trash

I'm surprised at you, my freckle-faced defender says. Invading your husband's personal correspondence like that. It's not exactly illegal, but . . .

I'm not saying I was proud of that moment. But it did the trick and I could concentrate again on my art practice.

Of course, she says, scribbling away. Your art practice. You mean Joel?

No. I mean, okay, yes. I sent him an email.

Joel held the painting in his hands for a long time, staring at it. His scrutiny made me nervous. I studied it alongside, with new eyes. How heavily I had relied on artistic licence to glamourize my scarred body. My skin on the canvas was alabaster, with just the shadow of a spread wing on my breast. My hair fell softly.

Beautiful, he said.

I nodded, Thank you.

And there's a wild animal on your lap. Is that a wolf?

I nodded again.

Interesting, he said. Romus and Remulus.

I said, What? Remus and?

He threw his head back. I can't believe I was adopted and no one bothered to tell me until I was twenty-five years old.

Joel, I said —

He pointed at the painting. And I see that you know exactly how that feels. He paced, becoming agitated. My adoptive parents are well-off, well-groomed people, they drive BMWs, but that doesn't stop you from wondering, who is your real mother? Your real father? Are they rich? Are they well-groomed? What do they drive? He leaned in, My stepfather had a nervous breakdown when he was an adolescent. A cautionary tale he would tell me at night. For three months he believed he was a goat.

He tucked the painting under his arm.

So you still want it?

Want what?

The painting. Is it still okay?

Oh, the painting. It's fine, totally fine. Eight hundred bucks . . . It's all good.

I pulled it out from under his armpit and placed it on the easel. This was not what I was hoping for. I needed a bit more affirmation than that. I was waiting for Joel to move forward with his plans to instate me as his artist-in-residence. In fact, I had done a walkthrough of my closet and set aside the clothes I would need in Seattle for a three-month sojourn there in the fall. Rain, but mild. I had ordered a pink umbrella that opened inside out and bought shiny red gumboots. A red cape. My art supplies were the hard part. How much to take? What to leave behind? I needed to know more about the studio space. Easels? Or bring my own? The residency would be kicked off by a gallery showing. One to start, one midway through and then one to close purportedly delineating the artistic journey I had travelled while in residence. Was there a hot plate? A real kitchen? Or a per diem to eat out?

But when I asked him to elaborate more fully, he tossed it off. Oh, that's Marguerite's domain. I don't step into Marguerite's domain. Big no-no.

I must have looked a bit crestfallen, so he quickly added, But we're all good. All good. Not to worry. He put his hand on my fair shoulder and squeezed, twice, two quick pumps then pulled his hand away.

But worrying is part and parcel of my DNA. I said, I'm sure your real mother drives a Ford Fiesta. Or worse, I added. Be grateful for the BMWs.

He brightened considerably. You think? He pulled a little paint sample chip from his pocket, a dull lavender colour called Inspired Lilac, and he handed it to me. He said, When you've got time, do you mind? Marguerite wants the gallery walls freshened up and you are the local pro. He chuckled. When you've got time, no rush. And he left with still no confirmation about the residency. But this little favour he asked of me? I was sure it boded well.

It was late afternoon by the time I got home. The sun had not yet set behind the mountain. Two weeks had passed since our last contact with Tully, since my email to her, and Blake and I had managed to call a truce. Cliff averted, danger passed. Once again it was like living with a moody brother, or needy handyman. The laundry, the meals, the lawn mowing, all of it went on and made this thing called a marriage endure. Past the expiration date.

I stopped for a moment on the pathway that led to the house and looked around for the raven that was stalking me. That dark shadow on the branch? Hard to tell. There were other birds, pretty brown ones, too small to count, a noisy squirrel, and a snake which slithered away from me into the woods as if I were the scary one.

CHAPTER 8

September 5, 2008

So. Tully was dead. That was the word on the street. My neighbours were whispering it in the lineup at the Buy-Low. Whispering and darting glances at me. Word gets around in a small town. Those men at my party last year, those brothers, those chicken farmers, the truck driver, they had met her, seen the child, seen the look on Blake's face, they had put two and two together. The child was a bastard, bastard of a bastard. I paid for my U.S.-grown avocados and Mexican pomegranates. A bag of organic coffee, a package of tortured chicken. At home, I found Blake in the driveway, in his truck. Just sitting at the wheel. Staring ahead, unfocused. I rapped on his window and he jumped. I went inside and poured a drink. Vodka, grapefruit . . . another shot of vodka. I poured a rum and coke for Blake. Blake came in and I held out his drink. He stared at it, then grabbed it from me and drank it down.

She shot herself, he said. On the bank of the South Thompson.

Shot herself. An image of the child flitted across my consciousness like a butterfly. I let it pass. Shot herself, my god. I knew what that meant. Her memory would haunt Blake forever. I turned to the counter and sliced the avocado in two. Peeled it and pitted. I mashed it into a bowl and ripped open a package of tortilla chips. Guacamole, I said. You need to eat. But when I turned he was gone and I was alone. Cheap taco chips, every one without exception broke when I dipped it.

That officious one who visits me bites the end of her pencil and chews. You know what they say about butterflies, the ones that flutter in Africa and cause a tsunami in Detroit?

What do they say?

They say they flutter in Africa.

That night, he came into my bedroom and stood in the dark at my bedside. I let him suffer until I lifted the blanket and he climbed in. I let him fumble through the motions. The sex was joyless, and a little bit erotic. The wetness of sweat and tears. I should write a song. Exhausted, he fell asleep enveloped in oxytocin and heart-ache. Blake was broken. And because he was, so was I. But I had been broken before. One limps on, it is as simple as that.

In the mail next day another card came addressed to Blake. Inside was a childish drawing of a blackbird, a raven or a crow, sitting on a branch, wings spread, a red berry in its mouth and two beady yellow eyes staring out at the viewer. CLARE in block letters on the bottom. And a note tucked in from Tully — we need to talk. Postmarked five days before her suicide.

Blake folded it in thirds, placed it in the kitchen drawer on top of the Visa bills and liquor store receipts. I need some air, he said and walked out the door. I heard his pickup start and watched out the window as he drove away.

Around ten that night my phone meowed. Drowsy from wine, I had fallen asleep in front of the TV. The phone call was Blake.

Are you sober?

Suddenly I was.

I need you to drive down to the police station.

Why?

I need a ride home.

I dressed up warm and clean. A solid citizen of the world in respectable grey trousers, an oversized black tunic. For some reason, for fun maybe, or design, I put a little pillow in the waistband of my slacks. Couldn't hurt, right? I made a pot of coffee. He could wait. I drank coffee, water, Gatorade. I was aslosh. I peed. I brushed my teeth, I gargled. I burped and burped. I have heard somewhere that burping reduces your blood alcohol reading. I smelled my breath against my hand. Peppermint and hand sanitizer. Truth be known I had never been more wide awake and sober. I got in my little yellow sports car and drove carefully down the dark highway, tiny white moths fluttering in the air. Hardly a soul on the road. At intervals a TV light glowing from a farmhouse. A luminant yardlight, a lonely cow bellowing.

The police station was bright under fluorescents. The officer on duty did not give my pillowed belly a second glance. Which was a lucky thing, as the pillow had shifted weirdly to the side. The station smelled of stale coffee. A mostly empty box of donuts on the counter. Clichés become clichés for a reason.

Blake was released without a fuss, some paperwork to sign, my name, my driver's licence, vehicle registration. I nearly put my hand out for fingerprinting but stopped just in time. Blake's licence suspended for three, several, eight months? Can't remember, it seemed forever. A thousand-dollar fine, all of it explained by a yawning sergeant. Yes, sir. Yes, sir. Three bags full.

We drove home in silence. When I pulled into our driveway Blake turned to gaze at me. I sat motionless with my hands on the steering wheel, looking out the windshield and waited for his apology, but instead, he nodded and said, You look cute pregnant.

The next morning I called my truck driver friend — forget her name — to help me ferry Blake's truck out of the impound lot.

Morning ablutions, glass of water, vitamins, squats, and face creams, touch-ups for any stray greys, makeup: concealer, foundation; blush, lipstick, eyeliner, mascara, my brows plucked.

I went through my ART Book and found a painting that

Frida Kahlo had done, a depiction of her friend's leap from a tall building, her friend's suicide. I could only stare at it and wonder. The blurb attached described it as a commission, from the woman's family, for a portrait of the daughter, a remembrance. They had not been expecting a depiction of the leap. There must have been quite a fuss. I tried to begin. A few marks. A splash of paint, green. Then red. The zone, the concentration, the inspiration, it all eluded me. I went back into the house and ordered more art supplies from Amazon. In a thousand years, I could never paint enough to use them up. Was I mad? The Buffalo called me in for lunch. Tuna sandwiches. Carrot cake. I opened a beer and I ate the sandwich, ate the cake. I felt starved. Could not seem to get enough food in me. Gaining weight.

And apparently, I was the designated driver.

The child's birth certificate was located. October 31, 1999.

Weight. Length. Mother. Father. Hospital. Attending physician. Birthmarks. Race.

The woman from child services placed it in front of us. Precious document. The room she called us into was low-ceilinged and close. Beige walls. Pale, flowery paintings. I studied the artwork, the mountain landscape on one wall. A vase of flowers on another. Pastel colours. Was this what the people who buy art, hang art, really want? The air smelled stale, of nervous sweat — was it mine? Pickle juice and swamp moss. I sniffed at my armpit; Blake kicked at me; I kicked him back, much harder, under the table. A fluorescent overhead and a dwarf-size table — meant for children I suppose, not dwarves — in the corner, littered with germy plastic toys and vivid tales of bullied turtles and shape-shifting caterpillars.

The woman wore bracelets on both wrists that tinkled and shimmered when she moved her hands. I wanted to slap her stubby fingers away as she pointed to salient details. My own nails were acrylic, black. I was completely in black.

Of course, the father named was Blake. I gave him a knowing look. He refused to meet my gaze. I sighed. Such a huge misunderstanding. I would be kind. I owed it to the dead woman's memory.

It's sad, though, I said, because my husband had a vasectomy several years ago.

The woman looked up at Blake for confirmation, eyebrows lifted in surprise.

I kicked him again.

He nodded, shrugged, waggled his head around in the most non-committal way possible.

Even so, she said, even if that is the case, of which I am not convinced, sometimes those procedures do fail. She leaned in, dropping the weight of her bosom, a thick blubbery shelf of flesh, onto the desk: Did you know that a man must ejaculate at least twenty times to clear the semen out of the vas deferens after a vasectomy? She rolled her eyes. But who counts, right? Anyway, there are ways of finding out. The woman smiled. Big mole on the side of her nose.

There are ways of getting those removed, I thought.

She reached down and pulled her boobs up off the desk. Shuffled her ass on her chair until the earth beneath her settled.

The child, apparently, was in the temporary care of a family, religious, Christian, already fostering three orphans. Was it rude of me to ask how much they were paid for each of the foundlings? The woman answered without a hint of shame, shameless.

Blake's eyes had never appeared so grey, grey as oceans, grey as steel. He smelled of wildfire and cottonwood. I wanted to take his face in my hands and turn it towards me, but he was at a distance I could not cross. Fully engaged with the awful woman, that dimpled smile. We want what's best for the child, she kept saying. Her mascara clotted, little pooches of eye bags. As if we did not. All of the children, everywhere.

All right then, I said. Bring it on.

We left the office and I drove us home in silence. Blake turned the radio up. Pipelines, truth and reconciliation. For forty-five kilometres we did not speak. The hard set of his jaw. He turned the radio off. He said, Slow down. I slowed. Then he said, Can't you even go the speed limit? I said, Shut up. At home, we were wary as hunted spiders. Wide berths. Blake chopped garlic. I stepped aside to let him. He stepped aside to let me fry. Dumped a package of frozen ground into the pan. We stood there and watched it steam in its own juices.

So, what now, I asked. Semen analysis? Porn mags? Jerking off in a doctor's office? Viagra? Big tits and wet pussies?

Are you that ignorant? he asked.

Uncharted territory.

And Roxanne at the top of the stairs in a flannel nightgown stained with soup. Every time you masturbate, she quipped, God kills a kitten.

This cannot be born.

DNA sample, he said. It's not about jerking off.

When the kit came, instructions for an inner cheek swab. I joked, Maybe we should send mine in, instead? I mean, JUST IN CASE.

He set me straight again. To be legal, it has to be done in front of witnesses.

Of course. I was only kidding.

None of this sat right. This moment looming was the beginning of the rest of my life. The rest of my shitty life.

Just do what you got to do, my friend. And leave me out of it. Just leave me completely out of it.

Leave who out of what? he asked. Then he remembered my existence and said, Oh, you.

When Blake went out, I texted Joel. Are you in town? Come over, I demanded. And he did. Good boy. He came over with a bottle of sherry. My new pal. My drinking buddy. I hated sherry. We drank it down. He wanted to talk about Art with a capital A. He wanted to talk about the Gallery with a capital G that he and Marguerite were arguing over in the village. He wanted to talk about Finances with a capital F.

I missed you, I said.

Oh, well. Stuff going on.

Me too.

Painting?

Not at all. I brushed my hair back away from my face, then remembered what it was covering, and brushed it back again. So, I said, not quite a shout, but loud enough, The woman is dead.

He tilted his head quizzically. What woman?

The mother.

What mother?

The child's mother.

What child?

I said, Never mind. I pulled out a checkers game. Want to play?

Before he could say, I would absolutely love a game of checkers with my favourite artist in the whole world, Marguerite beeped and he picked up the almost-empty bottle of sherry and wished me a fond adieu.

At the door, he winked. She's in heat.

And the opposite of in heat is out cold. That clever thought distracted me from the realization that I was in way over my head.

I went upstairs to Roxanne's room. She and the Buffalo were watching *Secret Diary of a Call Girl*. I sat with them and stared at the beautiful bad girl building lie upon lie.

I said, Can either of you explain this motherhood thing to me? The fixation, the obsession, the bewitchment? It must be hormonal. Is it hormonal?

Roxanne and the Buffalo exchanged looks.

The Buffalo stepped up to the plate. Well, I for one don't talk about my hormone parts with my employers.

Fair enough. I looked to Roxanne, expecting the usual nonsense. But what she gave me was this: We exist, therefore we breed.

I stepped outside. A raven swooped by, so close it almost touched my head. It landed in a tree by the house. I could swear that it had a nest high up in the crotch of that fir tree. Eggs, eggs, eggs. I threw a rock at it.

CHAPTER 9

One by one the world is being overrun with babies. And each pregnancy is lauded, bare bellies right up in your face, like a miracle, another miracle, and another, and if it is so miraculous how come there are billions of them squirting out? And everywhere you turn, the picture of fuzzy ultrasounds to endure. Movie stars, newscasters, the weather girl, the drugstore lady, CEOs, waitresses, doctors, dentists, lawyers. It never ends.

I signed up as a volunteer for hospice. I whispered to the comatose old ladies, You better hurry up and get a move on! There's a swamp load of babies out there on planet Earth waiting for space. The old ones would blink open their eyes, coming alive for the first time in weeks and croak, Baby? Is there a baby here? Even the old dying ladies wanted a baby!

Oh, I luxuriated in my childlessness. It was clean and pure and bright. I went back to hospice and said, Do not die. I command you not to die. They have no right to push you out of this overburdened, overpopulated world. You stay right where you are and don't let the babies in.

Baby? the old ladies croaked. Is there a baby here?

With my sketchbook open on my lap I sketched their beautiful cadaverous faces. I drew with precision every wrinkle, every crusted eyelid, every slack-lipped opening into the chasm of their fleshy gums. Back at my coop, I turned the sketches into lurid portraits. Joel recoiled at each without exception. But still, he pressed me for more, better, different. Marguerite was interviewing others for the position. Who was kidding who here?

Blake waited like the reincarnation of Buddha for the results.

I told him if Joel and Marguerite's offer of a residency fell through, that did not mean I would be available. In fact, I had applied for an artist residency in the Yukon and should push come to shove, he would have to manhandle the girl on his own.

He blanched. His thin red beard looked redder against the whiteness of his skin.

Of course, I continued, it's not like push will come to shove. That would be a medical miracle. Wouldn't it.

I don't have my driver's licence, he said. You can't leave me here without a licence.

Gee, I said, sucks to be you.

I was lying about the Yukon application. I don't know what I expected from Blake. Something a little more personal than requiring my driving ability would have been nice. Maybe I wanted to hear him say he needed me for other reasons. Not that I cared. Honestly, I did not. I bought a cowboy hat and wore it for a week.

My legal genius narrows her eyes and aims them at me. Something that sounds very much like "harumph" comes out of her mouth.

Your baby, I say, is having a poo.

That always diverts her attention.

When it pains me to look back on my life, I look away. It seems all I can recall are the bad acts, the missteps and barbed words and cold hard-heartedness jutting into my consciousness like rocks in a creek that I bump against as I float downstream. I'm sorry for the bad metaphor. But why do I feel like I'm a basically good person when every memory reminds me that I am not?

In the bedroom, early morning, I lay in the crumpled bed with Blake, my husband. My aging, try-hard, get-it-wrong-half-the-time husband.

He was between my legs. The top of his head a swirl of red hairs mixed with grey, pink scalp, a little dandruff. He stopped.

I'm sorry, he finally whispered.

What are you sorry about? It's not your fault. It's mine.

No. I mean, the other.

The other?

The child.

I knew then. What I had already suspected. There were no records. No vasectomy. And for me definitely no climax.

My phone meowed. I answered while Blake climbed out of bed and dressed. A call to renew Sirius. Sure. Why the hell not? From now on, Yes to every damn thing.

And the very next thing that happened was Clare.

What I want, what I claim I do not want. What I do not want, and what I claim I want. All this sent out into the universe. And the universe listened.

The results of the DNA were returned. I was there when Blake opened the envelope. The cartoon owl look on his face told me everything. He crumpled the pages in his hand. Cast his eye about wildly, not seeing me, not caring that I stood there watching. He pushed the crumpled pages into his pocket. He left the house. He was the father.

Well there you go, my clever little lawyer says. She is diapering her jumbo baby on the foot of my bed, the baby slick with diarrhea and diaper rash.

We are in the hospital. I'm pretty sure she is with me here, just learning of the DNA results. She has plucked this page up out of the shuffle, out of order in the sequence of events. Or is she here? I want her to know the results of the DNA. I need her to know that first, before she learns of other things.

Blake was still working as a plumber's helper while his computer business was getting off the ground, and since the suspension of his driver's licence, it was up to me to drive him to the plumber's house every morning, pick him up in the afternoons. I didn't mind. It wasn't like I had to get dressed. Just a sweater over my PJs, and bare feet stuffed into boots. Hair uncombed, no makeup, not even my teeth brushed. Blake on the other hand was crystal clean and ready for septic duties.

As we drove, we listened to the radio. Sometimes I would chortle at Stephen Harper's latest faux pas, sometimes he would hum to a song he liked. It was the only time we had together alone, but instead of being comforting it was awkward, like two teenagers getting to know each other, hyperaware of their bodies, their smells, their tics and facial expressions. An invisible presence sat between us. A third body.

If there was a question raised, it was usually mundane.

Can you wash my coveralls while I'm at work?

We'll see.

So what is Joel up to these days?

Nothing much.

The main plumber guy and the main plumber guy's truck were a twenty-minute drive from our house.

One morning Blake said, I made an appointment for winter tires.

And I said, Has social services found out you got a DUI?

His silence told me that they had. And that the girl's placement with us was being re-evaluated. I won't pretend that this did not fill me with glee. How they found out was not something I needed to divulge.

So what did you do? my charming tormentor asks me.

I am loathe to tell her. But I suspect she barely listens at the best of times, let alone when the air in the room is choked with baby powder and the smell of rash cream and baby pee, and the jumbo baby's legs are kicking so furiously in the air making her gurgle in joy. I let some words come that I hope will go unheeded.

I went into the studio and I went online and I took sleeping pills and went to bed I drove to the Yukon I burned his clothes I smashed his computer I cleaned the house I stopped talking.

I called my mother.

It was midnight in Paris. Seasonably cool, partly cloudy, a late September evening, half moon. So said World Weather International. I knew her number by heart though I rarely used it. She picked up. Her throaty voice, *Allo*?

I said, Mummy, it's me. I'm sorry to call so late. I hope I didn't wake you. I took a deep breath. Life is so complicated, Mummy, I'm sure you know that. Even simple lives are complex when you look back at them and try to find patterns and reasons and consequences that make sense. I paused. Maybe that's what art is supposed to do, make sense of life, find the coherence, make outcomes seem inevitable and satisfying — resolutions that actually resolve, or maybe art is only meant to entertain and distract. But if art does that, it does it self-servingly to serve its own purposes because life really is just a series of chaotic, mostly inexplicable events, and any coherence imagined is manufactured, or at the very most a function of habit or primal instinct and behavioural choices and relationships and emotions and myth-making, and what is formed and forming are as whimsical as bubbles. I'm babbling. I haven't talked to you in so long. I've missed your voice. But is it all and only about science? Because even bubbles can be scientifically scienced, but what is science anyway? Isn't science a series of false starts over and over again with what is contained in one end squishing out another hole, a house of cats and crows and genetic coding? Mummy, there's that monkey mind again trying to find the either-or, the black or white, the this or that and trying to pin it down. What won't be pinned down. Mummy,

I love you, I do try. And I'm sorry. Always and again. When you get this message, please call me back.

I sat on the hard chair in the kitchen with my iPad and waited. It was 3:10 in the afternoon in my world. The skies hazy with the forest-fire smoke from a different country, another world. I scrolled through pictures. Me and Blake on New Year's Eve (I was a gypsy), me and Blake at a Chinese restaurant (a geisha), Blake in front of a panorama of snow, my hand holding a giant shrimp, a bowl of raspberries; my yellow sports car when it was new, my hair when it was new, my toenails painted blue. I took a selfie of myself waiting. I texted the Buffalo, who was upstairs with Roxanne. How is the old crow? She texted back a thumbs-up. She texted again, Can you get us a subscription to Netflix? I texted back a frowny face. I put my iPad down. I waited and waited. I taught myself stillness and patience. I remembered hunger and anger. Blake was due home. I got in my yellow sports car and drove to the Hut and ordered a burger and poutine. I ate it in my car with the engine running and the radio on.

Our house was so dark. All the walls threw everything back at me and no matter the season, inside was always winter. The man I gave myself to was big as an animal. I told him this morning, I have to get out of here. He said, I don't trust you out there. He said, I don't think you know what you want. He said, Go to Paris then.

I fell asleep in the car; it was more like a hibernation than a sleep. Every time I looked up it was raining. All day long. The trees were so clean I wanted to lick them.

Later that night, the old crone was in bed, sucking on Turtles, watching TV, pay-per-view, something lewd. The Buffalo had left for the day. I lay down beside her. I pulled the crocheted afghan over my legs. We ate the chocolates and watched a young, muscular firefighter strip down to his jock strap. The old crone patted my hand. Again and again. She just kept patting. Gumming those Turtles and patting.

Mummy did not phone back. However, the next day one hundred euros were deposited into my bank account.

My youthful solicitor hands me the diaper-rash cream to hold. She purses her lips. Don't worry, she says, lawyer-client privilege. She puts everything in air quotes.

It's not a secret, I say. It's out there for anyone to know. My husband fathered a baby with another woman after we made a pact and decided we would never have kids because we were not cut out.

He probably feels so bad about it. I wouldn't hold it against him.

I stare at her. Are you really a lawyer?

Are you really a client? She scowls.

What day is it? I ask.

Tuesday.

Month?

Still November.

Year?

The year of my little wonder's birth, 2019. Little wonder.

The jumbo baby vomits, a huge and milky eruption.

What kind of a hospital is this?

Don't you know?

Not really.

Hmm . . .

Can you get me out of here?

Where would you go?

Home? Is there such a thing?

She tickles the baby's juicy belly.

I push the call button for the nurse. I whisper into the monitor. And before I drift off I hear someone talking. It might be me. I try to make sense of the words as I speak them. I'm begging you, God, I'm begging you for pain.

CHAPTER 10

Roxanne's breakfast tray came down untouched and when I went up to her with a special lunch of chopped Spam, she was standing near her bed, wild-eyed, ratty-haired and delirious, a magazine rolled up in her hand, swatting at the wall. I heard the Buffalo grunting in the bathroom.

What are you doing?

I'm killing mice now and I don't know why. Why am I killing mice? Mice have never harmed me. You know I've been alone here for a little while now, not sure how long but it feels like a minute, a whole minute.

I put the tray of mashed Spam and a plastic sippy cup of sweet white wine on her bedside. From the bathroom came the glugging sound of the flush.

The next day or so I found Blake sitting at the table in the kitchen eating a grilled cheese sandwich. The kitchen was hazy, the stench of burnt butter in the air. I turned the stove fan on. He had a non-alcoholic beer on the table in front of him. The TV was on and he was watching a re-enactment of a beach landing in a black-and-white war. He turned it up to hear over the fan. I turned it off.

He put his half-eaten sandwich down on the table. On his thumb a gob of mayonnaise that he licked off

You could at least use a plate. I held one out in front of him until he took it from me and put his sandwich on it.

Thank you.

He pointed behind me. I brought you something.

I turned. On the counter, a bouquet of flowers still wrapped in pink cellophane. A huge bouquet. Red ones, yellow, white. I recognized a rose, a daisy, something blue. The most beautiful bouquet he had ever given me.

Gee, I said, flowers.

You're welcome, he said. He turned the TV on again, I turned it off.

I stood in front of him and crossed my arms in front of my chest. You know, you told me once, and I remember it distinctly, you were juggling oranges on the beach in Puerto Vallarta and I was hustling those little watercolour sketches of palm trees to tourists, and I cut my foot on a piece of glass and you were so worried and I said, Just pour your tequila on it to sterilize and you did, then you laughed and you said... Do you remember that day? Do you remember what you said?

Blake shook his head, no.

You said, Let's never change. You don't remember that? I remember it so clearly. You wore cut-off blue jeans, and your calves were sunburned. And you said, The way we are now, this moment, is the way we should always be, even with all our faults and problems and cuts and bruises and mosquito bites. Let's promise to never change.

I let this sink in and after a moment I continued.

Well, I haven't, Blake. I kept my part of the bargain. I haven't changed.

He watched me as I spoke. He picked up his fake beer, looked at it and put it down again.

Are you done? he asked me.

I turned around and switched the stove fan off. Let the smoke have its way. The room was quiet again. Yes, I'm done. You have nothing to say? That is so typical.

As I began to leave him and his greasy sandwich, he spoke.

But I do have something to say, Frida. And that is that you actually have changed and so have I, and maybe you haven't noticed but we're not sleeping on a beach anymore in Mexico with sand in our hair. And maybe it's my fault that you changed from that girl you used to be. But we've got a house and a mortgage and car payments and insurance payments and your old grandmother to take care of and snow to shovel and lawns to mow and —

And your child to foster. Don't forget that little bit of info.

He put his half-finished sandwich down and picked up his sad beer.

I'm just curious, Mr. Dad. When I was getting my ster-il-a-za-shun done, where were you? If you weren't having your own government-sanctioned medical intervention performed, where were you all that time?

Who knows. Drowning my sorrows probably.

Drowning your fucking sorrows.

I picked the bouquet up. Blake stood as if to approach me. He wiped the mayonnaise off his lips with the back of his hand. Frida, he began.

I sniffed the flowers. I sneezed dramatically. Allergies, I said. I sneezed again and stuffed the bouquet into the trash.

When I open my eyes, my restless companion and her jumbo baby are gone. Just the dirty diaper in the trash as evidence that they have been here.

Blake spent the next day cleaning and rearranging the house. Washing windows, vacuuming, moving his things into my bedroom. His robe, underwear, socks, toothbrush, hairbrush, Old Spice, razors. Everything in his bathroom, into mine. The child would take his room.

I dug out from the closet a suitcase, the old-fashioned kind that women used to use for their cosmetics, square and small. What were they called? I went into the bathroom and began collecting my face creams and skin salves and makeup.

What are you doing?

I'm moving out.

Moving out where?

You'll see.

I stomp-limped out the door and made my way down the path to the chicken coop.

He watched for a moment as the realization of my intended move dawned on him. Are you crazy? he shouted after me.

I went to the hardware store in town and bought a hide-a-bed. The delivery man hauled it into my chicken coop. A strong-nosed, dark-eyed, pudgy forty-five-year-old with a bad hip. My doppelganger in a weird way. I asked him if he had any childhood scars, just as a joke really. He backed away from me. Only kidding, I said.

Well, to be honest . . . he started.

Never mind, I said, as he lifted his T-shirt and exposed his hairy belly.

Liposuction, he said proudly.

But his tiny scars were nothing to brag about and I told him so and he dropped his shirt with a scowl. I tipped him five bucks.

He snorted at me. Keep it, lady, he said. Looks like you need it more than I do.

Tomorrow the girl comes, I told him.

I hope she's a good cleaner, he replied. Got a lotta chicken shit.

I noticed a sour smell from my body. When was the last time I showered? Or shaved my legs? This robe was death personified. I would give it to Roxanne. I loped back to the house, drew a hot bath and added bath oil, what was left of it. I soaked and scrubbed. I picked at the pimples on my face until they were flat and raw. I massaged my gammy leg and rubbed aloe vera on the scar.

I walked out into the woods and wished I was dumb enough or brave enough to stay there. A wilderness woman, strong, self-sufficient. Waking to the whisper of branches overhead. A piny breeze, squirrels chirping. Early October. The sky was a tangerine globe. The crows and ravens were signalling danger or love or hunger or joy or god knows what to one another in the air, caw caw, honk honk, thwonk, rawk, screet. I wanted their language. I yelled, Hello. The trees were sending each other messages through the ground, through their roots. I wrapped my arms around a tree and listened. I heard nothing of note. Actually, nothing at all. And then even the blackbirds went silent.

At almost precisely ten the van arrived. Rattled over the cattle guard and stopped in the driveway. The child was being shuttled by one of those agencies that shuttle desperate children to their next temporary home. Or so I presumed. I had no experience of the official way of things. My own shuttling had been haphazard. Nothing signed, no interviews, no documents, no formalities. Just pack your bag, grab your stuffies, a short taxi to the airport and a long flight to Roxanne.

I was dressed in a long butt-hugging skirt that skimmed and swished around the ankles of my high black boots. Navy turtleneck. I looked killer, I must admit. My hair was huge. I knew it wasn't the style anymore but I didn't care about style. It was big and I'm big and the whole charade was threatening to overwhelm me and I would not let it. I had bleached my hair blond again too.

I crossed my arms and stared through the plate-glass window at the goings on, as a middle-aged woman with thick, framed glasses climbed out of the car. Pushing her glasses up her nose she looked around at our yard, our abode and spotting Blake on the step, she beckoned him over. I sulked at the window, watching, as Blake approached, nodding, shaking hands, crouching down to the child's eye level to look in the rear window at her and wave. The girl, staring straight ahead, sat motionless in the back seat, a doll in her arms, a dog at her side, while the woman popped open the trunk and unloaded a small suitcase and two cardboard boxes. She set them on the ground and retrieved a clipboard from the front and handed it, with a pen, to Blake. A cold October sun did its best to beat down as I watched him read it over.

The woman pulled a hanky from her sleeve and blew her nose while he signed and the child finally slid out of the back seat. She was followed by the dog, the same white dog I had first seen in Tully's van when I shot that deer and same I had seen again in the barn. The dog's fur thick and matted. Blake bent to it and the dog snarled. My new world unfolding before my eyes. The girl was dressed in satin, bright pink satin, and was wearing makeup on her child face. Spots of blush, pink lipstick, even eyeliner. Blake carried the boxes up to the front step, the woman following behind with the suitcase and clipboard, the child with the baby doll in her arms.

The child handler followed Blake inside and found me in the living room. She introduced herself, Trudy something, not a doubtful bone in her body. Her eyes were huge, magnified behind her glasses. She looked about the house. My very clean house. My extraordinarily clean, sparkling, shining, mismatched house with the old red leather couches. She made a note on her clipboard. Asked to see the child's bedroom. Blake pointed upstairs and we waited silently until she returned. Mama, I killed a man, I hummed until I ran out of melody and realized what I was singing.

This is Clare, the Trudy woman said. Your new charge until we make a final determination. And this is Fancy. The dog.

The dog eyed me suspiciously as I put my hand out to pat it only because it seemed that everyone was waiting for me to do that very thing. Fancy growled.

I expect you'll want to wash that makeup off, the woman said. Indicating the child.

Who did that? Blake asked.

The other child in the foster home, an older girl. The woman shrugged. How old are you, Clare? Can you say hello?

The child kept her gaze on the ground.

Nice pink dress, I said.

The child glared up at me. She knew a lie when she heard it.

And happy birthday in two weeks, Blake said. He had remembered.

The child hugged her baby doll a bit closer.

So anyway, Trudy, how long before you find the next of kin?

Now surprise bloomed on her owlish face. But father *is* the next of kin.

You know what I mean, I said. I mean "amenable" next of kin. Not a one-night-stand next of kin.

Ahhh . . . there is an uncle but he's in prison, it seems.

No surprise there, I interjected.

And we are still looking for the grandfather. But if you think the child might in the meantime be in trouble here . . . in the meantime . . . ?

A long pause then, and I felt Blake defiantly not looking at me.

We did get an anonymous call, Trudy said, but we don't have the resources to deal with crank calls. She smiled at me.

I'm sure she's good here, I said. Till better is found. We'll take care of business. I smiled back. I enlarged the smirk to show my teeth, my beautiful, Cloroxed, big white teeth. When did I get so smarmy?

Nope, Blake said. She's good. We'll take care of her. It's all good.

Yes, well, that was our impression right from the get-go. If we're wrong? She looked at me for confirmation.

Upstairs a thump, then another and a loud groan and a feeble, Fridaaaa?

Trudy looked at me expectantly.

Oh, that's just my granny. She's pretty old. Actually, she's dying. I'm sure that's no concern. Death happens. We're all grown-ups here. Most of us, anyway.

Trudy frowned.

My wife volunteers at hospice, Blake said. He shot me a dirty look. She's trying to raise awareness. About dying. You know.

Oh.

The dog grabbed the hem of my long skirt and tugged at it. I pulled back and heard it rip, yanked down, my butt half exposed. The child laughed. I hitched it back up to my waistline.

Well, that's the first laughter I've heard, the woman declared. I think we're all good here, right? She smiled around. You got your baby? she said to the child.

The child was swinging her baby doll by the foot, absent-mindedly banging its head against the wall.

All good, said Trudy, all good.

While Blake escorted his charge upstairs to her room, I lugged the boxes down into the basement, where I perused the contents. Tully's clothes and cheap jewellery, her shoes. All those shoes and yet when I met her, she was barefoot. Fringed handbags, camisoles, a scuffed leather jacket, a silk robe. The street clothes of a wanna-be courtesan. But everything old and worn, bought at thrift shops I suspected. The perfumes: Wind Song, Opium. I spritzed myself. Rose-coloured crop tops and padded bras. And from Victoria's Secret, her panties, bright, lacy, thong panties. Similar — no, not similar, identical — to the ones Blake had bought me a few Christmases past. And the gold-plated Buddha. My gold-plated Buddha. I had not even noticed it missing.

Here it was. My anger was simmering, bubbling inside me, a volcano threatening to blow. And something else, a feeling that I can only describe as a longing to shed my thick callous skin, emerge tender, raw, divested of my own hateful being. I stripped down and slipped the crop top on. My pale belly bulged out from beneath the hem. I yanked it off.

Upstairs I heard the water running in the bathroom. Blake was calling out to me but I pretended not to hear. When I climbed the stairs, I ran into the child in the hallway. Her face was mostly scrubbed clean and in her hand, she held a soiled damp washcloth. Blake was staring at her helplessly and she was staring back. A streak of blue eyeshadow was still smudged across her cheek. Blake, jittery as a feral cat, his pale forehead beaded in sweat, pointed to it and she scrunched her eyes closed and savagely swiped at her face, missing the mark entirely.

But was it really true, as the prosecution averred, that my whole life had been a series of futile attempts to tamp down the fury that festered? Who was that fury directed towards?

My legal eagle is watching me closely. Almost as if I have spoken these words out loud. Perhaps I have. Yet she has no response.

PART 2

Of Sticks and Twigs, Mud, Fur, Bark and Grass

The world is full of magic things, patiently waiting for our senses to grow sharper.

W.B. YEATS

CHAPTER 11

My first night in the coop I slept like a baby. Crying and belching and farting, my arms flailing, looking for boundaries, walls, a womb, anything to keep me contained. I woke with a headache, a wine headache, daylight filtering through my closed eyelids. I groaned and buried my head under the blanket. The coop was cold, dusty from old hay. The new cot was hard. When I opened my eyes the girl and her dog were standing at my bedside staring at me.

I screamed a little and sat up. I was wearing her mother's satiny loungewear. A swirl of dirty greeny gold. The girl wore old fleece pyjamas. Decorated in pink mice. The dog bared its teeth.

Something I can help you with?

An almost imperceptible shake of her head that meant no, or maybe not, or I'm not sure or does it matter?

Okay. Listen up.

The child lifted her head and waited. The braids she had slept in were tangled on her neck. Sleep crud in the corners of her eyes. Her bare ankles and shins poked out from below her pyjamas. Her feet were grimy with dirt.

I closed my eyes.

There are two kinds of people in the world, morning people and not morning people. Can you guess which kind of people I am?

When I opened my eyes, Blake was standing there next to her.

There are two kinds of people in the world, is right, he said.

Yes, I shouted. Those who cheat and lie and those who don't.

He took the girl's hand.

I had a funny dream last night, Blake. I dreamed I was a chicken and I laid an egg.

He scowled. Don't go crazy on me. The coffee's made. You look like hell.

On their way out past my workbench, the girl picked up a brand new package of coloured pencils and a sketch I had set there and carried them away. The sketch was one my mother had done, years before, when I was still a child. She had sent it to me in lieu of a visit I suppose, on a birthday, or Easter perhaps. It was of a rabbit. A rabbit in a jar, hunched over, hardly able to fit, his head and back and feet and ears all pressed up against the glass he was caged in. Fat and resigned, looking out at the viewer with shiny eyes, not even plotting its escape. So many nightmares.

I'd appreciate it if you asked, I thought loudly. For once my thoughts stayed in my head.

I needed the bathroom. I needed a shower. I needed coffee. I dressed in stretch-waist jeans and a sweater the colour of dead brain cells, the same clothes I had exiled myself in. I made a mental note to move some of my clothing in. I slipped Tully's bright silky loungewear under my pillow. It was embarrassing to be caught wearing it by the girl, but she had seemed not to notice.

In the kitchen, the new dad and daughter duo was finishing Cheerios together.

I found my robe on a hook, my own thick fleecy robe, pulled it on over my clothes to ward off the chill.

After an early poke of sunlight, the sky was promising more of its familiar grey gloom.

Is the Buffalo here yet?

Just arrived.

Have you taken anything up for Roxanne?

Cup of tea.

Did you leave me any coffee?

Right there in front of you.

I poured my cup to the brim. Added a spoonful of sugar, Creamo. Did not mop up the spill.

The girl, still in her pyjamas at the table, was watching me closely. I stirred my coffee and clinked the spoon on the edge, refused to take notice. Somebody, Blake no doubt, had placed *Hawaii* on her seat to get her up to level.

You know what I think? Blake asked the girl. I think it's time to get dressed and start the day. What do you think?

No answer.

You can help me in the yard, or . . .

I looked at him. Or what?

Or play in your room.

In her bowl was half a cup of leftover milk and sugar. She had her finger in the bowl and was absent-mindedly swirling a few soggy Cheerios around.

Are you going to ask her to finish her cereal? I said to Blake.

Why don't you ask her yourself?

I'm not in charge of her stomach, I replied. Actually, I don't seem to be in charge of anything that's going on around here.

Blake mumbled under his breath. I heard a vocalization that sounded like fuck.

What?

Nothing. He glared at me.

The girl put the bowl on the floor for the dog. The dog lapped it up and licked the bowl dry.

Dog saliva, biofilm, I said. Who gets to wash that?

The girl bent and picked up the bowl. She put it in the sink and turned the hot water on full bore. The water splashed up so suddenly and so vigorously, it ricocheted off the spoon and soaked the counter. The girl gasped. Was she that unfamiliar with running water?

Blake leapt to his feet and turned the tap off. I'll get it, I'll get it, he told her.

I drank my coffee and pretended it was April and I was in Paris.

Just go get dressed, okay? he said. And brush your teeth and stuff. He grabbed a tea towel and blotted up the water.

The girl shook her small hands, and drops of water flung out. She stuffed her damp hands under her armpits and with her eyes scrunched closed, she took one shuddering breath in and opened her mouth as if to speak, but no words came. She clamped her lips shut and left the room. The dog growled in my direction, then padded after her.

I poured more coffee for myself and drained the pot. When I turned, Blake was standing behind me with his empty cup out.

I don't know who you think I am sometimes, Blake. I'm human too. I have ambitions and dreams. I don't actually have the luxury of suddenly becoming a caregiver for someone else's child.

He went to the sink with his empty cup. He rinsed it out, carefully set the clean cup upside down on the drainboard. He dried his hands on the dishtowel.

He turned to me. I'll be outside, raking. Call me if you need anything.

And I had spent a fortune on art supplies.

Blake pulled his woolly green jacket off the hook in the hall and rammed his arm into the sleeve and went out the door. A waft of cold air breezed in.

I stood in the kitchen and watched out the window as he raked the fall leaves into a big sodden pile. Slick leaves, greasy with frost and rot and rain. From upstairs I heard the sounds of a house coming to life. The Buffalo and Roxanne shuffling about, water running, bedclothes rustling. A heavy step, a low bark. The girl had been with us for a day already and I wondered who and what she remembered from the party a year earlier. And too, what Roxanne had gathered was happening. I dreaded the duty but I knew that someone had to take charge, clear the air, give a heads-up on the new arrangement.

I heard drawers being opened and closed in the girl's bedroom overhead. Putting her few clothes away. The tick of the dog's claws on the wooden floor.

I took a breath and mentally composed an explanation, a re-introduction of the new houseguest. A rundown of who we were in relation to one another, and our roles, and rules and privileges. I stood at the bottom of the stairs with my hands clasped in front of me. I corrected my posture and breathed in. I called out, Could everybody come down here, please? I need your attention.

The girl appeared first. She was already dressed in blue jeans and a faded purple sweatshirt. Then the Buffalo in her trademark black housedress. Finally Roxanne in a muumuu. They looked at me and waited.

This is the girl, I said, and — I stopped, incapable of another word.

The three of them turned from me to each other to formally acknowledge what they already knew. The girl's eyes, which were the same rusty brown as her hair, went from Roxanne to the Buffalo and back to Roxanne.

She's grown since last year, said Roxanne.

The Buffalo clucked. And don't she look just like her daddy.

I turned my back on them and re-entered the kitchen. A place that had once been my sole domain now felt foreign. Cheerios, a dog bowl, an extra chair at the table with a thick book on the seat. That baby doll that she was surely too old for but still carried around, propped up against the butter dish.

I walked out to the yard and followed the trail to the coop. The day was bitter and I did not linger outside.

I texted Joel. Remember me? Hate to be a bother . . . where r u?

He texted back, Just crossing the border.

I opened a fresh bottle of wine and soon enough I was in a familiar world of acrylics and amnesia. But the memories that did surface only served to contradict the outrage I felt: at my predicament, at my marriage, at my life.

When my little lawyer looks at me inquisitively, I continue.

We had been dating platonically, Blake and I, off and on, for about two months before we found ourselves at a New Year's frat party. Blake was not a frat boy, nor was I a sorority girl, but the invite was unexpected, alluring, and I convinced Blake that we should go. Blake picked me up dressed in a navy suit jacket, pale blue shirt and a striped tie. I was in a little purple cocktail dress, in the days just before purple went from ubiquitous to a fashion anathema. But when we arrived, we realized, at least I did, that we were laughably overdressed. Ripped jeans, stained T-shirts, ragged sweaters. One girl, I'm sure she was wearing her grandfather's woollen underwear. Impulsively, and scared to death, I just dropped my purply sequined dress to the floor and presented in my black bra and pantyhose. Suddenly I fit right in, scars be damned. Blake, however, remained true to form, wouldn't even undo his tie, and I left him to it.

When he found me later, drunk in one of the bedrooms, in the company of strangers, he flexed his heroics and gathered me out of there. His warm, strong arms around me, I'm pretty sure he whispered, Frida, you're too good for this.

My dreamy-eyed counsel sighs. Is that when you knew?

Knew what?

That you were in love. That he was the one.

What I knew was, never to wear purple again. I close my eyes on her. Refusing the honest answer to the annoying question.

She frowns. When I met Kaleb, she says, I knew from our second date that he was the man for me. He's smart and funny and he had, has, the most beautiful brown eyes, with the longest eyelashes. Love is weird, isn't it? Just the smallest, most insignificant detail can set the neurons firing.

And you were pregnant, right?

She scowls at me. Just saying . . . love is not at all complicated. It just is.

A little snort escapes me. Thank you for your insights. Wondering, Had I ever, ever been that naive? I was no longer.

It must have been late afternoon, judging by the light crashing through the dirty pane of glass in the window. I had fallen back asleep after a nightmarish night, dark alleys, naked infants, piles of macaroni, the usual mess. When I opened my eyes Joel was standing at the foot of the cot staring at me. Time to put a lock on the door, I thought. Time to put up an actual door.

I was wearing one of Tully's red satin pyjama sets with an old flannel nightgown I had thrown on over it to keep warm. My first thought was, Oh god I haven't even brushed my teeth, I have no makeup on.

Forget the makeup, he said.

He sagged. He flopped down onto my cot. Oh god, he said, oh god, is there any sherry left?

We finished it a week ago.

If you only knew, he said.

Knew what? My first thought was that he was dropping me. Dropping me as a featured artist. I had bought that amazingly expensive pastel cougar painting from him. I had it framed and put it up on the wall. Bought all those art supplies. I had thrown myself feverishly into my art practice for four days now. I had sketches and scribbles and ideas pommelling me from every side, albeit, ideas that vanished under scrutiny, still . . .

Outside, the raven landed heavily on the sill, looked in and cawed. Memo to self, get a curtain.

I said, Your painting is getting dusty if you want to take it home with you.

My painting?

The one you bought last spring, remember? The portrait of me and my wolf baby?

Oh, that. Right. Didn't I already take it?

I pointed to it on the shelf. He ran his hand over it, lingering on the breasts.

If you only knew what I'm going through, he said. He traced the belly and between the legs.

What are you going through?

The ticking clock syndrome. She's desperate for a baby.

Yes, I know. You already told me.

You don't know the half of it. For a year now we've been screwing three times a day. Do you know how hard it is to get it up three times a day?

I had a different memory of the honeymoon days of endless sex, but no matter. I relaxed. This was not about me. I breathed more easily. No wonder he had not gotten in touch. Too busy spewing sperm.

Well, I said, trying to be funny, I have one you could borrow.

One what? He looked at me aghast as if I was offering him a penis or something.

Child. One child. Never mind. She's only a loaner.

He laughed uproariously. You see, the thing is, guess what? I'm important.

I wrapped my quilt more tightly around my shoulders. I guess we are all important in our own minds.

Important. Im-por-tent. Im-po-tent. Get it? Impotent. I can barely say the word without cringing.

You're not "important." You have those boys from your first wife. You showed everyone their pictures at our anniversary party. Little hockey stars. You were grooming them for the NHL. Remember? You bored us to tears. In a nice way, I mean.

Well, obviously, apparently, if science can be trusted, those boys are not of my loins. Ain't that a kicker?

Lucky Marguerite, I thought.

Luck has nothing to do with it, he said. It's like I'm not a real man.

I became philosophical. What's a real man? I asked. What's a real woman? What's a real human being for that matter?

Humans procreate, he said. That's what we are put on this Earth for. He apparently remembered then, albeit too late, my own childlessness and tried to smooth it over. Look, I'm sorry, I'm not talking about you. Obviously, you had your own reasons, and I applaud you for them. You don't need a little Frida Junior scurrying around in the shrubbery to prove you have a right to be alive. Cooking, reading a good book, cleaning, admiring the sunset, these are the things that make humanity tick.

Plus, I have an artistic career, I prompted.

He blinked. And nodded. You do. Absofuckinglutely. He leaned in towards me. His breath smelled tasty, like hot dog relish.

See, I'm not talking about you, I'm talking about myself, how I was cuckolded and lied to, and now Marguerite and the way she looks at me with that "let's get this over with" look in her eyes and into bed, hop-hop, or the kitchen counter, or the back seat of the car. She's got this thermometer thing that tells her the exact right moment, and I'm exhausted from trying to be a real man. It takes so much effort and I just want to be me.

I reached down to put my socks on. I had beautiful feet. It was a shame to cover them. You poor thing, I said. I made a sad face for him. Sometimes the only way through an awkward conversation is to immerse yourself. You shouldn't take it so personally. You're practically a real man, near as I can tell — I made a point of looking at his crotch — and Marguerite is a battle-axe. You said so yourself, she's a total bitch. You know there are silver linings in every cloud.

He squinted at me.

Think of all the EMS you can enjoy without consequence.

EMS?

Do I have to spell it out?

Emergency medical services?

Extra-marital sex. Extra. Extra. Extra.

He took a step back, away from me. I noted that. A step not forward but away.

I'm not talking about me, for god's sake.

And then, as if he had just noticed, he looked around my very humble abode, at the old hay and the nesting boxes and said, What are you doing sleeping in the chicken coop?

I scrambled for an answer that would satisfy not only him but myself. I came up blank until I blurted, Artistic retreat . . . a dry run for — I faltered — you know . . . our thing? Our residency thing? My voice had never been so small; it practically squeaked. I grinned, dog-like. He continued to stare at me, obviously unconvinced. To emphasize my point, I leaned over from the bed I was still in and picked a sable paintbrush off the top of the old poultry feeder. I waved it in the air in front of his face. I get my best ideas in the morning before I've even opened my eyes. I like to take advantage of that creative energy that bubbles up between unconsciousness and coffee.

Joel, I said, leaning in, I'd like to keep our relationship as professional as possible. Although sometimes, other things get in the way. I let the quilt slip off my right shoulder, my fair shoulder.

He looked and then looked away.

Of course, he said. That's what I want too. Professionalism.

Maybe one day I will paint you, would you like that? A nude. You can give it to Marguerite as a reminder of real man-ness.

He smoothed his little moustache, adjusted the gold chain around his neck. Maybe all women are bitches, he said.

Not necessarily in heat, though.

He smiled. Okay, I get it. You're trying to be funny. Ha-ha. At that moment his cell phone started playing the first bars of the *Pink Panther* theme. That ringtone warmed me to him and I reached to gently pat his thigh and hum along.

It's Marguerite, he said. She's having a fertile afternoon and wants me there now. Like lickety-split.

Where is she?

At her parents, in Agassiz.

But I thought you were impotent.

I am. Oh, yeah. But I haven't told her the results yet. I'm afraid to. I don't know how to. It would be the end of us. Of that, I'm sure.

I thought of all the ways a marriage can end and I nodded in sympathy.

He took my hand from his leg and held it. Wounded bird, he said. We are kindred spirits.

I leaned in quickly and he involuntarily recoiled and my puckered kiss landed half on his lips and half off. His breath smelled less like hot dog relish and more like mayonnaise. It made me hungry. My stomach rumbled. I tried to make amends by closing my eyes and yawning loudly. After a moment or two, I opened them and saw that he had picked up his phone. Be right there, he said into it. He clicked it off, put it in his pocket, looked at me and sang, da dum, da dum, da dum da dum da dum da dum . . . da daaaaa, then he winked. We're so bad.

CHAPTER 12

In the warm and cozy kitchen that I missed so much, Blake was pacing in front of the table under which the girl was sitting with her vicious dog. She had been with us for a week and so far had barely said a word. It seemed that we were accepting this as a normal reflex action to a traumatic event. All good. Time heals, Blake was saying, time heals. He cleared his throat when I stepped in.

I was just explaining the rules of the house. He smiled at me. His smile was crooked and dry.

Rules of the house? We had rules of the house?

On the table was a peanut butter and jam sandwich with the crusts cut off.

Bedtime by eight. He looked at me for affirmation.

I held my hand up and looked away. None of my business.

Do not disturb Frida. Let Roxanne sleep in peace.

The girl under the table was stroking the dog's paw with one finger. Over and over, one tiny perfect finger stroking the paw. The crazy dog had its head on her lap.

One hour of TV after chores are done.

Chores? I asked.

I had chores when I was growing up, Blake said. I mowed the lawn, took the garbage out. Didn't you have chores? Vacuuming? Dusting? That's what my sister did.

I thought back to the chaos of my childhood. No dusting that I recalled. Hot-rollering Roxanne's hair. Fielding phone calls from ex-lovers. Picking up the Chinese takeout. A wave of nostalgia overtook me.

How about just keep your room tidy until we figure things out, he leaned down to say to the girl. And added, Plus we eat together for one meal a day. A family unit. Six o'clock, washed hands. Maybe you can set the table?

Did Blake really say "family unit"? How could this be happening? The months and years of our life together had been so predictable, forgettable even and blurred with sameness. Now every word he said was sharp as a shard of broken glass.

It's not all rules of the house, Blake babbled on. This, as you know, is the kitchen, so help yourself to the fridge, see? Lots of food in there. He opened it wide. I caught a glimpse of some mouldy cheese, an avocado, two cans of beer before he shut it.

And that's the yard. He pointed out the window. Looks like we're in for a nice warm spell before winter hits. I could put a swing set up if you like. He faltered. You're not too old for swings, are you? Sorry, I don't know the answer to that. Did you bring any toys? We can buy toys at the Dollar Store, or at Treasure Trove. Do you like puzzles? Dolls? A new baby doll?

I became alarmed by the speed at which this fakery was proceeding. It felt like my whole excellent existence was being derailed. Of course, my life had been far from an "excellent existence" but I had a way of lying to myself when the need arose. The child hugged her knees and closed her eyes as if melting into the hypnotic cadence of his voice, his words, his assurances. I tried to slow the train down.

And stay out of the studio, I blurted.

Finally, from under the table, she looked up at me. The crazy dog licked its shaggy ass and whimpered.

With a start, Blake and I both realized that the dog, who had come with a plastic bag of kibbles, had actually eaten every bit of it the day before.

Dog food, Blake practically shouted. Any kind in particular? Alpo?

Alpo, I snorted derisively. Oh god no. Not for that little treasure.

The crazy dog was biting at a tangled mat of fur under her hind leg, her teeth clacking industriously.

It has to be organic, I said, savagely. Free-range organic chicken and lamb. The good stuff.

Blake swallowed.

See you at six, I said. I grabbed a beer from the fridge, snatched up the abandoned peanut butter sandwich and, blood pounding in my veins, I escaped to the toxic solitude of my coop.

Did he always do the cooking? my little analyst asks.

No, he did not. Normally I did the cooking but I guess you could say I was on strike.

Later, in the basement, I again sheepishly dug into one of the boxes of clothes and sundries that had belonged to the woman. I found a sweater dress that would never fit. It was a colour I would not have chosen for myself, a mustard yellow. It was tight on me, and stained. I found a robe swirling in flowers and leaves, parrots in the corners, satiny and bright, big fronds of fern and drooping purple orchids and nodding shapes of mangrove and fruit and god knows what, greens and lilacs and deep blacks. Wine-stained, torn. I put it on over the sweater dress. I found a bottle of jasmine-scented bath oil in the box. I recognized it as something I had once owned. I'd thought it was still in the guest bathroom.

Ten past six, I stepped into the kitchen. Blake had just dished up.

Thick mushy stalks of broccoli, frozen fish sticks heated in the microwave, frozen french fries warmed up in the oven.

I took my plate of faux fish and carbs into the living room. I wanted none of this charade and refused to accept that the Rules of the House applied to me. I turned on the TV and sat in front of it to eat. *The Biggest Loser* normally kept me from overeating. But not this time. I shovelled it in as fast as I could swallow. Told myself I was burning a lot of calories in the coop.

Partway through my faux meal, I remembered Roxanne and yelled upstairs, Roxanne! Dinner! Ding-dong! Five minutes!

The Buffalo left every day at 5:30 for her basement suite in town, so it was me who delivered supper. Roxanne ate in her room, and I always gave her a heads-up so she would be ready, sitting up in bed, pillow on her lap.

But before I could carry her plate up to her, she appeared at the top of the stairs and hobbled down, gripping the banister with two hands for support. I was astonished to see that she had combed and teased her thin grey hair into a donut-shaped corolla around her head, wrapped a silk scarf around her scrawny neck and was dressed in a purple floral shift that stopped well above her knees, some flimsy thing from her days as a beach bunny. Her knobby legs were pale, fuzzy with fine old-lady hair and bruised from blood thinners. She sat, not with me, but at the Formica table in the kitchen with Blake and the child. Tucked a paper napkin into her bodice. And then the old atheist clasped her hands together as if to pray and said, If I eat the broccoli, will I get dessert?

With eyes squeezed shut, the girl clasped her hands together as well and mouthed, Amen.

One late afternoon, I heard a knock, which I chose to ignore. I was in the bathroom tweezing my eyebrows and not expecting or desiring company. But immediately another knock, louder, and then a voice calling out, Police. My stomach twisted into a tiny knot. I went to the door and opened it. Two RCMP stood there, children from the look of them. The woman had braces, the man just the whisper of a moustache. I took a deep belly breath. It will grow in, I thought too loudly, when you reach puberty.

He put his hand on his waist, bringing attention to his side arm.

And? I prompted.

They were there to tell me that Tully's body had finally been found. The police boy: Quite a ways downstream of the "accident."

The police girl: In the river. I'm sorry to say, not in very good shape. Caught in a log-jam. Gunshot wound in the head.

I felt my knees begin to buckle and I steadied myself with the doorframe.

You okay? the police girl asked.

Of course not, I replied. But better than most. I may have giggled hysterically.

Anyway, it's the decent thing to do, shoot yourself in water. Saves a lot of bloody cleanup for the survivors.

Decent, I repeated.

Yeah, I get it, the police girl said. Nothing really decent about the whole mess.

Oh, we're still doing ballistics on the gun, the one they found on the bank. So don't go running off. We may need to talk again. But unofficially the case is closed.

I nodded and they left, having successfully delivered the parting shot.

I returned to the bathroom and studied my eyebrows, my face. I had been thinking lately about the nature of love. About infant attachment and need, the constituent parts of a love relationship that analysts and psychologists had tried to measure with love scales and personal characteristics that moved the needle. Good for them, because what all the brains agreed on was this: love was not easily defined and in the end was somehow greater than its parts. When my face was composed I went upstairs and stopped outside the girl's room and put my ear to the door. I wondered how much of the conversation she had heard. She had her little SanDisk on and was listening to something, I don't remember exactly. Fergie? Kanye West? Was it loud enough to have covered our voices in the hallway? I knocked and she turned it off. I said, I'm going out to the studio. I waited for a reply. Just so you know. The music came back on. Heard the refrain to "Big Girls Don't Cry." I said, Okay, then, and after a moment I left.

It was 5:30 when Blake was dropped off from work. I went out into the yard and stopped him there to tell him the news. That the police had been by, that the body had been found.

Oh, jesus, he said. Oh, shit.

Don't get carried away, please. Relax, I said. Breathe.

You're like a rock, he said. He hugged the rock.

I left it at that. What could I possibly add?

After Tully's landlord and an old aunt had identified the body, it was delivered to a funeral home for cremation. That was followed by a small service. A gathering which included the old aunt, a streetwalker friend and the landlord. I guess they wouldn't let the girl's uncle out of prison or maybe he didn't know or care. And at the last minute, Blake. Clare declined to attend and no one forced the issue. Blake said he felt guilty being there, almost like he was responsible. Expected angry accusations, but none came. He stayed in the back and didn't try to meet or talk to anyone. But the landlord, Larry his name was, sought him out.

A nice guy, Blake said.

I know the guy, I said, I met him. I know how nice he is.

Nice enough anyway, Blake said, right? He didn't give me a hard time about anything.

They had chatted for a minute, Blake gave him his card. Larry told Blake he was leaving the area, looking for someone to rent the barn out to. In the meantime, he had put pigs in there. Did Blake want the VW van?

No, no, no.

Larry nodded. Okay. I'll hang onto it then.

Two weeks later it was Thanksgiving and as no one seemed to expect much, I let it go. Maybe I roasted a chicken, or maybe Blake did. Then Halloween came, along with our eleventh anniversary and the girl's ninth birthday all on the same day. This time we spent it without friends, without neighbours, without extra women that Blake had fucked and without a deer that needed shooting. Blake bought an ice-cream cake for the girl and I bought a curly red wig and dressed as a clown.

And still no hysterics from child services re: Blake's DUI.

They must be overrun, he told me and tried to hide his smile.

I kept to the coop as much as I could, buffing my nails, sipping martinis, painting. Only going into the house to sleep or to watch TV and to raid the refrigerator while my pretend family watched cartoons non-stop. The girl on the floor with her savage dog, Roxanne in the rocker and me in and out like a fever. Pippi and Popper and Poopie and Pappy and God knows what ad nauseam . . . no more *Sopranos*, no more *Deal or No Deal*, *What Not to Wear*, *The Office*, no more. So much for house rules. Blake told me to get rid of the clown suit and grow up.

When I finally shut down the tube on McBoing-Boing the girl screeched. Most noise I'd heard from her since she arrived. Blake came running, strike that, came stomping downstairs, as if I had stabbed the kid.

I smiled at Blake. Reruns of McBoing-Boing? I don't think so. House rules remember?

He did not smile back.

That night I went down into the basement and rifled through the box of clothes and whatnot that had belonged to Tully. I told myself I was merely looking for useful things, like warm clothes for the girl, or candles or perishables, maybe kitchen stuff. In truth, it felt more like an exorcism. Did Tully keep a journal? Would I find it there? I sorted out some socks and undies, a pile of Tully's clothes, capes and lingerie, but near the bottom a little sweater, a child's sweater, with a ladybug appliqué that was splattered with blood.

I put it all back, all of it, and closed the lid.

CHAPTER 13

Blake was juggling the food, the cooking, the laundry. Library books, dog walks. He had to be tested for rabies after a bite on the hand. I said, Poor you. Luckily we had the Buffalo to babysit while I drove him to the hospital. Mostly, I kept busy in the coop. Sort of. It was difficult to see them together. The child and Blake. She was silent and queenly and he treated her with reverence. It annoyed me no end. He practically bowed when she came into the room. Whenever I appeared, Blake would disappear. An idyllic arrangement. She was a brave, resilient girl and try as I would, I could not remember ever being that courageous.

Blake had just dished up, and when I stepped in, he pulled a plate from the cupboard for me and dropped two mounds of beige-coloured food on it. Mashed potatoes in one pile and macaroni and cheese in the other. He had arranged a plate in front of the girl, a special plate. A child's divided plate, in good plastic he said, food-grade plastic, three divisions, purple, green and yellow. Suitable for a toddler, I told him, not a grown girl.

She likes her food to stay separate, he retorted, without looking me in the eye.

How do you know all this?

My little sister, he said. She always liked her food not to touch.

I mixed the two soft heaps on my plate into one comforting pile and took a spoonful. All the tension in my bones dissolved. I poured a glass of milk. Added a shot of rum.

Whose idea was this fabulous meal?

Blake grinned and poked his head sideways to indicate the girl who was eating heartily.

Sarcasm is the last refuge of a dirty mind, said Roxanne, toothlessly gumming her mush down.

But there was no sarcasm intended.

We ate our comfort food in silence until all the comfort slid down into our respective digestive systems and the crazy dog, Fancy, had licked the casserole clean.

I hadn't finished eating but Blake and the girl had. He gathered their plates and dropped them in the sink to wash.

He asked, How's the art coming? Have you heard from Joel?

Have you?

Why would I?

He needs advice on making a baby, I said.

Blake cleared his throat; no words came out.

Oh, the art. Look, the problem is — and I shifted my eyes slightly in the direction of the child — the problem is . . . a funny thing happened since the G-i-r-l arrived. (I spelled girl out with a capital G.)

What's that?

I seem to have dried up. Like there is a definite energy exchange that goes between the artist, the artist's work, the artist's inspiration, the artist's home life, et cetera. And the energy exchange that is occurring because of the G-i-r-l's presence here has shifted and I, unfortunately, feel it has drained. The energy, that is. Luckily it's not a permanent situation.

Normally after dinner, Blake and I would get a deck of cards out, tea or beer, depending on how much we had already ingested, and play a game of gin. I saw no reason to disrupt our marital ritual and pushing my plate to the side, I dealt two hands.

Done with your dinner now? he asked. Gin game ignored. My words ignored.

No, I said. There were still a couple mounds of comfort food left on my plate and I crammed one into my mouth.

Blake handed a dish towel to the girl who began vigorously drying the dishes he washed. She was stashing them away willy-nilly in any old place. Plates with cups. Forks with spoons. Had she never encountered a well-ordered kitchen before with actual cabinets? Nobody corrected her.

Meanwhile, the food I had so quickly ingested had gone down the wrong way. And I began to choke. Did anybody notice? Or care? Roxanne picked the dog-licked pot off the floor, put it on the counter and the girl put it away in the pots-and-pans drawer. Blake blanched. But nobody said a word.

I coughed and sputtered. I gasped and hacked. Leaned over a chair and tried to give myself a Heimlich.

What the hell are you doing? Blake finally asked.

Choking? I said. And continued my performance.

I'll call 9–1–1. He picked up the phone to dial. I slammed it down before he finished.

I'm breathing again now, I said, can't you tell?

What a relief, he muttered.

I found a little Tupperware in the lazy Susan, washed it (insurance) and put the rest of my unfinished mashed and macaroni in it to take back to my lair.

Goodbye, I said. Good luck.

Same, he replied.

Roxanne and the girl continued their cleanup as if I did not exist. But I saw the look that passed between them.

In the coop, I finished my leftovers, then got my good drawing paper out and made up lettered signs. I snuck in later that night when everyone was asleep and taped them to the maple-wood cupboard doors. Plates, Glasses, Cups. And then I went from bedroom door to bedroom door and listened to them breathe. You know that expression, You did your best? What a useless maxim. What is our best anyway? Is there such a thing? Why does no one ever say, You did your worst? Because, really, they are one and the same.

So what you're implying is your best is the same as your worst?

Well, isn't it? Isn't it just an arbitrary judgement laid down after the fact?

What?

I glance over at my radiant attorney. Today she is wearing a deep-orange sweater that hangs off her pale shoulder. I struggle to recall her actual qualifications.

Doesn't matter, she says. You're probably right. Anyway, do you still have the divided plates?

Are you kidding? I ask.

She frowns. Don't be peevish, I'm on your team. My Tinker will need a divided plate when she's old enough to eat.

I remember one dinner when I was a child, I tell her. I had been a bit rambunctious at the table and knocked my plate to the floor, where it broke. Roxanne, bless her motherly heart, plopped my food, mashed potatoes, something else, directly onto the bare table, plateless.

My team player makes a face of sympathy, or is it disbelief, and returns to her work decoding my defence for a crime I could not for the life of me remember.

And still barely a word from the girl since she arrived. He was such a fool, I thought. We were both being taken for fools. We tiptoed around her, we tiptoed around the dog. Stub of a tail and short stubby little legs. The dog watched every move we made. We were both afraid of the dog. Were we afraid of her as well? She was changed from the smart-aleck girl we'd first met. And who wouldn't be? Solemn at times, giddy at others. But always wordless. Mute. Eyes wide, staring off, as if seeing ghosts. I would turn to see what she saw, the hair on my neck prickling — nothing there. I turned the TV up to drown out whatever imaginary voices she might be hearing. I caught her once, under the table sucking her thumb, a nine-year-old. She was not my doing. And the closer Blake got to her, the further I retreated.

Children are like animals, my child/animal expert volunteers, they can smell emotion. It's not the words that matter.

I can smell emotion, too, I say. And the emotion I smelled was outrage with a hint of helplessness.

Oh stop it, she says. What you smelled was sadness. Nothing more, nothing less.

Blake was still mostly off the booze. No word on how much longer. I had a bottle of champagne to celebrate our back to normal if and when — but in the meantime in our house of ill-repute, he left me to be the so-called reprobate of the so-called family unit. And soldier on I would, raising the flag for so-called happy hour. I missed him telling me what a bitch I was, then forgetting about it in the morning. I was left with Roxanne as a happy-hour partner. She who forgot nothing in the morning and could hold a grudge for years. Meanwhile, Blake sober was unbelievably boring. And how stoically he ignored the cocktails I mixed for myself in front of him.

I went back down into the basement and pulled out the little blood-splattered ladybug sweater. I met the girl in the hallway on her way to the bathroom and I stopped her. I put on a friendly face, half-smile, half-nonchalance. I held the little sweater aloft as if it had materialized there on its own.

I said to Clare, Look what I found. Such a cute sweater. Do you recognize this? Is it yours?

She stared at it, blinking, then looked me in the eye and shook her head, no.

Okay. Well, should I wash it or throw it out? Do you want it?

She turned away.

CHAPTER 14

The weather, overcast with the gloom of November. House empty but for the Buffalo and Roxanne upstairs, their TV on low. Dawdling at the kitchen table with a cup of bitter coffee and a Google search of myself. I found a Frida Frank in Tanzania, a comely African African with a baby. I found myself, and a girl in Croatia. Not in a hurry to get painting. I turned to making up another faux envelope from Publisher's Clearing House which I addressed to Roxanne, placing a twenty-dollar bill inside. I did this every month — oh, I don't know why — maybe I couldn't bear the disappointment on her face when the envelopes came empty except for promises and requests. She never caught on that they would never send any money at all, let alone cash, and the twenty dollars seemed to give her a jolt of joy each time, which she loved to rub in, saying, I told you so.

The phone rang, the land line that no one used. Alternative Cremation Services. The silken voice of the director requesting, most tactfully, that it was time, past time, way past time for someone to come to pick up the ashes. Tully's remains. That jolted me awake. Why had no one done this yet? How can they have a service without remains? I was so far out of my depth. I poured a martini. They must have gotten our contact info from the police or child services. People in authority keep track of stepchildren now, orphaned children. Not like the old days. When Blake got home I relayed the message. His eyes widened.

I shrugged at him. It's not rocket science.

He waited till the next Saturday, when he called our truck-driver neighbour to drive him. I was relegated to keeping an eye on things. Euphemism for babysitting and making sure the dog didn't rip anybody to shreds.

Nervous while he was gone, I plugged in the vacuum to drown out the sounds in my head. Not to mention to suck up the tumbleweeds that were collecting in the corners of the rooms. But the crazy dog, Fancy, so afraid of the noise, yelped and hid shaking in a corner. The girl was watching. Did she know where Blake had gone? Her pale quiet face and big eyes told me that she did. I said, without looking in her direction, Take your dog for a walk please so I can get this place cleaned up.

She put her little red jacket on, the one that was at least one size too small, a collar and leash on Fancy and stepped outside.

Truth is it should have been a relief to be back in my house, alone and doing domestic chores, Blake gone for a bit, Roxanne comatose in her room, the girl and dog outside. But the pressure of the gallery show that I was not yet promised was weighing heavily on my shoulders. And something else as well that I was loathe to articulate.

Living room vacuumed, coffee tables dusted, kitchen floor swept. Hot and stuffy in the house. I stood on the deck and watched the trees do their photosynthesis thing. I saw a deer in the yard. I threw out a soft apple. My good deed for the day. That was a helluva walk the girl had taken the dog on. Just above freezing and the wet flakes were heavy with rain. When I went back inside, chilled and bored and something else I could not pinpoint, I saw that the girl and the dog had already slipped in the back door and crazy dog had shaken rainwater all over my kitchen floor. I hung the wet red jacket up by the fire and remopped.

Blake came home ashen-faced, holding in both hands a tin box filled with Tully's remains. Ash and bits of bone. He put them on the sideboard next to the piano. Never said a word about the cleanliness of the house. I went back to the coop, to work. Nothing occurred to me. I texted Joel. Come, I want to paint you.

If he got the euphemism, he did not let on. Sorry, my jeep's in the shop.

I went online to Amazon and found myself scrolling through girls' clothing. On a sudden impulse, I bought a pink down-filled winter jacket, girl's size ten.

Several weeks went by. Early December, Blake made an appointment for us with a therapist at the local family counselling centre. While the two men chatted — the weather, our sex life, apportioning of household duties, financial responsibilities — I remained mute. When the therapist offered up a sheet of "homework" for us to complete for the next session, I scoffed. No homework, no next session. No family, ergo no family counselling required. Blake set his eyes on the road as we crossed the Water Avenue bridge back over the Fraser, me singing "Fly me to the moon," till he told me to shut the fuck up.

It was coming on Christmas and Blake's daughter had been busy at the kitchen table all day. A Saturday. Coloured papers spread around her. Scissors, glue, crayons. An art project? I poked my head over to see better. Can I help? She covered the papers with her small hands. Hid them from my sight. Stared at me until I retreated. Fine. Fuck it, I thought. I won't ask. She won't tell. I don't care.

But I did peek again and saw that she was making cards. For the holidays. The glimpse I had was of towering black trees and a crooked sinister-looking house with a small figure standing in front. Faceless. Slump-shouldered, arms raised as if at gunpoint. For Chrissake. Her point was what? But I steeled myself to be complimentary if the moment should come that she gave me one. I would sing the praises of these gloomy childish-scrawling cards. I was not the devil after all.

She did not show me. She took them up to Roxanne. When she came down the stairs, her plump-cheeked little-girl face was flushed. The cards were all in sealed envelopes. She jabbed her finger at the corner of the envelope where a stamp would go. Quite the little authoritarian.

How many?

She counted and held up her hand. Five.

Domestic or international? (I could play this game too.)

She faltered. Clearly, she didn't know what I was talking about.

Roxanne appeared like a phantom at the top of the stairs, called out: International!

The child blushed and I rummaged through the drawer until I found five international stamps. Red birds or baby Jesuses? While she was considering, I chose the baby Jesuses.

Not for spite.

The girl took them, licked them and stuffed the cards into her backpack.

Later, I went through the knapsack. All the cards, all five of them, were addressed to Tully in Heven. What were we dealing with here?

I pulled out the old Christmas box. Tinsel, lights, a wreath. Hadn't I read somewhere that there were more suicides over the Christmas holiday than at any other time of the year? Each to their own. Personally speaking, we were determined to be, if not merry, then at the very least alive. Whatever that entailed.

The Christmas presents I'd bought online before the girl had shown up were still in their Amazon boxes. I carried them up to the living room. Socks, wool ones for him. And a camera. He used to be quite a good photographer, had given it up after we got married. Could maybe take it up again? But now the child has come, voila, his new hobby. I had bought myself pyjamas, a bathrobe.

Like a metaphor for staying in bed. Ha. The bathrobe was black, satin, cheerless and cold. I remembered Tully, how much haute couture she had displayed in a worn sweater and torn tights. That she killed herself haunted me. I looked in the mirror. What kind of fuss would there be at my suicide? Would I be much missed? I played the self-pity funeral game. Imagined the tears, the heartbreak, the wailings. But really, from who?

I pulled one of Tully's robes out of her box. Pale rose, flounced in pink ruffles. I put it on and went upstairs. Roxanne saw me and screeched, Oh you scared me. I thought there was a flamingo loose in the house.

I went back downstairs and stuffed it away again.

Blake and Clare drove out one afternoon and came home with a tree. A bent-topped, crooked-trunked thing, a fir I guess, or a pine. I had no idea. Forlorn in our sunken living room. It was under the power line, Blake told me, when I protested its demise. Destined to be cut. His nose and cheeks were bright with cold, his thin red hair dusted with snow. Clare smirked. Roxanne was giddy like a child, almost jumping up and down, wetting herself. Looked like I was the curmudgeon then. I washed my red Christmas shirt and the colour bled in the machine, spoiling the white towels.

That afternoon, Joel arrived unannounced. I'm ready for my portrait, he said. He looked pale and worn down.

I directed him to the centre of the coop. I said, Do you prefer to sit or stand?

May I lie down? he said.

Of course. The model's comfort is always my first consideration.

He undressed. His body looked soft and bony at the same time. Where Blake had muscles and a pouch of fat, Joel had skin and tender flesh. He could have been a prepubescent boy or even girl. I painted him that way, exaggerated the length of his hair, the eyelashes, the pinkness of his mouth. There is an occupational hazard for the artist when working on a portrait: falling in love with your model. And Joel himself, I could tell, was basking in the intensity of my gaze.

CHAPTER 15

The Merry Christmas extravaganza had erupted all over our town. Not so much Happy Hanukkah, though the child wore a Star of David, which I opted not to question; I had no problem with the scuttling of our worn-out traditions. Nor did Blake, who hung a menorah in the window and shrugged at me. What did I know about Judaism? Nothing, except for that date with Ari in Toronto one summer. And he was lovely, handsome, brave, furiously dark and I was wishing I had pursued him further, met him in London instead of Blake. That's the aphotic, sunless depth my thoughts were swimming in. I bought a plastic manger scene at the Lucky Dollar Plus, playing devil's advocate, I suppose. I painted a moustache on the Mary, glued tiny earrings on the baby Jesus, a top hat on one of the sheep. I saw the child watching me, suppressing a smirk. But I knew better than to acknowledge that, or speak to her, or inquire what was so funny. We had an understanding, and it was this: you leave me alone and I'll leave you. I set the blasphemed manger scene in the window for all the world to see. But when I looked outside, there was no world watching. A dark bird flew by and squawked. I hated our understanding but lacked the gumption to change it.

Blake's sister, Brianna, drove out one day from the Okanagan with her infant. She was loaded with the paraphernalia of motherhood. A stroller, diaper bag, baby-butt balm, Snugli, jars of applesauce and carrot puree. She pretended she was there to deliver gifts.

She unloaded the bag. Artisan soaps, an acrylic scarf for Blake, a huge doll.

Thanks, I said. Sorry to say I don't have anything for you. Wasn't expecting.

No, no, it's okay. She looked around. Do you have any tea?

I turned to put the kettle on.

You're not gonna like this.

I dumped the water out of the kettle.

Have you considered personal therapy?

Blake had told her, I suppose, that I had put the kibosh on family counselling.

I'm just trying to help, she said. And I'm here if you want to talk.

She laid a soft pink-and-yellow baby blanket down on the floor and put her baby on it to sleep.

I don't need therapy, I said. I'm totally fine.

Well, maybe not. Maybe you should consider that you are holding it all in. I know I would be completely devastated if my husband's mistress showed up with a child of his and then I had to raise it. I would go nuts.

I refrained from kicking her. The child is not an "it," I said. The child is a "she." When I walked past the baby, I accidentally stepped on a corner of the pristine blanket. Brianna flinched as if struck.

Are you okay? I asked.

Look, she said, this isn't easy for me. We used to be friends when you and Blake were first married. I thought we could be friends.

You're a Red Jacket star team-builder elite leader or whatever you are at Mary Kay. How could we ever be friends?

A hostile silence while I wondered if it was envy or disdain I felt. She and Blake had been raised by their mother, Dolly, a woman who adored them from the moment they were born and still does. Did Brianna have any idea the advantages a childhood like that bestowed on them? How easy to be a good person, a good parent, when you were showered with affection from birth. So fucking easy.

It seems my little lawyer disagrees. She says, That's not at all how it works. It's way more complicated than that. It's chemical and genetic and astrological and all of our experiences combined. Plus luck. She leans down towards me. Being a good person doesn't just happen on its own. You have to make it happen.

Oh god help her. You, apparently, are one of the lucky ones.

At this, she gathers her baby and leaves.

When Brianna viciously retorted, How is your scar by the way? Did that cream you bought help? I dropped my sweater off my shoulder and showed her.

Humanity. How it bristles and if we are very lucky it will leave us unscathed. If not, there will be scathings.

One dark morning, one dark cold morning before the birds were even awake, I left the coop and as a Christmas Eve gift to my husband, I stepped into his bedroom and climbed into his warm bed. Without hardly waking him, I went down on him until he groaned and pulled me up to embrace.

He whispered, May I repay the favour?

No, I said. It was a gift. Not a favour. And then I spoiled it all by saying, Don't say I never gave you anything.

I wasn't crying, so it annoyed me when he asked why I was.

I'm not.

You are, he insisted. Why?

Okay, it's happiness, I lied. Half-lied. It's because I love you so much. Are you satisfied?

And I suppose he was, because he turned away and closed his eyes and said, Go back to the coop.

I had believed so many years before that he would be the antidote. And I would be bathed in a safe, steady stream of uncomplicated adoration. What he didn't know about me he didn't care about. He never asked probing questions. He took everything I said at face value. I could manage like that. And for a long while, I did.

In a back wing of the Fraser Canyon hospital, amidst the hum of hospital beeps and pagings, my organized little lawyer carts in everything that she has been supplied with. From her faux leather briefcase, she pulls out those years-old depositions and affidavits, the confessions, the indictments, the injunctions, the diaries. Everything I have managed to blissfully forget which she is forcing me to remember. I suspect for a moment that she is not a lawyer at all, and I am not even in need of one. But that means she is there for other reasons. Reasons I cannot fathom. She rummages through for a moment, then goes, Hmm. Looks at me. Did you say that she was listening to "Runaway"?

No.

You did. But that song didn't even come out till 2010.

What are you the teenybopper music police?

I'm trying to help.

Well, don't.

She drops the folder on the floor beside her plastic-covered chair and stares out the window.

No baby today? I ask. I want to tell her I'm in pain. I want to tell her I'm sorry, but I can't.

She turns to me. Maybe I've not the right temperament.

To be a mother? I shrug. Bit late for that I would say.

I mean there are grace periods, honeymoon periods for every relationship, and then after that, when things go south, it's about respecting each other, mutual kindnesses.

Mutual kindness from the baby?

From you.

I hold my breath.

Don't say sorry, she says. I'll be fine. Just having a moment. She looks at me and smiles. She has a chipped tooth that always takes me by surprise. She says, Driving home yesterday up into the mountains, the highway quiet, trees all loaded down with snow, I saw two moose running on the side of the road. They stopped when I did. We watched each other.

That sounds great, I say. Lucky you.

It was. Totally great. Lucky me.

And just like that it was Christmas morning.

I expected the girl to be up early with tousled hair and rumpled PJs. Isn't that the way of children? Up early to swarm the tree, rip apart their gifts, swoon over Santa and tinsel and the empty cookie plate and dirty milk glass. In whose world? Not ours.

In our world Roxanne was the first one up.

Long grey hair hanging in sparse strands over her nightgown, thin legs splayed, she sat parked under the tree, broken baubles sprinkled around her. Gifts open everywhere, the camera I had bought for Blake, the cookbook he had bought for me, lavender soap and fuzzy slippers for the old one. And from the girl a small paintbrush. For me. With Blake's handwriting on the tag.

I stopped my grandmother in her tracks as she was about to open yet another gift labelled Clare. Santa came, she gushed. Finally found us. Her old eyes bright with greed.

And you've ruined it. I gathered the gifts and rewrapped. Rox watched mutely, chagrined I hoped. I pointed to the rocker and without a word, she pulled herself up from the floor and sank down in it.

In Japan, there is a practice called *ubasute*. Carry the ancient ones up into the mountains and leave them there in the wilderness, in the cold, to die. I would be a liar if I said I hadn't thought along those lines myself. Wouldn't we all be better off?

As if reading my mind, she muttered, You're mean. And then: I didn't raise you to be mean.

What did you raise me to be?

She read the fury correctly in my tone.

A good girl.

I smiled falsely at her. See how good I am? Anyone else would have slapped you.

Blake came down and the girl. Finally, it was all over. The boring monotony of materialism. Of expectations unmet, of hope extinguished for another year. Because I admit I had been almost eager myself. For years we had sworn off the bullshit, as we called it. Decorating our yard for the sake of the neighbours, but inside the house not even one plastic wreath, not even a box of chocolates. The pretense, the cost, the utter uselessness. We only revitalized the tradition for the sake of the child.

I'm sure it was my idea, though Blake tried to take credit. Waiting, expecting, opening, thanking. Pretending. And Blake's wide eyes did look sincere when he unwrapped the camera. A Nikon . . . NIKON. Cost a pretty penny. The girl, of course, was mute and cheerless for the flannel pyjamas covered in kittens and a beaded bracelet spelling her name. She perked up a little when Roxanne handed her a miniature bottle of Bailey's Irish Cream. Good god. And Blake's gifts to me, *The Little Lunchbox Cookbook*, and unbelievably, savagely, *The Complete Idiot's Guide to Stepparenting,* I managed to accept quite graciously. Though I couldn't help one barb: No panties this year? It came out more viciously than I meant.

But he brushed it off. You have lots. Never wear them out in a lifetime.

True that. But when it should have been over, when I stood to crumple the paper for the fire, when I reached for the broom to sweep up the dried needles and sharp broken ornaments that had fallen to the floor, when I retrieved the liquor bottle from the girl's pile with a warning look at Roxanne, Blake stopped me.

Wait, he said. One more.

I admit I thought then of the blue earrings I had seen in Spiritwood a week before, earrings that I had hinted at to Blake and even prepped the storekeeper — if my husband comes in — and when I saw the jewellery box he pulled from the branch where it had been hidden, I smiled. Warmly. At him. I'll fuck him tonight, I thought.

Blake held the box in his hands for a moment and stared at it. It was as if he were praying over it. Okay, enough of that I thought. Don't get maudlin on me. He never got the tone quite right, that man. Dramatizing to beat the band. But maybe it's a new wedding ring, I thought. I had taken the gold band off and told Blake I'd lost it. And still, I waited, because still I didn't get it. Not until he handed the box to the girl. And whispered, For you.

She seemed to know, I guess from the reverence that Blake was exhibiting, that this was something special. Really special. She untied the ribbon. So slowly. Picked at the Scotch Tape until the paper was released. Shining blue paper. She folded the paper. I tried to breathe. I told myself, breathe. I tried to marry my breath to my heartbeat. I looked out the window to watch the snow. Small inconsequential flakes that would only become consequential in numbers.

When I looked back, the girl had finally snapped open the box and revealed the jewel inside. It was a gem. Not merely a gem. A diamond. A small flesh-coloured diamond. Pressed from the ashes of Clare's mother, Tully.

I listened to Blake explain this, as if in a dream. How he had mailed the ashes off to this place that mimicked the actual process of natural diamonds with pressure, machine-made pressure. That he chose the natural colour, chose a bevel cut. That later she could turn it into a ring or a pendant. That he hoped she liked it and would treasure it her whole life. That it was expensive, more expensive than a natural diamond that size would have been but infinitely more meaningful.

Roxanne had quit her rocking and chattering. Goggle-eyed. Blake's eyes were on the floor. He had finally run out of words. He sat and waited, a half-smile on his face, a religious-y look. He turned to me in defiance, inviting me to protest, I think. As if I would. As if I had words. As if I even knew what I was feeling. As if it mattered to anyone at all. And still, we sat, this trembling tableau semi-circled around the child and the diamond. The amber diamond throwing what light it could muster, until one by one we dared to seek out the child's face and finally realized that she wore not a look of gratitude or surprise, not a look of love or loss or memory, none of that. What we saw was horror.

It won't bite, Blake said foolishly, and her head snapped up at him, in fear I think, and she bolted from the room.

My grandmother looked at me and for a moment our eyes locked. The old fool. I stared harder, ferociously, willing her to look away. But she would not. Then I realized that look in her eyes was almost like love. Almost she loved me. As if she knew who I was and what I was going through, and almost loved me.

I'm dying of hunger, she said. Will there ever be breakfast?

Waffles? I said to her.

And Blake shouted, he literally shouted, Sounds perfect!

I opened the new cookbook. Look, here's a recipe. Do we have any oat flour?

You can substitute, Blake suggested.

I can substitute, I said. I'm very good at that.

I turned for the kitchen, leaving the detritus I had started to clear for someone else to deal with. Thinking, I admit, fuck them.

On Boxing Day our neighbours arrived at the door, with a Styrofoam plate of Santa-shaped sugar cookies covered in plastic wrap. After they stomped their little footsies on the stoop for a minute or two, I invited them in. I had to. People think I'm such a bitch, but am I? Am I really? See how nice I can be? The middle-aged woman was newly married to the middle-aged man. Both of them recycled spouses, both in red sweaters. Both already tired of each other, looking for something juicy our way, I conjectured. When I thought of all the singles in this small town, the divorced couples, the separated, the never married and how they recycled through all available spouses. Used goods. God give me the city again. God give me the past with a wide-open future. God give me a clan, a posse, a warm body to claim me. God give me innocence.

This was very — inconvenient.

The girl refused to come out from wherever she had holed up, and the neighbours, who really only wanted to gape and gossip and gather ammunition for their titterings, finally left. Dancing and drinks tonight at the Local House, she called.

Don't forget your Styrofoam cookie tray, I called back.

Keep it, keep it, they shouted generously.

They were completely immune to insult. I watched them stumble over the discarded tree and I yelled, Happy Hanukkah! I heard Clare snort with glee from wherever she was hiding. The sound of that snort was like a sudden warm breeze through a chilly cave, an affirmation, an endorsement, of — me, yes, me, or at the very least of my seditious sense of humour, and it woke something in me that I believed had dried up and blown away. I followed up my shout with, Shalom! But there was no follow-up chuckle and I realized that she had no doubt been conferring with the dog.

My psychiatrist makes that clicking sound with her tongue and studies her notes. A discarded Christmas tree? Now, how did that happen exactly?

We had a row; I tossed the tree out into the yard.

The decorated tree?

Yes, the decorated tree. Tinsel, garland, lights, the whole shooting match. Our neighbours had to step over it to get to the door.

Funny, you never told me about a row. She stares at me and I stare back, willing myself not to blink. She is not an easy woman to intimidate or even annoy.

Hmm? she prompts.

When still I keep silent, she volunteers: Christmas. The sweaters always too itchy or too small. Was it about the child? And what did the child think of it all? Do you recall? Was there shouting? Swear words?

Look, the child was spared. We had our fight in the car. She was in the house, asleep. And if you must know, the fight was about money, the cost of the diamond. Nothing more.

Oh, there's always something more, she replies.

After I tossed the Christmas tree out, I snatched the diamond up and threw it out into the snow as well. I'd never seen such beautiful fury from Blake before. I, for one, was impressed. He retrieved it, of course, stuffed it back into its box and slapped it down on the windowsill above the sink. A perpetual eyesore.

Oh great, I said, let the precious woman's precious remains sit there and haunt me while I wash dishes.

Blake had no retort, though the way he looked at me when I said that . . . chilled.

CHAPTER 16

I was watching Clare in the yard chirping at unseen birds as if calling them to her. Good luck with that, I thought. But moments later as I watched, the ravens came. Three of them clustered high in the tree in front of Clare. They honked and squawked at her and she honked and squawked back.

When she came back inside I handed her a bag of sunflower seeds.

A week later, I saw Clare crouching near the feeder, her hand outstretched, sunflower seeds on her palm. Blake was crouched behind her. For a long time, they squatted motionless.

When the child came in she was aglow. As was Blake. A bird, it seemed, had landed on her hand.

What kind? I asked, trying not to sound as jealous as I felt. A golden-crowned kinglet? I prompted. A bohemian waxwing? I had no idea but was trying to appear like an expert.

Just a sparrow, Blake said, undiminished.

I hope you didn't harm it. I turned back to study my new painting. A portrait of my foot. In place of toenails, claws.

Two or three days later I was again in the house, blow-drying my hair after a much-needed shower, and I heard a knock. Blake was gone, the girl in the basement sorting through her mother's possessions, the Buffalo busy force-feeding Roxanne. I went to the door with my hair half-dry.

Standing on the doorstep, the same police children as before.

What now?

They had questions. Just a few. Could they come in?

No was just as good an answer as yes. I flipped a mental coin and let them in.

What is this about? I asked. Knowing that Blake sometimes drove his truck locally, even without a licence, when I was too busy to be his chauffeur. If he's in jail again he can stay there, I said.

The two teenaged police officers looked at each other.

Why would he be in jail?

I was ashamed to realize I had fallen into their trap.

A question had belatedly arisen in the minds of the excellent law enforcement system of our little town as to where Ms. Anatole Curry (a.k.a. Tully) got the gun that she used on herself. Because it turned out, rather awkwardly, that it was registered to Blake.

Whoa, my feisty lawyer says.

Whoa what?

That's some pretty lax police work, wouldn't you say? If that's how it really happened. Her gaze on me is steady and cool. Weeks go by, months even and they suddenly remember the gun? I don't think so, cowgirl.

I'm trying to remember. Get off my case.

Fine. Forget it. I watch her make a little mark on the page in front of her.

So, anyway, when I told Blake — months earlier, okay? — to get rid of the rifle that I had shot the deer with, that's where it ended up. It seems Tully, the sainted one, the model a.k.a. prostitute, had run into a bit of rough trade as they say, and Blake had given her his gun for protection.

No, he gave her the gun because you asked him to get rid of it, my little lawyer corrects, too smart for her own good sometimes.

I didn't tell him to give it to her, did I.

I'm not entirely sure what you told him. Nor what he told the police.

I press the pain button that releases morphine into my drip. I pretend to drop into unconsciousness. I do not want to hear another word from her.

But in my faux coma, I recall Tully's swollen lip, the scratches, the reddened cheek.

The police girl continued, the police boy took notes: How long had Blake known her? Where had they met? What has Clarabelle told you about the sequence of events? What were you doing the night of September 5?

Am I under suspicion or something? I said.

Just some routine questions, they said. But I had watched enough TV to know that when a cop says routine questions, it's time to lawyer up.

Where was I that night? I don't know. Where was Blake? He wouldn't know either. At the high school, probably, looking for affordable ways to upgrade their outdated computers.

I was probably in the studio. I may have been with Joel, the local gallery owner. I showed them sketches from my sketch journal, dated. The good ole wine glass series. The foot one. Naked me. Naked Joel. Satisfied?

They stared and glanced back and forth. Still, they remained.

I said, Sorry, kids, I wish I could be more helpful. Glass of milk? Cookie?

They sat and drummed their little fingers on the table. I wiped up the sticky bits of jam left over from breakfast.

The neighbours said they saw Tully leave in the car around noon. The landlord said the girl was in school or should have been. A pot of stew on the stove was cold. If they could talk to the girl it would clear up a lot of loose ends.

At that, I bristled. No, you cannot talk to the girl.

Why is that? the police boy asked.

Because for one thing, she's not here.

At that very moment, the girl opened the door from the basement, stepped into the kitchen with Fancy at her side.

When she saw the police she gasped.

The police children smiled. Well, look who's here.

The girl froze into a statue, a shaking statue.

We'd like to ask you a few questions, the police boy said.

No. You can't. I turned to the child and said, Go to your room.

And without a moment's hesitation, she fled.

Now, Mrs. Frank, was that really necessary?

Ms. Brooke. Frank is my maiden name.

We're not hurting anybody here. We like kids. I have a kid, the police boy said, as if it were some major achievement.

But do you have a warrant?

They looked at each other and visibly sagged. They did not.

They turned to leave finally. Then turned back. One more thing, the boy cop said. Shouldn't that kid be in school?

Yeah, his partner said. I would say so.

I'm so proud of you, my counsel says. Asking to see a warrant.

For some reason, that brings tears to my eyes.

That night I went back into the house and accosted Blake in the bathroom where he was washing up, preparing for bed.

Why did you give her the gun?

He wrung the facecloth out in the sink. Hung it to dry. Turned to me. Her lifestyle was dangerous. She was fearful living alone with a child. In her profession.

Profession, I scoffed.

He continued, You would not understand. Men do terrible things sometimes. They can. Especially to a woman in her position.

Some good the gun did, I said.

Blake didn't like it much when I said that. Didn't like it one bit. But it did make me wonder, ungenerously, how did a woman that skinny, that plain, get customers? What was it about her, about anyone, that aroused desire? Makeup can only accomplish so much, although from what I have seen on YouTube, the metamorphosis can be quite astounding. Some women become completely unrecognizable. Yet others look merely lost. I may have voiced these things out loud. Blake may have said, It's never about the makeup, you fool. I may have accidentally dropped his toothbrush in the toilet. I'd had wine. Not my finest hour.

She had a quality, he said.

What quality? I demanded. I'd always thought it was beauty that men lusted after. And I had strived in that direction and even sometimes succeeded. But he was telling me it was something else. Some quality. Tell me.

But he would not.

Tell me. Smell? Touch? What is it?

He leaned over the sink to gargle.

You've always liked skinny girls, I accused him.

He looked at me in the mirror. He spat the gargle juice out and turned.

If you must know, it was . . . her presence while I talked. It felt so good to talk and be listened to. She just really listened. And I'm sorry. For the last time, I'm sorry.

We stay quiet for a bit, my inquisitor and I.

Did he floss? she asks gently.

Oh yes. Since the child had been with us, Blake had gotten serious with his grooming. He shaved almost every day. Combed his hair, tamed it. Wore a clean shirt in the morning, showered at night. He slapped on aftershave. He smelled like a walk in the boreal forest. He smelled like a sawmill.

For some reason, she frowns.

No, he smelled good.

I'm not frowning about that, she says. I'm frowning about the police. Did they think he might have shot Tully?

You're kidding.

No. Did Blake really have an alibi?

Oh my god. Shut up.

Or maybe they think you killed her? Did you have an alibi?

What are you getting at?

Because you wanted to, didn't you? If you'd had the chance, you might have.

We stare at each other until the jumbo baby lets out a sudden wail.

I'm so thirsty, I say and it's true.

She picks up the little paper cup of water at my side and puts it to my lips. I grasp her wrist. My head is spinning. The slats on the window blinds are rattling like delicate bones. The woman is staring at the monitors. An unpleasant beeping.

Who are you? I whisper. Why are you here? Where are we?

I'll call the nurse.

No. Get out

Look at me, she says. It's okay.

A pain surges up from inside and again I press for morphine. A tall nurse strides in and manhandles me. Later, when I open my eyes, my little lawyer is gone. On the floor by my bed is a list. I struggle to pick it up and I read in her childish handwriting — Bills!! Due! Gas, parking, cell phone overages. Paper clips, Wite-Out, diapers. And then a total. Is this for me? Has she meant this for me to pay?

For a week, more than a week, eight days, maybe twenty minutes, she stays away. When she finally shows up I shout at her, I'm not paying for the jumbo baby's diapers.

Not diapers for Tinker, diapers for myself! she shouts back.

There are leakages. I'm trying to maintain my sexual dignity. Kaleb claims to love me like this but he's only kidding. You're lucky you never had to go through this. So lucky.

She sobs. She has never been so cruel. The nurse hands me my purse and I try to give her money, but she is already gone.

CHAPTER 17

The police released the gun. It was a legal firearm after all. And it belonged to Blake. He could pick it up at the station. Foul play had been considered and dismissed as a cause. And as per the police children's pointed admonition, Blake registered the girl for elementary, grade 3. Chatted with the teacher, bought her pencils and a pencil case. Signed her up for the bus route and one morning, 8:33 a.m. on the dot, the bus stopped at the bottom of the hill, almost directly in front of our property, red lights flashing, stop sign extended.

The driver beeped. I sauntered out from the coop and poured a coffee from the pot that Blake had set up the night before. The girl appeared, wide-eyed, dressed in blue jeans and a striped polyester sweater, relatively clean, relatively tidy. Blake had also made a peanut butter sandwich the night before; this, together with an apple, a banana, a little bag of chips, a box of Smarties, a cranberry juice box, an orange juice box and a Ziploc of dates and walnuts — enough food to last her a month — he'd packed neatly in a Flintstone's lunch box labelled CLARE in capital letters. I watched as Clare shoved it into her little knapsack and stepped out the door. I put my winter jacket on over my nightgown and made to follow and she turned on me. Shook her head, no. I stayed where I was, very happy to do so. Very happy to watch as she dashed down the trail, climbed up the steps into the bus, very happy to watch the bus driver pull the stop sign in, turn off the red lights and drive away. Nothing else that day made any kind of impression on my hippocampus except the moment that Blake woke up belatedly and rushed into the kitchen and I said, You missed it.

Next night, after I was sure Blake was fast asleep, I crept back into the house from my coop. I tiptoed past his (our) bedroom and heard his breathing, deep, relaxed, with that little whistle on the exhale that I had come to deplore. I listened for a few minutes before another sound intruded. The television.

As I suspected, the girl was sitting three inches from the TV, the volume down low, mesmerized by what she saw on the screen. I stood in the doorway to the kitchen and watched with her. I forget what.

My little truth ferret says, You really don't remember? Mickey Mouse? Donald Duck?

Smartass, I said. And then I did recall. It was a cartoon show called *Bad Dog*. It seemed that whenever the dog heard "bad dog" it would fall to the floor and pretend to be dead. Only coming back to life if someone said "good dog." Since her mother had died I had not seen her cry. But now, engrossed in a funny cartoon, the tears came. Waterfalls of tears cascading down her round cheeks, dropping on the bald head of baby doll. She suddenly noticed me and swiped her face clean. Shook her head, no. Violently shook her head. No.

I took a step back and stood in the passageway, leaned against the jam. I kept my eyes fixed on the TV, watching the cartoon for hours it seemed.

When I finally dared to look her way she had fallen asleep on the couch with the crazy dog curled on the floor at her side. Her lips were parted slightly, brows furrowed, her cheeks still damp with tears. Her vulnerability and innocence surrounded her like a shield and I was the venal intruder.

I slipped the pale grey blanket over her, hardly daring to even touch, and returned to my hard bed in my cold lair.

A few days later I approached the principal at the elementary. He was stapling things together at his desk. It was casual Friday and he was in sweatpants and sweatshirt, NOR in block letters across his chest.

Does your shirt say "either/or" on the back? I laughed.

My son-in-law's construction company. He smiled. Can I help you?

I'm sure you can, I said. And proceeded to introduce myself and offer my services in the art department. I gave him my resumé and a sample of my work, a neon study of copulating flowers. My application was impressive, especially for a small school in a backwater town like this. I was a member of the Federation of Canadian Artists. I had been juried, I had won awards. Also, as a postscript, I told him I was the daughter of Lulu Frank.

Who? he said.

On the wall over his head was a framed cross-stitch. Be True to Yourself.

For some nefarious reason, it pleased me immensely that my mother's fame had not reached the backwoods of this "happy valley."

He was studying my resumé. You don't say anything about experience with children.

Oh, I love children. Their spirits, their life forces, their innocence, their artistic ingenuity. And they're so cute. Most of them. Unless they're not cute. And even the ones who are not cute, are cute. They're like weird, smelly little animals. They need training, of course. They need to be reined in. They need firm hands. Gotta keep them away from bleach and guns and matches. I know that. I'm not completely ignorant of children. I was one once. And I'm sure they could teach me more than I could teach them. To a point. I —

I finally stopped talking. I'm not sure what had come over me. He stared at me for a moment. Maybe an hour.

Alas, he said.

Alas?

Our budget is completely stretched to the limit. At the moment.

Alas, I repeated. I liked the sound of it, on my tongue. I said it again, to myself. Alas.

He squirmed in his chair. But I'm sure we would be honoured, he said, if we could afford you.

Alas, money, I sighed. Alas, honour.

He narrowed his eyes at me. If you're really interested in helping the children, you can volunteer. Otherwise, don't waste my time.

Alas, I think not, I said. And left.

On my art table in the coop, I found a sketch. Loosely scribbled, not accurate, not careful, but full of energy and emotion. The kind of thing I was trying to tap into, that I had once been capable of. It was a lopsided white dog, with a lopsided blackbird standing on her back. The dog had turned her dog's eyes towards the bird with a gaze that, to be honest, looked like lust. The bird had one wing lifted, and the pencil strokes that raced in the air above showed it flapping. The bird looked resigned, unable to fly and probably unwilling to copulate with the dog. Maybe I was putting my own interpretations on it a little too much, reading more into it than it warranted. Maybe it was just a crude sketch of a dog and a bird. I pinned it to the wall where it could be seen from the window. Where the low winter sun would light it up. Where any passing crow or raven or blackish bird could look in and see a kindred spirit.

I determined then to offer my unsalaried services as a volunteer at the school. Start an elementary art department. After all, I needed to immerse myself again.

Was that the only reason? my psychiatrist asks.

I ignore her. I just keep punching the TV remote and hardly care that the bed is going up and down.

Was it? she insists.

Well, you obviously have a theory.

Just a thought. Maybe you wanted to be near the girl? Am I close?

And, well, yes, she was. In some secret cubbyhole of my glistening brain I wanted to show off a little, let her have a glimpse of me in my element. And okay, yes, I missed her.

And the way the principal shook my hand with so much gusto, saying, Welcome to the team, made me realize he had looked up Lulu Frank.

CHAPTER 18

Clare missed the first week of art, showed up the second. The group was a mix of kindergartners to fourth graders. The fun ages, so they say. That afternoon I decided it was time to introduce some structure into their scribbles. I asked the children to draw a favourite animal. Could be stick figures or simple splashes of colour. I drew some shapes on the blackboard. Rectangles for bodies and circles for heads. And before they could copy, monkey see, monkey do, I erased it all. Groans. Pouts. Hands waving in the air. But Mrs. Brooke! Ms. I corrected, Ms. Brooke. Now let's go. Let's see some real art for a change.

So they chattered, little tongues sticking out of the sides of their mouths in concentration, grabbing crayons, pressing so hard they snapped, fighting over purples and pinks. I strolled the aisles. I saw what might be a unicorn or an elephant. A rainbow. It was all rather wonderful, quite a bit of a rush, this creative energy I had birthed, yes, birthed. Patting their small, hard heads in appreciation, humming, picking up dropped crayons. They were all so proud of their work. And so intent.

And I was proud of myself.

Clare, head down in the back, was concentrating hard, vigorously colouring, her whole body shivering with the effort, one leg kicking back and forth, and when I finally reached her desk and looked down at her drawing I stopped. A stick figure woman, limbs at crazy angles, lying face down in a river, red splotches all around her and a flapping bird perched on her head.

I stared at it. The little blond girl who had drawn the rainbow was staring too and finally burst out laughing, pointing at it, That is ugly, so gross! Yuk! It's not pretty, it's ugly! Clare immediately crumpled it and closed her eyes. The children were laughing now, all but Clare. All the pleasantness I had been feeling not two seconds before drained away. As the children's snickering gained momentum something very close to fury washed over me for reasons I was not prepared to articulate.

I turned to the one who had drawn the rainbow. Rainbow, I snorted. Roy G. Biv? Not very original, is it?

And to another. Do unicorns really have eyelashes like a movie star? Bat, bat! Aren't elephants grey? Eyes on top of the head? Where are the brains supposed to go? Did you run out of room? No feet?

I tramped down the aisle, spewing critical nonsense, till one feisty little know-it-all stood up and said, I think you should give us a break, Mrs. Brooke, we're not Van Gogh!

The little brat. Van Gogh? What do you know of Van Gogh?

Starry skies, she replied, but her confidence had waned.

And his ear? How he chopped his own ear off with a knife! Blood streaming down the side of his face, head bandaged with a dirty rag? That he was mad and jealous and brilliant? None of that?

The children had stopped drawing by then. Some were whimpering, some bawling. I tried to control myself, but the train was coming and I could not get out of its way.

What have you drawn? I demanded, pointing to a mousy-haired first grader. What's your favourite animal?

She stared at me, whispered, A deer.

Well, that's not hard. Dead or alive?

Alive?

Naturally. Standing there in side view. Big brown eyes, big ears, antlers, bushy tail. But don't you think that's been done to death? Why not a wounded deer? Tongue hanging out. Bit of blood, or a lot of blood. You like red, don't you?

I like pink.

Another cliché!

Clare was watching me, eyes wide. The way she had thrown her whole body into her drawing and the strength of the emotion she had created, I realized something I had forgotten. Art is in the body, where emotions take root, not in the head.

I banged my hand down on the paper in front of me, slashed through it with a crayon. I grabbed the broom from the corner and dipped it in a pot of Ready-Red and flung droplets against the blackboard. See? See? I shouted.

The class grew quiet. I heard a rustling in the hallway.

Can we have a chat, Mrs. Brooke? When you're done here? The principal was standing in the open door of the classroom, watching.

Every round, soft-haired head turned to that figure of authority, eyes wide. And then, as if by magnetic force, their gazes returned to me.

When I'm finished, I told the principal. What I'm trying to get across is this: art is not just for an imaginary perfect beautiful world, everything perfect and in its place. My voice softened. I felt that magic moment an actor must feel when the audience is rapt, no need to shout, I had them in my thrall. The children, the principal at the door, even another teacher from across the hall.

It was wounded, I explained to the class. We knew it would never stand again. It had no chance of a life. It was suffering horribly in the ditch and I put it out of its misery. I shot it out of mercy. I put a bullet in its brain because it needed to die.

I admit I had gotten a little out of control. I could not stop myself.

I turned to the little crowd of adults at the door. The children want real scissors, real ones, I said. And bottles of glue, not glue sticks, and thicker paper.

We'll see about that, the principal said.

Alas! I shouted at him.

He met my smile with a sort of horror on his face.

I was breathing hard. I leaned forward to the little pink lover to console her. Real scissors I said, wouldn't you like that?

She recoiled. The children now were crying.

And the deer had a baby? she said. Her lip quivered.

It was a buck deer. A buck doesn't have babies! A doe does.

Some of the children were calling out in their childish high voices, I want to go hoooome.

I went back to my desk where I had prepared a bullet list for the afternoon activities. Distribute materials. Explain the assignment. A moment for quiet reflection.

Clare had slid under her desk. In actual, or feigned, misery? How is it possible I could not tell which? I whispered, I'm sorry.

She closed her eyes and smiled. Thank you, she breathed in the smallest voice I had ever heard.

Alas, sighs my clever one. It does sound like you lost control there. She is grinning at her phone.

What's so interesting?

Pix of our honeymoon in Paris and Tel Aviv. Want to see?

No, thank you.

The next day I returned to the school and cancelled my art classes, collected my smock. Not much in the way of regret on the principal's part. In fact, he snorted when I told him I was taking a leave of absence. Long as you like. Sarcastic sonuvabitch. Mrs. Pat will take over, he said and smiled. Big yellow teeth. There is help out there if you need it.

And there are dentists out there too, I thought. Or maybe said.

As I non-limped out his door, he said, Oh, one more thing. It did come to our attention that some of the art supplies went missing yesterday. The new pastels. The brushes. I'm not accusing you, but I should think, as the daughter of Lulu Frank, you would have the wherewithal to buy your own. Good luck.

I didn't miss the job. It was only ever a distraction anyway. Killing time. Looking for inspiration in all the wrong places. I was glad to be done with it.

Back home, nothing but the ticking sound of the dog eating dry kibbles from its bowl as Blake, with his magnifying glass, picked through the guts of somebody's laptop.

I told him the story and he stayed quiet.

Do you remember when they tried to change the word laptop to notebook? I asked.

I do, he said.

It was impossible to go to Staples and ask for an actual notebook without some salesman shoving a laptop in your face.

With the tiniest of screwdrivers, he released a wire. She spoke to you? She thanked you? Eyes glued to the broken motherboard.

Two words, I said. I wouldn't write home.

Next day on my workbench I found a box of new pastels, Property of Silver Creek Elementary, and three sable brushes.

My brilliant barrister has arrived and I show her from my personal file a copy of an injunction filed by one of the toddler's mothers. A protective order to keep me fifty metres away from the elementary school. Her preciousness had come home traumatized by the life lesson I had delivered to the kindergartners. I am outraged and so is my girl Friday.

But what she says is, So, am I your girl now?

I am taken aback but I immediately recognize my error and correct myself. Sorry, I should say, my woman Friday.

It's not Friday.

She's being churlish and I'm not sure why.

Is this about a retainer? Will that change your mood?

What it's about is this. I'm really tired of your labels: inquisitor, solicitor, interrogator, mermaid.

Had I said these things out loud? Her face is flushed pink with anger, so I tread lightly as I can. Well, then, if you're going to be so picky . . . what should I call you? Your Highness? What is the preference of your holiness?

For the briefest of moments she pauses, tsks and then says, How about my name, how about Belle?

Belle?

You heard me.

Ms or Miss or Mrs?

Just Belle.

And without another word she departs. I press a button to release an extra shot of morphine into my abused veins but I feel no relief.

It must have been about the time of the injunction that I began to be harassed by a neighbour who claimed a big white dog was trespassing on her property, leaving his "calling card" on her lawn. The dog was even responsible for the theft of a triple-A Alberta rib-eye steak from the deck, where she had been about to barbecue. She was a muscular, weather-beaten woman and had pounded on the door of the chicken coop until I opened it, at which point she jabbed her finger at me, hurling accusations in my face. She frightened me with the intensity of her conviction, I might even call it hatred; and I defended the dog, tried to, suggesting she was neither all that white nor all that big.

But when the woman's accusations became more personal I had no defence. What do you do anyway?

Nothing, I said.

You must do something.

I paint.

What, houses? She was staring pointedly over my shoulder at my naked self-portrait with wolf.

Oh, it's nothing, just a bit of art.

Art. She repeated that word as if it were a slur. When she finally left, I noticed the girl and Fancy in the yard quietly watching me. I whispered, Good dog, and waited, heart in my mouth, until I heard her lowly growl.

CHAPTER 19

About a week later, Joel burst into the coop where I was eating lunch, a tuna sandwich on white with mayonnaise and relish, and he said, I told her. She knows. Tufts of brown hair stuck out from the back of his head. Bands of pink rimmed his eyes.

It didn't take me a second to figure out what he was talking about.

I patted the cot. Are you hungry?

I offered my sandwich. He sat. He took a bite. He stood again. Took another bite.

I patted the cot again. He sat.

So, what did she say?

Oh, it felt so good to unburden myself. You have no idea. For weeks I've been carrying this around with me.

Well, good for you.

But then . . .

He buried his head in his hands. I retrieved the sandwich and finished it off.

I'm gathering she was not impressed with your importance.

He stretched out on the cot, his leg accidentally brushing mine.

Her exact words? "You pay a helluva lot of child support," quote, unquote. Not a word about my feelings of betrayal or what this all means for my sense of masculinity. No, just, "You pay a helluva lot of child support."

She's practical.

She's a battleaxe. But it's true. I do. I have done for eight years. But now I have to ask myself. I have to decide. Do I continue to pay a helluva lot of child support for two sonny boys that are not of my loins, or do I burst their bubbles and spill the beans? Of course, we know what Marguerite wants me to do. She's all about the money. Which, she says, will come in handy if she ever has to go for IVF.

Nobody *has* to go for IVF.

Exactly. Anyway, in the meantime she wants us to give it the old college try. Fourteen percent chance of success.

That's better than Vegas.

Joel laughed.

I laughed too. Not sure what the joke was, but it felt good to laugh. Laughing, even falsely laughing, releases chemicals in your brain that make you feel good. So I laughed and laughed. Until I realized that Joel had stopped laughing quite a bit ago and was staring at me. I wiped the spittle off my mouth and frowned in sympathy. Different chemicals released.

I'm not much of a father, he confessed. And I'm telling you that because I think you are about the only person on this planet who would understand that not being a good parent doesn't mean you're the devil.

I felt a little chill go through me.

Shall I stoke the fire? he asked. You look cold.

I watched him fumble with a piece of firewood. When he opened the stove box a blast of smoke came out.

You have to pull the damper, I said. A funny déjà vu dropped down on me.

Sorry, he said.

No need.

So anyway. The gallery.

I've been working. On a portfolio.

Yes, of course. But the gallery, the Valley Gallery, not the Seattle Gallery.

I waited. The heat of his leg had worked through his chinos and was seeping into my Lycra leggings. It would have been awkward to move my leg — it was the limpy one; also that would have been a statement and would have brought attention to the accidental contact, so I held my position instead and froze in place.

The money for the gallery might need to be reallocated. He pulled his leg away and I breathed again.

May I confide in you? he asked.

Again?

That Marguerite, he said. She can be quite the fishwife. If it weren't for the gallery I would have left her years ago.

He sat on the edge of my cot and pulled a tiny purple-coloured square from his pocket. Unwrapped the wax paper around it and took a bite.

But do you like my paintings? I asked. Does the fishwife like them?

Oh yes. Oh yes. Oh yes. My apologies. I don't mean to burden you. I just wish all women were as self-contained as you are. She, I should say we, are just not sure how to brand you.

It was then I began to wonder if his interest in me was strictly professional or was it more personal. And how many strings were attached?

He handed me the half-bit gummy and I licked it, tentatively. I'm not much of a pothead, I said, not anymore. Not since I got my sister-in-law's six-year-old stoned.

Joel startled and I continued, Accidentally. The boy got into my stash accidentally. He's totally fine. No harm done.

I handed the wet gummy back to him. He took it between the tips of two fingers and dropped it into the trash, then stood, looked about, leaned against the roosting rack with his arm stretched along its length, looking at me so seductively that it made me turn my head a little. I decided not to move, just to keep eye contact with him. I have wine, I said.

He frowned. He cleared his throat. You're an interesting case, he said.

I am?

He picked up the unfinished portrait of himself.

Is my nose really that big? he said.

It's not finished, I said. The nose will change. So will some other bits. I grinned.

Do you need another sitting?

I do.

Joel put the painting aside.

But maybe not at the moment.

The portrait still had his portrait eyes pointed in my direction, not in menace but in pity. I smiled weakly and felt a little flutter in my heart. A heart attack, an arrhythmia, indigestion, nothing to worry about. I decided to ignore it.

It's a matter of riding the line between realism and impressionism, I said.

Oh, I've made an impression, have I?

I had a sudden hunger pang and wished I had not shared my sandwich.

He heard my stomach. We should go out for coffee one day, or lunch, make a date of it, he said. A business date. Of course, I would have to run this by Marguerite.

Marguerite, of course . . . Run what?

Nothing, nothing yet. Just getting to know you better before we proceed. He looked at his nude self-portrait again. You know I can't help but wonder what my life would be like now if I had met you before I met Marguerite.

Guess we'll never know, I said. I threw in a sigh, for good measure.

When you fix the nose, could you have another go at my chin?

I nodded mutely.

On his way out the door, he stopped, and as if the thought had just occurred to him he asked, Oh, by the way, have you talked to your mother lately?

My mother?

Lulu Frank?

I know who my mother is and no. Why?

Just wondering. Just wondering.

After he was gone, I fished the sticky gummy out of the trash and took another little bite. Tasty. I took another. Had I talked to my mother lately? Hmm . . . I repeated the question over and over in my head until it became an alternate reality that I started to believe had actually taken place or would. Hi, Mummy. I've met a man with a gallery!

I turned to the portrait. I fooled around with the size of Joel's nose. Mummy, he wants to meet you. I directed my attention to the portrait's manhood. Mummy, I do believe he requires your professional endorsement. I found a bag of Oreos and ate them. Mummy, have I ever asked you for anything before? I laid down on my cot and imagined the wardrobe I would need to complement my burgeoning career. I imagined getting undressed in front of Joel. Getting into bed with him. Telling him that Lulu was on board. Would he still expect me to exercise and hike?

I fumbled through the bag of cookies and ate the crumbs. I slithered back into my house and grabbed the last piece of leftover French toast out of the frying pan, poured a large glug of syrup on it and ate it at the stove. I found old coffee and poured a cup. Three spoons of sugar. I drank it down. Sat at the table and stretched my bare feet out and touched something soft and furry and damp. I screamed. Under the table was the dog, Fancy, licking my toes, and next to Fancy, the girl, sitting straight as if in a yoga position, eyes closed, legs crossed. Her rust-coloured hair looked greasy, tangled. Freckles on her pale, fine nose.

I said, Oh, it's you.

She opened her eyes.

Are you hungry? I offered the rest of the French toast.

She ate half and handed the rest to Fancy, the vicious white dog, who gulped it down. She crawled out from under the table and with great dignity walked out of the kitchen, up the stairs, presumably to her room. The dog barked once and followed.

I sat alone at the table for a bit. Maybe longer. I wished I was clear-headed and wondered how long I would have to wait it out. I filled the sink with soapy water. At least I could accomplish that much. The diamond stared at me.

Was it a Saturday? Where was everybody? I felt like the last person on the face of the Earth. I whistled for the dog. No action. I thought of my art career. That Joel was going to promote me was seeming like less and less of a reality. Unless . . . I shut the doubt off, went to my computer and Googled Joel again. Same old shit. I Googled Blake. Dozens of Blakes, none of any interest. Googled Lulu Frank, her latest show an unqualified success. Googled myself. That Tanzanian beauty and me, that newspaper article again. That frightening picture. A covered gurney. A house on fire. I hated the internet and everything it stood for. I Googled stepchild.

Old English *steōpcild*. The prefix *steōp*, "orphan," comes from Old English verbs *astiepan*, "to deprive of," and *bestiepan*, "to bereave." The original sense is an orphan bereaving their lost parent(s).

Joel texted me, Don't forget our lunch date. Wednesday.

I texted back, astiepan/bestiepan. Let him chew on that for a while.

When I looked up, the Buffalo was standing in front of me

with her coat on, her black purse, her woollen hat, waiting.

Oh, it was Saturday. She had the afternoon off and it was already past noon.

I pulled some cash out of my wallet. Is that enough?

She shrugged. I pulled out a bit more. Is the old crone still with us? I joked.

The Buffalo took the money and left without a word.

Every day for a week or maybe less, Joel sent me encouraging texts, inspirational texts: Remember that the ugly stage of art is powerful, it leads to authenticity. To be authentic is to suffer. To suffer is to create art. Suffering is a circle that takes you back to yourself. Suffer on, my beautiful friend. Make mistakes. Get to the ugly stage. Above all, be present.

Jesus H, where did he get this shit from?

I always texted back: LOL

Always no response.

I ordered a bottle of Uberlube online and had it sent to Marguerite.

I signed the gift card, A friend.

I envied her and the 86% futility of her desperate attempts to make a union of sperm and egg. I envied her, but I pitied her too, because whatever choice she made was de facto irrelevant. Nothing she did caused a butterfly tsunami in Africa. Just fucking and hoping. Hoping and fucking. Was I ever that innocent? The joys and woes of attempted parturition. I should paint that, I thought.

When I looked in the mirror I saw pimples on my forehead and chin. Like a teenager, I was breaking out again. Would the horrors never cease?

While I was driving Blake to work one morning, he told me he had received a memo from the girl's teacher with an informal assessment of her progress to date. She is quiet and yet disruptive at the same time. (Ha. Hahahahah.) She is working at the expected level in mathematics, working at greater depth in reading. Working towards the expected level in social skills. Above her age level in science and nature by two-and-a-half years. Memory and organizational skills, advanced for her age, et cetera. Et cetera. Et cetera. Blah, blah, blah.

Yet the teacher was worried about her. Does she have any hobbies? Outside interests? We have multiple resources at hand: school counsellor, regional services, child care worker, intervention, collaboration, behavioural consultants. Please come in for a consultation at your earliest convenience.

School has certainly changed since my sojourn there, when a report card said satisfactory or not, pass or fail, I said. What a pile of bullshit, I added.

I stopped the car and waited for him to get out.

He opened the car door and said, You know you might have benefitted from a little bit of intervention yourself. He turned directly to me. Don't worry, you're fine now. It's all good. I left a printout on the table in the house. Can you take care of it?

I beeped. I don't know why I beeped, but it did the trick and he exited my vehicle.

At the house, I found the printout, folded it in thirds and put it in the top drawer of my desk.

I wrote an email in response: Thank you, Mrs. White. I will save your "informal" assessment for the permanent caregiver. In the meantime, my husband will be in touch regarding a consultation.

I texted Blake: Buy the girl a pizza.

It's all good, it's all good, it's all good. Were there ever any more useless words than it's all good?

In the meantime, Marguerite texted, one line: Are you a friend?

CHAPTER 20

The pizza was thick crust, an everything pizza. When Blake started to apologize, I sat down and said, Don't worry, it's all good.

The girl, with surgical precision, was picking the green peppers off, one by one, onto a little pile on the table.

Blake said, You don't like green peppers, I'll remember that.

She picked a mushroom off.

Nor mushrooms, I'll remember that as well.

When she reached for a pepperoni I said, Do you even like pizza?

She popped the pepperoni into her mouth.

Blake must have seen something on my face that I was unaware of because he said, It's finger food, not a problem.

Not a problem, I said, and picked the onions off. Will you remember that as well?

Roxanne, our mascot crone, gathered all the bits that the girl and I had discarded and piled them onto her piece. We watched as they dribbled down her chin and onto the floor, where crazy white dog slurped them up.

Table manners, I said. That's how I was brought up.

She said, Times have changed. And we've learned a few things.

Like what have we learned?

That table manners were invented by the upper classes to keep the riff-raff in line. She snorted in glee and wiped her greasy fingers on her lap.

I slapped her hand and thrust a paper napkin at her.

So, said Blake to the girl, interrupting the merriment of our family mealtime, Who was that boy I saw you hanging out with in the playground?

The table, as one, froze. Roxanne and I looked from Blake to the girl and back to Blake, who was smiling in a very weird way with all his teeth showing.

The child stood, dropped her half-chewed slice back into the box and, without a backward glance, left the room. Crazy white dog trotted after.

I was just wondering, Blake said.

What boy?

I don't know. That's why I asked.

Well, that went well, I said.

I poured a glass of red and swirled it in my glass. Blake eyed it as I sipped.

Should I take another piece up to her in her room? he asked.

Should you? You're asking me?

Actually, I was asking Roxanne.

Moi? Roxanne said.

We stared at each other. We were at an impasse. But our moment of utter indecision was aborted when the girl appeared before us and said, He knows magic.

She picked up the box of pizza, the whole thing, and carried it away to the sanctity of her bedroom.

Blake told me later that when he picked her up from school he had seen her talking to a boy in the playground. A tall boy, wearing a hat, a top hat. It looked like a magician's hat, and the boy was also wearing a tuxedo-style jacket, much too big for him, with long tails behind and a little red bowtie.

I'm glad she's found a buddy, Blake said.

No matter how inappropriate?

He shrugged. I used to like magic myself when I was a kid.

I thought nostalgically then of early-days Blake juggling oranges on a beach. He had rescued me from my corporate advertising job and taken me to Mexico for our honeymoon. We were in Mazatlan, at an old hotel, and had spent our first three days in a lumpy bed, oblivious. When we finally emerged Blake decided he would teach me how to juggle. I was hopeless. He didn't mind, he was so patient, starting me on three oranges, then two, finally just one. When I finally caught it, he laughed, threw his arms around me, shouted, You beautiful genius! Well done!

I've wished a thousand times over that I could return to those before-days when I was a beautiful genius.

That perks my naif up and of course, she asks, Before what?

I pause before I answer, then blurt it out, Before I got pregnant. If you must know.

She waits for more but I'm not ready. We don't know what our turning points are until they've turned. That's the sad fact of things.

Are you going to teach the girl juggling tricks? I was trying to lighten the mood, trying to be funny, but he frowned. I mean as a hobby.

God no, he said. It seemed he had come home with a drum set, which he had set up in the basement for the girl.

That evening the neighbour who had accused Fancy of stealing her T-bone steaks phoned to touch bases. You cunt, you bitch. You think butter grows on trees? Do you? Have you ever even had to make do? Who do you really think you are, anyway?

I had no answer to any of those questions and whispered I'm sorry and hung up.

It was already Wednesday and Joel was driving in from Agassiz to check on my progress before our lunch date. My first thought was not to the canvases I had prepped, I'm embarrassed to admit, but rather to my personal hygiene. The limpness of my hair, the winter pallor of my face, the pimple on my chin. Back in the house, I rummaged through my medicine cabinet for blush and mousse and pimple cream and concealer. Like an insecure child, I stepped into Roxanne's room for approval and she frowned.

What happened to your face? Do you have a fever? she asked.

I swiped at my rouged cheeks. No.

I hope you didn't squeeze that pimple, it will get infected. Come here, she said. Bend down, and when I did, she sniffed my head and sneezed, told me I smelled like artificial grapes. When I pulled a strand up to my nose, I realized she was right. Are artificial grapes bad?

Depends on who you're trying to impress.

I bristled. Nobody. Maybe I should cut it? I whispered, desperate enough to ask Roxanne for advice.

What were you thinking, my busy bee asks. A long shag? Streaks?

I was thinking, Change me.

When Joel arrived, tousled and sexy in the annoying way that men have when they reach middle age so effortlessly, I realized he was in the mood for a shoulder to cry on again.

So where are we going for lunch? I said.

Lunch? He said he had decided to keep the boys' true paternity a secret, but he was beginning to see certain characteristics developing in them that reminded him of the gardener he and his first wife hired when they lived together.

Like what?

Brown hair.

You have brown hair.

Blue eyes.

You have blue eyes.

Talking with their mouths full.

I decided to get tough with him.

Do you have a plan?

He blinked. He had been corkscrewing a bottle of white wine on my workbench.

A plan for what?

For the gallery? For the show? For my Seattle launch? I handed him two wine glasses. Let's do mid-February, Valentine's. That gives us plenty of time, right?

Okay . . . Hesitant.

Or even better, the Ides of March. I proposed a toast. To the Ides.

Again he hesitated.

Fine, I said. The first of April then, April Fish Day. Not a day later. To my launch. To my exhibition. To us.

Finally, we drank. He held his glass out for more.

That feels good. Doesn't that feel good to have a deadline? I said.

It was 3:45 and the bus was due. I stepped to the window and looked outside while Joel pawed through my canvases.

The school bus stopped and the girl got off, followed by a boy in a top hat. The magic boy. From my viewpoint in the coop, I watched them in the yard. The girl, the magic boy and then Blake, who appeared with a bag of oranges. The children threw their backpacks down and stood in a circle. Blake threw an orange at the girl and another at the boy and they tossed the oranges back and forth between them, their breaths steaming in the cold air, the white snow littered with orange balls.

Joel stepped up behind me and watched for a moment. I could feel his breath on my neck. When I was a father, Joel said, I used to play a game with the boys. I would tell them to pick a number from one to eighteen, and I would recount a story from my childhood on whatever number that related to. One day they picked eleven. The only story I could come up with was discovering masturbation in the bathroom with my adopted father's *Penthouse*. Of course, they told their mother about it, and she cut me off for a week. Joel laughed. Children, he said. Can't kill 'em, can't live with 'em.

He leaned in close and sniffed. I smell a fruit basket, he said. Juicy. He put his hands on my shoulders and began to massage. So tight, he said. Relax.

CHAPTER 21

I went to the drugstore for vitamin E cream, muscle relaxants and mascara. When I got home the little white dog was guarding the front door with a low growl. When I made to step past her, she lunged at me and took a nip. I stood frozen in place on my own pathway and called out, Hello! Hello! I shouted, Help. No help came. The crazy dog flattened itself on the front step, staring at me. I retreated back to my sports car, where I sat and listened to the radio. Snowstorm in PEI, Indigenous woman missing presumed dead, sexual misconduct from coast to coast to coast. I put the earplugs in and turned the radio up. I yelled again. Hours later it seemed, the girl materialized, the crazy dog wagging its shaggy-assed tail at her side, sweet and submissive.

I had a dog once. As a child. A little black-and-white collie. I called her Herringbone. She made such a mess around the house, leaving tufts of fur and chewing slippers. When it thundered outside she would sneak into my bedroom and climb into bed with me, shaking. I would tuck her under my blankets where Roxanne would not find her and stroke her head until she calmed down. Go to sleep, Herringbone, everything is okay. Then one day I came home from school and Herringbone was gone. Where is she? I asked my grandmother. Roxanne said, Gone. Gone where? Never mind, Roxanne said, she's just gone. I gave her away. Why? Always "why" you want to know! Because we're not dog people.

I thought again of that Japanese word for granny dumping. How elegant and doable it sounded in Japanese. *Ubasute*. If only the mountain were higher, colder, closer. If only she would just go.

Not actionable, my you-know-what says. Unless it leads to something. In which case it's called premeditated.

In the fridge, I found a package of old hot dogs. I took them out and cut them into tiny one-inch pieces and microwaved them into hard snapping shrivelled-up chunks. I piled them into a plastic sandwich bag. I had gotten all the instructions online.

I went outside and around the front and pretended to visit, knocking on my own door. Inside, Fancy ran clicking across the linoleum to throw herself at the door, barking like the crazy dog she was. I opened the door and threw a piece of hot dog at her and when she ducked in shock at the sudden missile, I ran to the coop, shut the coop door and hid. Lesson number one: Gotta start somewhere.

Joel let me know that he was on his way from Seattle and would stop in to check progress. He had an idea. He had a very big idea. It involved a collector he wanted me to meet.

I spent all morning staring at my work. Examining it. Critically. All by the book: composition, contrast, focus. Was it any good? I personally wouldn't spend a dime to own any of it.

Joel showed up morose and moody. I tried to comfort him. Glass of wine? He took it and knocked it back. Held his glass out for another.

Where is the collector?

Who knows. He sighed. With everything that is going on in this world, what is the value of art? he said.

I've got some new work to show you.

Pretty pictures in a pretty gallery.

I refilled his glass a third time and my own as well. Can I show you what I'm working on?

Why not? he said.

I had given up on a collage of medical receipts for all the prescription drugs I had taken over the years and was painting over individual Tarot cards, replacing each iconic figure and face with my own family — Blake and Roxanne and even myself, Fancy and the big-assed social services woman, the principal at the school, Tully, the Buffalo, the police girl. Even the truck driver. All of them represented.

Am I in here? he asked, laconically.

I showed him the Fool. His face, tight jeans, cowboy boots. A bulge in his pants. The gold chain he always wore around his neck.

He looked without seeing, suddenly blurted out, My boys have been expelled for bullying.

Oh. That sucks.

Will you talk to them?

Me?

Marguerite can't. I don't think she likes them very much. Plus you can give them the perspective from the other side. Like a victim impact statement.

I mulled that over for a moment. It's always enlightening to see yourself through someone else's eyes. I'm not a victim, I said, pathetically.

Oh, I know, I know. Though I'm sure you heard "Frida Frankenstein" more than once in the hallways.

My heart stopped for a moment until I commanded it to beat on.

What a disaster life is, Joel continued, undeterred. He picked through my painted-over tarot cards. Which one is you?

And there I was, my big dark eyes, bold unsmiling face, wearing chain mail, sitting on a green horse, the Death card of course. Light brown hair flowing behind, breasts leading the charge.

He glanced briefly. Great, he said.

I flinched.

Everything you do is great. Plus, to be honest, I was afraid you'd give me vaginas.

Vaginas are not good?

Vaginas are so last week. But you, you're brave and authentic. And by the way I'm going to need an artist statement.

Oh! Really? Are you kidding? An artist statement? And my little heart leapt in joy, a joy balloon taking flight. But shouldn't there be a contract first?

Oh, we'll get to the contract. No worries. Just make your statement pithy, yeah? And, yes, we are still wondering, Have you or have you not talked to your *maman*?

He squeezed his dark blue eyes at me and smirked. Next to every joy balloon stands someone with a very long and very sharp, pointy needle.

I presume she's still in Paris, he said.

Yes, still in Paris. Shall I call and tell her that vaginas are passé?

Funny girl, he said.

So did you call her? asks the relentless girl/woman at my bedside, eyebrows raised in query. Oh never mind, she continues. Mothers are tricky. They get a bit needy as they age, right?

I begin to disagree then think better of it. My own mummy was like the opposite of needy. So what did that mean? And when was the last time I spoke to her? Do voice mails count? Somehow I think not.

Transfusions are being administered, plasma or blood cells, or platelets. I have a recollection of myself as a foolishly naive young woman, her dark blond hair carefully coiffed, chin lifted in pride, sitting in a small Parisian café with an aching limb, a pulsing throb in the scar tissue of her neck and a portfolio of drawings spread out. Spread out before the artistic gaze, the terribly critical artistic gaze of her famous mother. What did I expect? Love? And if not love, then what? Acknowledgement? And if not acknowledgement, then at least forgiveness. As if demanding to be punished. As if it would help or, more to the point, as if it would hurt.

Forgiveness for what? Punishment for what? For the fire? My little lawyer sounds angry. But you were, what, five years old? Children that age are not to be held accountable.

And at what age, do they become accountable, I ask.

Eight, she says. Eight years old. And our session ends.

Blake came in, dressed in his going-to-work-on-someone's-plumbing clothes and said, I've been called in to unclog a drain. Can you drive me?

I lurched forward to grab my coat.

Oh, I can do that, Joel smiled. I'm just leaving. Let the artist work.

Indeed, said Blake. No fake smile there. No smile at all.

Joel shuffled my little cards and piled them into a manila envelope, to show Marguerite.

I watched him toss them into the back of his Land Rover. Blake in the passenger seat, Joel picking something out of his ear, starting his Jeep; they drove off together.

We settled into an uneasy routine. Every morning Blake set out a breakfast buffet of boiled eggs, toast, peanut butter, Cheerios, bananas, whatever was on hand, and let the girl choose as she rushed in and out of the kitchen getting ready for school. Blake and I took turns with simple dinners, baked chicken thighs or hamburgers. The girl was in charge of piling the dishes into the dishwasher. She kept her room tidy, the dog fed and watered, homework done. Blake worked when he had a call, did the girl's laundry, checked her homework, kept the driveways shovelled, the cars washed. I was in charge of the groceries, the vacuuming, the toilets. The girl seemed to enjoy reading picture books to Roxanne and we left her to it. When the phone rang, we all jumped.

The uncertainty of our collective future together felt like a tsunami on the horizon, a herd of buffalo galloping towards us. Blake was moody: short-tempered with me, solicitous and nervous around the girl and exasperated with Roxanne. He had lost weight and was not himself.

I spent most hours working in the studio, texting Blake obnoxious things like: So now is the winter of our discontent? which he would ignore. I put crusts of bread out for the raven. In my wildest dreams, I never imagined I would be drinking wine alone in a chicken coop when I turned forty-three instead of showcasing an exhibition in Toronto. This was not on my playlist.

I think Blake feared that I would leave him.

He stormed into the studio one night. And you? What are your plans?

My plan is this, I said — but at the very moment I began to speak I realized I had no plan that I could put into words. No Plan A, no Plan B. Maybe the April Fool's show. Could I get it together in time? I had no idea anymore. The only thought that occurred to me was, The crazy dog has not yet learned to heel and we are completely out of hot dogs. The next time I shopped I bought 100% organic, grass-fed Kosher beef dogs and then turned my attention back to my art and signed up for an online workshop.

The exercise for today is a self-portrait drawn with your left hand. Sixty dollars and this was the drivel I got. I sketched a fat woman in a bulging grey chemise. Lopsided angry eyes. Grey teeth showing in a grimace meant to be a smile. Big heavy breasts. And a belly. Prominent, proud. I uploaded it to the site. One comment, Congratulations! When are you due?

People. Fools every one. I was about to send a photo of it to Joel when I changed my mind and sent it to Marguerite instead with the caption, Good luck.

Inside the house I paced the kitchen from fridge to stove to table, brooding. I had the sketch in my hand and realized suddenly how much I liked it, how true it really was, how honest. I went upstairs and slipped it under the door of the child's room. I waited for a moment until she pulled it in. I put my ear to the door and listened. So faintly I might have missed it, I heard a giggle. As if a weight had been lifted, I felt light-headed and in a strangely unfamiliar way, light-hearted. I went back to my coop.

CHAPTER 22

When I got home one day from the salon, my hair layered, bleached, re-dyed or undyed or whatever the hell I was into at that time, the Buffalo was cowering in the corner of the kitchen where Roxanne had her pinned. Roxanne was accusing the Buffalo of theft. A pillow missing, a half-empty box of chocolates, a lipstick. She'd flung the TV remote at the Buffalo and connected. Buffalo held a paper towel to her eyebrow. There was blood.

Would you like a raise? I asked. You deserve a raise. Do you need stitches? I have glue. Just put pressure on it. I was babbling.

Roxanne showed no signs of remorse.

The Buffalo bellowed at me, That woman should be locked up!

Twenty dollars an hour?

I should call the police.

Twenty-five?

She rolled her beautiful shoulders and shrugged them in a maddeningly noncommittal way.

Twenty-five fifty?

I suppose, she snorted. She pulled the tea towel away from her forehead and looked at it. Hardly any blood at all, but I was pledged now to $25.50.

I led Roxanne upstairs.

Are you mad at me? Her watery eyes.

How many times had I asked her the same thing for my youthful transgressions? Are you mad at me, Gramma? Are you mad at me? And how had Gramma responded? With the devastation of silence. Which was what I gave her now. And locked her in her bedroom.

My tender sidekick looks aghast. She turns her attention to her jumbo baby. She whispers, Are you mad at me, Tinker? Are you mad at me?

The baby gurgles joyfully.

A big sigh from — is it Barbara? Maybe Bette . . . ? Anyway all is right in her world. Still right.

Enjoy, I think. While you can.

It was Clare who had been pilfering Roxanne's things, reclaiming the items she recognized as belonging to her mother that Roxanne had pilfered from the boxes in the first place. So we'd all been in there, we'd all had a go. All of us thieves longing to embody that grungy charisma. I admit, I had some of her clothes. And Roxanne had been collecting the shiny bits and baubles that caught her eye. As well as the ordinary detritus of life, the Q-tips and panties and chocolates and neck pillow. Clare had retrieved each thing. Had built a shrine in her closet. Corey, the magic boy, had joined her there with his monocle and top hat and white gloves. How do I know? Because I found them together one day in the girl's closet, humming. I had no experience.

One afternoon, while Clare was in the basement practising on her new drum set with Blake blowing on the trombone, I escaped from the noise in the house and the art practice in my studio and took a drive north, aimlessly, mindlessly retracing the route to Tully's barn.

I found myself following the South Thompson River and when I spotted out of the corner of my eye a bit of yellow tape on the bank, I stopped and got out. A scrap of police tape, left over from Tully's suicide I presumed. I walked down to the river which was running deep and slow with thin, crisp edges of ice gracing the shallow eddies, and I stood in the spot I imagined she may have stood and tried to conjure the despair she must have felt. They say souls linger, but for how long? I felt something amiss. Caught on a branch was what looked like a long strand of red hair. But when I touched it, it dissolved, merely a spider's thread reflecting the sun. A lone raven circled above me. I struggled up the bank to my car and drove home, where my growing concerns over the details of Tully's suicide were upstaged by some very irksome news.

The Buffalo had quit. She had been with us since we moved to Hope. Was recommended to us by the care home in town. She lived in a basement suite below the convenience store, and every weekday she drove her Morris Minor up the road to our place, with her shoulder bag heaped with the special crisps and coconut candies that she preferred. Did she really have a licence? Or even a work visa? We knew so little about her. We had hinted at the idea that she could move in with us, twenty-four-hour care, less room and board of course, but she wanted her own space for sanity's sake. She was very clear about that. As you please.

Is it the noise? I asked. I can tell her to stop.

I love the drums, she said, as if I had insulted her.

What about the trombone?

It's your grandmother.

Apparently, Roxanne had demanded private bathroom privileges and the Buffalo had denied her for reasons of personal safety, and Roxanne had deliberately pooped the bed.

The Buff shook her head at me, shook her finger. Your grandmother, she said. She's a selfish person. Self-centred. Arrogant.

Proud, I suggested.

Arrogant. Narcissistic, egocentric.

I thought you loved her. You always acted like you did.

The Buffalo sighed. I do. But I miss my family.

We're your family, I said. You're our sister, you're our mother. Our daughter. I really had no idea of her age.

You're not my family, she said. I have my own family. I have my own mother, my own husband, my own daughter. They miss me.

We will miss you, I said. Even more.

Your people, your family, your problem, she said.

I offered another raise.

She shook her head. The finger again, pointing. All day long in the chicken coop. What are you doing in that chicken coop?

All right, that's enough, I said. That's my business. How much do I owe you?

She told me a number. I had no way of knowing if it was true.

I went to my wallet and found it empty. I dug out the cheque book to write the final payment. I realized then that I did not actually know her name.

I'm sorry, this is awkward. Who should I make this out to? It's not . . . Buffalo, but . . . What is it, your real name?

She spelled it out for me, letter by letter. Beau Fleur.

So the beautiful flower went back to Jamaica. If I could have switched skins with her, I would have in a flash. To be in Jamaica in the arms of a warm and singing mama, full to the brim of family and song, all of us arguing and alive in front of a blue, blue sea.

And now I am the one cooking, diapering, washing.

Whenever anything distasteful happened and I complained, Blake would tell me, Just live with it for a while, you'll get used to it. For example, when he bought wide-bottomed Wranglers, for example, when he proposed that Roxanne live with us, for example, when we moved into this old house. Well, I did get used to all of that, but this abandonment would take some work getting used to.

All day long nothing happened to the sky. The clouds just

hung there and would not release. I missed window shopping. I missed Starbucks. I yearned for Seattle. I yearned to step out and spend money — Blake's hard-earned money — on face creams and copper pots, throw pillows, Stoli. But all around me were those impenetrable woods, lumbering, bending, coarse throngs of trees and branches and bushes and moss. The silence I was surrounded with was deafening until I heard the noise behind the silence. Squirrels that sounded like monkeys, doves that sounded like owls, screams that sounded like babies. Sorry to be so melodramatic, but honestly the air was thick with tension. The tension of unfulfilled precipitation, unfulfilled promise. Unfulfilled love. There I said it. The dreaded L-word.

And I watch my psychiatrist underline it and circle it in yellow magic marker.

I advertised for a new caregiver. Roxanne was quite particular. Had to be male, single, heterosexual, at least five feet eleven, under the age of forty-five. I actually found one who fit the bill, an Irish, vegan bodybuilder, and for an hour or more, there was joy in the House of Rox. But as we shared particulars we discovered first that he did not do "personal hygiene," second that he was at least ten dollars above the going rate and third he wanted a picture of his ward. When I sent it, we did not hear from him again.

One evening, I heard Roxanne talking to the girl in her bedroom. She was bragging about her legs, how shapely they were. Touched in three places only, she said, thighs, knees and ankles. How slim her waist was. She was telling the girl to lose weight, that bad things happened to girls who couldn't control their weight.

I walked in on them. The girl was sitting on the floor, staring up at my grandmother in confusion. Roxanne was yanking a cloth measuring tape tight around her own sagging waistline, holding her breath.

What bad things? the girl whispered.

Before Roxanne could answer I said, No. You won't be giving the girl any of your so-called advice.

Roxanne looked at me with a sly, pitying look, then looked at the girl. Need I say more?

I counted off the days left to Roxanne. One hundred? Four hundred? There was no way to really tell. Her name was already on a waiting list at the StarDew Care Home, but of course, it was impossible to know which would come first, death or care. And I counted off the days of our temporary arrangement with the child while the grandfather was traced. I knew for certain that something had to give. My studio work suffered. But I started exercises, pumping big cans of sauerkraut over my head. I needed to be strong, even if I didn't know for what. Even if it was only to make a beautiful corpse.

When my burly neighbour phoned and asked, Is this the stupid bitch with the stupid dog? all I could think to say was, Yes, wandering over to her yard later with a shovel and a bucket while she watched from her window and yelled at me through the glass, laughing, pointing.

Back home, in the meantime, in the interest of not being ripped to shreds by the dog in question, we continued our hot-dog training sessions.

And hot dogs are not cheap, I say to . . . Beverly? and watch her write it down.

I had a dog once, she says. I love dogs. But now I have a baby. No hot dogs for you, right, little marshmallow? She blows a breath into the jumbo baby's face and we watch the baby's surprise bloom into a laugh.

That night, when I went in to get Roxanne ready for bed, I found the girl at her side with a book in her hand, reading out loud to my grandmother. When I saw the title, *The Story of O*, I snatched it away and sent the girl to her room.

How could you be so ignorant? I asked Roxanne.

She closed her eyes and pretended to snore.

This is so wrong, I told her. Wake up, you're not sleeping.

It's not wrong, it's sexy and it takes my mind off things.

It's wrong for the child. Don't you get it?

Oh, she won't understand. It's just words.

She's smarter than you think.

Oh, just read to me, Frida, she said. I'm lonely. I need something. And I'm afraid.

I could not resist the plaintiveness of that request. Roxanne's fears and loneliness were like a herd of grey hippos in the room that were threatening to sit squat on me as well. I opened at random and began to read, hoping to distract her. But while O was tied up and tortured into orgasm, Roxanne cried, her mind not at all distracted. I want my Buffalo back. I want my beautiful flower.

Don't we all.

I sensed the end coming for Roxanne. Every loss takes a bite out of your soul, a bite out of your life. There was something very final about the air in the room, the way her breath was coming shallow and slow. I heard the wind rustle through the trees outside. If she died now it would save us a lot of money. Sorry to have had that thought, but I did.

I kissed her good night. Gently on the lips the way she liked it. I whispered, I love you. The long hairs on her chin tickled my mouth.

All night it rained softly, the way it does sometimes in winter, half-hope, half-fear, all of it rebellion.

But in the morning she was still alive: wet, hungry and loud.

No oatmeal again! I want pancakes! She handed me a pair of tweezers and commanded, Tweeze.

I met Joel at the Local House, a drinking hole that catered to a younger generation with posters of rock stars and movie stars on the walls, Kurt Cobain, Sid Vicious, Freddie Mercury and a pool table beneath a disco ball covered in dust.

We ordered silly drinks, drinks that made the bartender snort in disgust. I had a grasshopper and Joel a strawberry daiquiri. As if to insult, the bartender put an umbrella in. Joel loved it. But when Joel let his thigh drift up against mine under the table I pulled my leg away. Then I felt bad and found his foot with mine. Until finally we left each other's extremities alone and drank our cocktails and chatted. I complained about Blake, I complained about winter, I complained about Roxanne. We argued abstractionism versus figurative works, the nineties versus the fifties, movements and installations, Elaine de Kooning, the tyranny of love. Or mostly he did. I was tired of the labels and the movements and the afterwords.

He asked how the work was coming. He tilted his head to the side to listen. I made up a bunch of crap. Working night and day on a series as he had suggested. Going very well. So inspired by the nature I was surrounded with. The wildlife, the birds, the flora and fauna. Of course, everything was blanketed in snow but I had the intertubes to inspire me. Painting underlayers then scraping them away to repaint and enrich the overlayers, which, as he had suggested, would become underlayers themselves, painted over again and again, white and thick with implied meaning until a finished painting was created in the way memories are created, the way they change each time they are revisited then are stored back into our unconscious in that changed way and become our personal history.

What I didn't tell him was that I feared I had spent my life pursuing something I didn't want after all. Let alone deserve. With a dawning suspicion that I was talentless.

He picked the lettuce out of his duck sandwich.

And Lulu? he said, out of the blue.

I put my drink down. What about her?

She had a burning in Portugal, almost lit the whole town on fire. He shook his head in admiration. To have a mother like that. He was talking about my mother's artistic shtick. Create a work of art, sell it and then six months later set fire to it. That was the contract you signed when you bought one of her pieces. She would arrive with her small entourage to wherever the work was displayed and put a match to it. Lulu's Burnings, the media called it.

I dunked my cinnamon bun into my coffee. Took a bite. And another. Gone in a moment. It tasted so good.

But wait. My little lawyer stops me. I thought you said you were in a bar? Drinking girly drinks.

No. I said coffee shop. It's a struggle to sit up but I manage.

She stares at me. She has cut bangs and they look wonderful on her. But I tell her they are hanging in her eyes.

She looks at the ceiling. The jumbo baby is grappling at her breast with her tiny fingers and her fishy mouth, determined to find a way through the cloth barrier.

I begin again to tell her about my conversation with Joel, that he wanted to confide in me and before I could stop him, he leaned in and said, D-O-R.

Of course, I had no idea what he was talking about, until he explained, Diminished ovarian reserves, D-O-R.

Hello. What? Marguerite?

Yes.

Holy shit, I thought. But then, who cares?

Well, I care, he said. I care very much.

He put his hand on my knee, the knee of the bad leg, and squeezed.

Say the word, he whispered. Just say the word.

Ouch.

And then Joel said, Clarabelle.

I paused, mid-swallow. The way he just said her name out loud like that, in conjunction with Marguerite's diminishing reserves, as if Clare were a difficult puppy that had not yet found her forever home and one was waiting for her right around the corner.

The bill came. It sat on the table between us until I reached out and Joel stopped me. We'll just go Dutch on this, no problem. And he counted up the expense of his daiquiri and pink malibu and put that exact amount of money on the table, plus 10% tip. Fair enough? he asked me.

When I drove into my driveway I saw that a red Toyota was parked in Blake's space. Marguerite's car.

I opened the front door and smelled something burning.

I heard voices in the kitchen, a clattering of pans and a high, girlish laugh. Not the girl laughing, it was Marguerite. I stepped through the threshold into the room.

Ahh, the lady of the house is home, Marguerite said.

What's burning?

Sugar. Sorry. Your oven might be a bit of a mess. We made cupcakes. She beamed in the direction of the girl and put her hand out to pat the top of her head. Without seeming to, Clare ducked. The girl's hair had been put into two high pigtails. It was Roxanne's idea, Marguerite continued. Not the pigtails, that was mine. I mean the cupcakes.

And sure enough, there was Roxanne at the table eating blue-frosted cupcakes, her lips blue as the dead.

Where's Blake? I asked.

Doctor's appointment. I stopped by for my husband, who's apparently not here, and Blake left me in charge. She tilted her head to the side; her shiny black curls drooped to her shoulder. And where is Joel? Not with you? Never mind, she said. He'll come home, wagging his tail behind him.

She buttoned up her leather jacket. She turned to Clare. Bye, sweetie. Thanks for the super cool afternoon. Best day I've had in months. She patted Fancy, who completely allowed it. Then she pointed her finger at the girl and said, I think you are awesome and super, super cool. Let me know when I can hang out with you again. Maybe next time I come to look over Frida's paintings, eh?

To me she said, And you, my dear, you just keep up the good work. She wiggled her fingers at me and left.

Super cool.

The kitchen was a disaster. Roxanne took another cupcake. I put the mixing bowl and measuring cups and whisk and wooden spoon in the sink. I turned the hot water on. I turned the oven off.

The girl said, I'll do that.

No, you won't, I said. A bit harshly I suppose. I softened: So, how were the cupcakes? Super cool?

Too sweet, she said. And she handed what was left of hers to Fancy.

CHAPTER 23

It was dark, a crooked finger of a moon behind a solitary cloud. I heard Blake's truck pull slowly into the driveway, heard the crunch of gravel, heard the engine quit. I could tell from his squared posture and the moments he waited behind the wheel before he left the truck and entered the house that he had lost again at the poker table. I wanted to tell him that I did not care. I wanted to pinch him and wake him up to me again. I waited in the coop and watched the lights in the house go off and on from room to room. Bathroom on, off, the girl's room off, the bedroom on, off. A staccato of light that beat the narrative out plain. I watched until I saw the blue reflection from his laptop.

He texted me: I did great. Case you're wondering. Clare's asleep. I'm nodding off. I'll make the coffee in the morning.

I did not text back. I waited another five or ten minutes, and then I slipped into the house and up the stairs to the room he was pretending to sleep in. The door was ajar. I stood by the bed in the dark. I stood in front of him until he looked up.

I slipped off my nightgown. Am I fat?

He buried his head under the pillow. No, you're not fat.

All I do is diet.

You're not fat.

Before he could qualify the remark, I slid in next to him. He rolled over, giving me his back, and I pulled myself up against him — his smooth skin, the way my soft belly felt against his spine. I don't care about the money, I whispered

But you do, he said, very much. And so do I.

He didn't know me at all. At one point that had been a refuge. But no longer.

I whispered, Hold me, Blake. I'm cold. I miss you.

Please stop crying, he said. Just let it go.

Before morning came, before the dawn, after the twist of moon had gone wherever moons go when they are not shining, I returned to my coop, to my single bed.

I waited there until the coffee he had promised me was announced. The sun was slow and miserable to rise. The morning brought with it a change of attitude, of mood. Blake was cranky, rushed. The dog peed on the rug. We were out of the good coffee and had to make do with Maxwell House. There were only two eggs in the carton because I had not shopped in two weeks.

I did not appreciate all this being dumped on me. I have deadlines, I said. I have two art gallerists on my back. I have a huge art project on the go. Why is shopping my responsibility?

Because you eat, because you drink, because I have a job to go to, a job that I don't very much care for but I do to keep us in the food that it would be great if you would shop for. He slammed open the pantry door. No Cheerios? No Cheerios?

We don't even eat Cheerios.

Well, Clare eats them. That's almost all she eats.

It's just so bizarre how you expect me to take all this on when it is nothing but a daily reminder of—

Of what? A daily reminder of what?

Of what I can't have. Of what I gave up for a so-called art career which has turned to nothing but shit. Of how you betrayed me. Of how I am excluded from everything. Of a million things I can't even think of. Is that enough of a daily reminder?

Get over yourself, Frida.

I threw my cup of coffee in the sink. The cup broke. The coffee had been delicious and I missed it the moment it drained away. Okay, I'll shop. Is that what you want? I'll fucking shop.

Never mind, he said.

Has it occurred to you that I could leave you here, leave you at it to deal with your own situation on your own?

You mean leave with Joel? You and Joel? He snorted.

We're not a bad match you know. And Marguerite is desperate for a baby, why don't you help her out as well?

Blake stepped hard towards me as if he would strike. I stood my ground and waited. I closed my eyes and waited. My disappointment knew no bounds when nothing happened. I opened my eyes. He had held himself back; he turned and left me.

My psychiatrist lifts her head. I'm curious about this disappointment. What were you hoping for? Would you care to elaborate?

No, I would not. Anyway, isn't that your job? I say. You're the expert, not me. You're getting the big bucks, not me.

She clicks her tongue at me, turns to my little lawyer, raises her eyebrows and leaves.

I turn and see that my sensitive counsel has covered the jumbo baby's ears with her hands and there look to be tears in her eyes.

What's your problem? I ask. A little more belligerently than I meant to.

Nothing, she lies. I'm allergic to baby powder, such a drag. She uncovers the baby's ears, who blinks to realize she isn't really deaf. My little lawyer smiles at this, then smiles at me. She swipes a tear from her face and says, No worries, we're all good here.

While the girl made do with Raisin Bran, I searched her face again for the tenth, twentieth, hundredth time for signs of Blake, anything at all. There was the reddish hair, yes. The thinking wrinkle between the eyes, the dimpled chin, the freckles on his hand echoed on hers. But I figured any child on any street might have shown the same resemblance. The accuracy of the DNA test was 99.9%. Was he the 0.01% with a false positive? But as I scanned her features I saw something there that I had not expected, something of my own self marking her: I recognized a remoteness, a holding in, a tight shallow breathiness of sorrow and loss. What I recognized was my own true unadulterated self. DNA became irrelevant. I went shopping and filled the house with food.

When I returned I found the girl mopping the floor.

I watched her for a few minutes, and if she knew I was there she did not let on. We had one of those battery-operated mops that you press a trigger and the cleaner sprays out in front of the disposable mop head. She was seriously shoving that mop head back and forth over the linoleum, and the air was choked with the stench of cleaner. Crazy little dog was at her side sneezing and sneezing.

Okay, stop. You don't have to mop. It's not like you're our little slave.

She kept mopping.

See? I bought Cheerios. Don't you want some? Clare. Stop. The floor is plenty clean. My goodness, do you wash windows as well?

Back and forth on the floor.

I'll mop the floor, thank you very much, that's my job, not yours. It's not gonna make a difference, you know. Nothing makes a difference. Your grandfather, your real grandfather, your true blood grandfather will be found. You realize that don't you? And you won't have to put up with the likes of me. I was waiting, I admit now, desperately hoping for a quick disavowal of my remark, but she put the mop down and left the room.

That evening at supper, while we forked Blake's soggy noodles into our mouths, I noticed with a start that the windows now sparkled, and from my seat at the table I could see every snowflake that fell.

Next day Blake lit a bonfire in the yard. Fire sanitizes, he said. Fire heals. A big blaze to cheer. He and the girl looked like a poster advertisement for winter outdoor fun: daughter gathering twigs with Dad, while Mom busied herself inside, baking cookies, drunk. Dad and daughter stomping their boots in the snow. Cooking hot dogs on sticks. A little end table drug out for the buns, the mustard, the ketchup. Paper plates. A thermos of hot chocolate. A winter picnic. They watched the flames. I watched them. I was not baking cookies. Blake was burning the branches he and the girl had raked up off the snow from the last windstorm. Burning old newspapers, tax returns from eight years ago, empty boxes of Cheerios. The girl was showing off, acting as if she liked to work, hoisting branches into her arms that dwarfed her, dragging them to the fire, throwing them in and missing, getting caught in the smoke. And Blake, not interfering, not helping, letting her struggle. Then she was whittling a stick with a knife Blake had given her. No instruction. He didn't even watch. The knife was sharp. When Blake looked up to the kitchen window, I stepped out of sight. I opened the fridge and found another package of hot dogs. Pulled one out and placed it in the microwave, forty seconds on high. I ate it plain, standing in front of the refrigerator.

I decided to take the dog for a walk. Nothing bonds you to a dog like a walk. And we both needed the exercise.

Where are you going? Blake called out.

Never mind, I said. Nowhere. Just getting some air. I'm allowed, right? I'm allowed to get some air?

Taking the dog?

Free country, if she wants to come. When I opened the back-seat door, she jumped right in and I drove to the quarry.

She had so much fun sniffing and poking around. Hunting down rabbits and mice. A dog's life is not the worst of lives. But when I turned around later to head back home, she was not with me. I called and whistled. She was nowhere to be seen. I started the engine and beeped the horn. I retraced our steps and poked around rocks and cavities, stumbling and lost. By then it was dark and I barely found my own way back to the car and drove home.

I tried to ignore the tizzy and confusion of my husband and his child and my granny. Where were you? Where's Fancy? You left her out there? You left her? Never mind my own scratches and throbbing ankle.

Blake got in his truck and started it.

But when the girl whistled, that special bird-like whistle she had, Fancy appeared, panting and utterly exhausted, lapping at the water bowl, then flopping down to sleep at the girl's feet.

The looks that Blake gave me and the soundless sobbing of the girl, as she wrapped her arms around the wounded dog, told me everything I needed to know about love and blame.

I returned to my refuge, the only place I knew that accepted me without judgement, where I could fully lose myself. I had sketched a likeness of my mother at her dressing table. An oval mirror surrounded in frosted light bulbs. The type a movie star would have in her dressing room. Her lips slightly parted, cigarette in hand, staring at herself in the mirror, utterly frightened by her reflection it seemed.

Clare found me in the coop later. I was sitting on the edge of the bed, hands in my lap, just staring off into space. I had been that way for a while. I looked at the girl. Her hair needed a good wash, her baggy socks crumpled at her ankles, but she stood sturdy and straight, Fancy at her side. She studied the painting I had just completed.

She spoke first. Self-portrait?

I looked at it again and realized she was right, it looked exactly like me in that mirror.

I nodded.

It's pretty good, she said. I like it.

I nodded again. Thanks.

Clare continued. You don't have to say anything now, but I just want you to know that we don't have to keep Fancy if you don't want to. 'Cause I know she gets you into a lot of trouble. Stealing people's food and running off and making messes in the house. But she can't help it and she's really a good dog, for me anyway, but not to everyone 'cause she doesn't really like other people that much, but I guess that's not really fair to you. So. (She swallowed.) Maybe we can find a really, really, really good home for her? A place with land like this she can run around in?

She stopped talking, then continued. Just wanted to tell you that, so now you know.

Fancy thumped her tail on the floor. Clare turned to leave and I called out, Clare.

She stopped.

I will never get rid of Fancy. Not ever.

PART 3

The Last Meal

When falsehood can look so like the truth,
who can assure themselves of certain happiness?

MARY SHELLEY, *Frankenstein*

CHAPTER 24

Fancy knew how to tell time, and every weekday she would bark at the door to be let out just before the school bus stopped at the bottom of our driveway. The girl would emerge and Fancy would run down the trail to greet her. The girl, in snow boots and toque, wearing a backpack filled with books, trudging the hard-packed trail up to the house, Fancy jumping all four feet in the air to greet her. I could see the trail from my coop studio window. One afternoon while Blake was gone I stepped outside as the girl and Fancy crested the snowbank. She stopped short, startled.

I have something to tell you, I began.

The girl crossed her arms in front of her chest and glowered at me. Fancy flattened herself on the ground, ears pricked back against her head and matched the girl's glower. A short, sharp wind blew through the yard, left a moment of stillness, then circled back. The trees whirled in response.

This is not easy to say and probably not easy to hear, but — I glanced around the yard for at least one friendly encouraging eye, a chirp of support, a squirrel nodding in the trees, any sign at all — stepmother, I blurted the word in her direction.

I don't know what made me say that. Maybe Marguerite's shameless interest in Blake's child, maybe just something about the dog's attachment. Maybe her way with all animals, or maybe it was Blake and his bourgeois desire to turn us into a family. Hoping, I suppose, that the girl would bless this self-revelation with her usual aplomb. It was not courage. It was anything but. Maybe I was trying to prove something to Roxanne. What I didn't acknowledge was that perhaps it was the girl herself and the heat that radiated from her, the way I felt drawn to it, and the realization that mothering her might be mutually beneficial. In the end, it was just another one of those things I blurted out without thinking it through.

I waited for a response.

Again the wind blew and the trees relented. I stood my ground against it. Having made my declaration, I froze in place.

The girl, immobile, gave one slow blink as she stared at me. The ends of her hair blew about in the breeze.

Finally, she said, Whatever.

And as she skipped away from me, I called out, Look, this is who I am. I'm not changing, just because "whatever." We're talking compromise on both sides, right? Right?

She turned. Can you please cut me some slack?

I had so much to learn.

My pal the Barbie doll studies me, thinking hard.

I'm thinking, she says.

Don't hurt yourself, I reply. I shuffle my hips from side to side to relieve the pressure of lying flat on my back. I struggle until I'm sitting upright. The tubes are an ongoing annoyance.

Being a mother, she says, it's not something you learn, it's something you do.

Everything is something you do, I say. Doesn't mean you can't learn about it too.

Barbie nods. You're the cabbage, she says, you got the head

She's patronizing me with that old joke, the one I used to hear from Roxanne and still use myself. I let it go.

The next morning, woken by the pressure of a full bladder, I hear in the distance of the woods the soft howling of a lone coyote. The bed is lumpy, not quite clean, but warm. I revel for once in a wakening not sullied by memories of a bad night passed in argument and hostility. Wakening, too, from a happy dream of singing spontaneously with my father the song "Walking in a Winter Wonderland." Perhaps this really happened when I was very young, before he left us. I don't recall. But the feeling it evoked was real.

The next day was a Saturday and it was lunchtime and the tomato soup was getting cold and the girl was not in her room. I put out a side dish of saltine crackers and called out again, Lunch!

So you fed her? My bedside companion asks and makes a note.

My little lawyer is back and I am so relieved to see her. But sometimes the things she says make me wonder. I stare hard at her — is her name Bailey? — hoping she will see the look of insult on my face. Of course, I fed her. I am not a monster and even as I say that, I find that I am wishing it to be true.

Good, she says, just asking. Tomato soup? Good. Homemade? Never mind. And the name is not Bailey.

I found the girl in the yard with her magic friend, Corey. They seemed to be fighting over a photograph that Corey was holding over his head while Clare tried to grab it. When I got closer I saw that it was a photograph of Clare as a baby, sitting in her mother's lap. All right, that's enough, Corey. Give the picture back to Clare, don't take things that aren't yours.

Clare grabbed the photo, stuffing it back into the pocket of her pink parka.

Yeah, Corey.

Ah, we're just fooling around, Corey said.

Well, don't. By the way, Clare, I just want to remind you that child services is still looking for your grandfather. Kind of a tricky guy to locate but they're determined because point of fact they are not at all pleased to hear about Blake's DUI. Not that I blame them. Though you think they'd have better things to do. But anyway, bureaucracy. So. Okay? Got it?

No response.

Do you know what a D-U-I is?

No response.

It's when you drink and drive. It's very bad. Not that he hurt anyone. And it was only two or three beers and I'm not condoning, but he had just heard about Tully's suicide and he wasn't thinking properly and he got caught. I paused. Of course, there are worse things in the world. And I went on to enumerate them. Evil, premeditated things like racism and ageism and dysentery and dementia and wasting your whole life and feeling sorry for yourself and being a fraud and destroying the rain forest and girls killed on the Highway of Tears and . . . I can't remember now everything I said or thought, but finally, the boy said, Okay. Thanks. We get it.

I took a deep breath in.

There's tomato soup in the kitchen. And crackers. For both of you.

When I turned to leave them, exposing my back to their eyes, I half expected to be struck down before I reached the house.

Wow, so melodramatic, my drama queen intones.

You don't know what it's like to be reviled.

But were you? Were you really reviled?

I close my eyes on her. Her youth, her innocence, her questions. And when I open them again, moments later, she is gone as if she has never been, and I am in a familiar tangle of tubes and beeping monitors and bleached sheets.

It took me awhile to finally notice the little red bumps along Clare's hairline and the constant scratching, I knew then that my first test as stepmother was to address the fact that the girl had lice. At the drugstore, I conferred quietly with the chemist, though he had no notion of confidentiality and loudly directed me to the lice aisle. I bought a bottle of Nix Crème Rinse along with shampoos and conditioners and paper towels and Febreze and hair dyes and other things I had absolutely no use for, hoping I suppose to camouflage the one thing I needed. Of course, there was no working barcode and the girl at the till had to pick up her store-wide microphone for a price check on Nix for lice. I stared straight ahead.

Back home with my remedy, I hemmed and hawed for two hours. Invading her personal space, I was a newbie at this. Her door was always closed. On the door a note: Do Not Enter.

Blake was away on a hard-drive job, so I went back to the girl's room and knocked. I waited a moment, then opened and peeked in. Knock-knock, I said. She was on her bed, listening on headphones to her new little MP3 player. Fancy, curled into a comma beside her, woke and jumped down and greeted me. A low growl in her throat, but her stubby tail wagging. I put my hand out to touch the dog's cold nose and let her sniff.

What are you listening to?

She looked up startled.

I heard the faint sounds of maybe Spice Girls, maybe Backstreet Boys, they all sounded the same. When I was her age it was Madonna. And for a whole month, Cyndi Lauper. I withheld judgement.

I showed her the bottle of Nix and waited for her to read the label. For lice, I said. Those little insects living in your hair and sucking your blood. Probably driving you crazy. This will kill them. It won't hurt. A pause. Can we take care of this?

Her long red hair was a tangled mess. A rat's nest.

Can we? She asked.

Take charge, Frida, I told myself. Like it's all a *fait accompli*. Don't leave room for waffling, or stubbornness, or disobedience. Funny concept that.

I left and went into the bathroom and turned on the taps in the tub to pull the warm up from the basement. Tested the water. I put a towel down on the floor for us to kneel on. Plucked the spray showerhead down to reach. Put on my rubber gloves. I waited and turned the water off.

I called out, Clare? How many times had I spoken the girl's name since she had been with us? In these few months, not many. Not many at all. I'm in here, Clare, waiting.

She came in.

Do you know what lice are? Nothing to worry about. Just tiny insects that feed on the blood in your scalp, lay eggs on your hair and make you itch. Little parasites.

I motioned for the girl to kneel down and lower her head into the tub.

Parasites are just things that are not part of us but live on us, feed on us, need us to survive. And take whatever they need with no regard for their host. But we've got their number.

I could not stop talking, that's how nervous I was. I rechecked the temperature. Too hot now? I cooled it down. The back of the girl's neck was bare and downy with wisps of rust-coloured hair drifting about.

I had lice too when I was your age. More than once. And Roxanne was not exactly gentle. But some people are not meant to have children. Don't know how to care for them. But we try.

The water seemed too cool then and I added more hot. How's the temp? I asked. Is it too cold now? Should I make it hotter? Is this too hot?

She lifted her dripping hair and without looking at me shouted, Just do it!

I took the gloves off and sprayed her tangled hair. With a dollop of conditioner, I massaged the girl's scalp. Rinsed and combed it through. Then I doused her head in the poison.

The feel of her scalp under my fingers. The bone of her skull. A sudden memory of a woman, my mother I'm sure, showing me that soft spot on my baby brother's skull. Putting my small hand on it to feel the soft hollow indentation. Saying, Never touch this, be very careful. It's still open, his skull hasn't closed yet. I stopped mid-rinse.

Are we done? she asked.

No. I scrubbed at her scalp, rubbed the Nix through right to the ends of her hair.

Must be done, she said.

Okay. Let's rinse, I said. I turned the taps on again. I let the water flow over her head, gently massaged. Her skull was strong, hard, bony, as a skull should be. So what do you want to be when you grow up? I continued dousing her head with water.

No reply.

A doctor? An artist? A lawyer?

Are you finished yet?

I turned the water off, pulled a big towel off the rack. I'm just saying you have a lot of potential.

A small pause. That's what Marguerite says. She thinks I should study fashion design or be a model.

Oh, really? I draped the towel over her head. Can you do the rest? Before she could respond I left her there, kneeling at the tub.

In the coop the next day I found a sketch on the bench. A big-breasted woman with a chicken head. Underneath, in block letters: THE STEP MOTHER. I nearly laughed.

I kept at my canvases. Joel kept zooming in and out, edging around about Marguerite's dilemma though he was smart enough not to spell it out. I ignored him until one day I said, Just fuck right off about it. Okay?

He blinked at me. Okay, he said. Got ya. By the way, who have you sent invitations out to?

No one.

Not even Lulu?

No. Not even Lulu. Anyway, invitations to what?

To, to . . . to the show, to your solo exhibition.

Oh, is that settled now?

It will be . . . it could be. He was stuttering and I ignored him.

I gessoed plywood, huge boards, painted them over in layers of zinc white, cadmium yellow, then white again, activating the dried surfaces with large scrawls of black ink and charcoal, letting my hand wander freely. Not even Lulu. Not even Lulu — pounding like a drumbeat in my head.

Then he added this bombshell. He was leaving Marguerite. He would tell her after the exhibition. He knew she would pull funding if she found out before. And he and I could take charge then of our own lives. Without you-know-who.

I kept to my studio and scrambled through my paintings. Deer, ravens, nakedness, wolves. Nothing pretty. Everything raw. They were utter shit. I had to start over, but there was no time.

And then my next official stepmom duty was to find the girl's dirty laundry sitting in a pile outside the door to my coop. I knew what the pile meant — mothers do their daughter's laundry, not fathers. Did no one in this household give one rat's ass about the time crunch I was up against? I gathered up the clothes, pyjamas, T-shirts, underwear, socks, jeans, gathered them all up into my arms and carried them back to the house, down to the basement, to the washer. I held the bundle up to my face and breathed in the waxy, sweaty smell of her dirty clothes. I dropped the clothes into the washer. In the pocket of the hoodie, I felt something hard. I put my hand in and pulled out a rock, an old Kleenex and a barrette. A pink barrette in the shape of a butterfly.

CHAPTER 25

Today, a rare visit from my garrulous psychiatrist. Send in the clowns. The scent she wears announces her entrance and I relax. She is a wonderful talker and I can simply listen as she tells me things, for example, about an elegant experiment she is spearheading that involves rats. It seems that not only do they have a strong maternal instinct and will fiercely protect their pups from threat (Is this supposed to be a Freudian message? If so, I ignore), but they also have a quite well-developed sense of humour. She and her colleagues discovered this by tickling them and recording the chirps and chortles, videotaping their tiny teeth bared in laughter.

This is truly astounding and I can't help but ask, Tickling them where?

In their armpits, silly, she says. Isn't that wonderful?

Yes! Wonderful, I repeat. And it is wonderful to hear about the laughing rats and to not have to spill my own, less humorous, beans for a change. But with a sigh, she stops talking and tilts her head in my direction. Your turn, she says, and I must fill the void while she sits waiting, pencil in hand, all ears.

Days went by. No word from Joel. I was too proud to reach out aside from sending one photo of a work in progress. Which he did not reply to. Blake's work on Joel's computer system had been curtailed. We saw another IT truck in front of the gallery, another artist on Marguerite's website, gushing, making overtures, posting thumbnails.

Meanwhile, winter, it just kept on snowing. A joy for some, anathema for others. You can guess where I was on the continuum.

And? my shrink asks.

And . . . one day Blake's sister invited him and Clare to join her and her family on a little ski holiday. His sister's baby girl was now eight months old. Her son, the same one I disastrously babysat some years prior, was now twelve, and she wanted the cousins to meet up. So Blake's daughter was now considered a cousin. The wonders of sperm when released into a functioning vessel would never cease to amaze me.

Blake felt a little guilty, I could tell. So he put on his big ol' cheery voice and said, Hey! You can work on your art, right? Not to mention somebody needs to be here for Roxanne and the dog. You'll be fine. You'll be better off without us. You'll see.

I grinned at him, showing teeth.

He loaded all his old ski equipment into the back of the truck. All the winter wear he needed, and Clare's. He had just gotten his licence back, could finally drive legally. And off they went. Good. Three days on my own. I had been waiting for this: solitude, world under my own control, quiet to work, dreamscape valley of loneliness, but now it was here and something else had come in with it, a dread — I'm not sure of what — like a rock in my heart place, like there was a precipice in front of me and all I had to do was tilt a little and down I would go.

I watch my psychiatrist scribble and I change tacks.

All morning I banged around in the studio, organized my brushes, set my colours out in a sequence of warm to cool, stared at canvases. I checked my phone. No word yet. A three-hour drive, they'd get there by happy hour. Check-in. The pretty snow, the lights glittering, the gaiety of it all. The whole atmosphere so alive, so young, so deliriously out of this world, so puffy-jacketed and mussed hair and red-nosed that it made you, pale and coiffed, in your regular street clothes, want to kill yourself. In our valley abode, the snow was segueing into rain. Up in the mountains, it would be snow.

I went back into the house. Mopped the floor. Fancy eyed me, suspicious.

When my phone barked, I grabbed it up, expecting a word from Blake. It was Joel. He was on his way over. Wanted to check out my latest oeuvres. I had been working on small, surreal self-portraits on canvas that had been painted, collaged onto and embroidered over. A visual diary of sorts. Frida, the Octopus Lady. Words stitched on: My arms have a mind of their own. Eight octopus arms and my face painted on the head, with a lopsided smile. Because I knew if I didn't keep drawing myself, I would disappear completely.

He would love this as much as I did, I was sure of that. So very sure. And yet, maybe not so very, very, very sure. I had still not gotten a firm commitment.

I went down into the basement, found the boxes of clothes and things that belonged to Tully. I pulled out a dress, a knitted sheath of red and black with a big black zipper running neckline to hem, inviting a pull. Soiled, of course. Still holding on to her particular salty-animal smell. I slipped out of my leggings and long tunic and pulled the dress on. Snug across the hips and breasts but if I didn't zip it all the way up, it fit. I looked in the mirror. I said, Voluptuous, tried the word on for size. Pulled the zipper down a bit, to cleavage. Said again to the mirror, Voluptuous. I half believed it. Would Joel?

I had just finished shaving my legs, dress and blush on, when, not Joel but Marguerite arrived, in a rush, checking her phone. She was on a spa weekend with her old high school girlfriends, who were waiting in the car for her. Girlfriends, spa weekend. I turned those concepts over in my mind. Where's Joel? I asked.

She narrowed her eyes at me. Why do you ask?

Isn't he representing me?

She looked at my red dress. I pulled the zipper up an inch or two.

We're a partnership. She continued to stare. I pulled the zipper up another inch.

Self-portraits, I said, directing her attention to my artwork. A visual diary in three mediums. Me as octopus, me as turtle, me as snake. You like? I may have raised my voice a little. She had thrown me off balance.

She laughed into her phone and blew kisses. She looked up. Frowned. She pointed her manicured finger at the stitcheries I had laboured over. Is that all you've got?

It's hard to find the time, what with . . . you know.

Either you want this opportunity or you don't, Frida. She looked at my octopus arms again and at the bug-eyed balloon head I had drawn in my likeness.

I was hoping . . . we both were hoping that you would incorporate some of your mother's little sketches and whatnot in a collage-y way. Wasn't there some guy, some cut-and-paste guy? She picked up a few postcards I had on my counter, the promotional miniatures they gave away at Mummy's shows and exhibitions, souvenirs of the burnings: huge, abstracted butterflies and flowers meticulously rendered in teeny tiny happy faces. I used to admire the incredible patience this would take, drawing hundreds of those tiny happy faces that would only go up in flames six months later until I realized she used uncredited assistants for that tedious work. In the end, the originals were worth their weight in gold, and collectors lined up to buy them. Why? Because they sold exorbitantly priced tickets to the event that more than covered the cost of the original painting, with Lulu of course getting a cut of the proceeds. Everyone made a killing. Win-win. Was this cathartic for her? It was not for me.

Marguerite stared at my self-portrait as an octopus. I never used a brush smaller than two inches. She stared at me. You want my advice? Call your mother. My god, what are you waiting for? Nobody makes it on their own, Frida. Just get her on board. Jesus Christ, do I have to spell it out? It can't hurt. Obviously, it can't hurt.

She turned back to her phone and let herself out.

I waved as she drove off in case she looked back, then slammed the door shut. Maybe I'll be the judge of what hurts and what doesn't.

Upstairs I let myself into the girl's bedroom despite the hand-lettered sign she had posted on the door: Stay Out. The tranquility of her space surprised and soothed me; I had expected a mess, a childish chaos. The room was painted white, the small bureau with its round wooden knobs white, the bedframe, something we had hastily found in a garage sale, also white. Curtains, ceilings, all of it ghostly. On the bed was the quilt she had brought from home, a faded patchwork applique of butterflies, surely someone else's handiwork, no doubt second-hand. On the shelf below the window, an array of found items and assorted treasures. The skull of a bird, a striped rock, the diamond. And under her pillow, folded neatly, I found the new smiling-kittens pyjamas Blake had bought her just a week before, that she had worn all weekend day and night but had probably forgotten and left behind. My mother had sent me PJs one Christmas, dotted with mice. At twelve years old, they were way too small and too babyish for me, but I kept them under my pillow for months.

I looked around. In the closet several small outfits, dresses and hoodies and tops hanging on the pole. On the shelf below were placed her runners and sandals. The soiled clothes in the hamper, the baby doll she had come with, a beaded bracelet in a tangle on the white bureau. I stretched out on her bed. I too had once been a girl who pretended to believe the world benign and the future under her control.

I thought of Roxanne's pills, the cornucopia of pills that I had closeted away on a high shelf in her bedroom. Pills for everything under the sun, diabetes and high blood pressure, anxiety. A mix of beta blockers and anti-depressants and sedatives and tranquilizers, all to be carefully administered in measured doses. That old hypochondriac.

I thought of the concept of luckiness. I thought how easily I had been left behind. Was it a sort of spite I had in mind? What a terrible admission, realization.

But when I opened the door to Roxanne's room, my miserable plans of self-annihilation turned into a bunch of hoo-ha.

Rox sat splayed, legs akimbo on the floor, tangled in her quilts, surrounded by her medical contraptions, the things that kept her alive or let her know at least that she was still a beating heart, a breathing lung, a human, in the act of being. Blood pressure cuff. Oxygen tube. Asthma spray. Aspirin, nitroglycerin, bandages, Febreze. Daily pill dispensers. Sani-wipes. Tissues. A box of candies. A tin of cookies. A vibrator, for god's sake. Makeup. Lipstick. Sunscreen. Expensive facial creams. Tweezers, nail clippers. Most of it on the floor. But most disturbingly, all the plastic medicine vials of pills. Everything I had thought safely stashed up on the high shelf. Everything I wanted for myself. All the bottles opened up, all the pills dumped out, all mixed up together with the candies and the cookies, and Roxanne was feeding handfuls to the dog, who was salivating at her side.

I slapped her knobbed hand away from Fancy as she extended another palm full of pills. One little blue one looked a lot like Blake's Viagra. Jesus H. I yelled. Hey!

She grabbed my foot and squeezed hard. I fell.

What the hell are you doing? I yelled at her.

Immediately contrite. Have I been bad?

Yes, you've been bad!

Fancy's lonely. She wanted a happy pill. Where's the girl?

Roxanne was tearful. Angry, confused. Just as I was.

I hope you're happy, I hissed.

I'm not, she said. Thanks to you. What did I do wrong?

Indeed.

I clipped a leash onto the dog's collar and carried Fancy out to the car. I drove to the vet, a place I had already spent too much time and money at. In my car, Fancy vomited. I stroked the top of the crazy dog's head and said, Good dog, good dog. You're a good dog.

At the vet's her vitals were taken and the vet shook her head at me in disgust. Time will tell, she said. But probably okay.

If Roxanne had an incident while I was gone so be it. It was on her. It was on Blake and the girl for leaving the dog behind. For leaving me. While I waited at the vet, my harassing neighbour called me up, spitting into the phone her insults and accusations. She had just ten minutes ago put a T-bone out to barbecue and now it was gone. I was a bitch and a whore and a useless waste of skin. I know, I told her, I know all that. But Fancy, she's a good dog and she's with me.

Back home, Fancy wobbled upstairs. I listened for any noise, any clue from the old crone. Quiet. I poured a Scotch. I went online. Nothing there, nothing in the remotest sense of value. Emails from Amazon and Zulily. Painting gurus offering workshops in Tuscany at crazy prices. The ski hill Blake had taken the girl: 15 centimetres of new snow, 120-centimetre base. All runs groomed, all chairlifts open. Lessons and rental packages. Those doctored photographs of warm wooden cabins, a yellow glow at the windows, with fresh blue-white snow and that sky. The impossible blueness of that sky that only appeared at altitude.

The doorbell rang. By the time I got down to it, the visitor was gone but on the step a cardboard package from Amazon, addressed to Clare.

I gathered Roxanne snoring in her rocking chair. Woke her up. Said, Get your pull-ups on. Get dressed. Hauled some warm clothes out for her, yellow sweatpants and yellow fleece sweater.

Are you getting rid of me now? Her eyes were round and soft as tennis balls.

No. I wish I could. We're going skiing.

My grandmother grinned.

Put your teeth back in.

For what purpose was I headed in that direction? To deliver the package, yes, but beyond that I had no idea. I just knew I had to be there. I grabbed the girl's kitten pyjamas and the dog, sedated and goofy, and with Roxanne belted in and also sedated I headed out

Three hours and ten minutes later we arrived at the narrowed streets of the ski hill. Snowbanks piled high in the ditches, skiers with their skis over their shoulders strolling along with no concern with how they might be holding up traffic. I stopped at a little convenience store and grabbed some wine and chips and pull-up diapers for Roxanne and got directions to the Powder on the Mountain Condominiums. Parking at the entrance was reserved with numbered spaces for guests, so I parked on a side street two blocks away, in front of the sign Beware of Sliding Snow, Park at Your Own Risk. I had seen that once, watched from a restaurant window as the snow slid off a pitched roof and landed whoosh onto a parked car, a young woman running out of the café, hysterical, her baby still in the car. Luckily unhurt. I might have yelled out loud, Jesus! You stupid fucking bitch! I'm pretty sure I did yell that, and possibly more. Because I remember the other diners turning from that exciting, snow-shrouded spectacle outside the window to the hot and loud screeching spectacle of me, safe inside, and Blake shushing me in alarm.

It took forever for Blake's sister to finally buzz us in after I shouted my cheerful hello into the speaker in the hall.

The first thing I saw was a fixed smile on Blake's face at the sight of me. A smile that didn't quite reach his eyes. And from the girl a squeal of joy, which may have been for Fancy, or even Roxanne, or maybe the PJs I handed to her. Well, it wasn't my neck she threw her arms around.

I also had the Amazon package in my hands. Here, I said. Missed Christmas, but here it is. Her eyes widened.

Christmas just goes on and on in your house, doesn't it? Brianna said.

The girl opened it in front of us. Inside, a junior makeup kit, three shades of blush, five eyeshadows and three tubes of lipstick, pink, red and purple. To no one in particular, but me, in general, she squealed, Thank you, her cheeks pinking in pleasure.

Everyone ignored her then and started in on all their boring ski anecdotes, moguls and tree wells and powder. Brianna's boy whispered, Did you bring your stash? and Brianna hissed, Stay away from my son. I ignored the comment, dove into the taco chips and drank more wine.

Brianna and I didn't like each other, that much was clear. And was my little joke about her husband and her tits really that offensive?

My psychiatrist raises one eyebrow. She has told me, more than once, that truth is healing. Truth is important. Truth is freedom. Over and over again, she admonishes me, Please Frida, try to be truthful. Not only in your words but also in your thoughts.

But this is what I've learned about truth. It's not truthfulness we must strive to attain. Truth is too malleable, it's fluid and even contradictory. Truth is completely subjective. All we can strive for is honesty.

Brianna had served a big pot of chili. Just enough for all of us, now that I was there with Roxanne. We were drinking wine, dozing off. Blake was playing Mexican dominoes with his nephew and Clare. Brianna was breast-feeding her baby and when the infant dropped off, she just left it hanging out there for all to see. (Indeed, the milk spurting from her plein-air nipples was a sight I would not soon forget, the round white spongy globe, the blue veins, the expression on her face that was half bliss, half smirk.)

And I said to the husband, I bet you'd like to get a latch onto that.

And instead of an easy laugh at my joke, the man stopped licking his lips and blushed. He swapped the look of infantile hunger on his face for fear and abruptly left the room, and I realized the truth and said out loud, My god, he sucks on them too!

Sister-in-law Brianna had yanked her startled baby away from her tit and snapped her blouse closed in fury, and the evening festivities were pretty well abandoned.

Which is when she said, I just realized I'm the only real woman here.

Everyone left the next day, although another night had been paid for. No refund. Blake in his pickup with Clare and Fancy, me with Roxanne in the car. I was hungover but not sorry. Her words haunted me, pricked me. I could not let them go. I just realized I'm the only real woman in the room. I kept repeating it to myself as I drove. Mimicking the high-pitched silkiness of Brianna's voice. She was referring to my childlessness and, even more, to my hysterectomy. In a moment of weakness years and years ago, I had confided in her about the operation, how I hated doctors, despised hospitals, was a coward in terms of pain. Yet to be done with those heavy cramping periods, blood clots the size of my fist... Ovaries, schmovaries, I had laughed. I had felt the same before my tonsils were removed, yet once gone how often did I think of them? Fair to say, never.

I had gone on and on to Brianna. Such an innocent, a naif child, she needed a bit of toughening up. I felt it only right to educate her in the full spectrum of femaleness. And I had taken advantage of her stunned silence and elaborated. Would they use the parts they pulled out of me? Surely, they wouldn't go to waste. It might have been in the category of too much information. Brianna was one of those unscarred, unpleasant types whose most regretted experience was hiring the wrong caterer for their wedding.

How sympathetic she had sounded. Never mind, never mind, at least you'll be done with the curse. But then at the ski hill, to have it thrown in my face like that. The only real woman, my fucking ass. Do ovaries make you a woman? Does having a baby or two make you a woman? I rolled the window down and spat. I clenched the steering wheel and hiccupped with tears. I put my hand between my legs, felt my loins, still there, warm as a peach, essential and desirous. Open. Wide open. Maybe the car swerved a little. I corrected immediately but Roxanne turned to me and pointed a long bony finger in my face. Don't play with yourself while you're driving. Didn't I raise you better than that? Oh God, bless the old crone. Nothing removed, nothing pulled — even she was more a woman than I.

CHAPTER 26

The nurse swabs my mouth.

My surgeon is lounging on the edge of the windowsill. Deep-blue scrubs. Wavy brown hair. His arms crossed in front of his chest, his feet crossed at his ankles. I suppress an urge to ask for his autograph.

All yours, doctor, the nurse says and sashays out to her station.

He studies me from across the room. He is telling me I have to do my bit as well. He means it. He says, We're a team here, I mean it.

I nod.

He says, You better start pulling your weight.

Okay, I say.

I'm not kidding, he says.

Okay, I say again.

He looks at the bundle in the basket by my little lawyer's feet. What did you have?

A baby, she whispers.

He sighs.

Good luck, he says. To the both of you. He steps over the papers on the floor but stops at the door to say, By the way, you owe me a congratulations as well.

New dad?

No. Ten days sober.

To my little lawyer I say, Close your mouth.

On Monday, Corey got off the school bus at our stop with Clare leading the charge. Her cheeks were pink and her lips pressed together, half-smirk, half-secret. I watched from the doorway of my studio. I thought of all the children that came home from school to a plate of cookies and a glass of milk. Or was that just a myth? I had no personal experience. My own childhood was ketchup sandwiches one day, goose liver pâté the next.

I looked through the pantry. Blake was partial to Pepperidge Farm cookies — he had a box of Tahiti Coconut and a box of buttery Chessmen hidden away on the shelf behind the Oreos. I pulled them out and set six of the expensive cookies in a circle on a big green platter. Blake's fake beer in the fridge. Popped the tabs on two of those, set them out. Maybe I was getting the hang of this after all. Snacks, I yelled, then retreated back into my studio and congratulated myself for a job well done. Parenting was turning out to be a snap. I squirted a tube of mustard yellow paint all over a panel and pretended to paint.

Sometime later, the yellow scraped off and a green slopped on, I heard a scream from the house. At first, I froze. To be brutally honest, I do not consider myself heroic; certainly as a child, I was not. Once I saw a man shoving his girlfriend around. He was yelling, I love you, you bitch. I was ten years old, and it was in the street below our condo. The woman spotted me up in the window watching and shrieked, Do something. I dropped out of sight to the floor below the sill. What could I do? I was only a child.

I walked quickly to the house, to Clare's bedroom. The girl, the magic boy and Roxanne were situated around a Ouija board, a small stub of a deer horn, the Tully diamond and a shining black feather resting on it. The boy was dressed in boxer shorts and socks, bare-chested, showing his skinny ribs, pale arms held rigidly at his side, tender fists clenched. Clare was in her T-shirt and undies, her whole body quivering. But it was Roxanne who demanded the most attention. She was flat on her back, practically naked, her lumpy pudding body drooping softly at her flanks. Her wispy hair, as if electrified, made a corona around her skull. The bones of her cheeks jutted upward, pink mouth agape, eyes closed.

What's going on?

The girl and Magic Corey were both breathing hard, wide-eyed. In fright or excitement, I could not tell which. Roxanne was as if dead until she opened her eyes and whispered, I disappeared.

You're right here, you didn't disappear.

I did, she said. She sat up. I went someplace foreign. I went to Morocco. I was young. I had a tambourine. Little Lulu was at my side, collecting money for coffee. She was so cute shaking the tin can, calling out, *S'il vous plait*. Roxanne looked down at herself, her drooping breasts. I'm old again.

I looked at the girl and at Corey. Neither one of them spoke.

I'm old again, Roxanne said.

Put your clothes back on. All of you.

They did as they were told, the children thin and awkward as broken sticks, the old crone fumbling with her nightgown.

I gathered the talismans from the board. The raven feather felt cold in my hand; the diamond, hot; the horn, hard as bone. Harder.

I wanted to tell them that it was impossible. That they were making it up. That Roxanne had an overactive imagination. That it had been a *trompe l'oeil*, a trick of the light, a sudden shadow. But the chill in the room and the palpable yearning stopped me. To disappear into an earlier time, who wouldn't wish for that? To wish so strongly that it might almost come about.

I folded the Ouija board and put it high on a shelf. Don't it always seem to go.

Later, when I told Blake, he shook his head, No.

But maybe, I said.

But no.

That night a storm dropped down like a curtain over our play. For hours the snow accumulated, heavy, wet, damaging. In the early morning, the temperature dropped and the trees and power lines bowed down, laden with their frozen burden. All day our electricity flickered and struggled until just after dark when the power and land line went out. Blake's phone was dead, unable to be charged, mine was at 35%. I stumbled through the hallway and kitchen drawers looking for flashlights. I lit candles though the smell of the wax, the small flickering flames, filled me with dread. I made sandwiches for our supper.

What I am not telling you is this: At some point that evening, in the dark, the snow still falling, I heard the front door open and Roxanne's shuffling gait as she stepped outside. For ten minutes I pretended I did not know. Until I gathered what was left of my humanity and went outside with a light and found her huddled under a tree, gasping in the cold. I led her back to her room.

Her favourite meal was macaroni and cheese and the next day, to soothe my guilty conscience, I pre-empted the kitchen duties to make it. Joel phoned and I put him on speaker, grating cheese into the cream while he ranted.

Everybody is pregnant, he said. Everybody has the hugest belly — fourteen-year-olds, fifty-year-olds, all the Madonna wannabes — it's like they're stalking us. And Marguerite, goo-goo at every stroller. When I was a kid, my dad took us out to the country one day, to get a taste of rural life, of nature. We went to a ranch, all the pretty cows mooing away. You know what we saw? A total horror show. Prolapsed uteruses, calves being pulled out by their legs on chains by tractors. Now you tell me, what self-respecting cow would volunteer for motherhood if that was known? Can you tell me that? Thanks, Dad, thanks for the nature lesson.

I stirred the béchamel sauce into the macaroni casserole. I sprinkled it with onion bits and Parmesan. I turned the oven on to 350 degrees.

I have to go, Joel. I'm in the middle of making dinner.

The oldest mother in the world, a sixty-six-year-old, had twins! IVF. And she isn't the only one. Talk about desperation. Even men are trying!

I looked out my window. My friend the crow was there, watching. You should see this big black pet bird I have outside, I said to get him off the topic.

Ravens? Crows? Know what they do? They steal eggs, they steal baby chicks. Not to raise them, oh no, but to eat them. Oh nature. There are two kinds of people in the world.

I stopped mixing the macaroni. Only two? I asked.

He stuttered for a moment. More than two, of course. There are millions, but the two kinds I'm referring to are — those who are living and those who are dying.

My breath came in shallow. Which kind are you, Joel?

He lowered his voice so that I could barely hear him. I'm dying here, Frida. I'm dying.

I'm sorry to hear that, I began.

He cut me off. I told her. I told Marguerite everything, the truth.

How important you are?

Oh, she already knows I'm shooting blanks, he shouted. What I told her was, I'm tired of working the odds. Fourteen percent, my ass. Tired of it. It was not a pretty evening. And if I can be completely honest —

Please don't be completely honest, Joel.

The sex, all that sex wasn't even that good.

I'm sure there were interesting moments —

Hey, wondering . . . Joel said. Can we talk face-to-face?

When I looked out the window again, the crow was gone and there was Joel, phone to his ear, waving at me. I left the casserole in the oven and met him at the coop door.

Hopping from foot to foot, Joel looked distraught or nervous or both, big-eyed and pathetic on the step. Rain was falling on the beautiful snow and everything was sodden again. Mush. Blake was off to his weekly poker game, to lose. Roxanne was in bed, Clare was sequestered in her room.

Joel, in turns chuckling and then serious. Marguerite, he said.

What about her?

He wagged his head side to side, took a deep breath, blew it out through rounded O lips.

Is she . . . having an affair? I guessed.

Oh god, I wish. May I come in?

I'm not really dressed. I don't remember what I was wearing, something elasticized. Old lady pants, comfort clothes that made me wish I were exactly dead. I looked down the driveway. Where's your Jeep?

Oh, he pretended surprise. I parked it down the road a ways.

I didn't ask why, but he volunteered, A bit of exercise never hurts. His beautiful leather shoes were sodden, the hems of his slacks dark and wet.

It's all set for April. Correction, almost set. Almost all set.

Okay . . .

He looked at me. I won't be long.

I have a casserole in the oven.

He took my hand. How is the work coming?

I had no idea what was going on. I let him in. I showed him

what I was working on, the underbelly view of a blackbird with you-guessed-it for a head.

Painted mostly by imagination, I said. Not easy to get a view of the underbelly of a crow. It's called *Self-Portrait as the Underbelly of a Crow.*

It was mostly black; there was a pinkish opening for what I imagined might be bird genitalia, and a couple of tiny nipples.

Joel nodded and looked. At the painting, at me. Back and forth. He scratched his head.

But do ravens really suckle their young?

Cute as he was, I was starting to dislike Joel and, even worse, distrust his opinion.

He nodded. He looked about rather wildly. Didn't you tell me once you were a nurse?

No.

Are you sure? I almost remember you saying that you studied nursing in school.

I studied painting.

Okay. Well, that's okay.

I decided, for once in my life, to keep my mouth shut.

Look, I don't remember exactly what we talked about the other day on the phone. I was drunk. I probably said some things that were way out of line, so let's take two steps back and start again. All right?

Okay.

I'll just say it, he said.

Or not.

The clinic wants another sperm sample.

And?

And . . . And . . . I can't get it up, and she can't get it up, and I remembered you telling me how you studied nursing and here I am.

He sat on my cot. He had brought a condom for the sample. I sat by him. And not knowing how to say no, I did as he asked until he hardened, gasped and sighed.

Thank you, thank you. You can forget all the competition, he said. Don't worry about the competition, the young up-and-comings. We'll keep this between us and just keep working, and if Marguerite withdraws support we'll get the funds some other way. Right? The point is, the thing you have to remember is this: April Fish Day. Just show up. You and your mother, Lulu, just show up. We don't have to set anything on fire. It's all so simple.

CHAPTER 27

It turned cold again and whatever snow had melted in the rainy days accumulated once more, not quite in force, but still. Almost ankle-deep. Blake bought two pairs of snowshoes. Not that I walked out much. I didn't have the time for it, or more to the point the inclination. I was obsessed with my failure to get a firm commitment from Joel and Marguerite. What really did they want from me? Would any mediocre piece be acceptable if Lulu were included? I tried to squelch the thought, but it would not be squelched.

I sent my mother an email. I told her Blake and I were loving Hope and the wild spaces we were surrounded by. And Roxanne was doing pretty good, considering, but she missed her daughter. I kept the fact of the girl's presence in our home unspoken. It was too tender, too temporary, too "mine" to share.

I segued instead into a wordy confabulation about my artistic successes, with a tiny photo of my self-portrait breastfeeding-the-wolf painting. I told her that my gallerists thought it might be fun to include her in the launch of my world-class exhibition. They very much admired her talents, her burnings and installations, and her stamp of approval would be . . . The words crawled out of my fingers like tiny ants scrambling for crumbs of love or admiration. I felt craven. I wrote, Mummy, isn't this what you've always planned for me? An artistic career of my own?

Her response took two days. Splendid! *Bonne chance!* And nothing more.

When a woodpecker knocked on the telephone pole and sent Fancy shivering into a corner with some ancient archetypal fear I shivered with her, having a few of my own.

I went to the coop and laid a drop cloth down, I was studying the vista outside the window, the white snow, the blue sky. The day was crisp with cold, and the zinc-white bank of snow and the Prussian-blue sky floored me. It was impossible to replicate so I was simply standing there with a tube of zinc white and a tube of Prussian blue, drowning in the frigid beauty of nature, when I caught sight of a big man knocking at the front door of the main house. I started to duck down but he'd already noticed the light on in my coop and my movement, and he waved. I stood straight and went out to greet him.

At first, I didn't recognize him. He was groomed, his eyebrows tamed, his hair combed back, his chin clean-shaven except for a goatee. Wearing baggy blue jeans, not clean exactly but not coated in grime. A thick plaid loggers-style jacket. But when he spoke I recognized his lazy drawl. Tully's landlord, Larry.

After our hellos and how did you find me and what a cold spell, he said, This is awkward. Shall we go inside?

Standing in the freshness of the whites and blues, I was disinclined to do that, could have stood there for an hour until he froze in place, but I opened the door and gestured for him to enter.

On the spot, I formalized a brand new policy. Never offer a drink to anyone who shows up with the line, This is awkward. I checked over his shoulder before I shut the door. His pickup truck was in the street, not at all crashed in a ditch, just parked normally. No wounded animals in sight. No blood on his fenders. No ravens circling. I forgot my policy and offered him a drink.

A beer if you got it.

I fetched two. And we stood in the hallway, each of us with a can of beer.

He jingled keys around in his pocket. It's about Tully. He took a long sip.

I braced myself for the worst. Even from the grave, she could not leave us in peace. Then I remembered she was not, in fact, in a grave but was somewhere glimmering upstairs in the girl's bedroom. What about her?

Can I trust you?

I drank. I wiped my mouth with my hand. Trust, what a funny word. I said, No. I wouldn't.

It doesn't matter. It's just that when she, ummm, killed herself, she left behind a couple of unpaid bills. He drained his beer.

I'm not surprised.

A broken lease, unpaid rent . . .

So?

Legally it should have come out of her estate. But seeing as she didn't really have an estate . . .

I guess you're out of luck then.

Look, I don't want to sue anybody, not the kid, or the father, or you. You could just be nice about it and pay what she owes.

I took his empty beer can out of his hand and did not offer another.

Had he already rented it out? my clever lawyer asks. Had he tried? Did he have proof of advertising? Did he have a lawyer?

Bingo, I say to her. He had nothing. Not a leg to stand on.

I could be nice or I could be not nice, I said. I just don't see how it's any of my business. I finished my own beer. I dropped them both into the trash can; hell with the ten cents. I continued, And isn't it enough that we've been paying out of pocket ourselves for the girl these last three months?

Ahhh, the girl, he said. The girl. How is she?

Fine, all things considered. Children are very resilient, I added. A total guess, I really didn't know but I had to say something. I had been resilient as a child, yes, but was that enough? Is that what life is about, resilience? What happened to thriving?

He was looking over my shoulder, and I swivelled my head. There she was. Scowling as only she could scowl at her mother's former landlord.

Hi, Clare, he said. Remember me?

She nodded once.

You've grown. He scratched his eyebrow. Hey, I brought you something.

He rummaged around in the pocket of his thick faded jacket until he produced, with a flourish, a rabbit's foot or a cat's paw or maybe even half a mouse. It was grey and furry. Was it my imagination or was it still bloody at the stump?

After a powerful hesitation, she took hold of it between her thumb and forefinger.

Don't say I never gave you nothing. Hey, by the way. For old times' sake. And from the other pocket, he retrieved his phone and said, Smile. Before she could even frown, he snapped a picture. Perfect, he said. And never mind about the rent. I'll suck it up. He winked at us and left.

The girl was staring at the amputated appendage in her hand and began a low hum deep in her throat. I reached out and took it from her, dropped it into the crazy dog's salivating mouth where it disappeared *tout de suite*.

Good dog, I said.

We exchanged a glance, the girl and I; she exhaled, I inhaled. I closed my eyes. When I opened them, I was alone.

CHAPTER 28

One afternoon Blake barged upstairs where I was clipping Roxanne's toenails while she slept.

They found him, Blake hissed, he's coming. Blake had his laptop in hand. I had Roxanne's foot in mine.

Who's coming? The iceman? I scraped the grime from beneath Roxanne's big toenail.

The grandfather. They found the guy in New Delhi. He's making arrangements to fly in.

I nicked Roxanne's toe with the clipper and she kicked out in her sleep.

You're kidding.

I'm not kidding.

When?

Who knows when. When his schedule allows. Soon I imagine.

Roxanne's toenails were long and curved, thick as claws. I gathered the bits and dropped them clattering into the waste can.

He shoved his laptop in my face. See?

I looked at the email, then wrenched Roxanne's other foot into my lap.

This is what you were wishing for, Frida. Are you happy? Are you happy now?

Of course, I'm happy. I'm always happy. I'm a very happy person. I clipped the next toe over.

It means we'll be alone again. Just you and me.

And Roxanne.

You, me and Roxanne. Like before. Back to our old normal.

I scraped more grime.

He scrolled through his laptop. We have options. I mean, Roxanne won't last forever.

Right. And neither will I. Neither will you.

We could sell this place. We could do some travelling.

Hmmm.

Look, he said, Machu Picchu. The pyramids, sea dragons in Sydney. Look at them.

I looked at Blake's laptop, then I looked at Blake. His eyes were practically popping out of his head scrolling through pictures of weird fishy-looking things on his computer.

Look at these guys, look at them. Sea dragons, but they call them weedies 'cause they live in the seaweed, and they half look like seaweed and half like sea horses but bigger. All orange and purple with these bumps and pokey things that stick out and a snout that sucks food in like a straw. They're amazing. Total homebodies living in the same patch of seaweed their whole lives practically — and the males carry the eggs on their tails and give birth. The males do! You know who would love weedies? You know who? She would love them so much.

He stopped talking. He turned to the window. We don't have to travel, we could just stay home. We can stay home and just keep busy. That's the thing, right? Keeping busy. Like we used to do. I could try hang-gliding again.

I looked back down at Roxanne's foot in my lap. Three more toes to go. I pushed at a cuticle. You're in my light, Blake.

Well, what's your big idea?

I don't have a big idea. Why do I suddenly need a big idea?

Your show, right? Isn't that your big idea?

Okay, yes. It is, actually.

But then what?

Then what indeed. I picked up the emery board and began to sand Roxanne's heel.

I'm waiting, he said.

Okay. Fuck Machu Picchu. I'm not hiking the fucking Andes. And fuck the pyramids.

We stared at each other. Roxanne banged her foot up and down on my lap.

But if we do your weedies don't we have to learn how to scuba dive first?

A moment passed. Blake snapped his laptop closed. He stood. He marched to the door and turned back. What are you doing this weekend? Got any plans? I hope not. 'Cause I do have plans. I'm taking Clare to meet my parents. They don't even realize they have a granddaughter yet. I hope that fits with your schedule. I trust it does. 'Cause that's what we're doing this weekend. He left the room.

I could have told Blake any number of things to dissuade him from this course of action. It seemed more appropriate to loosen the connection with the girl rather than strengthen it. Did he consider even for a moment how awkward this was for me? And honestly, what would the girl gain by this? But, I had a bit of a crush on Blake's father, and I relished a change in scenery. I relished more than just a change in scenery. But it was hard to put into words.

A long whistling passing of gas. Mummy, Roxanne called out in her sleep, smacking her lips, Mummy, you ate all the cake.

I would take my paints with me. I would take this step by step.

In preparation for our trip, I knew I had to bathe Roxanne. Oh, how I missed the Buffalo. Lumbering and inefficient as she was, still she was a buffer. Every time I was forced to minister to the pale and sagging, lumpy and hairless nakedness of my grandmother's body (a plucked chicken), every time I wiped it clean, towelled it dry, powdered the spots and creamed the rashes, plucked the chin hairs and pencilled the brows, I was confronted with a reality I was not ready to accept. But how stoically she submitted herself to all this. I give her credit for that. When she was irritated, she pinched me, and I pinched her back.

I had given up the daily bath and settled on weekly. Much easier, but who knew there was an old person smell nothing to do with externals. It emanated from the eroding hormones inside and smelled like she was embalming herself. It took a special soap to cleanse it away, something like pomegranate, or maybe persimmon. I steeled myself. As I suppose she did as well. First, she pretended to be dead. I poked her in the ribs, hard, once, twice, until finally she woke from the dead.

Ouch, she squawked.

Get up. Bathtime.

Why?

Why? Because you stink.

Spritz me with a little Opium.

We're out of Opium.

I don't want a bath.

I don't care. We're going to Marshall's cabin for the weekend and it would be nice if you were relatively clean.

We are? Why?

Why, why, why. Because.

Because what?

Because Blake's parents want a look at his progeny, that's why. Okay? Got it? Don't worry about it.

She rose and shuffled along, head bowed, as if to the gallows. I filled the tub with lukewarm water, dumped a capful of bubble bath in, which made enough froth for her privacy not to mention my own sensibilities. I hefted her up in my arms; she weighed next to nothing. I tipped her over the edge of the tub into the water and released her. In she went all bones and sag. I watched her flounder for a moment. The tub was filled nearly to the brim and she was having trouble keeping her head above water. After several moments of struggle and with a certain amount of difficulty, she managed to right herself. She sputtered and groaned loudly in bliss. I think it was bliss. How strong you are, I said, as she gasped for air.

Of course, I was not going to sit by and watch her drown, but I have to confess the idea had slipped into my consciousness where I let it linger for more than a moment.

You might be getting the idea that I hated my grandmother. Nothing could be further from the truth. I adored her. Admired her. I even envied her. At least I had, once. But were those feelings reciprocated? Not a jot. Like a carapace, I bore her disappointment. Kept my soft turtle belly hidden.

Bedside sits the young woman who calls herself Betty or Barbara, or is it Belinda, who claims to be working on my defence. But I struggle to remember not only her name but if she truly is on my team. So young. What could she possibly know or understand of my struggles? We are both quiet for a long time.

I'm sure now that her name is Belinda and I say it out loud. Belinda, I say — and she looks up — You don't have to be here if you don't want. I like that you're here, for the most part anyway. But it's not a command performance. Why don't you go home? Even as I say these words I dread that she will obey them. I pray she will disregard.

For a long moment, she studies me.

Do you know the Welsh word *hiraeth*?

I don't.

And she explains. It is homesickness for a home you cannot return to, or that never was.

There was a place on the lake where a gazelle had fallen through the ice and trapped there, half-in, half-out, had died. The ravens and eagles had swarmed in alerting me to the carcass. Now it was just a flag of hide and bone. Fancy had lost her fascination with the remains, all the good scents and bits of flesh picked clean. I called her to my side, and she started to obey, but then lifted her head and darted back down the trail. Fancy! I called. She ignored me. I saw, then, the small silhouette of the girl coming towards us. I froze in place. Would she speak to me? Would she smile? Was it me or the dog she was coming for?

I woke.

CHAPTER 29

We packed and readied. The girl was ecstatic. Snacks for the road! Three pairs of thick socks! Where was her makeup kit? Blake already had the truck gassed up, oil checked, snow tires on. He must've been plotting this weekend for a while. His parents' cabin was tucked away in the next valley, over on the bank of a small river. Marshall was a woodsman and Blake, an egghead, a computer nerd, must have been a disappointment to him, but still, Blake idolized the old man. He would watch nature shows, always trying to get up to speed with his dad so that when he went to the cabin he would have something to contribute. Did you know that the biggest fish ever caught in Lake Huron was a ninety-eight-pound walleye? His dad would look at him blankly and ask if he could chop some kindling for the fire. Adding, as Blake stepped outside, Don't cut yourself. Then he would wink at me.

Marshall had tried to teach Blake to shoot and had given him the 30–30 that I had used to kill that wounded deer on the road. The deer Tully had run into. The same rifle she had shot herself with. But Blake did not take to guns, nor did he inherit the blood lust. Unlike me, apparently. At the trial, Marshall had scoffed at the prosecutor's suggestion that I was comfortable with guns and therefore violent by nature. Bullshit, he said. Total bullshit. Court was recessed for the day. Were any of the jurors impressed?

Myself, I admired the old man. Wished he had been my early influence. I even wished he had been my own father instead of the one I only knew as a smudge of love that vanished. I might have made something more of myself. Or conversely might have failed more spectacularly. In an alternate universe, Marshall and I might have been the couple that set out to conquer the world. Fry bread, prairie sunshine, mountains, the way the earth opens up and leaves you to it, alone, racing hard across the landscape, cactus, a saddle for a pillow, a moon for a light . . .

Watch the road, Blake yelled. I swerved back into my lane.

One thing I did know, Marshall kept horses on his river property that belonged to a rancher neighbour who needed extra graze land. A rough pair of ponies, cowboy-broke, that Marshall treated as his own. The one time he had given me the chore of feeding them a bucket of oats I had been stepped on and bitten.

The girl leaned her head against the window and watched the trees fly by. Every branch, every hollow, her eyes flickered; once, an eagle, its white head shining, on a treetop and she gasped and pointed.

Blake described the cabin to the girl. No electricity, no cell, no running water. A wood stove for heat. This wouldn't phase her. I knew that his dad liked to hole up there away from Dolly sometimes and fish, or shoot squirrels and ravens for fun. Nobody cared to mention that tidbit, I guess.

And Blake loved his mother, Dolly. He doted on her. And for the most part, Dolly kept her condition under wraps. Alzheimer's, dementia, her slender frame gently shaking in wide-eyed confusion.

When we arrived we saw that Marshall had brought their motorhome for himself and Dolly to stay in to allow the four of us the cabin.

The cabin was outfitted with a double bed against one wall and two bunk beds on the opposite side. The girl slipped up to the top bunk easily and set her little pile of clothes at the foot, her red flashlight, her book of puzzles and stories. Roxanne tried to commandeer the double but I moved her over to the single bunk, below the girl. Don't bang your head, I said when she banged her head.

Mice abounded.

In the cabin the first night, it might have been midnight, we had been asleep for hours, nothing much else to do there, and I felt a shoving, snuggling and a sudden smell of lavender. I sat up and in the moonlight that came through the window, I saw that it was Dolly. In her nightgown, eyes closed, a dreamy smile, curling up against me. Dolly, I said, what are you doing here? At that, Blake woke. And without a word he gathered her up, small as she was, and carried her back to the motorhome where Marshall was asleep in bed.

Can't I stay with you? I heard her pleading.

No, Mama. You can't.

I remember how difficult I found the evidence of that particular mother-child love when I first encountered it. I mocked it. Kept looking for the chink, the falsity. The skeletons in the closet. The more I peppered Dolly's and my conversations with barbs — You don't recycle? Is that what happens to a woman's hair when she gets old? That green is not your colour, sorry to say. — the more she seemed to warm to me: admiration galore; compliments on my hair (I love that colour), my weight (had I lost?), my clean house. I used to taunt Blake sometimes, When did you stop sleeping in their bed? You were eight? Is that even legal?

He never rose to the bait and now I give him credit for that. Myself, I never questioned my motives. Jealousy, when I think back. Motives are what occur to us after.

That night from their motorhome came the sounds of lovemaking. Lovemaking? Animal sounds, high pitched, female. If Blake was awakened by it, he never let on. Thank you, God.

In the morning Dolly brought her cup of tea out to the little porch under the awning attached to the side of the motorhome and sat in the fold-up chair that Blake had set out for her. The ground was frosty but there was only a dusting of snow. She smiled at me. Some platitude, beautiful day in paradise. I looked around. It was true. Cottonwoods, bare-branched and glistening in frost. The river was freezing up in thin squares of grey ice, flowing slowly south to the Columbia, to the sea.

How did you sleep? I asked, and her eyes clouded over.

Very well, I think. She laughed. I guess if I don't know for sure then it doesn't matter.

Marshall stepped out, unzipped himself and turned to piss into the bushes along the bank. Eyes right, he shouted. He looked over his shoulder at me and winked.

I turned away. I had once admired his machismo, but it jarred on me now. Not sure what had changed, the thought of gentle Dolly in his rough hands perhaps.

Blake came out of the cabin with a roll of toilet paper and headed to the outhouse, and Marshall rolled his eyes at me as his son walked by. In a low voice, he said, He never did learn to piss outside. He laughed. When you tire of Blake, give me a call. Marshall didn't care, or notice that Dolly could hear him and had flinched and swatted at her ears as if besieged by gnats. How many years had it taken to learn to swat his words away?

I turned on him and said as pleasantly as possible, Don't you ever disrespect my husband again. And don't you disrespect your wife.

He looked at me. I felt the full force of his masculinity exuding from him like a squall. I held myself from falling into it.

All right, he said. Okay, Now I know who you are.

Did he?

I suppose you hold it against him, he said.

Hold what?

The kid.

You don't know me. You don't.

I know you well enough. Well enough. And more to the point, you don't know my son.

What don't I know then?

The boy is loyal to a fault, and I do mean fault.

And what you don't know is that boy is actually a man.

Marshall ignored me and whistled for the horses.

As if on cue, Blake came obediently out of the outhouse. We watched him step down to the river, watched him wash his hands in the icy water. Watched him turn and look at us, eyebrows lifted.

What are you guys staring at?

Marshall whistled again. Soon enough the two horses trotted up, expectant, full of animal trust. Marshall stroked their necks, let them smell his hands. Picked a rope up off the fence and looped it around the brown horse's neck.

This is my real baby, he said. Just green broke. Mostly quarter horse, with a touch of Arab. Gentle, muscular, elegant. He nuzzled her neck. The horse allowed this, not quite melting into him, but pleasure softened her body. She kept one wary eye in my direction.

Blake looked on with pride. My dad is so good with horses, he said. It's like magic, the way they trust him. He should have been a cowboy. Me, they run roughshod over. I never learned the knack. He put his hand softly on the hollow below my neck, the place that melted into the shoulder. With an effort, I kept upright.

Clare was watching from the cabin window.

It's not a knack, it's not magic, I said. It's practice. That of course, was pure guess. Because to me at that moment it did look like magic.

That afternoon I set up my sketch pad while Blake and Dolly played dominos and Roxanne wrapped herself in blankets on the porch, drank wine and watched the river stop flowing.

The girl came out to the paddock. Marshall saddled the dark pony he called Midnight and stepped up into the saddle with a grunt. Old hips, he said. Not even fourteen hands, he said. Too small for me. I should buy it and give it to the little girl.

What do you know about horses? he asked her.

Lots, she said. Horses are very smart and big. But it's been a while since I rode. I used to ride all the time. I'm sort of an expert.

Marshall pulled his foot out of one stirrup and instructed her to put her foot in and climb aboard.

I can ride on my own, she said. I'm not a baby.

I'll be the judge of that, Marshall said. He pulled her up behind him and set off at a brisk walk until Midnight decided it was time to trot. The girl screeched in fear and Marshall told her to shush, she was frightening the pony. Bouncing up and down at a trot, until Midnight stretched out into a smoother canter, they circled the paddock, with Fancy leading the way.

She'll fall, I said.

It will be a soft landing in the snow anyway, Blake said.

But the girl did not fall. Satisfied that she had found her seat, Marshall dismounted and let her take the reins while he held the lead rope and led them around in the same circle, the pony's breath steamy in the frosty air, until the horse stopped. Midnight pawed the ground down to a piece of earth and lowered her head to nibble up the withered grass that lay exposed. The girl's little kicks with her heels could not make the pony budge.

I pulled a deck chair out and began a river study. The vista shades of grey, the white that was not really white but blue and lilac and even pink. I had an idea for a series of watercolour nature sketches that might complement the larger abstracts and oils.

Dolly wandered over. How much longer do you have her?

Another week or so.

You'll miss her, I imagine.

I scribbled up a black poky bush, riverside. Oh my goodness, what a bundle of joy, of course we will. But inside my head, my thoughts were jumbled up like a dropped puzzle. How do you miss something you've never had?

I continued, To be honest, Blake and I are really looking forward to time alone again. Once she's gone and my show is over, we'd like to travel a bit, put the place up for sale, buy our own motorhome and take off south down into desert country, bandito country. Hollywood, Vegas. Blake even wants to learn to scuba dive.

Oh dear, Dolly said, I don't recommend that. But your show? What's your show?

Clare had finished with her ride, had brushed the pony down and was hanging about nearby, listening. She filled Dolly in.

Frida has a big art show coming in April. She's going to be famous, even more famous than her mother in Paris, and everybody will want to buy one of her paintings and I already know which one I want. She looked at me. The octopus one, can I? I'll pay you back when I get a job.

I'll buy it for you, Dolly said. How much is it?

This was getting completely out of control. Oh my god, I said, stop.

But Clare had turned her attention to the river and she left us.

Dolly glanced to the side to locate Marshall. Then she whispered, I always liked Roxanne. Does she know she's only got a week left?

With a jolt, I realized her misunderstanding. Roxanne isn't dying, I said.

She's not? Oh hooray. I'm so happy to hear that. Roxanne, she called out, and gave her a thumbs-up.

I laid a shadow down from the solitary tree. Isn't this great weather, I said. I love the cold and the fog and the damp. I shivered. There were times when even I was outraged by my personal cowardice.

She leaned in to look at my sketch.

You have such a great talent. You should take up art.

I turned the sketch over.

Oh, I'm sorry, she said. That was intrusive. She sat down at my side and we watched the river freeze up in slow-moving chunks of ice. I've always wanted a grandchild from Blake. What a lovely girl she is too. Will you buy her something from me? I mean aside from an octopus. She handed me a hundred-dollar bill. Anything you think. A dress or a computer or a bow and arrow, I don't know. You know her better than I do.

I took the bill. It fluttered in the breeze. I held my breath, waiting for the old woman's musings to fade back into the cerebellum of her rattled mind. Is it time for lunch?

But she would not stop. I'm sure you would have been a great stepmom. You have all the right instincts. I was so sad when Blake told me that you could not get pregnant. She reached to pat my hand, which I quickly pulled out of reach.

He told you that? I turned on her, to meet her gaze, to force her to stop.

Yes, she said. He told me that.

Did he tell you why?

Yes. You had your tubes tied, she whispered.

She had the greyest blue eyes. Just a hint of cloud. Did he also tell you I had a T.A.?

She furrowed her brows. What is a T.A.?

And in truth, it is one of those phrases I have a little trouble vocalizing. Therapeutic abortion, I said in a rush. Did he tell you about that?

I knew he had not, because he did not know. No one knew.

I waited for the flinch, but none came.

It was Blake's. And he didn't tell you because he doesn't know, and he doesn't know because I never told him.

And maybe I was trying to shock her, or force her into some kind of outrage or recrimination; or anything because I proceeded to spell it out right there. How I found a clinic, on my own. How it was mostly legal if you met the right parameters. The parameter I chose was mental instability. The doctor never probed further. I expected him to, but he did not. That's how convincingly unstable I was.

After that, a scheduled appointment, don't eat the day before, no coffee, arrange for a ride — it was like being on a wheel. Maybe not a wheel, maybe a staircase, an automatic electric staircase going down. A steep staircase going down to a hole, to a chasm, step by step, and each step was rather inconsequential until you reached the bottom step, the very last step, and jumped. The jump was the thing you could not reverse. Like gravity.

I chose to endure the procedure awake, conscious, unanesthetized. I wanted to feel it, to experience it. Penance? Or clarity. The way they say you should die undrugged.

A big room, a hellishly big room, a string of beds side by side, and on every bed a woman, an unconscious, oblivious woman snoring with unconsciousness, and the doctor and the anesthesiologist going from woman to woman, from bed to bed, with that horrific sucking vacuum thing and a bloody barrel. Could that be right? A barrel? No. I must have been a bit delirious. It pulled and pinched. And then the emptiness. And after that, and after that I had my tubes tied. Belly slit open, a tiny incision — below the bikini line, the doctor said, so proud, as if I would ever be caught dead in a bikini again.

I stopped talking. I don't know how much of that I actually told her. But I do remember that she watched me as I spoke, never took her eyes away. I gave her a little grin when I was done. No harm, no foul, I said. Having no idea what that cliché meant. But I had to say something to bridge the gap.

Dolly nodded. The silence between us stretched.

When Blake was little, she said, and he would cry, I would put a spoon to his cheek and collect the tears and drink them. She stood. She turned to me: Brianna told me once that you tricked Blake into marrying you by pretending you were pregnant. I really scolded her then because I knew that wasn't true. You're not the tricking type. But you were pregnant. And he didn't even know.

Yeah.

Tell Blake, she said. About the T.A.

For what? What in this world can he do?

She toddled off without an answer but then turned at the threshold to her trailer as her face lit up in sudden joy. Barbie dolls, she called out to me. That's the thing.

I tore the sketch up.

I climbed up the wooden steps to the cabin door and went inside, sat on the edge of the bed trying to settle my thoughts. I fell back onto the thin mattress and stared at the wooden ceiling where I could hear the buzz of a thousand flies that had come back to life with the heat.

Blake came in. What's the matter?

Nothing.

What are you doing in here?

Thinking.

About what?

Nothing.

Why don't you talk to me? Why don't you ever talk to me?

But I could not. Besides I had done enough talking it seemed for a lifetime.

Blake's probing was cut short by a gunshot then. Marshall target-shooting at birds and squirrels, a hobby of sorts I suppose. I was too engrossed in my own memory of events to pay much attention. Till Fancy barked, high-pitched, frantic. And just after, we heard Dolly yelling, Young lady, get off the ice!

And when we ran out from the cabin, we saw that the girl was gingerly slip-stepping out into the middle of the river where a raven had fallen. She paid no notice to Dolly's shouts, and though the ice was thin as paper she seemed to float above it and was able to reach the wounded bird without the ice breaking. Blake stepped onto the ice but broke through and stood helpless in the icy shallows waiting as she made her way back with the bird in her hand. I yelled something useless at Blake. You're soaking wet, you'll catch your death. But all of our collective attentions were on the girl and her rescued raven.

There was a feeling in the air of a close call, a diverted catastrophe, and we were frozen in the moment of that thrill. Blake wrapped his coat around the girl and led her back into the cabin. She had a pure look of triumph about her when the bird flew off, and I found myself wishing it was my coat around her shoulders.

CHAPTER 30

On the drive home Sunday evening, Blake turned the heater up full blast in the truck. When I complained, he said, Take your sweater off if you're too hot.

It's all about you, isn't it, Blake, I muttered. But the three of us took off our sweaters and jackets and dropped into heat-induced comas as he drove.

Finally back home and out of the stifling truck, we unloaded our gear in the hallway and the girl ran upstairs for a shower. Me first, she shouted.

Don't use up all the hot water! The house was cold and I turned the thermostat up.

Is it your turn to cook tonight? I asked Blake.

He looked at me. Can you? I'm bagged, I'm really bagged.

It was unusual for Blake to shirk his duties like this and I searched his face for a clue. He went straight up to his bedroom, dropping his dirty clothes on the floor on the way.

Marshall had given us a trout for our supper, a beautiful rainbow that he had pulled out of his little camper freezer for us to take home. I knew how much Blake was looking forward to this meal, so I found his recipe and tried to follow it, dusting the fillets in flour and cracked pepper and pan-frying them in butter, with lemon slices alongside. Clare and Roxanne gobbled up their suppers and before I sat to mine, I took a plate up to Blake. He was in bed, the sheets and blankets tossed around him, his face red and sweating, half-asleep. Not hungry, he said. It's trout, I reminded him. Not hungry, he repeated.

Monday morning after the oatmeal and sandwiches and Clare was off to school, I called Dave the plumber and told him that Blake would not be coming in, had caught a chill.

It's going around, he said. Give him a cup of coffee with a shot of whiskey in it.

I made a pot of ginger tea with honey and lemon and took it up to him. He was burning up and I went in search of cool cloths, Aspirin, hot soups and tea. The house stilled around us. No trombone, no drums. Paint dried hard and stiff on my brushes. For the first time in a long time, I felt necessary, purposeful, needed.

Roxanne came in while I was changing his sweaty pillowcase. She had a peeled onion in her hands. She said, Put this in his socks to draw the fever.

An onion?

It works, she said.

But he's not even wearing socks.

What is he wearing?

Boxer shorts.

Blake and I tussled for a minute or two until the onion was tucked into that familiar softness between his legs. And it did seem to help and he slept better that night. I camped out on the armchair in his room.

Next day when I came up from the kitchen with Jell-O, he was standing by the bed. He had a slipper in his hand and when I stepped closer, he threw it at me.

You tax collector, he snarled. You goddam tax collector. Before I realized what was happening, he grabbed me and threw me to the floor, sat on my chest and put his hands to my throat. I prepaid, he shouted. Every year since I was born I prepaid.

Roxanne appeared in the doorway. Silent and pale, in a long white diaphanous nightgown, she stared down at him. Blake saw her and screamed, then whispered, But I'm not ready. I'm not ready. I'm not ready.

He loosened his grip on me and buried his hot face between my breasts.

While we waited for the ambulance, I wrapped ice cubes in a cloth and put it to his forehead. He murmured something about horses, that he had bought a lot of horses, a hundred of them, good swimmers. He looked past me to Clare, who was now standing in the doorway. You and your little girl will love them.

Is this my fault? She asked in a whisper.

No. Never. I put my hand out to reassure her with a touch, but she dropped to the floor and commenced an incantation, a fairy tale, a nonsense poem of made-up words and sounds, finally saying, Daddy get better, you have to, until Blake relaxed into unconsciousness.

The next day the hospital released him, said, Come pick him up. My truck driver friend, Sharon, went immediately and brought him home. He had been pumped full of antibiotics and returned to us with instructions to take Aspirin, rest and stay hydrated.

My little lawyer is watching me closely.

That was an interesting week, I say to her and reach for my little paper cup of orange Jell-O.

She nods, Yes, very. Not only that but you remembered her name.

Whose name?

Your truck driver friend. Sharon.

I never forgot it, I say. Did I?

How small my mental victories are, how generously she commends them.

If Blake had not gotten sick I might have confided in him as Dolly had suggested. I mean about the pregnancy and the abortion. But the moment for that passed, even as the memory did not. And I realized I was still hoping for something. People call it closure.

I Googled the doctor, found his practice, his address, his phone number, his email. I phoned the clinic and made an appointment. I drove to his office in my yellow sports car and tailored suit and parked in the lot reserved for the Patients of the Greenvale Clinic. All others would be towed away.

Sat across from his desk. Crossed my legs. Put my purse in my lap and patted it. Calf leather. He was in a soft, pale blue shirt, khaki pants. Short, curly dark hair with flecks of grey. A handsome man. On his desk, he had a portrait of his family: wife, four kids. Round-faced boys, girls, hard to tell — they all had long hair and T-shirts with slogans.

He looked at his notes. What can I do for you, Mrs. Brooke?

I said, Do you remember me?

He smiled, a small smile, looked at me quizzically. Glanced at my scar, then back to my face. His right eyelid twitched and he put a finger up to settle it. Frida Brooke. Hmm . . . not really.

Not at all?

He gathered his carefully scattered papers into a pile, lined them up and straightened them with a snap on the desktop.

No, I don't. Should I?

I suppose not. I was only your patient for a week. Consultation, procedure, sterilization, follow-up. Quite a while ago. And you probably do so many. It's all good. It's okay. I leaned forward. I just wanted to see you again and —

I stopped. As if with a will of its own, my hand stretched out and presented itself palm up on his desk, available, as if hoping another hand would touch it, but another hand did not. I pulled my hand back into my lap. I should not have come.

He glanced down at his papers, then looked up at me. I understand that sometimes it's hard for a patient to pinpoint the pain, to locate where the wound actually lies. Am I right? He waited. There are other doctors, good doctors, doctors trained in this that I could refer you to. My advice? Don't let it fester.

He stood. He pressed the button on his phone. He said, Nurse, is my next patient here?

I left him.

What had I gone there for? To confront him? Educate him? Or was I hoping he would comfort me, inform me that there were so many reasons not to give birth. The world was already choked with humanity. It was merely a union of egg and sperm and not a soul, not yet, not a human, not even a baby, not yet. And I believed all that too. Still believed it, and yet. Who in those parades and courtrooms shouting for the right to control our own bodies, who acknowledges the trauma, the grieving, the pain? Did this doctor? Probably not, because he also had the pleasure of delivering babies, that particular life-affirming joy, and he had his own, so it was easy for him to get on with the other business. His life had balance. Mine was skewed. I wanted to blame him, absolve myself. Blame someone, but I could not.

I sat there in the parking lot in my little yellow sports car until the last patient left the clinic and the weak sun went down. I waited till the parking lot was nearly empty. There were three vehicles left. A rusty red pickup with a white canopy. A dented green Subaru. And a pearl-grey Mercedes XL. I reached for the carton of homegrown organic eggs in the back seat and one by one egged the Mercedes.

My little lawyer looks at me. I don't know if I believe that.

Believe what you like.

Frida, she said, don't go crazy on me, okay?

The next day the police came. My heart raced in my chest as I prepared myself mentally to be put under arrest for vandalism or worse. I summoned up some courage or maybe just a facade of indifference and pretended I was surprised, even pleased to see him. What can I do for you, officer? He was at least old enough to shave.

I'm here regarding the death of — and he consulted his notes — Ms. Anatole Curry. May I come in?

Six months since Tully's death and still they come a knockin'?

We got a new staff sergeant digging through the files. Showing everybody who's boss.

Okay, I said, unevenly. At least the vandalism was not the issue.

Leave your boots on, I said, though he had made no move to remove them.

My anxious lawyer is leaning forward, engrossed in the tale.

My stomach hurts, a hot, pulsing pain. I want to take a break, go to sleep, drugged, but she will not let me.

What happened? she insists. What did they want?

It was about the fingerprints on the gun. Child-sized fingerprints on the gun had been found and recorded in their files. So what? I thought. Who were they kidding? I'd seen the child in action. She couldn't keep her fingers off anything. In the pantry, in the bathroom, in my purse. She was a tactile creature and her mother was a suicidal mess and were they actually looking for a scapegoat?

He wanted to question the child. He wanted to ask her some questions. He wanted to know if she picked up the gun after her mother killed herself.

The raven banged against the window, as if trying to get in. The policeman jumped in alarm, said, Where's the girl? Can we talk to her?

You may not.

Relax. This is not an interrogation, just a friendly question or two.

I took a step towards the officer. I stared at him hard. I said, Don't ever think for one second that I would let you come here and interrogate that girl without a damn good search warrant. Friendly question or two or not. Now get out.

He put his hand on his side arm.

Please, I added.

He nodded. He left.

Behind me, I heard the quiet click of a bedroom door being closed and the whoosh of wingbeats.

This is not what you told me before, Miss What's-her-name says.

I may have misremembered.

She sighs and makes a note on her yellow pad.

But every memory is true in essence, if not in fact.

Blake was watching a war movie, volume muted. Soldiers running across a moonscape, thrusting bayonets into boys they called enemies.

I turned away. My heart was doing its thump-a-thump thing and I said without looking at him, You knew from the moment she was born that she existed. I paused. Didn't you.

He didn't speak. He didn't have to.

I knew as well. In fact, Blake had told me, in his way. Left his cheque book out once or twice, and after my breakdown had hidden it in his bottom drawer under paper clips and rubber bands.

I look at my little lawyer who is watching me with concern.

I said to him, But you never met her until that day last year. Is that right?

Just once, he said. She was a newborn.

We turned back to the TV, where men were now being blown up out of ditches.

Finally, Blake spoke. She's wondering if her grandfather has been found yet.

And you told her what?

I told her, Yes. Yes, he has. And he's coming from New Delhi to get you. You know what her response was?

I shook my head, no.

She said, I hope his plane crashes.

And with a little jolt, I realized I had the same wish as well.

Little bodies flying through the air. It looked so real.

I felt a tingle in my wounded shoulder. When I turned, the girl was standing at the top of the stairs, in her pyjamas, listening.

Can't sleep? Blake said.

I can, she said. When I want to, but it's better not. And she turned and disappeared down the dark hallway.

Good night, Blake said. Soft as a sparrow.

Ditto, she said, her small voice resonating in the house.

And I whispered into the ether, Ditto.

CHAPTER 31

Joel and Marguerite did not return to Seattle as he had promised. Instead, I discovered they were staying in a fancy new B and B in the centre of town.

I drove up to the Hummingbird and parked my yellow sports car in front. A cold, sunny day. The walkway was shovelled but icy. I stepped carefully, with a stack of canvases wrapped in brown paper in my arms, followed the arrows to the back suite: Rufous.

Joel opened the door to my knock. Look who's here, glancing at and then ignoring the package in my arms.

The room was hot, airless. On the walls, tiny watercolours of hummingbirds. I dismissed them as elevator paintings with a pang of envy.

Good timing, he added and winked.

Good timing?

Just finished eating, ummm, breakfast, he said. It was three o'clock in the afternoon. A smell of hairspray and lotion in the air. I sneezed it away.

How'd you find us in our little hideaway?

Are you hiding?

No, of course not. Great to see you.

Funny, 'cause I thought you were going back to Seattle.

Unfinished business, he said.

The gallery? Isn't it done?

We're looking for property, believe it or not. Notwithstanding Marguerite's own horror show in high school, she thinks this would be a good place to raise a child. He whispered the last bit, looking out at the verandah.

I whispered back, What child are we talking about?

Our future child.

I thought her reserves were diminished.

There's still hope. Yesterday she went to get her follicles stimulated.

This was brand new territory for me and I said the first thing that occurred. Did she come?

Don't be a smartass. But I could see his mind churning the idea over. What matters is the expense. Oh, baby. And probably hurts like hell, I'm sure you can imagine.

Actually, I cannot imagine.

Oh, don't be like that. Not everyone is cut out. He paused. Well, I'm just repeating what Blake told Marguerite.

That stopped me in my tracks.

Marguerite had come home raving about that little girl in your care. With a little guidance, a little grooming . . . she sees so much potential.

Potential for what?

To make something of herself, of course. He frowned at me. Kids are not plants; you have to engage.

In the yard outside the bed and breakfast, a black raven cawed in the snow. I watched its belly swell with every caw. Calling out to his raven buddies, flying away in search of them.

I handed Joel the wrapped canvases and he dropped them onto the rumpled bed.

Muchas gracias, señorita, showing no intention of unwrapping them.

Another big black bird swooped by the window.

Did you want to have a look at what I'm working on? I indicated the wrapped canvases with my hand held out, palm up.

He took a deep breath. The thing is Frida —

It's sort of a new direction for me —

The thing is —

I'll tell you what the thing is, I squealed. The thing is . . . I spoke to Mummy! I spoke to Lulu.

Joel straightened, eyes wide. What? You spoke to Lulu? When? Where?

She's in Paris and she's doing her thing. So great to talk to her. And I told her about my solo exhibition at your gallery, and guess what? She wants to come. She totally wants to be there.

Joel's eyes got even bigger. Say what?

Of course, she's busy, sales and burnings and the actual painting work and all of that, but April first is looking good and she's ecstatic. She's gonna get back to me.

Marguerite! Joel rubbed his hands through his hair, then spread them wide. Give me a hug. Give me a fucking hug.

We hugged. I chuckled.

Marguerite, he called out again. Can you come in here?

Marguerite was on the tiny icy verandah, charming the owner with her bright blue eyes, her curly black hair, her chatter.

We stood in limbo until Marguerite stepped back into the room, her small hands wrapped around a giant cup of coffee.

She said, Oh there she is, my friend, in all her glory. She looked at the wrapped package on the bed. So what have we settled on? Nudes? Ravens? Nude ravens? She laughed. Sorry. I don't mean to jest but has Joel informed you of our very reluctant decision?

Joel interrupted. Wait. Tell her your news, Frida. Tell her what you just told me.

Marguerite tilted her head.

Tell her, Joel repeated. Come on, don't be shy.

And so I told her.

And Mummy is ecstatic, Joel added.

Marguerite stared at me, wordless, and Joel giggled. Told you, Maggie, told you.

On their bed was a book, *The Three Stages of Childbirth*.

So, did you want to have a look at these? Again I pointed to the wrapped package on their bed. Or . . . ?

No, no. We're all good. Take them home, keep them safe. We're good, we're all good. We'll draw that contract up and next time we see you . . .

I retrieved my canvases from their mussed bed. They were both beaming at me and I tried my best to beam back. As I left, I heard Joel mutter, Oh my fucking oath.

So? I say to my child-bearing smarty-pants.

So, what?

Are you going to scold me?

Would it do any good?

It might.

What's done is done, Frida. You of all people know that. But I'm actually a little curious about the three stages of childbirth.

You're the baby maker. Don't you know what they are?

The jumbo baby is latched onto her breast, has fallen asleep but will not release. Nor does my little lawyer seem to care. Her small breast is plump with purpose.

Labour, push and out everything comes? Is that it?

I realize then, just because a woman has had a baby doesn't make her an expert on childbirth. On anything at all. So I tell her: dilation, expulsion, placental.

Humph, she says. Didn't I just say that?

I remember a session with my little lawyer just before she gave birth, her huge belly bumping and crawling like there was an animal inside trapped under mud. She was so proud. She asked me, Do you want to touch it, feel it?

Of course, I didn't. But when I did not completely recoil, she took my hand and put it on her naked belly. Something caromed against my palm, and I snatched my hand back and slipped it under the cold, steely bedpan where it belonged.

I am starting to get a sense that my little lawyer is more than just a lawyer, or should I say less. Is this all my delirium? I look at her. She's wearing jeans and a pink T-shirt stained with damp circles of leaked milk. The shirt reads Greenpeaks, plant a tree and save the earth. The bangs have been swept to the side.

CHAPTER 32

Though we both knew the child was only a temporary addition, Blake seemed determined to make the most of it. I found him in the basement one morning with a stack of plywood and boards, hammer and nails. At first, I had thought he was making me a painter's easel so I was a little disappointed when I realized my mistake. He was building a tree house for Clare to play in.

Clare's such an outdoorsy kid, he explained while he hammered away.

An outdoorsy kid. I repeated that in my little head. The best kind of kid, an outdoorsy kid. I could hear so plainly how his mind worked. And I, not an outdoorsy kid. It was difficult to admit, but I was finally learning that not everything was about me. Except of course, when it was.

I had a cigarette in my hand that I was putting a match to. Blake looked at me and dropped his saw. What the hell are you doing? You don't smoke.

Back in the day I did. I took a drag, remembering how it used to calm my nerves. I coughed.

Put that damn thing out. Come and help me, Blake said. You look like the cat that swallowed the canary. Hold the end of the tape and settle down. What's going on with you?

Nothing. I'm just excited. Guess what? (We paused.) I've got a contract. For my show.

Really?? Blake said. Wow. A signed contract for your show! Well done, Freed.

Well, not quite signed, not yet, but it's coming.

I told you, Frida. I told you.

Yup. You told me. You're always right. I held the end of the tape. He made a little mark and sawed.

Clare and Corey were sitting under the tree that Blake had in mind for the playhouse. Blake had already set a ladder up and Clare and Corey were trying to train Fancy to climb it. Clare sat on the third rung with a dog cookie in her hand, calling, Good dog, come, good dog, come. Corey was behind, trying to lift Fancy's front paws and place them on the rung. Fancy stood there, stubbornly frozen, drooling at the dog treat that Clare had extended.

What darlings, I thought. What innocents, what hopelessly hopeful little people. I shouted at them, Use a ramp, sillies.

Clare swivelled to look at me. Brilliant, she said. And to Corey, I told you.

Everything I wanted was imminent. My exhibition, my validation as an artist, my self-respect. And so I passed the next few days in a state of utter misery.

I have been lying in bed, staring out the window at the parking lot for hours, it seems, waiting for my little lawyer to show up. The room has become unbearably stuffy. I switch my gaze to the pale green wall. I push the channel changer for the TV. From *Dr. Phil* to *My 600-lb Life*. I turn it off and sulk. I buzz the nurse. She comes in to replace the drip, not gentle, unsmiling. You buzzed?

What time is it?

Ten minutes past the last time you asked, she says.

The nurse bustles around my head, doing something awful to

the pillow, uncovering my shoulder, not a bit disturbed by the scar.

Is today a visiting day?

Every day is a visiting day, she says. You know that.

The truth is I know nothing fully. But there's no one here.

You shooed them away.

Who? Who have I shooed away? But I will never admit to any nurse that I do not know the simple answer to the simple question. Who has come to see me and who have I shunned?

The nurse sets a tray of Jell-O and mashed potatoes or some other white goo in front of me. I eat it. I hear her talking in the hallway to another hospital worker, nurse or orderly or doctor, they are all the same. I hear her saying, Look out for that one, she's a little nutso.

I swallow down the hurt. But am I? Who is the real judge of that? And if I am, have I always been?

When I look up from the meal, my exhausted counsel is here. She is practically dragging herself, the jumbo baby in her arms hanging heavily off her hip. The baby crying. My lawyer crying.

I can't make her stop, she says. She's been crying for an hour. I'm so tired. She's fussing and fussing, her diaper is changed, she's had titty, I rattled the rattle, I don't know what to do with her. I'm dead on my feet. Can't you help?

Where's Kaleb? My senses are on high alert. This is not in my wheelhouse.

Kaleb is working. He was up all night with her. I was up all night watching him be up all night with her. I haven't slept in three weeks. Please. She holds the jumbo baby out to me. And drops her on the bed on my chest. The jumbo baby howls. My little lawyer turns to go, telling me that she is desperate for a coffee, a cappuccino, a nap, a glass of wine, something, anything. I'll be back, she says.

And she leaves.

I pull my good arm, my untethered arm, out from under the sheet, wrap it around the baby's body. She squirms. She cries. I make shushing noises. I pat her back, she burps. I wait for a nurse to relieve me. I can't reach the call button with my arm around the baby. I put my lips to her head, her fuzzy, dark head. I hum into her skull. The crying slows. I hum a bit more. The crying slows a bit more. I begin to sing that moon song, that "Fly me to the moon" song and as we play among the stars, the baby goes quiet. Her eyelids slowly blink, then drop. I hum. Her long dark eyelashes on her cheeks. She sleeps. I am being tested.

In my fertile years, I endured my mother's occasional probing phone queries about me and the state of motherhood. Without preamble, she would start right in. Are you on birth control? I very much hope you're on birth control. You must not rely on condoms alone, do you hear me? Pills and condoms, you must use both. Don't take chances, Frida. And I did not take chances. I did use both at the same time. But what was she getting at? Was she afraid that being a granny would age her? Or maybe her motives behind the admonition were more insidious. Maybe it had something to do with me and what she saw in me. Or rather, what she did not see.

Other people, girlfriends at the time, young mothers themselves, would encourage me in the opposite direction with that old cliché, a ticking clock, a ticking biological clock, a clock which cannot be reversed, or they would tell me: It's a window, Frida, open to motherhood, and the window is closing, but you're still able to fit through. You can still squeeze through.

I would laugh. What did they see out that window? A sunny day, a swing set, a wading pool? Well, I saw a heap of disposable diapers polluting our planet and a chubby toddler growing into the CEO of a corrupt brokerage firm.

But just before I married Blake, I quit the pill and immediately got pregnant. I panicked then and took matters into my own hands in terms of motherhood. The window was firmly shut, locked in fact. The little newborn booties my girlfriends were saving for me would go unworn.

CHAPTER 33

The coming Sunday would be Roxanne's eighty-fifth birthday. It was also Valentine's Day, though Roxanne refused to share the event with any Hallmark bullshit. We were taking her out for a birthday dinner, period. She'd be the same age that her sister had been when she died. Roxanne kept repeating this, like a mantra.

I remember that day very well when her sister was found dead. Roxanne had phoned, wailing. Blake had said, Go stay with her, I'll be fine. He had a Y2K conference to attend in Calgary, so the timing worked. I went to her little condo. Put my sleeping bag on her couch. Drank with her, did her laundry, ordered takeout, as she launched herself into a violent, hungry depression. Egg rolls, pizza, which she gobbled up despite her grief, alternately sobbing, breaking plates, ripping photos up, then Scotch-taping them together. There were boyfriends, even at her age, a hairdresser, some guy who played bridge; she shoved them all away. Until one morning she dusted herself off, looked about the condo and noticed me at the table squeezing the dregs out of a box of wine (my other source of nourishment during those dreadful two weeks) and said, I'll come live with you now. And she came to us, sharing the small house I was living in at the time with Blake in Vancouver.

And though she should have settled in as the dependent, I found myself reverting to the neediness of a child thrust into an incomprehensible situation where the patterns of behaviour, the rules of engagement, the mysteries of life are withheld; it mortifies me to remember how cravenly I sought her approval, love, recognition.

The celebratory dinner was planned for a local restaurant, a semi-fancy place that served food.

What kind? Rox wanted to know.

The kind you chew and swallow. I poured vinegar into her denture glass and swished it around. Now that the Buffalo was gone it was up to me to see that she was diapered and lipsticked, wheelchaired and pearled. I sprayed her armpits with deodorant

My last meal, she whispered.

I combed out her curls. I said, Don't be so superstitious, you'll live to a hundred.

And so will you, she retorted spitefully and added, But if you're wrong, and we both know you've been wrong before, this may very well be my last birthday.

She looked so pleased with herself that I couldn't stop from saying, And I bet the very next day after you die the Publisher's Clearing House will come through with the big million-dollar cheque for you.

That shut her up.

Joel emailed to inform me that in a few days, he would be on his way through and wanted to take a quick peek at what I was working on. He had the contract ready and would bring it with him. And he wanted Lulu's contact info, for promotional purposes.

I slept not at all that night and the next morning I woke the girl up early and led her into my office nook.

It's not even eight o'clock, she whined.

I said to her, Do you want to meet your step-grandmother?

You mean Roxanne? I already know Roxanne. I wanna go back to bed.

No, no, that's your step-great-grandma, I mean, my mother. In Paris.

Lulu? Her eyes got wide. I thought she wasn't talking to you.

Of course, she's talking to me, I'm her daughter. I had a feeling that Roxanne had been gossiping about me and I tried to squelch the annoyance I felt. Here, comb your hair and try to look presentable.

It was ten after seven in the morning in B.C. and ten after six in the afternoon in Paris. Lulu would be just sitting down with her second or third glass of wine.

Was that all a ruse? My blank-faced lawyer asks.

What do you mean, a ruse?

I mean, were you using the girl to get what you wanted from your mother? Was she there for you to hide behind? I don't know how to put it, but were you trying to manipulate Lulu's emotions to get what you really wanted from her?

Get out, I shout. You have no idea what I really wanted. What I really wanted was for Clare to meet my mother. Like she met Marshall and Dolly. To know me better. And I wanted my mother to meet her. To see that my life was not this empty nothingness she probably imagined.

Actually what you really wanted was for Lulu to come to your opening, my lawyer says, her face betraying no emotion whatsoever.

It is possible to want more than one thing at the same time, I shout.

Two nurses quiet me down and my little lawyer waits. I remain mute until she apologizes for her assumptions.

So tell me, how did the Skype go?

Not well. Not well at all.

Clare seemed shy in front of my mother, who was ablaze in colour and paintings and cats. Lulu's hair was dyed bright pink, her dressing gown awash in orange polka dots and her lips painted red. Behind her on a tufted yellow couch lounged a young man dressed all in white.

Frida, Frida, Frida she kept intoning as if to remind herself of my name. *Quel plaisir!*

She sounded stoned or drunk and seemed on the verge of sentimental tears.

Look at me, she said, doing all this fancy technology. She lowered her voice. That's one reason I keep Daniel around. Daniel, on the couch, groaned.

You look good Mummy, I said.

Merci, *ma chère*. But oh my poor hips. And you too look good! How long has it been since I've seen your darling face? She turned, Look at her, Daniel. That's my daughter, all the way in Canada. What a miracle all this is. And she's lost weight! Isn't she so very nice looking?

I decided to nip this conversational disaster in the bud.

I want you to meet someone, I said. Her name is Clare.

Allo, Clare. Nice to meet you. Now tell me, who are you?

Clare did not respond but shrunk lower, almost out of the camera's eye.

Are you babysitting, Frida? Are you that broke? Is this about money?

No. It's definitely not about money. Clare lives with us, I said. Sit up, Clare, and say hello. Come on.

But Clare shook her head, no and stayed partially hidden, saying nothing.

Is there something wrong with her? my mother half-whispered. Is she mental?

No. She's not "mental." Christ. She's just a bit shy suddenly.

But why do you have her with you?

I have her because . . . she's Blake's daughter.

Your husband, Blake?

Yes. My husband, Blake.

Your husband, Blake's daughter?

Yes, my husband, Blake's daughter. Jesus, is that so difficult to grasp? And I'm her — I stopped.

Stepmom, Clare declared suddenly losing her shyness

Lulu had been sipping on what looked like a martini and quickly set it down. I was wishing I had a martini of my own nearby.

And guess what, Clare announced. It's Roxanne's birthday tomorrow and we're taking her out for dinner. She's eighty-five years old!

It was Lulu who had now gone quiet.

And how old are you? Lulu finally asked.

I'm nine.

We sat there in silence watching Lulu work the numbers in her head until she came to the correct conclusion that I had been cuckqueaned.

Cuckquean, my dogged counsel repeats.

It's a word, I tell her, look it up. And she does.

So, if I may ask the obvious question, where might the real mother be? Lulu said.

Clare startled, her eyes wide. I should have anticipated this question, but I had not.

It's complicated, I said and Clare blurted, It's not complicated, she's dead. And with a quick swipe of her hand, she shut the laptop down on our Skype session and left the room.

The jumbo baby at our side is sucking on her little fist, rooting in hope of sustenance which her mama is ignoring.

So you never even got to ask the big important question. About your gallery show. About Lulu coming.

No, actually, if you must know, I did not. And when I Skyped her back, almost immediately, she did not answer.

February 14 arrived on schedule as promised. I know because I watched the sun rise on it. Roxanne woke and began sipping Baileys while the girl pencilled in some eyebrows for her.

Roxanne was in a tizzy and I was trying to help her choose a dress. Nothing fit, nothing suited. I noticed how thin she had gotten over the past year. I handed over a polyester chemise that no longer fit me. Might as well put it to use. It was blue, modest and age-appropriate. But she tossed it aside with the others and from the back of her closet pulled out a sequined black cocktail dress, spaghetti straps and a ruffle, the dress she had worn to her sister's funeral.

And I'll help you choose your outfit too, she said.

God no, I said.

But then she unzipped a garment bag and retrieved the dress she had been left at the altar in. A swirling, gold-coloured gown that shimmered and flowed in the light, a sling of gold buttons up the back. So gorgeous that I gulped. But as I reached for it, she yanked it back, frowning. Never mind, she said. I'm sure it won't fit.

Can Corey come to our party? Clare asked.

Of course, he can, Roxanne said. The more the merrier.

Merry was not what I was expecting.

Later, when Joel texted that he was on his way, I groaned out loud. But Blake said, Just invite them to dinner with us. He seemed a little confused by my reaction, but that was his problem. I had enough of my own.

I took three half-hearted deep breaths and then went to my closet. I examined half a dozen outfits, which were either too tight, or too bright, or too old-fashioned, or so colourless and grey they made me feel like jumping off a bridge. Shoulder pads, my god. Blake was no help. It's just your grandmother's birthday, he said. Wear anything.

Nothing as appealing as Roxanne's gold wedding dress had been.

I marched back into my grandmother's room and said, Just let me try it on for god's sake.

She scowled. All you had to do was ask. Far be it from me.

And with a slight rearrangement of two or three buttons, I was dressed by the House of Rox and I was beautiful. I stood in front of Blake and waited, wondering what he saw, if he saw me as I was seeing myself at that moment, if the woman he once loved so fiercely still existed. And without looking up from his computer he said, You look great.

I presumed Clare would wear the pink satin she had shown up in but she stepped down from her room in torn-at-the-knee jeans, a black T-shirt with a rainbow unicorn. Hair in two wonky red braids.

In response to my scowl, she said, This is the style, Frida. Everybody wears ripped jeans.

I'm not ashamed to admit that I sent her back up to her room to change. It's my grandmother's birthday. Please show some respect. She scowled at me and stomped back to her room. Came down ten minutes later in a lace-collared polka-dotted, cinch-waisted chemise with a giant red bow in the back. One size too small. She looked amazing. Ridiculous. A plucky cherub that I could hardly take my eyes off.

We hired our lady truck driver to convey us. Dressed to serve in a blue suit jacket, white shirt and blue tie. Damn, what was her name? When she stopped at Corey's house (extra charge?), he was waiting in front in a black cape. Hair curling long around his ears. Braces, white cotton gloves and on his head a short top hat. Hi, Corey, our driver said. Put your seatbelt on. Clare opened her door and in he slipped, grinned at her and said I have a new magic trick to show you. Well, magic boy made a lot of food disappear.

When Joel and Marguerite arrived, late, already oiled, they were accompanied by Joel's sons from his previous marriage. How smart Joel and his boys looked in grey turtlenecks and blazers. But Marguerite seemed determined to steal the show in a bright red sheath. Tight in all the usual places. She staggered to her seat right next to Blake and leaned into him. I saw how he inhaled the smell of her hair or, rather, hairspray. She chattered non-stop and drank freely. Girly drinks and wine. She looked so alive, festive, uncomplicated. I looked down at myself and felt overwrought in gold, wondering if Joel at least would flirt with me.

Aren't you trying to get pregnant? I finally asked Marguerite after her second drink.

I guess we're not trying all that hard anymore. Are we, darling?

Sssshh, Joel mouthed in my direction.

The silence settled. Until Marguerite started up again, about Trump's orange hair and the tornado in Tennessee, that she never did get to visit the Notre Dame, about Joel who threw a hissy fit if his shirts were not ironed.

I don't think Frida has ever seen an iron, said Blake. Laughter.

But at least I've seen the Notre Dame, I countered. Less laughter.

Wait one little minute, madam, my psychiatrist says. You're mixing things up I'm afraid. Trump, the fire in the cathedral, that's now. We're talking about then.

Now . . . then . . . I still don't iron, shoot me.

She narrows her eyes at me. You need to take this seriously.

Or what? You put me in the Ding Wing? This is rather funny, and I try to laugh until I realize how much it hurts. Until I realize no one else is laughing with me.

A tall, stooped young man in worn-out jeans and T-shirt appeared and loomed over us.

My name is Troy and I will be your server tonight. He looked at us in our finery and said, Well, happy Valentine's to you all.

No, said Roxanne. It's happy birthday. To me. Can you take our picture?

Blake handed over his cell phone and we all squished in, Marguerite's breast grazing Blake's forearm. Me at the far end sandwiched between Roxanne and Corey.

Troy continued. The Valentine's special, I mean birthday special tonight is surf and turf, a ten-ounce filet mignon topped with an aged blue-cheese dressing with wild chanterelles and roasted garlic asparagus on the side and a six-ounce broiled lobster tail in garlic butter for forty-nine, ninety-five.

I glared at Troy. Thank you, Troy. He would go far, I could tell.

He put a paper placemat down for Clare, with a Cinderella wicked stepmother outline to colour in. A pack of crayons. In her polka-dot dress, she blushed right down to her fingertips. Joel's teens tittered.

Roxanne said, None for me? And he quickly laid one down for her as well. She grabbed a crayon, scribbled colour onto Snow White's face, wildly ignoring the lines. Corey pulled Clare's placemat to himself and drew glasses on Snow White, boobs on the dwarves, tongues sticking out.

Oh, it went, on and on, and when boy-toy Troy asked for our order, Roxanne, upright in her wheelchair, glass of champagne in her hand, in clinging black-sequined attire, proclaimed loudly, It's my birthday, probably my last and I want — we all want — the special.

Nine filet mignon, wild mushrooms, brie, roasted asparagus, the works.

Troy skipped back to the kitchen.

And then some awkwardness from the teens about Corey's sexuality. Blake called them rude, and Joel intervened on their behalf, and Clare set the table straight saying, Anyway he is so gay, and Corey with great dignity elaborated: But that's not exclusively how I define myself. I contain multitudes. He tipped his hat and from somewhere, his pocket or his sleeve or thin air, he produced a big yellow gumball, and when Clare closed her eyes and opened her mouth, he popped it in.

Roxanne applauded, Do me, do me! And he did.

I don't remember every detail of the evening. I had another wine, maybe two more, maybe four. Marguerite tipped almost over, leaning on Blake. She was drinking from his tumbler of Scotch, leaving her lipstick on his glass. He seemed not to care. Neither did I.

The meals came, juicy and red and swimming in financial collapse. We ate what we could, drank even more.

Joel asked the girl about school. Did she like it? The girl nodded. Did she get a lot of homework? The girl nodded. And just when the dialogue should have run its course, Clare volunteered that the homework for the month was to do a biography on a famous person, a musician or writer or artist. Guess who I'm doing, she said.

Rambo, suggested Joel.

You mean Sylvester Stallone? Nope. Guess again.

Elizabeth Taylor! From Roxanne

Nope.

Madonna, from Marguerite.

Albert Einstein, from Blake.

Until Clare said, Gramma Lulu.

A bit of a stunned pause.

I was gonna say Lulu, that was my next guess, Roxanne said.

And all of them beamed, chuckled and beamed, and nodded. Everyone but me.

Guess what. You'll get to interview her in person, Marguerite said.

Really?

Tell them, Frida. Joel was rummaging around in a briefcase he had brought with him. He pulled out a manila envelope. Everyone looked at me.

I stayed mute.

Well then, I'll break the news, Joel said. And he repeated my little falsehood, my tiny lie, and told our group of merrymakers that Lulu would be making an appearance at my exhibition at his gallery in Seattle. The media had already been informed. The promotional posters were being printed up. And there was already a helluva buzz in the air about it.

So voila, Joel said, we celebrate tonight, not only the beautiful birthday girl, not only Valentine's, but the final and official contract approval. He lifted up his briefcase and pulled three pages from a manila envelope, laid them on the table, uncapped a lovely fountain pen and with a dramatic ceremonial gesture, signed each page, using Troy as a witness.

The whole shooting match was then passed to me. Trapped in my little lie I signed to a small smattering of applause, and Joel slipped his copy of the signed contract back into his soft leather briefcase, handed me mine and ordered another round of drinks.

Of course, the bill was left in front of Blake, and I watched him blanch. Marguerite blew kisses as she left, then leaned in to whisper to me, See if you can borrow Roxanne's black cocktail dress for the event. The one she's wearing now. It would look so good on you. Very chic. A little scarf around the neck there. The art world will all be there with their cameras, you don't want to disappear.

My psychiatrist sighs, I almost hear her mutter, Oh god. But is she oh god-ing me or Marguerite? I have no idea. She puts her pen down and checks her watch. The look on her face, as if she's disappointed in me. She stands.

Wait, I say, listen. I was drunk.

I know, she says. And so what?

We do things when we're drunk, or anxious, or stressed that we later regret. This is a given. It's called being a human being.

But what what did you do? she asks. What did you regret doing?

Nothing I couldn't fix. And I hear myself telling my exacting shrink how I slunk out of the chicken coop the next morning, hungry, hungover, makeup smeared and contrite, in search of Scotch tape for the contract I had torn in half the night before.

Is that what you were contrite about? she says. A torn contract?

I was contrite about everything, I shout. All that meat I ate that sat in my belly like a bomb, all that wine. I really don't recall and don't want to recall every last little thing I was contrite about. All I know is that I did not want company in the morning.

For a moment we are quiet together, my psychiatrist and I, until I continue. But the girl, that clever little girl, she pinned me down at breakfast. She lowered her head and frowned at me.

Did you lie? she asked. Did you lie about Gramma Lulu?

She came right out and asked. And that's what you're wondering too, isn't it?

And did you? my psychiatrist asks. Did you lie about Lulu?

Yes. I did. I had to.

Why?

Because I wanted the validation of this show more than anything in the world, I tell her.

More than anything in the world? That's a lot of wanting.

Yes. More than any fucking anything. I wanted to believe that the sacrifices I made were for something. Not for nothing, but they were for something.

The sacrifices, she repeats. She writes it down.

I leaned back in my bed, exhausted, full of self-pity but proud that I could open up and be so honest, so vulnerable. I felt like a turtle flipped upside down. The big white tender belly of me on display. Surely this would shut her up.

Okay, she nods. And nothing more?

Jesus Christ. Isn't that enough?

I guess what I'm wondering is, Who did you make these sacrifices for? Did you want to explore that a little?

A turtle belly to poke. An onion to peel. I banged on the call button for the nurse.

But in the meantime, the lie I had launched was gnawing away at me. I retreated to the coop and turned my attention back to my art practice. At least I tried to.

CHAPTER 34

When I found a spot of blood on the girl's sheets I went to Roxanne. At her side was a bowl of milk toast, buttered, with cinnamon. A comfort breakfast that I had brought up to her. She sat up and clanged her spoon on the bowl. Please inform the cook that I like a little more sugar on my milk toast.

I watched her eat for a moment, dribbling onto the blanket, and told her about the spot of blood. I said, Is it possibly her period? What should I do? She's only nine, that's much too early, isn't it? I was feeling overwhelmed by my role in this hormonal watershed moment and listened attentively to Roxanne while she lectured me about cow's milk and insulin and bacon fat, saying, Send her in to me and I'll have a talk with her.

I struggled to recall my own pubescent experience. Is that what you did for me? I asked. Have a talk? Did I understand what was going on? Should I buy her some pads? I'm only asking you because — I stopped.

Because suddenly I remembered.

It was indeed Roxanne who supervised my first "spotting." She had been stern, almost angry, pushing me into the bathroom with a box of Kotex. Later, a book for adolescent girls landed on my bed to detail and illustrate the facts of life. I took from it what I needed to and let the scientific bits pass. But a year later, at thirteen years old, my period inexplicably stopped. And Roxanne, noticing the box of Kotex had not diminished, grilled me. Her first assumption — that I was pregnant. I was a chubby girl, tall already, scarred and acned; not one boy had even looked twice at me, let alone approached. I was shocked by the accusation, but Roxanne would not let it go.

She made an appointment for an examination. A doctor she knew of. Someone discreet. Someone who could take care of business. This particular scenario was not explored in that teenage sexuality book.

She drove me there. I was nearly comatose with fear when she shoved me out of the car. It was after 8:00 p.m. even though the office hours on the door clearly stated nine to four. I rang the bell and he buzzed me in. Terrified. Elevator to the third floor. Second door on the right, maybe the third, maybe the second floor. All a fuzz now.

He was an old man. Seemed like. Probably the age I am now. We were alone in his examination room. No one else even on the floor. He motioned for me to undress, slip the gown on and climb up onto the table. I had never worn a gown like this. I did not understand its purpose. The first thing he did was rip a hole in the paper that covered my breast, which he mauled. The chubby bump. After that, the usual, which was all brand new to me then, feet in stirrups, scoot down, knees apart, relax. I stared at the ceiling in a sort of shock I suppose. I felt cool air on parts that had never felt cool air before.

Roxanne had assured me he would take care of business. What could that business be? But when he tried to examine me, he could not. The doctor. His wispy grey hair, the bushy eyebrows. He told me he could not get in. I was too tight. Could not get in to examine. And perform whatever it was he needed to perform. He wanted me to relax. He kept saying, relax, relax. Do people ever relax when they're lying here like this? He told me he knew how to make me relax. It took so long. Until finally, I did relax and he left the room for a few minutes, left me alone. Then came back and finished the exam, told me what I, a virgin, already knew. Not pregnant. Get dressed, he said. And to my grandmother, who was now waiting in a chair by the elevator, his final word: Tell her to lose weight. She slipped him some money, tried to, but he waved it away. Lose weight was the diagnosis. And I did. A lot. And my period returned.

The next time it stopped was for the more common reason, apart from menopause that is. And two-and-a-half months in, I did have it taken care of. Not with this doctor but another, Dr. Mercedes. No funny business this time. Nothing funny about it at all. Blood is thicker than water, Roxanne used to say when I would pretend I was the neighbour's child.

There is a sudden kerfuffle in my room. My little lawyer, who has just arrived, suddenly stomps back out again into the hallway. I try to move my arms but I cannot. Are they paralyzed? I hear her confronting one of the nurses. She's not an animal. Got it? Got it?

The nurse says, Jesus who took your muzzle off?

The nurse comes in. Fusses with my arms until they are mine again and under my control. I expect you will be good now, won't you?

To my little lawyer, I say, Hi.

She sits and sighs. Unstraps her Snugli. Stuffs a pacifier into jumbo baby's mouth. She throws a newspaper onto my bed. There's an article, a headline. Thousands of fetal remains found in doctor's garage.

Isn't it complicated enough as is without this? she whispers.

It's okay, I tell her. It's all good.

At the drugstore, I bought an assortment of pads and tampons, light flow to heavy. I felt nostalgic for the paraphernalia; my own flow had stopped, menopause had come on early. At the bookstore, I bought *Your Blossoming Body*, a graphic novel about puberty and what to expect. Glancing through, I even learned a few things myself.

And on a whim, at the last moment, I bought a book called *Final Exit*, on euthanasia.

Back home, I put all these things in front of the girl's door. All but *Final Exit*, of course.

I returned to the coop and climbed into my cot, pulled the Hudson's Bay blanket up to my chin. I could smell the prairie on it, the sheep, the mountains, the hayfields and tang of gunsmoke. The promise, the deceit. I opened my new book. First thing I read was a quote from Isaac Asimov. "No decent human being would allow an animal to suffer without putting it out of its misery."

But the question seemed to be, Who was the sufferer, and who was the suffaree?

CHAPTER 35

I was on my bunk in the coop reading *Final Exit* when Joel texted me to stop by their new gallery in town. He had a surprise. I put a bookmark to hold my place in the "Cyanide Enigma" chapter, then drove out and waited for him to notice me in my yellow sports car parked in the street out front. I was not in a very receptive mood. I had accidentally bumped the placard advertising the opening of his gallery in Hope and my solo exhibition — *With Lulu Frank*, in large letters — in Seattle.

Finally, he saw me and rushed out. He tapped on the driver's side window. I rolled the window down partway. He leaned in. He was shivering in the cold, hopping from foot to foot.

I think we got off on the wrong foot back there last week, he said. My fault. I'm on edge, all this stuff with Marguerite and the appointments and my sperm versus other people's sperm. Can you imagine?

I could in a way.

Come on inside. Don't worry about the placard. It's cardboard and plastic. It can be fixed. What's between us — and he thumped his hand back and forth between his chest and my window — that's what I worry about. Something broken between us, being fixed.

I knew what was broken, but I don't know if he did.

He opened the door of my car. He put his hand in and under my elbow. He lifted slightly until I yielded.

Got a surprise for you inside.

I followed him into the gallery.

My mother, he said. My real mother. I found her. Or rather, she found me. Hazel, can I call you Hazel? Say hello to Frida Frank, I mean Frida Brooke, my artist.

And there she was, a tall, lanky woman with a long brown braid streaked grey down her back. She glanced my way, then back to Joel. The way she looked at him. Her eyes never left his face even as she said, Hello.

He shuffled nervously in front of her, glancing up now and again, then, as if burned, looking down.

By her appearance, the worn woollen coat that hung on her frame, scuffed shoes, it seemed the woman was not rich, not even a little. She smelled of cigarette smoke. She reached out and tried to touch his hair. He flinched. I turned away to give them privacy. It was a horribly intimate moment that I did not know how to witness. Joel put his hands in his pockets. The woman said, I don't want to interrupt your work, you have a meeting. I'm in the way. Her voice was husky and charmingly damaged.

No, no, Joel said. Just that I was so shocked to finally meet you. But Frida is probably busy as hell.

I did not corroborate this lie. We stood there in silence for a bit.

We've been catching up, Joel said to me.

Not really, the mother answered. That would take a lifetime, wouldn't it? Her eyes could not leave his face.

He turned and went to a drawer under a table. From my vantage point, I could see that he was opening a brown envelope, the type a bank gives you cash in. He pulled out a few bills and shut the drawer. Folded the bills quickly into a tiny package and pushed it at her. Without hesitation, she took it, let her fingers graze his hand for a moment. He pulled away; she slipped the money into her coat pocket.

Stay well, she said. I'm so proud of you. Keep in touch. And she left.

He had several canvases propped against the wall in front of him. Buxom Asian women in striped bikinis. Partygoers drinking on a basket boat in the mist. Bui Van Thong scrawled hugely across the bottom. We studied them together for a moment. On the back were the photographs the artist had painted from.

I said, Your mom seems nice.

He shrugged. She's nothing to me now. It's too late. Now, it's about this. Moment by moment. Choice by choice. Outcomes are not inevitable. Outcomes are based on choices. This will be the birth of your new life. Your second life. The life you deserve. The chance you deserve. It's like a brand new day. He handed me a bucket of paint the colour of cream cheese. Marguerite thinks the lavender is wrong. Do you mind? He leaned in to kiss me, and with as much regality as I could muster, I allowed it.

When I got outside again it was an hour later, maybe more. I had repainted most of the gallery walls the colour of cream cheese. Outside, the sky had purpled and dulled. Missed another sunset, I thought. We are allowed a finite number of sunsets in our lives. At dusk every day the finite number grows smaller.

I got into my car and with a start realized I was not alone. Hazel was sitting in the passenger seat.

Sorry, sorry, she said, didn't mean to startle you. Her neck was long and graceful, her hand thin, with long fingers. She was holding the money Joel had given her, a hundred dollars.

She was hoping I could give her a ride to the bus depot in Kamloops, willing to pay for gas of course. She was on her way back to Fort St. John, where she had a job waiting. She was holding a small knapsack on her lap, had she been expecting to spend the night?

It was a two-hour drive, but I agreed, insisted there was no need to pay.

She told me she recognized me though we had never met.

Something in me that rang a bell. She smiled. Kindred spirits, am I right? I remembered that her son had said the same thing to me, yet how different each of them was not only from me, but from each other.

As I drove her along the winding roads to her drop-off, she told me about the circumstances of her pregnancy, that she had been raped at the age of seventeen. She had been drunk and a lot prettier then, she bragged. Anyway, she gave the baby up, all those questionable genes, and did not prosecute. I wanted to reassure her, wanted to tell her I understood and that Joel had turned out okay in spite of his hidden genotypes but she brushed my words aside. It's not really about him anymore, that train left the station a long time ago. She said that she ended up marrying the man who raped her and it had been okay while it lasted. She said, Don't tell Joel. Not sure he would understand. She added, I've never told anyone that before, but you look like someone who can keep a secret.

We drove along. I asked her what job she was going to, and she told me, butcher, like her own father had been and still was. He really pushed me in that direction, she said. I felt like I had no choice. It's okay. Not what I wanted to do with my life, but it's okay.

What did you want to do instead?

Figure skater. Funny, right? She glanced at me. You're lucky being an artist, you got to choose your own way, you got to be yourself.

She watched me drive for a moment. She might have been waiting for me to corroborate my luck, but no corroborating words came to mind. Too busy being myself I guess. We drove the rest of the way in silence.

Thank you, she said when she got out. I thank you from the bottom of my heart.

It was after ten when I got home. I had driven north to Kamloops with Joel's birth mother and left her at the bus station to wait. Had slipped forty dollars into her coat pocket and driven home again. She had no regrets, that's what she told me. No regrets. But I heard the prideful lie in her voice.

Coping mechanisms, the sophic one at my side says. That's what they call them.

God help me, even the very young have opinions.

Blake was sitting up in the dark watching TV. *Ancient Aliens.* All the menstruation equipment I had bought for the girl was on the sofa. It seemed that the girl was not on her period after all and that Blake had asked her point-blank. I winced to think of my own cowardice in that regard. Apparently, Tully held nothing back from her and the girl was completely cognizant and fully prepared.

What was the blood then?

She cut herself.

How?

With the axe. And at the look I gave him, he added, Hey, I'm new at this too.

The treehouse was complete and every day after school, Clare would gather her snacks and homework and climb the ladder to her little lair, with Fancy scrambling up the ramp to join her. I would stand at the kitchen window and watch her. A small pleasure in a time of anxiety. I suddenly remembered the barn she once lived in and the ladder she climbed to her loft bed when she lived with her own real mother.

Blake kept checking his inbox for an email from the grandfather with arrival info. But so far, nothing. Perhaps the man was not really interested in taking on this responsibility. Who could blame him?

The show was looming like a storm cloud in the distance. How many days? How many weeks? I knew better than to count them. Every morning I stepped into my studio and prayed to my muse. Prayed, begged, pleaded. I played Mozart on my cell phone. I burned rope incense that came all the way from the Himalayas. I heard once of an artist who surrounded his work with rotting apples to invoke that elusive vixen the white goddess. The only time I stopped was to eat and, yes, to drink.

In the kitchen I overheard Blake telling the girl to leave me alone in the studio. He told her I needed uninterrupted time and lots of space. That art was more important than people realized, especially in this day and age. That when the world around us was going to hell, when we were broke and the people we loved were dying, when there was sickness and crime and terrible people in power, we needed art more than ever. I left the hallway where I had been about to vacuum and retreated to my studio, to save the world from the sound of things. Didn't somebody's God do it in a week?

Once there, instead of going to my "work" I went to the window and looked out at the house, at the kitchen window. A small houseplant blooming pink on the sill. The girl was still listening to Blake. I saw his lips moving, his shrugs and other body language that meant he was wrapping up. I saw her turn her head to the kitchen window, the same one I was staring through. Our eyes met. I turned to my canvas, lightheaded. The painted splotches mocked my efforts. I put two ripe bananas on the windowsill. I waited. The fruit flies came.

Meanwhile, the girl continued to work on her biography of Lulu, asking me all the usual questions: date of birth, place of birth, education, husband. I always directed her to Roxanne. And I knew that soon enough her research would uncover the fire.

CHAPTER 36

After a warm night, the weather turned cold again and it started to snow. The wind was up and the flakes were crowded, criss-crossing in the air. Nothing drastic, just the usual last gasps of winter. Spring was definitely on the horizon. I was slopping paint around in the coop Thursday morning when Blake came in and informed me the girl's missing grandfather had finally contacted him and would arrive on Saturday.

This Saturday?!

Yes!

I don't have time for this, I shrieked. My show.

Who cares? he shrieked back. Just do whatever. A light lunch. You know, sandwiches and a pot of tea. It's not about you.

But somehow I believed it was about me and my culinary abilities, so Friday afternoon I combed the ethnic aisle at Buy-Low for Indian fare. The lady at the till price-checked every item. She said, Oh you must be doing one of those international dinner club things and got lucky with Indian. There was that concept of luck again. Eighty-two dollars worth of mango pickles and pappadums and ghee and you name it. The next day, recipes printed off, I spent the morning preparing the "light" lunch instead of working in the studio where half my panic resided. The girl sat on her heels on a chair and watched me cook.

I gave her a spoon to stir the lentils, and after she had sloshed all over the stove and the lentils were thoroughly stirred, I said, Why don't you just go make your grandfather a card? He's come all this way to . . . take you home with him. India. Maybe you can ride a camel. I dropped a dough ball into the rose-flavoured sugar syrup. I thought to myself, India is not so far, not really.

She glowered at me.

And no, I said, his plane did not crash.

She put her jacket on instead and went outside. The heavy quiet that filled the kitchen after the electricity of her presence made me turn the radio on. The distractibility of fake news, drum beating and puffery.

I cooked on. When I was done, I had paratha, paneer, dahl, yogurts, spiced samosas. Gulab jamuns. Did I know what I was doing? Not a clue. But my kitchen had never smelled so good. For Fancy, I had a plate of cold hot dogs at the ready.

He was expected at one o'clock. Twenty to, I took my apron off and fluffed my hair. Lipstick. A grey turtleneck, black slacks. A silk scarf. I knew he would be early and I wanted to be ready. I set my hot dishes in the warm oven. I put the cold dishes outside on the back deck. I called out to Blake, It's almost one. He was in the yard re-shovelling the path to my studio. He whistled back at me in response. I called out, Don't you want to shave? Nope. I went up to Roxanne. I told her to stay where she was, that our guest was coming. I yelled out the door to the tree where the girl was in the branches playing Go Fish with a sparrow, It's time to get ready. I heard the clatter of the treehouse ladder as she descended.

At one o'clock I put the kettle on for chai. The girl was taking her time getting dressed. At one-thirty I turned the oven off, at two o'clock I brought the yogurts in before they froze. At two-thirty I called Blake in, Don't you have an email or a text number for him?

He did, and he emailed. No reply. Texted. Same. We sat in the kitchen and waited. Blake began singing low in his throat,

"Pack up your troubles in your old kit bag" – It was past three o'clock — "and smile, smile, smile" — Another text went unanswered — "What's the use of worrying?" — I poured a cup of cold chai — "It never was worthwhile." Soooo —

Shut up, I said. Just shut the fuck up. Smile, smile, smile.

I'm hungry, I said.

We're all hungry, Blake said. We're all very, very hungry. And he called the girl down.

She descended step by step in shiny black patent leather shoes, wearing the same pink satin dress she had worn when she first came to us. The dress seemed wildly out of place. Childish and overdone. I could see the pale-red downy hair on her bare legs. A scabbed knee. I wanted her in the ripped jeans I knew she preferred, the sparkly T-shirt with the faded unicorn. In the girl's hand was the card she had drawn, herself on a camel under a yellow sun, holding the doll she called Baby. She slammed the card she had drawn down on the table. I propped it up against the pot of red poinsettias.

That's nice, I said.

It's not nice, it's terrible and I don't really care. I don't do my best drawings when I'm told to draw something. I thought you of all people would know that.

But it's really good, I said.

It's not really good. It's fake. Don't you know fakes when you see them? We stopped chatting then.

Okay, Roxanne, I shouted. I know you're standing there waiting for an engraved invitation.

Oh, am I allowed? Roxanne appeared in gold kitten heels and a T-shirt that read I'm a virgin, but this is an old T-shirt. She looked around. Where is he?

Who knows. I put my dishes out on the table with the little bowls of chutneys and coconut and chopped peanuts and said, Oh just help yourselves. I'm not your servant.

And they did, we all did, all of us greedy to fill our empty bellies. The buffet was a little dry, a little overspiced, a little sweet and a little greasy; no one complained, it was delicious.

That night Blake came into the studio where I was stretched out on the bed with a glass of wine.

So much for all our getaway plans, he said.

So much.

I know you had your heart set on Maui.

Maui, Kansas. Doesn't matter. I've had my heart set before.

He touched my shoulder, the wounded one. Want a massage?

I should never have said that about riding a camel. I should never have condescended to her about the card she drew.

Probably not.

I let my dressing gown slip down off my shoulders. In some lights, the scar shone white and ghostly. At other times it rose red and fiery. Tonight it was the ghost. No amount of makeup could conceal it, though my grandmother had tried. I refused to be ashamed. I told myself it was my personal mystery, my flag of survival. Years gone by I used it to separate the wheat from the chaff in the lover department. Though I undressed in the dark, made love in the dark, there would always come that moment when my would-be lover would switch the light on or place his hand there and recoil in confusion, asking, What's that? I separated a lot of the wheat from the chaff.

Blake traced the outline of it with his fingertip. The wheat.

And so we were saved. For the time being at least.

CHAPTER 37

It was late afternoon when the police children left, and the house still reverberated with their presence. Even Fancy sensed that something was amiss, growling at the door as it closed behind them. They had stopped by with more questions about the girl's whereabouts at the time of Tully's suicide. What time, who saw her home alone: neighbours, witnesses, babysitter, school? I felt as if I were underwater trying to converse with the moon. I answered what I knew, as honestly as I could. Everything in slow liquid motion.

But what's your point? I finally asked them.

No point, they replied. Just dotting our I's. Suicides always need to be followed up on.

A factoid I knew very well.

I take a deep breath. I can't remember what I've told my little lawyer. Yes, about my nervous breakdown, but did she know I had also tried to kill myself?

No, I did not, she glowers.

Well, now you know. Pills and exhaust fumes. Why? Take your pick: my floundering art career, my tubal ligation, Blake's infidelity and the baby that came of it. I had more reasons than God. Blake found me in time, unconscious in the garage and took care of business. I think he was more distraught than I was, although I did have a raging headache for a few days. The police did their due diligence, their follow-up, and I was put into counselling. Roxanne and Blake brooded over me like mother hens for six months until I popped back into normalcy, at which point my "event" was put firmly behind us. Never to be mentioned again.

My roomie of the hour holds her small hand up in the air to stop me. And I'm just finding this out now?

I shrugged it off. A momentary lapse. Not that important and I survived it, didn't I? None the worse for wear.

But suicide attempts are not small things, my bedside counsel insists. And then what, what happened after the police left?

Nothing much. Nothing at all, really. A frog is stuck in my throat, and it takes a moment to clear it. Just a little kerfuffle over liver.

My little lawyer drops her pen, stands and goes to the window. Oh do tell, she says. I can hardly wait.

Fancy was still agitated, so I put her bowl down filled with kibbles. And as a treat, I opened a can of Purina Liver and Fish. Spooned the wet gop on top, gagging at the smell. Fancy sniffed disdainfully and lay down in a corner and stared at the door, waiting for Clare to come home from school.

I remember being fed liver as a child. Refusing to eat it, the smell overpowering. But not allowed to leave the table until I did. After an hour, desperate to pee, to play, to sink into an oblivion of television, I put a forkful into my mouth and chewed, swallowed. Tried to swallow. But it would not go down and I immediately vomited it back up onto my plate. Roxanne forced me then to eat what I had regurgitated. Is this a memory that has congealed over time? An ordinary power struggle between caregiver and child congealed into a poisonous tangle of hate and powerlessness? Lost in these thoughts, and staring at the dog's dish of horror, I picked it up from the floor and brought it to my nose to smell, a madeleine moment of the dark side.

The girl, now home, stepped into the kitchen and shrieked, Don't!

Fancy barked. I dropped the bowl.

That's dog food, she said. You don't eat dog food. Plus it's liver, it's gross.

The way she was looking at me, like I was one of the deplorables. I was so embarrassed that I went on the attack. Maybe there are some facts of life that you don't realize, I told her. Number one. You don't have to eat liver, because you don't have to eat anything you don't want to eat. I, on the other hand, was raised differently. Go ask Roxanne if you don't believe me.

Even though it was true, I heard how churlish it sounded. So be it. I turned to the sink and put my hands under the tap until it ran hot.

And I don't mind telling you, I'm really tired of having the police show up.

I was waiting to hear the girl's footsteps stomping out of the room, desperate to put the whole exchange behind me, already rehashing what I should have said, what I could have said, but instead of her stomping footsteps, what I heard was a gagging sound.

When I turned, I saw that the child had spooned up the dog's liver and chicken puree and was desperately forcing herself to eat it.

Miss Betty Boop is quiet, until she raises her eyes to look at me. Have you no control over yourself? Apparently, I did not.

A few days later I was slashing bands of black across a canvas I had painted pink when my phone meowed. Expecting, dreading a call from Joel with more questions and demands I was loathe to answer, but as the phone meowed on I gathered my courage and answered with, Okay, what is it now?

But it was Clare. That took me aback. I knew that she had both Blake's number and mine in her notebook, and it startled me that she had chosen my number to call. Had she forgiven my awfulness over the liver? Three sleepless nights I had spent vowing to change, vowing to be the good, loving, kind, self-sacrificing stepmother/guardian/wife that one sees in Hallmark movies and reads about on Facebook and knowing I would only ever be the same old bitch I had always been. But, now, here she was, phoning me. As if I were forgiven. Facebook, here we come.

Hello, darling, I said.

Don't call me darling. Can you pick me up? she asked. She'd had a run-in with her social studies teacher over the biography she was writing about Lulu. The teacher had accused her of fabrications — fires, scars, dead babies, burnings — and insisted she write a proper biography without fantastic embellishments. Lives can be interesting without all the drama, the teacher told her. What were Lulu's hobbies, for example, did she enjoy cooking?

Cooking? I said. I was flabbergasted.

It's not fair. Call her and tell her it's all true! Tremulous and silvery, her childish voice was so authentic to my ears that I found myself speechless. So she knew.

The teacher came on the phone then and nervously told me that my daughter seemed to have a hyperactive imagination, and it might just be best to pick her up and bring her home and let her settle down. I could hear Clare's shuttering breaths in the background, striving to swallow the outrage she felt. I put my paintbrush down and immediately went to her rescue and we drove home in silence.

The next few days (weeks?) were a blur of emotion and activity and its opposite, lethargy. Half of me wanted to embody the brilliant, creative, outrageous mature artist that the universe was waiting for. Half of me wanted to vacuum and peel potatoes. But the other half, the main half, concerned the child.

When Joel mentioned one day that Marguerite was a little afraid of me, I had to laugh. Of all the emotions I had ever hoped to inspire in those around me, fear was not one of them.

You have a powerful life force, he said. Imperious. Not an easy woman to ignore.

I pretended this was a compliment and I said, Thank you.

I watched Joel shuffle through the drawings, paintings, canvases I had given him over the last little while, his face completely impassive.

He sighed, oh he could sigh so big. He yawned. Huge open mouth. I coughed in his face and he shut his maw.

It's funny, he says, that we haven't heard back from Lulu. I have a two-bedroom suite reserved for her at the Fairmont Olympic, but it would be nice to know how many we have to plan for.

Did you call her?

The number you gave me was disconnected.

Ah.

I see she's orchestrating a burn in Wilmington.

Wilmington. How the mighty have fallen.

Frida . . . do you think she would consider a burn at your opening, one of your pieces?

Are you kidding me? I was aghast.

Sort of. Never mind. Marguerite says —

Marguerite says, I mimicked his whiny voice.

He cleared his throat, dropped his decibels. Marguerite suggests this is your domain. If you read your contract over, it's written in there, pretty plain. You will make the arrangements for Lulu's attendance. Sorry to go all legalese on you. He thumbed through my drawings again. You do have talent, he said. Don't squander it. Okay?

I showed Joel to the door and watched him gun his Jeep with a dramatic show of machismo. I tried to imagine myself doing the same in my little yellow car, revving the engine, spitting gravel, zero to forty in ten seconds flat. The fantasy amused me no end.

I returned to my art piece, *Black on Pink*, and added a bird's head in my likeness. How lifelike it looked. How perfect. I dropped a dot of zinc white on its eyeball. I swear I saw it flinch. When I turned, the child was standing there, her hands in front of her, cupped, holding a small frog, which leapt from her palms onto my workbench.

Happy birthday, she said. I had completely forgotten.

Above the earth a heaviness settles down, deep clouds, warmonger-grey, and a stripe of open silver cuts through them, which is the sky, the key. Everything under it — the fogged parking lot, the barren cottonwoods, the thick-waisted nurse, the rain-streaked window — everything is complicit in the threat.

It's nice she remembered your birthday, don't you think? Did you give her any credit for that?

There are moments when I find my little lawyer really hard to bear.

Hmph, she says again.

I turned back to the lilies and pears, the nudes and canoes, the geese, the sunsets, more geese, all the paintings Joel had damned with faint praise. I opened the wood stove and pushed them in. What a noise they made of protest. I kept aside the ones that defined me. The suckling wolf and pregnant raven, the frogs and bucks done in my image. And of course the self-portrait as an octopus. It was promised.

It was snowing. The crows were celebrating on a branch, or complaining. I could not tell the difference. It seemed the geese were back. Or were these the ones who never left? Hungry, alert, suspicious. Welcome home. Build your nests. Guard your eggs.

That night I dreamed again of a baby. Huddled with cold, fallen asleep on a hard bench. I laid a towel over his chubby body. But it was the dog's towel and somebody, even the baby, reprimanded me for that insult.

CHAPTER 38

At last, an email arrived from the grandfather. He apologized for his no-show. An abscessed tooth, but all sorted out and he was ready to reschedule. He lived in New Delhi, Illinois, actually. Had already set up tap dance lessons and a Christian summer camp program for the girl. He believed in structure and discipline. He had a theory that he was curious to test out. That without consequences for bad behaviour, a bad child will turn into a bad adult. Which is what had happened to the girl's mother. She would be kept busy, kept clean and kept fed. His next opening in his schedule was the thirtieth. A Thursday.

Blake sent back a thank you. And promised to be in touch after we checked our calendars.

Later that night I got up and crossed the dark yard and went into the house up to the bedroom where Blake was lying with his eyes open. I said, Text the grandfather and tell him no. His services are not needed. He cannot have the girl. I was panting with the exertion of these words coming out of my mouth.

Blake said, Calm down, Frida. I already have.

Next morning when Blake informed the girl of our decision, she threw her arms around her dad's neck and squeezed, Yippee, and to me, she gifted a little thumbs-up.

The day after we cancelled, I had a fight with Clare. She had discovered her private things had been touched and rearranged and had stomped down from her room and thrown a temper tantrum. Told me I looked like a witch. A big fat witch. She said, I'm glad you don't have children. You would be the ugliest mother. They would hate you.

Stung, I shot back, No wonder you don't have any friends.

Sobbing, she fled to her room, the sanctuary I had apparently violated.

Blake, his mouth set in fury, his teeth clenched, demanded I go apologize. He had never been so clear, not even on acid, not even the first time he entered me. That surety — should I call it love? — frightened me. I went.

The girl was in her bed under her blankets. Fancy, as usual, was by her side. I fed Fancy one of her hot dog bits. Fancy swallowed it whole and returned to her vigil while the girl stayed hidden in the covers, a lump.

I said, I apologize. I'm sorry.

On the bedside table was what she had wanted to keep private, what was so precious to her that she had erupted in vitriol and insult. A note to her mother. A private note to her dead mother that I had read. Dear Mommy. I'm rily soory. Pleese come back. Clare.

Barbarella has brought takeout. Two steaming bowls of phở for us. She slurps and chews, then puts her empty bowl down. I stare at mine and wish I had the appetite for it. The room smells of spicy beef and that jasmine conditioner she uses.

Thank you, I say.

Here's a little advice, she says. If you want to look good, you have to forgive everyone, quote, unquote.

I contemplated the child's note. No apology, no matter how poignant, could bring a dead woman back. But don't all children live in a world of fantasy and fairies? I had, at her age, set out tiny walnut shells full of water for fairies to bathe in.

Eat your soup, Bo-Peep says, while it's hot.

I took a tour through town, looking at all the "For Sale" signs in the yards. Places with rusty swing sets and decrepit snowmobiles, canopied boats in the driveway. Cluttered, cramped places that people raised children in, watched TV in, grew old in. When I turned homeward, struck again by the huge dark forest behind our house, the river behind and the sky above it, I noted a police car just pulling out of our driveway. For a moment, I froze and then I went inside.

The house was quiet. I went up to Roxanne's room and stood outside the door, ear bent to the panel and listened.

Roxanne was talking.

You're only nine? I thought you were ten. Nine is better. But I don't know for sure what they do with nine-year-olds. I know there used to be electric chairs, get all strapped down. Saw this movie, they put this cream on the head clamps and flipped the electric switch but forgot the water and the smoke and the smell and the shaking —

I slammed the door open. The girl was backed up against the window, frozen in fear. Roxanne was not paying attention, sitting on the bed painting green shadows above her eyes.

Frida, she said. You missed all the excitement. The cops were here. They found a pink butterfly hair barrette in the bushes by the river.

I looked at the girl. The statue of the girl. Her hair was hanging long and loose, half obscuring her face. It could have used a couple of barrettes.

To Roxanne, I said, What the hell are you talking about?

When Tully shot herself. Or did she? There might have been witnesses. She rolled her eyes towards the girl shaking behind her.

She wasn't there. She was at home in the barn. I'm sure there's plenty of garbage in the bushes.

She was there, Roxanne whispered. She's not telling the whole story. I think the police are on to her.

Stop your nonsense. What are you trying to say?

Nothing. Believe what you like. It doesn't matter, and I would never in a million years put a little girl in an electric chair. But what's-his-name might change the law. Hard to say.

Suddenly, I was remembering that spidery red hair.

The girl fled. I went after her. I stood outside her slammed-shut bedroom door. We have to talk, Clare. Don't listen to Roxanne. We have to talk. I dropped to the floor. When you're ready, come and find me. Just don't believe anything Roxanne tells you, it's all bullshit. Okay? Okay? I heard a blanket rustle as she and the dog climbed into bed.

I went back to Roxanne, who still had Clare's makeup kit open on her lap, her lips purpled, her sunken cheeks rouged. Before I could stop myself, I slapped her across the face and she tumbled back against the headboard, gasping.

I left her there.

When Blake got home that night, I told him what had transpired. He called the police station. Just routine questioning was the answer he got. The new sergeant likes to go by the book. We just take direction, they said, until something new comes along.

What did you tell them?

I told them to leave us alone or I'd file a police harassment charge.

The girl did not appear for dinner that evening, and when Blake went with an apple and a donut to tuck her in, I sat in the hallway and listened to him reading from their book of fairy tales and fables. Once there was a hard-working girl with a wicked stepmother and a heart of gold. But was it the girl or the stepmother with the heart of gold?

In the morning, I took a cup of tea and a bowl of cinnamon milk toast up to Roxanne. I found her half-delirious on the floor. She could not get up. She had soiled herself and scraped her arm. The thinness of her skin, the blood caked on her arm. She had not pushed her little alert button. She had just lain there waiting.

I didn't want to disturb anyone, she said.

It was clearly time. I called the StarDew for an update on availability. Roxanne was next in line and it looked like something might open up in a week, maybe less. It turned out to be less.

The day was strange already. Full of fog and quiet. Inside and out. No TV turned on. No radio. No thumping and groaning from upstairs.

I made a pot of coffee and found Roxanne's favourite cup, the cat with sunglasses, and filled it halfway and then added thick cream, two spoons of sugar. I took it up to her. She was pretending to sleep.

I know you're awake. Here's your coffee.

I'm not going. It's snowing again.

It's for the best, Roxanne. You know that. It's a lovely place.

Full of old people.

You're old.

I'll be good, she said.

It's not about being good.

Though in some ways it was about being good. Unfortunately, I doubted she knew how. How many times has this conversation been repeated around the world?

I packed her clothes and meds and jewellery into a case, as much as I thought she might need.

You might meet someone, a man, I said.

If I do, I'll change my will.

I'll miss you.

Is there booze allowed?

Of course. Though I knew it would be rationed.

TV?

Of course.

Where's the girl?

In her room.

I want to say goodbye.

When I turned the girl was standing there. She had the mail in her hand.

Roxanne's face lit up. All the catalogues and sweepstakes and lotteries she had won. On every envelope, You are the Grand Prize Winner! A million dollars. Send a one-time processing fee of twenty-five dollars to retrieve.

The girl spread it out on the bed for Roxanne to go over. And then the little bump of expectation, opening the envelope from Publishers Clearing House. But I had forgotten the twenty dollars this month and her disappointment was palpable. She swallowed it down.

You collect my mail and bring it to me, Roxanne told the girl. I'll share with you when I win.

Clare nodded. The horror from the day before forgotten. Blake had soothed it over with tales and signs and donuts. Or so it seemed. Buried deep perhaps. But I saw that Clare had forgiven Roxanne in a way that I never could.

Roxanne pushed all her mail to the floor. I'll need to get my hair done. And a new wardrobe.

I don't have time for this, Gramma. I just don't.

So now that you're getting rid of me I'm Gramma again. What do you have time for then? she replied. She sank back into her pillow. This will be the end of me. I suppose that's what you want. She sipped her coffee. Too sweet, she said. And it's cold.

Good luck, I said to the attendant when I wheeled her up to the front desk, her purple suitcase stuffed with her clothes and jewellery and makeup.

Roxanne stared straight ahead, mute.

Hi there, the attendant said to her. You're just in time for movie-star bingo.

No response.

The attendant shrugged. We've seen it all, she said. She'll be fine. And she wheeled my grandmother down the long hallway. Without turning, the attendant gave me or the world a thumbs-up. Roxanne gave me nothing. Nor did I call out an adieu.

That night I again took up my post outside the girl's door while Blake read her to sleep. He was telling her the tale of Iron Henry. A tale about a spoiled princess, a gold ball and a frog who had once been a prince. I heard him tell her the prince had a servant named Henry, who loved him dearly, but when the prince was turned into a frog poor Henry had three iron bands wrapped around his heart to keep it from breaking.

The girl must have fallen asleep by then, because Blake stopped reading and I never got to hear the happy ending.

CHAPTER 39

With Roxanne gone, I found myself suddenly in the position of being the oldest female in my clan. It ages you, that does. It forces a sort of maturity on you, and responsibility, not for any reason you can point to but as a simple matter of being next in line. Now, instead of the sensation of Roxanne looking over me, judging me, informing and instructing me as if I were a child, I was the one at the top of the heap. Three weeks to go before my show, a world-class city to impress, and my focus had not so much shifted but expanded to include the definition of myself as not only a wife and stepmother but also a matriarch, with the biggest artistic event of my life fast approaching.

Problem being, I had not yet managed to confirm Lulu's attendance. Online I kept running into digital posters promoting the affair with pictures of a resplendent Lulu in front of a burning, and even pictures of myself tucked into a corner.

Blake and Clare had just finished a late breakfast of pancakes.

Not hungry? Blake asked.

No. I finished my coffee and put my coat on. Outside the air was cool and fresh and perfect. I backed my yellow sports car out of the driveway. I saw Blake at the window watching me drive off.

The care attendant met me in reception. Your mother, she began.

Grandmother.

Right. Has been calling for you.

I'm here.

I walked down the hallway until I found her door. Her name, her number, a posy of plastic flowers on the wall beside in a crèche. I had a bottle of apricot brandy for her and opened it when I arrived. She had one teacup and one plastic water glass. I poured hefty quantities into each. She was watching her tiny TV, a VHS of *Last Year at Marienbad*, in which she claimed she had had a role. Small, but significant, she said.

She told me how the director had made the actors, all of them, meditate before a rehearsal. She closed her eyes and took in a deep rasping breath and held it. I was just about to push the call button when she exhaled. Like that, she said. She leaned in: Reality is not real. The only real reality is death.

Real reality, I mocked. Had another drink. Is there fake reality?

She nodded. There are things that happen that we think happen but actually don't happen.

Like what? I took the bottle out of her hand.

She hesitated. People come into my room at night, but in the morning there is no one here.

They come and go, Roxanne.

She opened her mouth as if to speak, then shut it.

Out her window, the sky was cold, blue. Winter, still, forever it seemed. The single fir stiff in the breeze. In her room the smell of boiled cabbage and baby powder.

Here it is, she said. This is it.

I glanced again at her movie, the scene she was in. Standing straight and unnatural, a mannequin, a long shadow cast before her.

No such thing as truth, or memory.

I watched it with her. Over and over she made me rewind to watch the scene that she was in. A fleeting tall, thin woman, serious, indifferent, cold.

She turned it off.

I had brought a photo album with me. Photographs of her visiting her friends' graves. She said, Get rid of those photographs. I look so old.

I scoffed. Maybe you look old but Christ, you're standing, you're still alive. Imagine how your friends look underground.

I was thinking then of the things that could kill us, young, old, in-between. Like my baby brother, the one that died in the fire. The fire that I set, playing with matches, lighting candles they told me. I still remember it like a movie that someone has described to me. Vivid, frightening, shameful. But something bothered me and would not go away.

I turned a page in the album.

I'm trying to get a commitment from Mummy for my show.

She's busy, Roxanne said.

Oh, I don't know. Not that busy. Since her sales fell off, her burnings have fallen off, and without burnings, her sales have fallen even more: Catch-22.

Well, it's not my business, Roxanne said. You made sure of that when you put me here.

I turned another page in the album.

Did my mother smoke?

Roxanne coughed, flailed out in search of something. I pressed a tissue into her hand and asked again. Did she smoke?

I don't remember. She reached to pat my hand and I pulled it away.

But look at that. I pointed to a photo of my mother in bed reading, a cigarette in her hand. The baby asleep on her pillow.

She looked. It's just a picture.

She's smoking. That fire . . . I was always told that —

Roxanne hissed at me, We don't dwell in the past. She snapped the album closed. You of all people should know that. Or do you want me airing your own dirty laundry?

I opened the album again, leafed through pictures of myself in my twenties. Lounging on Blake's lap. The two of us in a canoe. My brown hair. All those smiles.

Finally, I asked her the question that I had vowed not to ask. Roxanne . . . when the police came to the house . . . did they show you the barrette they found?

Oh yes.

What did it look like?

I told you, it was a pink butterfly.

Like this? I said. I pulled the barrette I had found in the girl's hoodie out of my pocket.

Exactly, Roxanne said. That's the one.

I put it away. We sat quietly together for a while. When she reached to pat my hand the second time, I let her.

I closed the photo album, put it on a shelf in her room.

Listen, she said. I've been practising for when they ask. And she began, One hundred, ninety-three, eighty-six, seventy-nine . . .

I looked at her quizzically.

The dementia test. I'll tell you the trick . . . subtract ten then add three. One day they'll be coming for you too.

This may be the best advice she ever gave me.

I tucked her in. I kissed her papery cheek, but when I tried to pull back she gripped me hard and forced her lips onto mine. Soft, wet.

That night I put the girl's clothes in the dryer with a vanilla-scented fabric softener. I stood in the basement and waited while they dried. When they were done and still warm, I folded them carefully into a small pile. I went through Tully's trunk again. I found a green sweater that I knew would never fit. It smelled faintly of cedar shavings and gin. I put it on. I squeezed myself into it. I took the little pile of clean clothes up to the girl's room and left it outside her door.

I waited for Blake with a glass of wine at the ready. A plate of cheese and crackers. His favourite music on, Van Morrison. But by the time he got home from whatever hard drive he had been installing, my conciliatory mood had done a one-eighty.

He walked in the door, smiled to see the flowers, the wine, and I said, What the hell do you talk to Marguerite about?

My anger had taken on a life of its own. I was half-drunk, riding a roller coaster that I did not know how to stop.

He had come home with a pair of binoculars for the girl, as well as cedar boards and hardware to build a birdhouse outside her window.

Did he notice what I was wearing? He didn't say.

We talked about nothing, he said. Just computer stuff for their gallery. He drank the wine, ate the cheese.

Not me? Not the girl?

What are you getting at?

What I'm getting at is Marguerite thinks we don't want her. She thinks the girl is up for grabs. That's what I'm getting at.

Blake looked at me, maybe he even noticed the stained green sweater I was wearing and how lusciously I filled it out. He said, Well is she? You tell me.

The bouquet of flowers I had bought for him had only barely started to wilt.

Just after eight, the girl was dropped off from Corey's. She saw us together in the living room and yelled, Sorry I'm late.

We looked at each other. Are you late?

You said eight o'clock. It's ten after. Will I be punished?

No. Of course not.

She frowned.

Did you eat? Blake asked.

She nodded.

Get enough?

I'm still hungry.

There's peanut butter in the kitchen. Help yourself.

She came back into the room chewing on a giant piece of bread smeared in peanut butter.

So did you have fun, I asked.

Yep. But Corey's mother is so annoying. Everything has to be so perfect. Knives on the right side, forks on the left. And she's always bugging Corey. Did you practise your violin? Did you write a thank you note to Auntie Joan? So perfect. She won't even let him wear the same socks two days in a row.

We looked at Clare's feet, at the sag of her mismatched socks.

Corey says I'm lucky to live here. She wiped her sticky hands on her jeans. She looked at the green sweater of Tully's I was wearing. I smiled, a thin smile.

Can I go to bed now?

Brush your teeth. Okay?

I know, she said. I always do.

And from me, Your clothes are in front of your door. Clean.

She paused on her way up the stairs. Omigod I hope you didn't put my pink sweater in the dryer.

No. I laid it out flat to dry. That's what the tag said.

Phew. Mama never read the tags. So thanks.

She ran back down the stairs towards us and wrapped her sticky hands around Blake's neck and hugged. And to me: Sorry to say, green is not your colour. And she was gone.

The next afternoon, it was a Sunday, a little rain, a little snow, I made a sandwich. Cheese, ham, mayonnaise, avocado. Brown bread with a pickle. On a plate. Sketched it and put the sketch under the door of the girl's room. Like magic, she appeared and began to eat. I was still basking in the glory of our imperfect parenting when we were interrupted by a car beeping outside, one, two, beep-beep. When I looked I saw Marguerite's red Toyota and Clare jumped to her feet.

Where are you going?

Marguerite is taking me for a mani-pedi. She put her half-eaten sandwich down and ran out the door.

Marguerite, Clare, a mani-pedi — girl bonding — completely not in my wheelhouse. I recalled the time Blake had bought me a gift certificate for a spa day on Valentine's, oh many moons ago. Facial, manicure, pedicure package. I agonized over it for a week and then gave the certificate to the Buffalo, who agonized over it not at all and came home skin glowing, parading around the house barefoot for two days showing off her pedicure, her sturdy toes painted red, her skin smelling of orange blossoms. Blake was confused and more than a little annoyed. I couldn't explain, except that I knew somehow I did not deserve a spa day. Had my just desserts improved since then? The best answer I could summon was no.

Ten minutes went by, a half-hour, until I reached out and finished her sandwich.

When Clare got home, I said, Well?

She showed me her stubby, bitten fingernails. I wanted pink but Marguerite chose blue. She said it was more grown-up.

It's nice, I said.

She shrugged. Everyone there was so old and they kept asking me how I liked school and all these dumb questions, and they thought Marguerite was my mother and they thought it was so cute that I kept calling her Marguerite and not Mommy. I don't think I'll do that again.

She took a step towards me, stopped. Good night? she said, like it was a question.

Good night, I said, and I held my palms up for a little hug as if in answer to her question.

But her eyes widened and she took a step backward, waved and ran upstairs to bed.

You should have just grabbed her in a bear hug, my little lawyer says. Instead of leaving it up to her to decide.

For once, I realize she's absolutely right.

CHAPTER 40

It's funny how we rationalize our actions. Survival mechanisms I suppose. A way to stay sane and not jump off the proverbial cliff.

My forlorn lawyer tilts her head and watches me, waiting I suppose for what she dreads is coming next.

It could have been considered a rescue. You know? Except no one saw it that way. Not the jury. Not even my defence, I suspect. Maybe Roxanne did, but she was useless at the trial. I look at my lovely counsel. She's pretending to study her notes. But what do you think? What do you really think?

She looks up at me. You don't want to know, Freddie, she says. And I let it go at that.

Joel was pacing, running his hands through his hair. His opinions on my art shifted neurotically from one exaggeration to another. One visit he loved everything, the next he hated. The worst was when he merely liked them. And Joel could be very demanding. I started to feel a little sorry for Marguerite.

Well, take it or leave it, I said. I'm the artist in this duo. Right?

He was stretched out on my coop cot, his shoes off. A smell of Swiss Emmenthal in the air. And hay dust. I wrapped my trademark scarf around my neck.

He said, You don't have to hide that scar. It's not that bad. Marguerite has breast rash, you should count yourself lucky.

I really don't think you should talk about Marguerite's breast rash. I think that's private.

Joel lifted his head off my pillow and frowned. I thought

we shared confidences here.

That's her confidence, not yours. Moron.

He settled back onto the pillow.

So how's the house hunting coming along? Damage control.

Slow, he said. Very slow. She's quite particular. He cleared his throat. And the money. It's not as cheap here as it should be. And those goddamn follicles cost a fortune. Cleared his throat again. But I'm humouring her, right? Isn't that the idea? God, I'm so tired all the time.

What are we doing, Joel? What the fuck are we doing? I was thinking this even as I felt about to succumb to his superficial charms. He eyed me with a look that was half-flirt, half-challenge. He had luxurious eyelashes that he blinked at me. He took his glasses off. His breath smelled eggy. Will you kiss me?

I'm not hungry, I teased. And then, Okay, but just a little. Let's not make a meal of it.

Oh for chrissake, he said, never mind.

My god, I said. You're so fucking sensitive.

He put his glasses back on. Frida. Frida, Frida.

What?

Do I need to ask you, yet again, what commitment you have gotten from your extraordinarily hard-to-pin-down mother?

No, you do not need to ask.

Well, I am asking.

Well, don't. You'll be the first to know.

He frowned. He looked quite sad actually. I leaned in and pecked him on the lips. There, are you happy?

Frida, he sighed.

We were a pretty pair of fools.

But more importantly, in the back of my mind, I could not stop worrying over what the girl might be hiding from us. Our lives, all of our lives it seemed, were nothing but a pile of hidden truths, terrible secrets.

A few days later I woke up late to a winter thaw, snow melting and the bizarre sound of chickens clucking. I looked outside my coop window. Saw five red hens and the girl jumping up and down with glee trying to catch them. The squawking and flapping, the hysteria, Fancy adding to the frenzy, the chickens flying up onto branches to escape the pair.

I stepped into the yard. Blake looked at me with a sheepish look. Is this okay, Freed?

So what are we, farmers now?

We have chickens! Clare shrieked, Corey is going to be so jealous!

One by one the chickens marched into the chicken coop. Just like they owned the joint.

And if he thought this would send me scuttling back into the house, into my bedroom, into my bed, the one he was sleeping in, he was right. But I didn't know it yet. I stuck it out one more day with the cackling and the chickenshit before I gave him that satisfaction.

My final night in the coop he crept in after I was bunked down and the chickens were roosted. We lay there together and waited for sleep or dreams or understanding or any emotion at all other than the one overtaking us, the fear of stepping off a familiar cliff into the abyss.

You left the girl in the house on her own? I asked.

Fancy is with her.

Fancy is a dog.

Well, you sleep with chickens.

Slowly I inched closer, until we were touching, skin to skin, and I settled up against him in the bunk. He waited, I heard him breathing, and then he put his hand on my thigh and began to drift off.

Did you put the baby monitor in her room?

Ssshhh, he said, it's all good, I'm falling asleep.

And so was I. He waited a moment, until he thought I had dropped off, before he said, You know you left your phone in the house and it was ringing and I answered it. Vernon, Goldburgh and Kanat returning your call. Goldburgh wants to fax you a fee schedule.

I snored a little, pretending sleep and he went on.

I know we've been through some rough patches. But we're good now, aren't we? I told them that. I told them we're good now and did not need their services after all. He massaged my head a little and soon enough we were both fully asleep.

He had once told me, early on in our life together I deserved better than him, that I had lowered myself in marrying him. I remember that I did not reject this analysis of our relationship, though I should have if for no other reason than largess. But now I saw what was really true, that he had lowered himself in marrying me. Maybe not lowered himself, maybe that's the wrong conceit, better to say missed the mark, like his love and commitment and attention was an arrow aimed at a glorious target and he had missed the mark and hit me instead.

In the morning when I awoke, with Blake snoring beside me, the girl was there as well, lying on the floor alongside the bunk, nestled in a pile of hay with her patchwork bed quilt over her, Fancy at her side. Both of them fast asleep. On her pillow next to her head were mouse turds.

That day I moved back into the house.

When I finished with the breakfast dishes I turned and saw the girl lugging her quilts and pillows down the stairs while Blake was manhandling a foamie up from the basement.

What's going on?

Blake raised his eyebrows and rolled his eyes towards the girl.

I'm making up a bed in the treehouse, she said. She was giddy with excitement. It will be awesome. Do you have any extra flashlights? And can I take some snacks? I might need another blanket; do you have another blanket I can take? It might be cold out there.

You're moving into the treehouse?

Not moving. Don't be weird. It's for camp-out, not forever. It's only when I feel like it. Is it okay?

I guess. Sure. I shrugged. Far be it from me. Anyway, I doubted it would amount to much, darkness makes cowards of us all.

But after dinner that very night, with the sun already set, her teeth brushed and her pyjamas on, she filled a zip-lock with raisins and dried apples, another zip-lock with dog cookies, and waved at us in the kitchen as if she were embarking on a full-scale mountain expedition.

Okay, good night, she said.

Good night, we echoed.

She squared her shoulders and opened the door, turned the flashlight on to light the pathway to her treehouse. Not even a moon to light her way.

Are you sure?

She nodded.

Then take this. I handed her my cell phone. If you have any problems, give Blake a call on his phone. The number is in the contact list.

Or I could just walk back.

Or that, too. Yup.

But she took the phone and left.

Half-hour later when she had not returned, Blake, who had been in the habit of tucking her in every night, looked at me.

I said, Go, go tuck her in.

I think back and imagine, what if our tale of familial harmony had ended at that moment, with nothing further to disrupt and dislodge? I'm certain I could have made it work. It felt like more than a second chance, it felt like a cosmic opportunity, my slate of missteps wiped clean. Forgiveness. I had served my time before the mast and was found capable. More than capable. But our story was far from over.

For the next while, Clare spent every weekend night sleeping in the treehouse. In the morning she would bring my cell phone in to be charged. Come evening she would load up again with snacks and dog treats. She looked tired but claimed she was getting the best sleep, the foamie was comfy and she wasn't even cold.

Blake continued to tuck her in. He said, I had a treehouse when I was a kid, but I never had the guts to actually sleep in it.

One day, I checked my cell phone and saw some outrageous long-distance calls on it. The number was very familiar. It was Lulu's.

I'm working on my biography, she said. I didn't know it would be expensive.

Well, it is. So stop.

And guess what, Clare said. Lulu told me she's coming to your show. She said she wouldn't miss it for the world.

She showed me the confirming text, with arrival times and flight numbers. Daniel was coming with her. I could hardly believe it. Neither could Joel. We texted back and forth the happy dance, the heart emojis, the xxx's and ooo's. It might very well have been the happiest day of my life. Certainly Joel's. For the first time in a month of Sundays, I breathed. But at night, when my unconscious took over, I knew better.

CHAPTER 41

I had forgotten about the baby monitor in the kitchen on top of the fridge. The batteries had been dead for quite a while and it was not much used anymore, but I put fresh batteries in and decided I would give it to Marguerite if she ever got pregnant. And I hoped she would. My own happiness had spilled over into the most luxuriant feeling of generosity towards humankind.

When I turned the monitor on to check if it was working, I heard rustling sounds coming through the speaker. The other half of the monitor was still in the girl's room on a shelf. I heard the window close. Heard Fancy licking her paws. Then Corey's voice. He had come home from school with her, to do homework together.

Where's the diamond?

Right here.

Put it in your other hand.

Why?

Just do it. And the feather?

I got it.

Sit down, like this. Like a yogi and close your eyes. Repeat after me: fifth of September, 2008.

A pause. I can't.

Why can't you?

'Cause it's stupid.

You're afraid?

No.

Yes, you are. Don't lie.

I'm not lying.

I don't like liars, I don't like lying.

You lie.

I do not.

Yes, you do. You haven't even told your parents that you're gay.

I'm only ten!

So what? I'm only nine.

But your lie is more important.

I crept closer to the fridge, afraid to listen, afraid not to.

Maybe I'll do it then, Corey said. On my own.

You're not allowed.

You gonna stop me?

I don't have to, 'cause it won't work anyway.

Give me the diamond, Corey said. Give me the feather.

Make me.

Noises, rustling.

Asshole, from Clare.

Then whispers, chants, vocalizations that I could make no sense of.

Time travel is bullshit, said Clare, loud. Everybody knows that but you. Stop being stupid.

Everybody knows a lot of things that are wrong. Everybody used to think the world was flat.

Maybe it is.

Maybe you are.

And your magic tricks are stupid. They're not real either.

Fifth of September, 2008, fifth of September, 2008, fifth of September, fifth —

Stop it. Get out. Get out of here. Get out of my room, get out of my house.

I turned it off. A door slammed upstairs. In a very short time,

Corey came down. Straight and pale. Holding his crushed top hat in his hand.

Hi, Corey. Are you leaving already? Need a ride?

I'll phone my mom.

Is everything okay?

Not really, he replied. And left.

A little while later, I was vacuuming an immaculate rug when the girl appeared. I turned to see her suddenly standing in the room. She held her hand out to me.

Look, she said.

I expected to see the tiny yellow diamond, but in her hand was a green frog no bigger than the nail on her pinky.

See? she said.

I nodded, relieved. It's cute. Where did you find it?

In your fern plant. Look at it, she demanded.

I looked closer. The tiny green frog was missing a back leg. She put it on the rug. It pooped, then hopped unevenly and not far.

Can you fix it? she asked me.

I snorted. That would take some kind of magic.

The girl flushed. I immediately regretted the remark. I hadn't meant to refer to magic. Well, it's hard to know looking back what I meant exactly.

The tiny green frog hopped under the couch and the mood in the room darkened. I tried to lighten it. I pointed to the table. See? I said. I bought you a new box of crayons.

She looked at them, longingly I thought.

The frog will be okay. He'll find his way back to the fern. He'll do his hopping thing with one leg, it's all good. Can't be helped. Might as well move on.

She sat at the table, sideways on the chair, not quite ready to succumb to my gift.

Corey's a nice boy, I said. I'm glad you two are friends.

She dumped the box of crayons out.

He's really into magic, isn't he?

She fingered the crayons.

He'll outgrow it, probably. Not to worry.

She scribbled on the tabletop with a crayon.

Did you guys have a fight?

She stared at me.

I'm not prying, I said.

Yes, you are.

Fine, you don't have to talk about it. None of my business. I started emptying the dishwasher, hung a coffee cup on a hook.

She picked another crayon up, a purple one.

I said, Please don't colour on the table. I have lots of paper.

She stopped what she was doing, ripped the little paper cover off the purple crayon and snapped the crayon in half.

When I was a kid, I loved a new box of crayons. Not that I got many. I hated it when they broke. I hung up another cup.

That's the difference between you and me I guess, she said.

One by one she went through the waxy heap of crayons, picking each one up in turn, ripping the covers off, and snapping each in half, ripping and snapping.

I wanted her to confide in me, wanted to be the type of person that she could trust enough to do that. But I had no idea what type of person that was. Should I be blunt? Or tricky? Serious or light? Pretend nonchalance or would she see right through that? I wanted to tell her that I understood, but I knew that was another lie, that I could never understand what it would be like to witness your mother's suicide. I thought about lies. I wanted to reassure her that without them we would become defenceless, worse than that little three-legged frog. We had to take care of ourselves first and foremost.

I may have said some of these things out loud because when she was done breaking the crayons she sniffed the air and scoffed at me.

You smell like my mother.

I don't.

You do so. That's her perfume.

I flushed in shame. She looked me up and down. You dress like her too. Is that my mother's sweater?

And it was.

Are you trying to be her? 'Cause you're not and never will be.

I leaned on the sink and stared out the window. Marguerite wants to take you shopping for an Easter outfit.

Whatever.

Wouldn't that please you?

I hate Marguerite. All she ever does is talk about diets and losing weight. As if I'm fat, and I'm not.

I know that. I took the plunge. So what do you want to talk about instead? Music . . . school . . . the fifth of September?

The girl stood up, staring at me with hate.

I dove again into the deep end. When I was a very young girl, I lit a fire. That's what they told me anyway, and even though I don't remember that, I believed it and . . .

And what? What? She was still staring at me, but now her face was wide open, like an empty, shining crystal glass waiting to be filled.

I said, Never mind. There are things we can change and things we cannot. I turned back to the dishwasher. She was sitting again, breaking crayons again, banging her heel. You won't tell me because you're a coward is what I think.

I won't tell you because it's not important, I lied, knowing somehow that it was.

What's important then, crayons? She swept the broken pieces

onto the floor. We stared at the confetti of waxy rose and ocean blue and sunset luau until Clare broke the spell.

A fire you lit killed your baby brother, right?

I froze at the sink. She knew about the fire, I realized that. But to hear her say it out loud like that . . . for a moment, I felt paralyzed.

But it was an accident, right? Police don't put kids in jail for accidents, right?

I stooped down to pick up one half of a broken purple.

Or do they? She insisted.

Do they what? I found the matching purple and put both pieces into the box.

You heard me. Do they?

Put kids in jail? Obviously not, I said. Look, let's colour something together.

Not even if . . . someone shot their mom? She giggled. Shot her and killed her?

Blankly, I repeated, You shot your mom?

At which point her facade crumbled and she shouted, Why are you so mean? And she fled.

That night she retreated early to her treehouse, no good nights, no little waves. Blake watched her go, then turned to me.

What happened?

When I told him, his face stiffened and he stood, reaching for his coat, ready to go to her, to soothe her or distract her with their book of fairy tales and fables.

I stopped him. Blake, let me.

A brief moment passed, and I thought I saw his face soften. You? On that ladder, with your leg? And after what happened?

Yes, me. On that ladder, with my leg, after what happened.

Don't you think it's better if I go?

It might be, I tell him. But this is on me.

He stopped buttoning up his jacket. She's very particular, he said. There's a bedtime ritual we follow. And he sketched it out: book, two pages, blanket, not too tight, a forehead kiss, hug, sweet dreams and a pat for Fancy. In that order.

My little lawyer is wearing a soft plum-coloured sweater, her long red hair slightly mussed on her shoulder. She is watching her baby, who is sleeping soundly at her feet. She looks a little sad and I cannot bear to see that. I turn to the window. A while back someone had thrown an apple core down and every day I watch it to see what creature might discover it. If maybe a sparrow or a chipmunk would light on it, to peck the seeds or take a nibble, or a maintenance man would sweep it up into a trash can. But it lay there untouched, every day a little more shrivelled, a little browner than the day before.

My lovely lawyer raises her eyes and I continue.

The ladder was more challenging than I had anticipated. Blake had spaced the rungs closer together to accommodate little feet, and mine were not little feet. Nor did the slight limp I had grown used to on level ground help in my ascent. When I finally reached the top, a mere seven feet in the air, it felt like a hundred and I was breathless, though maybe not with the exertion. I had been rehearsing in my mind the bedtime ritual.

The entry was merely a scrap of cloth tacked up. I knocked on the door frame and waited for a response. When none came, I squeezed through the entrance.

Clare was already in bed, covers pulled up to her chin, her flashlight aimed at a book, Fancy at her side.

Where's Dad? she said.

In the house.

Why are you here?

To tuck you in.

I waited. I sat back on my heels and waited. I ignored the ache in my joints. I was prepared to wait till dawn, if need be.

Finally, she responded. Well, do you know how to do it?

I do.

CHAPTER 42

In the oven was a honey cake full of cinnamon and ginger. In the Crock-Pot a stew. The house smelled like someone had put her apron on to take care of her family, and dinner would be hot and meaty and dessert would be sweet.

I made a sketch of the little brown cake, steam coming off and slipped it under the girl's door.

She came down to the kitchen and I cut her a slice, put a big spoon of whipped cream on top and watched as she ate it.

Her resiliency amazed me and I vowed to keep it intact.

The girl said, What do you want me to call you? There was whipped cream on the downy moustache of her upper lip.

That's a good question, I said. Any ideas?

Let me think about it. She licked the cream off.

All at once it was April first. April Fish Day, April Fool's. Two weeks earlier, I had hired Sharon, my truck driver friend, to transport my paintings across the border to Marguerite's gallery. Frida as Buck, Frida as Raven, Frida as Octopus, Frida as Wolf. Joel had texted a picture of the display and it looked amazing. Now the day had arrived. I woke late and panicked. I banged on the main bathroom door. Get out of there. I need to get ready.

I heard a tap, on, off, a flushing, the tap again, the sound of a spray.

Did you hear me? I banged again.

Finally, the door opened and Clare emerged, spritzed and

creamed and rouged. Her hair still a tousled mess, her lips stained with the lipstick she had dabbed on, then tried to wipe off. She smiled. She had lost a tooth in the night and there was a bloody gap in her mouth. She worried the space with her tongue and grinned. It's under my pillow for the tooth fairy.

Oh, good lord. Who was kidding who here?

I stopped Clare in the hallway and put my hands on her shoulders. I looked her in the eyes. I said, Clare. I need the truth. The honest to god truth. Is my mother coming or not? Is this for real, or is it something you made up?

Geez freaking Louise! Doesn't anybody ever believe me? Her plane already landed. Phone her up if you don't believe me.

I took a deep breath. I don't know which I was more nervous about, my show or seeing my mother again after all these years. I rehearsed in my mind what I would say to her, the questions I would ask. The questions I would not ask. And what she would say to me. Would we hug? Cry? Would we know each other the way mothers and daughters should know each other?

I drew a hot bath and added Epsom salts and soaked for twenty minutes to relax. I steamed my face and washed my hair. All the procedures and rituals, the scents and soaps and moisturizers, exfoliants. I shaved and bathed.

I went into Clare's room. Braids or ponytail or loose? I asked.

Loose.

Do you want barrettes?

Her rust-coloured eyes widened. No. Thank you.

So I brushed her hair until it gleamed and she protested, Aren't you done yet? I chose an outfit for her that she rejected. Can I at least pick my own dress?

Yes, yes, yes.

I phoned Roxanne. We'll pick you up in two hours. Be ready.

Blake had his suit laid out on the bed. The same suit he had married me in. Pale sage green and it still fit if he didn't use the middle button. Laying next to his suit was the yellow daffodil tie, the one that Clare had found in the thrift shop and bought for this occasion.

I packed snacks for the trip, donuts, carrot sticks, cheese sandwiches.

I tried on Roxanne's black sequined cocktail dress, then chose one of Tully's gold-and-green caftans. I had lost weight and it fit me loosely, the way I liked it. One more look in the mirror, an hour to go before we left and a three-hour drive ahead of us, the border to cross, when someone knocked on the door.

I opened it and there she was.

She looked as I remembered her; it had been just about a year. Her black hair was longer. Like me, she had lost weight. The landlord was in the street leaning against his truck, waiting, watching.

She and I stood and stared at each other for quite a while.

Got a gun? she said, then laughed. Just kidding. Take a picture, it lasts longer.

The landlord lit a cigarette, blew the smoke in our direction.

What the fuck is going on?

She laughed. I almost went to my own funeral, she said. Not everybody gets a chance like that. She laughed again, such a merry woman she was turning out to be. She put her hand on my arm. It's all good, relax. May I come in?

The girl came down the stairs at that moment and saw her mother standing in the doorway, in three dimensions, completely alive. The girl was dressed in feathers and leaves. She had metamorphosed into a creature of the woods, or so it seemed to me until I cleared my vision and saw regular cotton and regular shapes. Earth colours, moss and oranges. A sound like a wail came out of her, and without hesitation, she threw herself to the floor at her mother's feet and flung her arms around Tully's legs.

Her mother patted the top of her head. Honey, honey.

The girl squeezed tighter.

Try not to snot on my new boots, honey, okay? They're suede.

Clare did not let go.

I missed you too, okay?

Clare kept her grip.

You're hurting me, Clarabelle. Don't squeeze so hard. Can you let me in?

Clare did not, could not, it seemed, let go.

Tully turned to the landlord leaning on his truck and shrugged. He shrugged back. Wow. I didn't know I was so popular, she said. And with Clare still attached, she scuttled over to the couch, sat down and motioned for Larry to come in.

You're not dead, I said.

Sure hope not.

They had your body. They found you in the river in a log-jam.

Wrong body, I guess.

But we cremated you. Blake brought the ashes home.

Wrong ashes.

There was a funeral.

Not mine.

This can't be possible.

It can't be but it is. It happens, I suppose. 'Cause here I am.

Then who is this? I reached for the diamond that had been sitting back in its little velvet box on my windowsill since Clare and Corey's magic ritual had gone awry just a few days before.

Got me, Tully said shrugging. Ya got me.

We sat in the living room, me and Blake, Tully and Larry the landlord, Clare and Fancy, and listened to Tully tell her tale while Joel texted and texted: Lulu's here! With bells on! Where are you? I turned my phone off.

Tully had left Clare in the house one crazy afternoon, when she was out of her mind, out of control. I was going through a very bad patch psychologically, she said. Very bad. You have no idea. Things were burned, threats made, stormings off, et cetera. Hungover, bills piling up, another STD — Larry grunted — I couldn't take it anymore. I just couldn't.

She gave the girl Blake's phone number and said, Don't wait up for me. She picked up the gun and made some excuse about an evil raven that needed shooting.

It was all I could think of at the time, I was totally off the rails. Coming down off a coke-and-fentanyl high if you want to hold that against me.

She wanted to travel, she wanted money, she wanted freedom. She wanted so much in her life and nothing was turning out the way it should.

Even birth control pills can make you suicidal. Did you know that?

I did not know that. How interesting, I said.

Least she's given up those pills, Larry muttered.

Everything was so interesting.

And Larry, the ass, had been talking about this eighteen-year-old barista like he wanted to bang her. And I told him, go right ahead.

So she put twenty bucks on the table for her daughter, grabbed the gun Blake had given her, drove away in her VW van and stopped at a place not far from the house where the river parallels the road. It was still running pretty good for early September. She wrote a note and left it in the car. Note said: Blake gets the girl and Larry gets the clap.

She crawled through the bushes, down the bank, and was trying to get up the nerve to do it. The gun was so long and awkward. But weirdly enough, a raven swooped down and began cawing at her. Circled her and cawed. The evil raven. She pointed the gun into the sky and fired at it. That was when Clare came scrambling down the bank.

She told the girl, What are you doing here? Go home. I told you not to follow me. Don't you ever listen? Go back home. Tully continued, The funny thing is that at that moment what I really wanted was to kill that raven, not myself. When I loaded the gun again I wasn't thinking about putting a bullet in my own head, god that would hurt, and I admit I'm a bit of a coward in that direction, but when I lifted the gun to shoot at the raven Clare ran at me and grabbed it out of my hand and it went off. Just like that. Hit me in the shoulder just above my heart. Right here, she said. And she pulled her sweater down to reveal the scar.

She leaned forward as if she were telling the plot of a really good movie. How she screamed and dropped and rolled into the river. How it hurt but nowhere near as much as childbirth. She smirked at her daughter.

Then you watched your mama fall backwards, bloody, into the river and get swept away and sink out of sight. At least that's what I imagine happened, right Clarabelle?

Clare nodded. I looked for a long time.

You're a stubborn one, Tully said.

We sat in silence for a while, digesting. Imagining the girl wading in up to her knees, her mother gone, borne under and away. The girl running up and down the bank and into the river trying to find her, crying and calling, Fancy barking at her side.

Fancy was panting in the corner. I could hear Blake's heart thumping, or was that mine? And in syncopated tandem, the faucet in the kitchen sink began to drip. Ping . . . ping . . . ping.

You have to tell the rest of the story, Clarabelle.

And from the few words the girl managed to volunteer and the questions that Larry prompted her with, we gathered that Clare had known something was wrong and had bicycled down the road till she came to the car. The raven circling overhead. And heard a shot. Ran down and saw her mother with the gun in her hands and so on.

That's when I killed her, Clare said.

Kids, gotta love 'em, Tully said.

Larry the landlord got up from his seat. He went into our kitchen and opened our fridge. He said, While I'm up, does anybody else want a beer?

Tully did. She popped the tab and took a long drink.

I went into the kitchen and found a bottle of gin.

Now you're talking, Larry said.

Blake put the kettle on for instant coffee.

After an hour or more, in shock at the river's edge, the girl had walked back up the bank to her bicycle and pedalled home with Fancy running at her side.

The police found the abandoned car. They found the note in the abandoned car. They found footprints on the muddy shoreline that led straight into the river. They found the gun in the shallows, they found drops of blood. They found Clare back home in the barn washing a coffee pot. The barn was so clean. They told her the news and took her into child care custody. Later, they found the body washed up on a log-jam, a young black-haired female with a gunshot wound and called it a done deed. Tully on a successful suicide mission. They questioned Larry, they questioned Blake. Later still they found the pink barrette.

Pretty shoddy police work, I say to my little lawyer.

Yes. Or pretty good magic, she replies.

I look at her.

Just kidding, she says.

Tully, badly wounded, had briefly passed out and been carried downstream to a bend in the river where she came to, caught an overhanging branch and pulled herself out. She climbed the bank to a gas station that had a pay phone still in order. She called Larry collect. He came to get her. He patched her up. He had some good drugs too.

Such an exhilarating feeling to be free and alive, Tully said.

Free?

You know what I mean. No offence, Clare. It was a time in my life when I needed to be free.

We let that sink in.

She continued, I was a bit desperate at the time. I'm better now. Got a second chance. Plus, I have Larry.

We let that sink in as well.

And the barista?

Larry grinned and stood. While I'm up? he said.

I poured shots of gin for myself and Blake, but he stuck to strong black coffee. Larry and Tully helped themselves. I unpacked the snacks and sandwiches I had readied for the drive to my exhibition. I put them on the coffee table and watched Tully and the landlord eat as if they hadn't eaten in a month. I rescued a donut for the girl before they all disappeared.

Tully was on a roll. With her mouth full, she said, I know I am really fucked up. I don't deny it. I should punish myself, go stand in the corner and contemplate my flotsam and jetsam, right? And I don't care. And don't get me wrong, I like pretty women as much as the next guy, just not all of them.

Larry the landlord laughed. We'll have to check that out, he said.

It's from a movie, she said. I just love that line so much.

But where have you been all this time?

Larry dropped me off with his brother in Castlegar while the funeral stuff was going on.

That creep, Larry mumbled.

Then we went to Paris. Paris, Las Vegas. She became almost

giddy describing the adventure. Cobblestoney streets, a little Eiffel Tower, the spa, cock-o-van.

But how did you get across the border? Supposedly being dead?

Oh, there are ways. She laughed. Afterwards, Larry got a job in the oil patch and I sat around and got — She stopped.

Sat around and got fat and lazy, Larry offered. She was nearly skin and bone, picking at a spot on her cheek. Don't do that, Larry said.

And you didn't let us know? You didn't think to let Clare know? That you were alive?

It all happened so fast. And then I realized, like I said, that I was free. Maybe you've never felt trapped before and you don't know what it's like to get a second chance at a new life. Larry showed me the picture he took of her here. She looked okay, taken care of. And Larry was taking care of me and we had an opportunity. I had a man at my side, I had a black dress. It wasn't like anyone was looking for me, it wasn't like I had committed a crime.

I served my honey coffee cake and cream. Black coffee and cream.

This is delicious, Tully said. Mind if I help myself? Before I could answer, she cut herself another slice. Anyhoo, I'm here now. Aren't I, Clarabelle? You glad to see your mommy? Ready to come home now?

What?

Go on, get your things, Tully repeated.

Wait. What's going on? I said.

To Clare again, Go on.

Clare stood for a moment, confused, looking from Blake to me.

Don't be all day about it, Clarabelle, please, she said.

Clare went upstairs.

No. Clare lives here now, I said. Right, Blake?

Absolutely.

Well, that's great, and I thank you for your service but she's coming home with us, now. We'll get a room set up, all that jazz. I'm her mother, that's my kid and I'm taking her back.

Larry chuckled.

I stood. I don't care if you're the Wicked Witch of the West. You can't just waltz in here after all that bullshit and think you own her. I remembered the girl had asked me, not a week before, about the police putting kids in jail. I said, Clare thought she shot you.

She did, the mother answered.

She thought she shot you dead.

Not a very good shot, I guess.

I may have grabbed Tully's arm then, I may have grabbed it hard. I do remember that she squealed, Hey! It may have been Blake who pried my fingers off her. That's not gonna solve anything, Frida.

Well, what is? I shouted at him. Tell me, what is? Child services? She's the fucking mother, who's going to deny her?

Wow, Tully said, pointing her finger in my direction. Be careful lady, be very careful.

It was then that Larry piped up. I could go either way, actually. But here's an idea, how about we let the kid decide.

The girl came downstairs then in that pink satin dress, now even smaller on her than before. She had her backpack stuffed with her things; she had the doll she called Baby. She went back to her mother and sat at her feet.

She would not look at me. I could not look at her.

Let the kid decide, Larry said again. Looks like a no-brainer to me.

Decide what? Clare asked. Her voice tremulous.

Sweetie pie, Tully began . . .

Listen to your mother, Larry said.

I have a question to ask you. You can think about it for a couple of minutes if you have to. But —

No, I said. No questions. You can't put that on her. You cannot do it. I stood. Take her away. She's all yours.

Oh, Jesus, Blake said.

The five of us grew quiet then.

Oh well, said Larry. Oh well. How about think of this as a blessing in disguise. Life is way, way simpler without kids, no offence, Clarabelle.

Tully patted Clare on the head. Not sure I like your hair like that. Let's get it layered. She then turned to me. You still got the boxes of clothes and stuff I left behind, I see.

The blood rushed to my face in shame and anger.

No worries, she said, you can mail it later. Here's our contact info in Surrey. We'll let you know when we have a place. She handed me Larry's new business card. Handy-Man. Anyway, the caftan looks good on you.

Clare, with her baby doll clutched to her chest, a doll she had pretty much abandoned since living with us, called out, Fancy! Fancy! Come!

Oh, Christ, is that dog still alive? From Tully.

I heard the landlord mutter something about not for long. And the little family unit left.

Clare turned in the driveway, looked at me finally and paused. I held my breath. She said, Thanks. Tell Corey thanks.

Outside my hospital window, in the parking lot, a black raven thumps down on the white ground, the hard ground where a groundskeeper has plowed it nearly to gravel. The raven bounces with the impact of his landing. A harbinger of death or symbolic mockery of the selfish child, perhaps the creator or symbol of the lost soul. A psychopomp escorting souls to the afterlife.

PART 4

An Irresistible Impulse

As I look back and connect the dots,
all I want to do is go back and hug my scared
young self, who took a lot of steps out of
impulse, not knowing what will happen.

ARFI LAMBA

CHAPTER 43

Every catastrophic act we look back on and try to explain seems at first as inconsequential as a small pebble in our shoe; it's just there, to be dealt with later. Until suddenly, and it is sudden, it is too big to deal with, and regardless of the cotton-and-wool words that we surround it with, it changes our lives. The explanations, excuses, are only "afterwords" we use to navigate the slick, land-mined, potholed road of our own making. We only realize what we have done, what has happened, after we have done it. So the afterwords are conjured up to explain, to dull, to cocoon the pebble, the pebble that is still and always will be stuck in the shoe.

I changed out of the caftan. Found a grey hoodie, a pair of black sweatpants. Blake watched but said nothing. Joel texted him: Where the hell is she? Everyone is waiting: Lulu, Lulu's boyfriend, Lulu's hairstylist. Christ, even the Buffalo is here, all the way from New York. And Lulu is looking very annoyed. No one is paying much attention to her.

What should I tell him? Blake asked me.

Does it matter?

Another text from Joel: Frida's the artist. She's the one. It's a non-event without her. My credibility is at stake here. Come on, what's going on? Who the hell does she think she is?

Tell him, good question. I have no idea. Blake turned to his phone and clicked it off. I wandered around the house in a daze.

Blake said, Sit . . . sit and talk to me.

But I could not.

This is your moment, he said. This is what you've been waiting for. You can't let this one go. He followed me around the house, dogged my steps, yapping in my ear. I know you're upset.

Upset?

You have to move forward, Frida. Don't you get it? Clare is gone. Don't you think it's killing me too? Don't you know that? For chrissake, your mother is there waiting for you. Don't you at least want to see her? Isn't it time you let bygones be bygones?

No, I shrieked. It is not time.

At one point, I forget when, I noticed the diamond and picked it up. Well, that was a big waste of money, wasn't it, I said.

Don't do that, Blake said. Just take a deep breath and relax.

I grabbed up my phone and called Roxanne. We're not coming.

Why not?

Because, I shouted.

After a moment, she said, It's just as well. I have nothing to wear. Anyway, it's karaoke night. Can I talk to Clare?

No. I hung up. I picked up my car keys.

Where are you going? Where are you fucking going? Blake shouted.

At the police station, I stood in the anteroom and demanded a full explanation. She's not even dead, I insisted. How could that not be a crime? Nobody apologized or even admitted any culpability. Mistakes happen, humans are fallible. The police children shrugged at me and shuffled their paperwork. We find what we are looking for, the police girl said. We're not rocket scientists. I admired her shameless veracity. She told us that the body was probably that of another young woman, a young Native, an unsolved murder. The police boy said they were looking into it. They had a shoe, they'd check the DNA, the data bank. She might have been a prostitute, not a high-profile case. We have to prioritize, he said. A movie star wanted for murder in California had killed himself in the local motel. We'll get to your issues when we can. I threw my coffee in his face.

Everyone stood.

An hour later I was released. You're lucky this time, they said. Daring me to claim otherwise.

I gave him the diamond. For the Native girl's mother, I said. Get it right this time, I may have shouted.

I heard him mutter, Get the bitch out of here, as I turned to go.

My little lawyer settles her jumbo baby face down on her lap and begins rather roughly patting the baby's back. Her hands are freckled, pale. Funny, I have never noticed that before.

I believe some of that, she says. But really? She still has faith in the system it seems.

The jumbo baby saves me from any more of her mother's skepticism and belches up a great milky eruption. Her mama coos, What a good girl. Her pink wool sweater is covered in baby puke, she doesn't even care.

I lost my faith in the system long ago.

I went to children's services. It might have been the same day, maybe not. The timeline is muddled in my head. It might have only been a phone call. I look at my beleaguered confidante hoping she can help clarify but she is staring at me soundlessly.

As I remember, I stood in front of the woman with the huge breasts and the jangling bracelets and the mole on her cheek. I said, Don't you realize that she might be crazy? Don't you realize how selfish she is?

She's the mother, was the mole woman's response.

I drove up into the mountains and walked out into the woods where I used to take Fancy for dog adventures. The big tree where she used to stop and sniff. Found a still life of dead daffodils, eggshells, white dog fur. All around me was white snow. White torture is a type of psychological torture, sensory deprivation, isolation, loneliness, where everything is white, the empty room, the clothing, even the food, white rice. But out here in the woods, I rather liked the effect. I told myself that. I stood there until the coldness seeped in, and then stayed there a bit longer.

From my bed, I can see that my lawyerly sidekick has polished her short nails, a pink so hot and bright it lights the room.

And with those fingers she is playing itsy-bitsy spider for the jumbo baby, who watches mesmerized from the basket on the floor by her feet.

One dark, cold day, very soon after the catastrophic gallery opening, with no decent thought in my head, no solace in the studio, no way out, no way in, and Blake, the phantom of a man I once knew ghosting through the house for socks and books and beers, giving me long, pointed looks, I got in my car and drove.

My tired girl has fallen asleep in the visitor's chair, snoring, mouth agape, drool leaking from her lips, with the baby stuffed into a Snugli on her chest. In my dream, I am standing undressed, half-naked, on trial. The prosecutor has a theory that she is expounding on. That I had an uneasy relationship with food. Blake, on the witness stand, denies this, No, no, no. But when Joel gets up to testify, he confirms: Yes, a very uneasy relationship with food — and he produces a tuna sandwich as proof — she's an artist after all. I squirm to hear him say the word artist and one of the jurors clears her throat. I know I am doomed.

When I wake, it is my psychiatrist who is staring at me on high alert. She purses her red lips and makes a little clicking sound that always signifies something, but I know not what.

Tell me, Frida, do you know the difference between an action that is uncontrollable and one that is merely uncontrolled?

No.

The truth, please.

But aren't they the same, all these judgement calls? My voice rises. You're the shrink, don't you know they're one and the same! You're the professional head-shrinker. The professional tickler. An action is an action, that's all it is and ever will be. I seem to be shouting.

Calm down, she says, and then, I cannot help you if you will not help yourself.

But why do I need help?

Don't you know? She smooths the scarf around her neck. She rolls her eyes at my ever-steady companion and says, All yours.

I listen to the telltale hum from the monitor beating out my rhythms. Nurses gossiping in the hall. I feign pain, try to feign sleep.

No, you don't. You must tell me, my little lawyer commands. I need to hear it from your lips.

I reach from my hospital bed and pull the pages from her hands because I know what is coming next.

She glares at me.

What a hot room, I say. I feel queasy. I vomit into the bedpan. Still, my little lawyer waits, such a patient, foolish, brave little soul. Faces, events, memories are still emerging out of the fog in my head and they are hard to stomach.

Where did you drive to?

Isn't it obvious? Every time my thoughts circle the event they back away, refusing to land, yet unable to fly.

Just say it.

Okay. I was sitting in my car with the engine running and my phone meowed. And it was Clare. And the text read: Hi. That's all, just, hi.

The nurse comes in to change my bandage. They have a new bit of technology now, it's a vacuum that they place over the wound to aid healing. But the nurses can't quite figure it out and have to Google directions. Great. Another vacuum to empty me. My lawyer leaves me in peace.

CHAPTER 44

I had run away once from Roxanne. Hid in a garage down the street with a pocket full of peanuts and jelly beans. Watched the windows of the neighbour's houses jealously. How warm the yellow light looked. Kids bouncing on beds. Shrieking laughter. Then all tucked in, lights out, and after a solitary moment in a dark garage, I went home. Roxanne had not even noticed I had run away.

The devoted legal aide at my side gets up from her chair. Her jumbo baby is overflowing the tiny basket she has been stuffed into and is starting to fuss. She pushes a pacifier into the baby's mouth and the fussing ceases. She leans over me in my hospital bed and puts her slim arms around my girth and I let her. Not much else to do but bear it and wait it out. I hope it helps her.

I'm trying to forgive you, she whispers.

Forgive me? For what? I ask. And by the way, are we still on the clock?

She unsnaps her jumbo baby's diaper. I force myself to stay present. The diaper. A thick rectangle of cotton decorated in flamingos. Her voice. When you've come to your senses you can let me know. Action, sound, rustle. She drops the soiled diaper into a plastic bag. The jumbo baby waves her chubby legs in the air. The nurses in the hallway. A brain tumour discovered in someone's temporal lobe. A liver transplant still touch and go. A viral infection, flesh-eating disease, leprosy. It's a beautiful world out there.

I think of all the crimes I have committed, ones I have faithfully recounted and the ones I have not. The ones that are fixable and the ones written in blood and stone. Ten years ago a parade of witnesses had taken the stand, some to vouch for me, others to testify against. It had been unbearable, dreadful, fascinating to hear my life exposed like that. Everything small seemed huge when testified to under oath. And the huge things. Well. That's like a black hole I prefer not to get too close to. How often I have wished to go back in time, to the time before, to right things, but realize too that once straightened out and on my fresh path, innocent again and guilt-free, there will be other crimes, maybe worse ones, as yet unknown, unnamed, to surprise and unhinge me. I knew I would never return to my former life. A premonition all too real. And besides, what was there to return to?

This is what happened.

I got the text from Clare at 7:44 p.m. It was just past 8:00 p.m. and fully dark when I ramped onto the Trans-Canada Highway. Tully and Larry and Clare were living in Surrey, outside Vancouver. I texted Clare back as I was leaving Hope: Hi. And waited. Nothing. Then: We forgot to say goodbye. Though I had not forgotten at all. I texted her: Are you okay? I texted her: Do you want any of your things you left behind? Your new pink coat?

It was Larry who replied: Leave Tully's kid alone.

She hates mushrooms, I texted back, and barrettes. I texted again: How is Fancy? No reply, I had been blocked.

By the time I got to Chilliwack, it was raining hard. I timed my breath to the wipers on the windshield. Just outside of Abbotsford, I saw the flashing lights of a police car trailing behind me. I pulled over. The officer came to my window and peered in. Licence, registration. I handed these things over.

Was I speeding?

No. In fact, you were going pretty slow.

Sorry. Is that a problem?

Not a problem. Your busted tail light is a problem. He looked at me. Where are you headed?

Just a tiny pause before I answered, To visit a friend. In Surrey.

I'll give you a warning for now, he said. Get that light fixed. And keep up with the flow of traffic.

Thank you, sir . . . Officer . . . take care.

He turned and smiled at me. Thanks, ma'am. And you as well.

By the time the so-called felony was accomplished, and the full reality of what I had done had hit me, it was two in the morning and I was back on the Trans-Canada driving east in a daze. Transport trucks by the score, it seemed, were passing me, laying on their horns or crowding me over. I pulled into a gas station and filled the tank. Bought some supplies. I had my purse. I had a coat, a flashlight, a half-cup of cold coffee, a quilt. And in the seat beside me, strapped in, asleep, a passenger. A very small, very young, very neglected child. In point of fact, suddenly, a baby.

At Marshall's cabin, I found the key he had hidden above the door jamb. I lit the kerosene lamp. Found some kindling and started a fire in the wood stove. I went out to the car for the sudden baby and brought her inside, only half-asleep now and squirming. She looked to be about ten months old, maybe six or eight? Anyway, less than a year, more than a month was the best I could come up with. I had heard of babies making strange and wondered if this one would. She would be hungry. I had grabbed the empty baby bottle I had found alongside her car seat and brought it with me. I had bought disposable diapers at the gas station on the way out of town. Milk, blueberry smoothies, a jar of applesauce. What do babies eat? In the cabin cupboards, Dolly had stockpiled some food. I cleaned the bottle, opened a can of sweetened condensed milk and poured it into the baby's bottle.

She grabbed at the bottle and stuffed the nipple into her mouth but yanked it out at first sip. Made a face, then tried it again. A can of spam, a can of tuna, a mickey of apricot brandy. The baby stared at me, not making strange at all. But wary-like. I tried some sounds, some talk, some song. I hardly recognized my own voice, quivery and high-pitched.

I stared into her deep blue blinking eyes. Wispy blond hair. A tiny mouth ringed in a red rash, tiny ears. Her fingers curling and uncurling, dirty. I wanted to hold her but did not trust that I knew how. I was shaking. Whatever we had going on between us was in the tender stages. An uneasy truce that I was loathe to break. Slow. The horror of what I had done was starting to seep in. I would take her back. Of course, I would take her back. But how? Where? I could not even remember the street I had found her on.

She started to whimper; her lips pulled down in a trembling scowl. I gathered my courage and picked her up. Overcome by the smell of her. The baby smell of — how to describe — fresh bread, earwax and the briny salt of the sea. Her legs were bare and cold, and her diaper was sodden. I breathed her in until she squirmed to be free. I laid her down on the bed to change her. I knew that much. And when I pulled the wet diaper away I saw that she was actually a baby boy! That set me on my heels. A blond-haired baby boy. He kicked his legs in the air. The new diapers I had bought were too big but would have to do. I slipped one under his bum and taped it closed. Still, he would not smile, and I knew enough not to smile at him. Animals see teeth as a threat, don't they? Isn't that the way it works? So I hummed a little. "Fly Me to the Moon," I tried. He kept his eyes on me, wide, alert and seemed to relax. I picked him up for a cuddle and like a wooden marionette, I placed him on my chest, stroking his head, keeping clear of the soft spot. The folds on his neck were grimy, he needed a good wash. He needed things. I named him Johnny in my mind. I said, Johnny you're a good boy, you're a very good boy.

My hospital room is so still, so quiet, beyond quiet. As if all the airwaves, every molecule and atom of living noise-making organisms had been sucked out of it. I am watching Belle in this vacuum, and she is watching me.

Belle, I say.

So you do remember my name. She says this so coldly, I am taken aback.

Yes, I remember, I do. Sorry it took so long. But you've changed, you've grown. You're not a chubby nine-year-old anymore. I force a laugh. Belle Star. Clarabelle. How could I have missed knowing you? Are you a lawyer? You're not a lawyer, are you. Are you? She won't answer. I sense I've made another mistake and I am desperate to fix it. I try to make light of it. Of course, I really did know who you were, somewhere deep in my unconscious. Of course, I did. You've been by my side all this time.

She stops me. I don't really care what you knew deep in your unconscious.

And now she is talking so quietly to me that I must strain to hear. I hated you for months, she says. For years. But I missed you and loved you and my head was like a top, spinning through so many different emotions, everything a contradiction. It was like bright colours when you mix them all together, they turn grey. I waited days for you to come and get me. I sat by the door and waited. I could never understand how you could let them take me in the first place. I thought you cared about me. And you let them take me. And then you went and rescued somebody else's baby and not me. She is crying, and so is her baby. But you know all that, don't you?

The nurses come to calm the fuss. Because I am the victim, I am the vulnerable one. It's me, the one at risk, the one who must be guarded and cared for and watched over. This is what I tell myself.

But you seemed so joyful to see her again. How could I stand in the way of that?

Joyful? Wouldn't you be joyful if the mother you thought you had shot dead suddenly appeared again, alive? Wouldn't you?

It was a question I really had no answer to.

Clare continues, My therapist says it will still take time. That I have to pay attention to my feet. Pretend I am a tree, and my feet are roots and they are growing into the earth and one day, I will wake up and feel grounded. One day.

We both look at our feet. I'm sorry, I whisper and look up. But Blake . . . ?

They "shared me." She snorts, narrows her eyes and shrugs. Whatever.

Everyone wants to know why I did it. And how. Why and how. Why and how.

It was not planned. Of course, it was not planned. If I'd even had a plan it would have been, what? To rescue Clare and bring her home to us. I had looked and looked for their place. I wanted to see evidence of child neglect that I could justify in my righteousness. We had bonded, Clare and I, and then she was gone. I wanted to know that I meant something to her. But had I?

Before I found Johnny, I had scoured half the streets in Surrey. Not the fancy places, not the rich places with the two-car garages and bay windows, but the rundown parts of town where the yards were left untended, old motorcycles parked out front, garbage cans tipped over. I was looking for Larry's pickup truck. I realize now it was exactly what Tully had done when she had come looking for Blake, but she had been successful. I was not. Clare was not spotted out in a yard pouting and dismal, nor was Fancy spotted chained to a tree.

I became exhausted, mentally exhausted driving around Surrey like that, lost in a maze of streets, desperate, still a bit drunk I think, and still grieving. Wishing I could go home, but home to what? The nothingness that waited for me?

I pulled over on some stupid side street wondering how and where and when I would find my way, and I saw across the road a really decrepit abode, chipped paint, a boarded-over window and a woman, scrawny, pockmarked, sitting on her front step smoking a cigarette, a beer can at her side and her phone in her hand. It was already dark and starting to rain again. She was weathered and trampy looking, if I can say that, though at the trial my lawyer had advised against any character judgements. Still and all. Her child, or someone's, was in a dirty car seat nearby. The woman rose, with her cigarette, her phone, her beer and stumbled into the house, leaving the baby untended. I watched the baby for so long, and then the rain turned to hail. And still, the baby was left out in it. I beeped the horn, and no one came to the rescue.

I don't remember what I was thinking. Nothing really. I just did it. As if I was not really in control of my body, every movement automatic and even feral if I can describe it like that. An instinct, an impulse that I could not resist. It was as if I was watching someone else do what I was doing myself. I kept thinking, the woman will come out and stop me, the woman will come out and see me and stop me and rescue her baby. But she did not. I heard the sounds of some awful music in the house, loud, metallic, thumping. I picked the baby up still in his car seat, damp with rain, and without thinking twice put him in the passenger side of my little yellow car, strapped him in and drove off. Just like that, I drove off. So that's my "how." My "why" may be more obvious to you than it is to me. And when you figure it out you can let me know.

It was only a day or two sequestered in the cabin in the woods (or was it less?), before Blake and Marshall drove into the yard and found us. That's their tale to tell, how they rescued us. Maybe my yellow sports car had been spotted. Maybe Blake knew me that well. Maybe it was coincidence or a guess. And yes, rescued. Both of us, the little baby boy that I called Johnny and me.

Clare picks up her jumbo baby and holds her close, letting her pull at her silver earrings. Clare is murmuring, You're the cabbage, you've got the head, you're the cabbage, you've got the head. The baby stares, enthralled.

My legal ordeal around the baby abduction business had been a nightmare. I'm recalling it now for Clare in technicolour. Sixty days in a correctional facility. I wanted just to get it over with and plead guilty, but my lawyer advised against and we went with the irresistible impulse defence. In other words, not guilty by reason of temporary insanity.

The jury lapped it up and thus followed several months in a psychiatric ward. I took their vitamin Bs, their anti-depressants, I exercised. Group therapy was a horrible experience that I lied my way through until they let me go.

Blake was waiting for me at home with bells on, as if we could take up where we left off and return to the status quo. A few weeks passed in that charade, until one morning we sat down at the table and realized we were out of Cheerios.

We had both continued eating them, as we did when you were with us, Clare, almost religiously every morning, but every time we sat down to our breakfast, those bowls of cereal were like salt on a wound. The day we ran out, we stared at each other until I drove down to Hilltop and bought a family-sized box and carried it out to my car. But instead of going home, where Blake was waiting, I drove away. I carried those Cheerios around with me for months. Until a mouse chewed a hole in the corner and the little bugs got in and I disposed of them. So, don't tell me that you had no impact on our lives, don't ever tell me that.

Clare packs up her child and the child's accoutrements and nods. Okay, she says, all right then. That's better than nothing, I guess. As she leaves, I hear her murmuring something that I strain to hear. Is it thank you?

At once I realize that it is not my story Clarabelle has been trying to unravel all this time, but her own. For a moment, I am relieved. I've told my tale, my sorry tale, the gaps are filled in, punishment meted out. But when I hear voices in the hallway, the grumbling girlish protest of Clare's voice and the telltale lilt of my psychiatrist in response, I fear that they are not yet done with me.

That week of anticipation before my gallery show, when I still had Clare, shines in my memory like jewels in a nest of wool. So much I have forgotten, so much I am forced to recall, the hard stuff and the insignificant all mushed together. For example, I remember a shopping trip to the Buy-Low and the lady at the till who smiled at us.

I was pushing the grocery cart and Clare was loading it up with everything she liked. Frozen chicken strips. Red apples. Chattering away.

I figured what I should call you, Clare had said to me at the till.

I waited for her to say, Mommy, or Mother, or Mama. I admit that I shuddered at the thought of it.

Freddie, she replied. It's like your name but it's better.

The woman at the till grinned.

Clare then remembered one more thing.

What?

Alcohol. For my pierced ears.

You don't have pierced ears.

I will when I'm a little bit older. I want two on one side and three on the other. You can't stop me, Freddie.

She's got that right, the woman at the till said and smiled at us.

After a moment Clare speaks. I have a funny memory too. Coming home from Corey's one night and that old cowboy song "Waltz Across Texas" was playing and the light was turned down low. And you and Dad were in the living room and you were dancing. Every time I hear that song I remember that.

I laugh. Well, I guess you don't hear that song too often, do you?

Almost never, Clare says.

Blake appears at my side. I haven't seen him in years. He's lost weight, his hair has thinned. But he looks good, probably better than me. Has he come to . . . what? He takes hold of my hand, his is warm and dry and familiar. He's here to tell me to be brave. He's here to tell me he lives in Kelowna now. And he has met someone, a dental hygienist. She's in the hallway and he beckons her in. The woman he has met looks as pink and fresh and plump as a cherry.

When are you due? I ask.

January.

They are both glowing. I wish her luck. And happiness, I add.

Now Blake is holding Clare's jumbo baby, his granddaughter, I realize.

For years, I avoided contact with everyone that mattered to me. My stubborn pride, my stubborn shame. With Roxanne's inheritance and sales of my own paintings, I set myself up with a small gallery in Vancouver, artworks and antiques. I called it Frida's

Fire. At ten in the morning, I opened for business, at five in the afternoon, I closed.

It was a life, of sorts. And might have continued in that state of limbo until my mother, out of the royal blue, sent an email. My heart raced, quite erratically, when I saw her name in my inbox. It had been more than ten years since our last brief contact and much longer since we had come face to face. I deleted it immediately, before reading. Then pulled it from the trash.

She had cancer. She wanted to see me. Was in distress and did not want to go to the grave without settling the score. If I cared to see her again, she would let me handle the flight arrangements.

I did not know what to make of this. The score. I tried to squelch the cauldron of feelings that was bubbling up inside me, but they would not be squelched. Finally, days later, I responded, Yes, come, and booked her flight.

I prepared myself for her visit. Prepared myself for the truth as she saw it, for our tears and guilt. Or would she insist on that age-old myth that I could never verify? I closed Frida's Fire early the day of her arrival and went back to my apartment to cook and coif and bathe and rein in my emotions. She had a score to settle. But so did I. In a very short while I would learn the truth.

I waited days, or was it merely hours, until I stopped waiting. All the wonderful dishes I had cooked for her: a duck in orange sauce, a crème brûlée, I watched it all congeal and then threw it all out.

I stayed shut away in my apartment, not opening my gallery, staring at her email, waiting. Another week passed before I finally found the guts to contact her and demand an explanation. In it, I asked the question that had been festering inside me my entire life. Was it you or me, Mummy, that had set that fire? Whatever you tell me now, I will believe.

It was two days before a response came. From her lawyer with a cc to the new husband, a Monsieur Daniel LeBlanc.

Lulu is deceased, he wrote. She died in Belgium at her own request. We are sorry for your loss.

I turned the lights off in my apartment, turned the heat down. I reread the email a hundred times. The legalities involved, the consultations, the procedure. But the gist of it never changed. Sorry for your loss. I shut down my computer. I tied a scarf around my neck and put a blanket in the back of my car and drove the Trans-Canada, a highway I knew too well. Hours later, as if on autopilot, I found myself back in Hope. Back at the old homestead. Not the most rational choice but being the living, breathing, erring human being that I am, I was not very rational at the time. It's easy to critique these things after the fact. My voice sounds shrill, even to my ears. I seem to be taking this out on my shrink.

And she is listening closely, so I apologize for my churlishness.

No worries. Go on, she says.

I try to choose my words more wisely.

Our old house was dark. It was late at night, the inhabitants no doubt in bed already. The shrubs in the front looked pruned and tended. The tire swing was gone. A triple life-sized ceramic frog sat on the porch, with "Welcome" stamped on his forehead. I circled to the back and found the treehouse in the yard. The ladder was half-rotten but it held me as I climbed.

Inside the little fort that Blake had built for Clare when she was ours, I lay down, wrapped myself up in the blanket I had brought, finally fully, very nearly content.

The old couple who lived there didn't find me until two days had passed. Found me feverish, delirious, groaning in pain. My cunning appendix had burst and with it went my last defence. The old people were not amused.

None of us were amused, my little lawyer says. She pauses. I have a confession to make, Freddie. Lulu didn't contact you out of the blue like you thought. It was probably my idea.

Probably your idea?

We'd kept in touch over the years. She blushes to the roots of her red hair. Are you mad?

Doctors have done studies and now hypothesize that there is a connection between complicated appendicitis and psychotic disorders, memory loss, selective amnesia. Perhaps that is true. But which was the cause and which the effect? Something had to give and an organ burst. Cause, effect, cause again, and effect again. A simple cycle of life that I might never fully understand. But I think it did happen the way it should, painful as it was until, in my confusion and denial, I came face to face with Clare again, who pulled from me the tangle of both of our stories. Until the point where they diverged. And then converged again.

My psychiatrist is lecturing me. Children cannot choose their lives. But grown-ups can, much as they might think otherwise. Another wondrous piece of wisdom that I pretend to absorb.

What do you choose, Frida? No answer? Well, think about it, and she turns to discuss my prognosis with my advocate, with Clare.

I finally understand that my future depends on the one basic question they must sign off on. And that question is: Am I a danger to myself or to others?

Their voices rise and fall. They don't seem to agree, and I don't blame them. Even I don't know the answer to that.

My psychiatrist asks if I have anything more to add.

I suspect this question is important, but I am at a loss. I am grateful to be alive, I offer, but is that enough? Probably not. So, I tell them the story of Iron Henry, the fable I had read to Clare so long ago, the night I tucked her in. But was it the frog or the prince, or maybe the servant, whose heart was wrapped in iron bands to keep it from breaking? I choose the frog. When I finish, I see that no one is taking notes. It seems note-taking is over.

How serene my psychiatrist looks, her brown eyes rimmed in kohl. Her serenity is almost an affront. Clare's brow is wrinkled in that thoughtful frown I know so well. I struggle for a look of cheerfulness, innocence and optimism until the struggle annoys me and I give way to whatever it is my face is trying to reveal.

You look worried, Clare says.

And I suppose I am.

Freddie . . . And she clears her throat. It seems she has a favour to ask. She has written a picture book for Tinker. And before I can congratulate her and bring the session to an end, she says, Now, listen, it's your turn to listen: see it starts like this. And for several minutes, her voice rising then falling, editing even as she speaks, she describes the forest, the sea, the sky and all the otherworldly characters contained within. I listen. I can barely follow her convoluted plot but somehow I can see quite clearly the wonderful world she has created.

It is of course, a child's picture book, in need of pictures.

As if on cue, a sound outside my window steals my attention and I look towards it. A fluttering of small birds chirp in the cedar trees. A blue-black raven has landed on the shrivelled apple core and is stabbing away. In the shrubs nearby a golden buck stands, immobile, wary. A community of creatures in tune with one another. As if their survival, their lives, their nascent well-being depends on it. No doubt it does.

ACKNOWLEDGEMENTS

I want to thank and acknowledge the people in my life who wittingly or unwittingly helped in the creation of this book. I also want to acknowledge the town of Hope, B.C.: I have played fast and loose with your township; I hope you're okay with that.

My first reader, and first editor, who gently and enthusiastically endorsed and strengthened this novel from the start, Michael Kenyon, thank you. And to Wendy Atkinson, whose support and initial concerns helped launch a draft that was infinitely more publishable. Robyn So, my keen-eyed editor, thank you hugely, your instincts and spot-on questions and suggestions were invaluable. And big thanks to my teachers at UBC, you opened up a world of writing possibilities.

To my husband George, thank you beyond words, for being there for me, for letting me hole up in my cave to write and for your considerable strengths and even weaknesses which have made our life together more than memorable. To Cameron, thank you for the island years we spent with our babies and for your abiding friendship. To Forest and Chloe, Maralee and Lorrie, a thank you is not enough for your love and for bearing the brunt of my mothering style and for teaching me what it means to be a mother and a stepmother. And to Ben, thank you, your open heart is a gift.

To my brother Claude, I thank you for your brilliant and funny mind, as well as your steadfast belief in my work. I hope to earn it. And to my twin brother Johnny, thank you for being a lifelong fount of amazement and inspiration. And to my beautiful grandchildren, your innocence and enthusiasm light me up. You give me joy. Grow on.

Thank you to the artist Wendy Toogood, for your friendship, your generosity and your wonderful, inspirational artwork. Vive the octopus!

And lastly, a hug of thanks to Frances, that crazy little dog of mine, always by my side and loyal to the bitter end.

AUTHOR BIO

Deirdre Simon Dore is a Canadian writer. Her short fiction has won, among other awards, the Journey Prize and has been published in numerous journals and translated into Italian. Her plays have been produced in Vancouver and Calgary. Originally from New York and a graduate of Boston University, she has an MFA in creative writing from UBC. After homesteading on a remote island in B.C., she moved inland where she acquired a woodlot licence on which she planted trees and learned to use a chainsaw. She lives near a large lake in the interior of British Columbia with her husband, black lab and assorted livestock. She has two children.